Memory
and
Metaphor

Andrea Monticue

Cover design copyright © 2019 by Niki Lenhart
nikilen-designs.com

Published by Paper Angel Press
paperangelpress.com

ISBN 978-1-949139-09-9 (Trade Paperback)

10 9 8 7 6 5 4 3 2

FIRST EDITION

Dedication

This work is dedicated to Red and Claire,
for all the wonderful things they've done for me;
and, of course, to Beth,
without whom this would never have been accomplished.

Acknowledgements

There is no way I could have written this book without the help of some very smart and wonderful folks.

I would like to thank Sherri Shimshy, EMS Nurse Specialist, for her advice on emergency medical procedures on foreboding alien worlds and what emergency medicine might look like in the future; "Joanne's Sci Fi Fan Friend Who Studies Evolution for a Living," for answering my weird questions regarding exo-evolution; Joanne Kerbavaz for putting me in touch with her professional scientist peers who were willing to answer my questions; Steven Templeton for explaining some of the finer details of malware and androids; and of course all the friends who were willing to beta-read or in other ways supported the project: Eva Moon, Hannah Storch, Mike Curtin, Jennifer Bob, Mary and Tonya Baut, Lisa Schoof; I would also like to thank SFERO, the San Francisco Esperanto Regional Organization, for patiently listening to the Esperanto versions of stories that take place in this universe. And finally to Steven Radecki of Paper Angel Press for recognizing talent when he sees it!

PROLOGUE

A SABOTEUR PRACTICED HER TRADE deep within a naval spaceship located somewhere between Rigil Kentaurus and Delta Pavonis. It had cost her much to get this far, pretending to be a stupid enlisted woman in the Kentauran Republic Navy, but now she neared the end of her mission. The bomb was set and primed, and all she had to do was wait for the signal.

She was going to die when the bomb exploded, but she had no regrets. She especially felt no guilt about killing the people she had pretended to call friends. They were ignorant and classist, rude, and condescending, ignoring the pain and suffering of the poorer cultures surrounding them. Their leaders manipulated elections, trade markets, and entire economies for the benefit of the oligarchical few. They had sent their spies to undermine the society she loved and had spent her entire life serving. They set off riots and demonstrations, blaming them on "students". They sold arms to enemies of her homeworld and trained ungrateful insurgents in guerrilla warfare. They acted like they were the interstellar police. Their naked imperialism was disgraceful. She would be remembered as a martyr for the Party, drawing blood for the cause.

An encoded message came through her Endocranial Processing Unit. There was the signal! Her heart and mind raced as she set the detonator by hand. Then, in spite of her courage and dedication, she found herself involuntarily backing away. It didn't matter, as there was nowhere to hide.

She had nothing to fear from death because she knew that she would live again to draw more blood for the homeworld.

"With this blow," she whispered, "I hereby avenge the deaths of my family and compatriots, and continue the battle for justice and against the lies of the imperialists who —"

She never finished the sentence.

1

KRS Zephyr
about 12 light-years from Rigil Kentaurus
Kentauran calendar: 23 Pagoniámina, 1382 PS

T HE THUNDER AND RUMBLE OF AN EXPLOSION echoed through the fifty-four thousand metric tons of the frigate Kentauran Republic Ship *Zephyr,* causing all 180 men and women of the ship's company to instinctively grab something and search the bulkheads for cracks.

"Hydraulic systems A and B are down," the operations officer reported without even a hint of panic.

"Damn it, what was that? Damage control, report!" Gabriella Souza, the commanding officer, looked at the retreating smuggler in the tactical display, accelerating away at nearly fifteen gravities. "Lock onto that ship!"

"Unable to lock, Ma'am. No hydraulics to the weapons control."

"Give me an intercept trajectory and tell that pilot to heave to or we'll open fire."

"She's at full acceleration, ma'am. They'll be able to hit warp in about twenty seconds.

"Calculate probable route. Get ready to engage warp field."

"Automatic safety protocol. We are unable to go into warp with only one working hydraulic system. Shall I override?"

For just a moment, Souza's hunter instinct to follow the prey competed with her rational instinct to keep her crew safe. Chasing a smuggler is one thing, but endangering her ship and crew for so small a prize was quite another. She knew that if she gave the word, the crew would follow her lead without question into a highly dangerous situation. That wouldn't stop a board of inquiry from hanging her out to dry.

"Negative," she said dejectedly as she watched the smuggler accelerate towards freedom.

THIS IS DAMAGE CONTROL, came the voice over her EPU. WE FOUND THE SITE OF THE EXPLOSION: MECHANICAL CHASE NUMBER ONE, SECTION THREE. THERE'S A CASUALTY.

Only one? Souza felt relief that it wasn't more, and silently thanked the designers and engineers of spacecraft everywhere.

HOW SOON FOR REPAIRS?

CHIEF PUŠKARIĆ SAYS NINETY MINUTES, MA'AM.

AND THE CASUALTY?

SHE'S STILL ALIVE, BUT BADLY INJURED. HARD TO TELL THE DIFFERENCE BETWEEN BLOOD AND HYDRAULIC FLUID IN HERE. TRANSPORTING HER TO MEDICAL NOW.

"Tactical, any way we can predict where the smuggler went?" Souza asked.

"Not without more information, ma'am. I'm running the data now and will give you a weighted probability list."

"Navigation, what's in that direction?"

"Nothing, ma'am, until you get to the Lesser Magellanic Cloud."

Commander Souza was now pacing behind her seat. "Damn it!"

Lieutenant Commander Guérin Lagrueux's voice came over her EPU so that only she could hear it.

IF I MAY SUGGEST, CAPTAIN, FINDING OUT WHY WE EXPERIENCED A HYDRAULIC FAILURE WHICH WAS TIMED SO FORTUITOUSLY FOR THE SMUGGLER IS A HIGHER PRIORITY THAN CHASING IT. WE DON'T KNOW IF THERE ARE OTHER SURPRISES WAITING FOR US.

Lagrueux's fluid Auschrodt accent was soothing, but it still took several seconds for Souza to calm down, weigh the risks, and come to a conclusion.

YOU'RE RIGHT, COMMANDER.

Out loud, she addressed the flight deck crew. "Stand down from battle ready. Commander, find out why the hydraulics failed, and find out if anything else is about to fail. I want a report in one hour."

Guérin Lagrueux set his EPU to address all senior officers. LIEUTENANT ĐOÀN, GET A FORENSICS CREW INTO THAT CHASE. I WANT TO KNOW WHO, WHAT, HOW AND WHY. LIEUTENANT BRUNO, I WANT A SHIP WIDE SEARCH FOR ANY EVIDENCE OF SABOTAGE.

THAT WILL TAKE A WHILE, Bruno responded.

YOU HAVE FIFTY-FIVE MINUTES, LIEUTENANT.

*   *   *

"Let's hear it. What happened?" Souza demanded, still bitter an hour later.

Lagrueux cleared his throat. Face to face meetings like this always carried extra gravitas compared to chatting over the EPU. They were in the Captain's office, sitting across a small table from each other.

"The forensic team," he said while sending a link to the file from his EPU to hers, "found burnt ceramics and electrical components." Lagrueux stopped himself from going into unnecessary details.

He was twenty-five centimeters taller than Souza, and since the Navy was his second lifetime career, fifty years older, and often needed to remind himself that she was his skipper, not his daughter. He was tall and lanky, while she was shorter and sturdier. The filial imagery was hard to shake, especially when they were speaking in private like this.

"An explosive device."

This was not exactly a surprise to anybody, but the mention of it still caused Souza's gluteal muscles to flex. She pulled off her cap and ran fingers through her short, dark, curly hair.

"Apparently. Fortunately, Lieutenant Bruno's team didn't find any others. They are beginning a search of personal lockers and work spaces for parts."

A bomb could only mean one thing, Souza thought: *a saboteur.* Either some port maintenance personnel or, and this thought was most abhorrent, someone on her own crew.

"Was it detonated from within the ship?"

"We believe so. Lieutenant Đoàn did find components which might have been part of a radio, but it was inconclusive. We performed an analysis on all radio frequencies which could have penetrated the hull, and found nothing, but we're still looking. They would have been recorded by the sensors. Further, Lt. Đoàn suspects that the device was activated from close by."

"The crew woman who was injured?"

"Crewman Carol Simmons," Lagrueux said. "She is, of course, our primary suspect."

Souza tried to remember if she knew the woman. She was about to query the ship's database when Lagrueux sent a photo without prompting.

"She's been assigned to the Zephyr for one and a half standards. But at the moment, the only solid evidence that she's involved is that she was at the scene. She's a q-trician with experience in system controls. She would know how to disable the ship without causing excessive damage. We found explosive residue on her skin and uniform, but she was in close proximity to the explosion, so that doesn't prove anything. We also found plenty of her DNA in the chase, but mostly in the form of bio-contamination. That is to say, she bled all over the place."

"Why was she in the chase?"

"Routine maintenance. Chief Puškarić gave her the task. There are two things we need to seriously consider, however. One, when we called for Battle Ready, Crewman Simmons should have terminated her project and reported to the electronics shop. She requested to stay in the mechanical chase."

"Do you know why?"

"Not yet. It's my intention to talk to Chef Puškarić about it as soon as he's finished with repairs."

"And the second concern?"

"While we were visiting the planet Maheux, she was out of contact for a little more than a day."

"Well, doesn't that just make things a whole lot more interesting," Souza said and sat back in her chair.

She set her EPU to check the ship's shore leave records and noted that Simmons had not been marked as missing or AWOL. Being out of contact for that long wasn't unusual, especially for sailor who'd been enjoying herself and was perhaps sleeping off a night of excess. However, in this era of automatic digital records, nothing went unnoticed.

"What's her status?"

"Massive head trauma. Dr. Bradford does not expect her to survive."

"Can we do a download of her EPU?"

"Unfortunately, no. It, too, was heavily damaged, and it died."

"Be that as it may, when … or if … Simmons dies, I want that unit removed for a very detailed analysis. Meanwhile, do an in-depth background check. See if there's anything in her finances or personal correspondence to indicate that her loyalties may have been compromised."

"Yes, ma'am." Lagrueux found it unnecessary to mention that he'd already assigned that task to a marine security officer.

"Meanwhile, tell Chief Puškarić I want a meeting."

"Yes, ma'am. Anything else?" Lagrueux stood to go.

"I'll chat you if I think of anything."

*   *   *

The hydraulic systems were repaired and operationally checked before end of watch, and they were back online 30 minutes later. Lagrueux waited until after Puškarić's crew finished the repairs and clean up before approaching him.

Puškarić stood and saluted, smearing hydraulic fluid across his forehead in the process. "Good day, Commander. What brings you here?"

"The captain sends her compliments and asks that you join her for a conference."

"I'm on my way. But you could have chatted me for that."

"Yes, I could have. A moment of your time, chief."

"Yes?" Puškarić looked at Lagrueux anxiously. It was never a good thing when the XO said that.

"Crewman Simmons. What is your evaluation of her?"

Puškarić nodded. "She's competent, learns quickly, though a bit of a trouble maker. She's not the worst of the bunch, though, nor the best. Lately she's been rather withdrawn. Hasn't been participating in the usual crew banter."

"Did this start after our last visit to Maheux?" Lagrueux asked.

"It's difficult to say when it started. She can be moody — On top of the world one day, looking like a dejected puppy the next."

"Why did she request to stay in the mechanical chase when Battle Ready was called?"

Puškarić stood nearly as tall as Lagrueux, but with wider shoulders, olive skin, and dark eyes. He shuffled his feet, clearly uncomfortable with the conversation. "Yes. That's unusual, but occasionally necessary. She had opened several key juncture boxes, and wanted to stay and make sure everything was closed correctly."

"Is that according to specs?" Lagrueux referred to the collection of tomes containing Naval operating specifications.

"It's a gray area."

Lagrueux nodded. Far too many gray areas existed in the naval specs for his tastes. "This morning — Did she seem anxious to you?"

Chief Puškarić made a noncommittal gesture. "The crew always seem anxious to me. I can make their lives miserable or not. Maybe her rackmates would be able to answer that question better. How is she doing?"

Lagrueux considered all the possible replies he could give and settled on the blunt truth. He shook his head. "Dr. Bradford doesn't expect her to make it."

2

KRS Zephyr
about 5 light-years from Rigil Kentaurus
9 Teleftmina, 1382

S HARON MANDERS WOKE UP SCREAMING.
Then stopped because she couldn't remember why she was screaming. It hadn't been much of a scream. Mostly it was just the thought of a scream, as very little sound had left her dry, raspy throat. She also didn't remember being in bed, but she was.

Sharon tried to remember going to bed, and discovered that she couldn't remember much of anything at all. She opened her eyes with a squinting, fluttering, almost painful motion. The room was dimly lit from some light coming from outside her field of vision. She could also see what looked like LEDs, and hear the soft humming of electronic equipment.

All of this went through her mind in mere moments before the lights came on, causing her to close her eyes tearfully.

She heard the sound of a door opening and sensed that somebody entered the room.

"Simmons!" a man said with a sound of total surprise.

Sharon cracked her eyelids open and tried to sit up. That is to say, she sent the signals from her brain to her spinal cord to start the process of sitting up, but nothing happened. It was difficult to tell where her body stopped and the rest of the universe started, as if her entire body was paresthesic and unresponsive.

The man was about thirty, clean-shaven and had short, neat hair. He looked horrified, paused only a moment and then became very busy studying medical instruments and mumbling to himself.

Hospital. I'm in a hospital. Something happened. Am I paralyzed?

She could see an IV bottle of clear fluid connected to her arm. The words on the label were too small to read.

Sharon made another effort to sit up and her muscles tried dutifully to respond, but this only brought on dizziness, pain, and a reaction from the man.

He said something in an accent that was so foreign that Sharon didn't immediately understand, but concluded that it was something like, "No. Don't try to sit up."

"Good idea," she mouthed, but it sounded hoarse, dry, and unrecognizable, so she sucked on her tongue to generate saliva. She wanted to examine her head with her hand, but her arm felt like molten lead, and responded by going in random directions. She let it fall back down.

"Simmons," the man held a light in front of her face. "Follow the light with just your eyes."

Sharon still didn't quite understand the words, but the gesture and intent was obvious. She understood by the cadence and patterns that the man was calling her *Simmons*.

Who is Simmons, and why is he calling me that?

Her name was Sharon Manders, though at the moment she felt lucky to remember that much, because the rest of her life was a vast darkness. She concentrated on following the light.

"Good," the man said, though it sounded more like "goot". A name patch on his well-pressed shirt read *Bradford, MD*. "Listen to me carefully, Simmons," he continued. "You had a nasty head wound and brain trauma. Do you remember being injured?"

Though she could tell the man was speaking some form of English, it was like listening to somebody with an extreme regional accent like Creole or Appalachian. Sharon parsed out what she did understand and filled in the gaps as if it was a verbal crossword puzzle. She tried to say *"No"*, but her tongue still felt huge and as if it was upholstered with sandpaper. She tried to shake her head, but only managed a minor tremble.

Dr. Bradford mumbled some more, then produced a cup and a spoon. He offered her a spoonful of ice chips. "Here, let these sit on your tongue."

The ice melted in her mouth, lubricating her tongue and throat. It felt marvelous.

She swallowed the cold fluid and her larynx no longer felt like a gravel road.

"No," she finally whispered.

"Your EPU died," Dr. Bradford said as if it should mean something. "You'll have to make do without until we can grow you another."

Sharon could feel the spot in her head that had been damaged. It was numb. Or more accurately: it was more numb than the rest of her body.

"Simmons, this is important. You've been in a coma for twenty-three days. Your body will take some time to recover. Don't try to move yet. Get your equilibrium back."

Sharon wanted to tell Dr. Bradford that she wasn't Simmons and that, beyond that, she couldn't tell him who else she was.

Did the head wound have something to do with why I woke up screaming?

"What do you remember?" the doctor asked.

While pondering questions of memory, Sharon's mind made wild associations between faces, places and events that seemed fantastical, she realized that her eyes were closed and she'd fallen asleep. The dreams hinted at a past life in which she did important things.

She lay there, listening to gentle electronic beeps and the occasional muffled sounds of human speech coming from beyond a door while sorting out the dream images.

As she opened her eyes, the room lights came on dimly. With great effort, she carefully rolled onto her side. While this was a vast improvement over her previous attempt at fine motor function, there was still a sense that her body and brain were learning to cooperate again. She had to concentrate on one movement at a time. When she finally succeeded, she saw that she was the lone occupant of a long, narrow room with half a dozen empty hospital beds.

It was a medical room, but beyond that she had no idea where she was. There were no windows. She was looking at a handle-less door. There was some writing on the wall, but it was too small, and the room was too dark to read it.

The door opened by sliding sideways into the wall. Dr. Bradford walked in, causing the room lights to brighten.

"Good evening, Simmons," he said with a forced smile and his strange accent. "Glad to see you're back among the living." He started mumbling to himself again.

Sharon made a successful attempt to find something akin to a voice. "Uh … hi. I'm not Simmons."

Bradford continued mumbling for a few seconds then looked directly at Sharon's face. "I beg your pardon?"

Sharon spoke again, this time doing her best to duplicate Bradford's drifted vowels and mutated consonants. "Hee. Uhm net Zeemuhns."

After a few moments of awkward silence, he said, "Well, then. That will certainly come as a surprise to everybody else." He pulled up a chair. "Who are you then?"

Sharon was overcome with the feeling that she had said the wrong thing — that she should have kept quiet about her identity. *But why?*

"Sharon Manders. Was there an accident? Maybe we were mistaken for each other."

Bradford chewed his lip, mumbled some more, folded his right arm across his chest and rubbed his jaw with his left hand. "Not unless you and Specialist Carol Simmons have identical DNA."

Sharon struggled to figure out what all this meant, and her brain was too sluggish to give concrete responses.

Bradford looked worried about something. "What year is this?"

Sharon had no idea, but numbers seemed to form in her consciousness. "Thirteen?"

Bradford kept a straight face. "Thirteen what?"

Sharon shook her head. "I dun' know," she said with a puff of breath.

"What else do you remember?"

Sharon tried to remember anything. Her mother. Her job. The president.

She asked, "Who's the president?"

"The president of what?"

Sharon almost said the name of something … a country. She closed her eyes trying to conjure up images of important things.

*   *   *

Sharon ran, swam, and even jumped rope while singing some inane rhyme. She mastered one physical skill and moved to another. She threw a ball, performed some archery, and rode a horse. Her body was remembering how to do all these things. The year was nineteen —

Then she woke up.

*   *   *

In an undisclosed location on a planet several light-years from the *KRS Zephyr*'s current location, five people met in a concrete room. Their activities were known to only a few in the highest of offices on their home worlds. Due to the nature of their business, their EPUs had been permanently disabled with a combination of pharmaceuticals and electroshock. They were so worried about being spied upon that they didn't use electrical power from the city, but generated it locally.

"The attack on the Kentauran naval vessel went according to plan," a man with an angular face said. "The personnel swap went off perfectly, and the explosion occurred exactly on cue."

"Excellent," said a sandy haired woman. "How long did it take them to repair their ship?"

"Not long," the angle-faced man said. "Their crews are well trained. According to our asset on the ship, they were operational inside two standard hours. But it gave us just enough time to ascertain the nature and degree of the damage. The bait ship was able to evade capture and return to its base."

The sandy-haired woman turned to another person she knew only as Giatrós. She didn't even know the person's gender, but decided to use male pronouns in reference to him. The sandy-haired woman wondered if the he was a woman disguised as an effeminate man, but one condition he had placed on his cooperation in this project is that there would be no inquiries into his personal life. That hadn't stopped the sandy-haired woman from trying, but her queries turned up very little. Giatrós always looked worried that somebody was going to figure out his darkest secrets and broadcast them on the 'Nets.

"Well, Giatrós. Would you call this a success?"

Giatrós inclined his head. "Yes. I believe you have that which you desired."

What he didn't say was that it came at the cost of not only a human life, but also of one of his assets.

These people have no idea how much work goes into creating an asset, he thought. *Which had to be completely destroyed after one use in order to hide the evidence. They are barbarians of the worst sort.*

The sandy-haired woman turned to the fifth person in the room, a young man of about 20 standard years, and asked, "Is your project on schedule?"

"Yes. It'll be ready before it's needed. I only need to perform some stress tests."

"Good," the sandy-haired woman said. "The target date is coming up. The entire population of Kentaurus celebrates like frat boys during their new year's Solstice. We launch in fifty-one standard hours. Get back to work."

As the others filed out of the room, the sandy-haired woman sat in contemplation. She could sense victory, and it would be hers if she didn't rush it. The Kentauran Republic was the oldest government in the sector — and had the largest military by far. Going against it head-to-head was a fool's errand, but as long as it existed, it remained a threat to the existence of her own way of life. Recruiting the disenfranchised among the Kentaurans produced limited and untrustworthy results. Creating assets for attacking the Kentauran infrastructure held far greater promise.

✳   ✳   ✳

As Sharon opened her eyes, the room lights came up to half strength. *How did they do that?*

The room was empty, and some of the machines had been turned off. She felt stiff and needed to stretch. The numbness she had felt earlier had been replaced with a feeling of being bruised all over. She put her arms slowly over her head and extended them surrendering to the stretch reflex. She felt the blood rushing into her extremities and, when she finished, she felt surprisingly better. She was also starving. No doubt the intravenous fluids supplied all of her nutritional needs, but they did nothing to fill the void in her stomach.

After evaluating her condition and situation, she decided to try to sit up again, and in a long drawn out process of remembering how her body was supposed to behave, she managed to roll over on her side and push herself upright. That's when she discovered she was in a green hospital gown and that she was attached to a catheter.

When she thought about it, neither of these revelations surprised her. What did surprise her, however, is that there was a band of thin, tough fabric around her waist which was attached at the other end to the bed by a narrow cable that looked like steel. The cable was just long enough for her to stand up and walk around the bed … if she managed to stand up.

She explored her injuries, running her hands over her head and torso. Most of the wounds had healed sufficiently that they were no longer covered in bandages or held together with stitches or staples or glue or whatever they had used, but they were still quite tender.

She sat there for about five minutes before Dr. Bradford walked through the door, followed by another man who looked to be about thirty years old, wearing what looked like a military uniform.

"Welcome back, Simmons!" the new man said in the same accent as Dr. Bradford. "We've missed you, and we're glad to have you back in the world of the living. The electronics department hasn't been the same without you."

Sharon smiled, thought briefly about standing up and then abandoned the idea. She wasn't that strong nor coordinated yet, nor was she dressed for visitors, and the catheter and cable prevented much movement.

"Good to see you sitting up, Simmons," Bradford said. "You're making remarkable progress."

Sharon studied the new man's face, trying to remember it. He was obviously important, but also a complete stranger.

"Thank you," she managed to say. "It's good to be back. I think." She held up the cable and looked questioningly at Bradford. "Why am I tied to the bed?"

"That's just a precaution," Bradford said. "Captain's orders. We need to make sure you're secure."

Before Sharon could respond to this, the new man said in an earnest voice that demanded to be listened to, "Simmons, do you remember who I am?"

Sharon's heart beat faster, and some machine made a warning sound: *This was important!* The man also wore a nametag which read PUŠKARIĆ. While Dr. Bradford wore a single shoulder epaulette with two stripes, Puškarić had none.

A pin on his collar showed some animal — a centaur? — a stylized seven-pointed star surrounded by a laurel, and the letters KRN. None of this meant anything to Sharon.

"I'm sorry," she shook her head in defeat. "But I really have no idea."

"That's okay" Puškarić said. "Dr. Bradford tells me that you literally came back from the dead, and the process isn't quite complete."

The three of them regarded each other awkwardly, the two men wearing forced smiles.

"The electronics bay hasn't been the same without you, Simmons," Puškarić repeated. "I've had to take all my ire out on McKenzie, and he's feeling a bit brow-beaten."

Their weird accent was becoming easier to understand, but Sharon still had to do some mental translating.

She had no idea what to say or do. These strangers obviously assumed some intimacy with her, and expected her to know how to behave. Panic rose in her gut and she struggled to contain it. Whatever the issues were, she did not want to embarrass herself further in front of these people.

She smiled and improvised. "I'll be back on my feet ASAP, sir."

The two men exchanged a conspiratorial smile and Sharon wondered what she'd said wrong.

"If you'll excuse us," Bradford said, "my patient and I have some work to do."

Puškarić made congenial noises and departed with expressions of "get well soon!".

When he left, Bradford mumbled some more, as if he were engaging in some private conversation with somebody else while looking at her.

Bradford came to some conclusion and said, "Lesson one, lass. You don't call a chief petty officer '*sir*'. He's Chief

Puškarić." He pronounced it *PUSHK-ar-itch.* "Do you understand?"

Sharon realized that they expected her to conduct herself like a fellow military person. She nodded and made a feeble attempt at saluting him.

Bradford tsked, took her right arm and placed it and her hand in the correct position for a proper salute. "Thus. Done crisply."

"Thanks. Em … Do I call *you* sir?"

"I'm an officer, so yes." Bradford looked disappointed. "Do you have any idea whatsoever where you are, lass?"

"None at all."

Bradford pulled up the chair and sat so that his face was level with Sharon's. His eyes showed signs of distress. "Do you still think your name is Sharon?"

She just shrugged, worried that any other response would get her into some kind of trouble.

"Do you remember anything at all?" he asked.

Sharon did her best to pull up some memory, any memory, from the dark fog that was her past. "Nothing."

There was more of the infernal mumbling from Bradford, which was getting annoying. Then, "You might be back on your feet ASAP, but unless you can get your memories back — all of them — you won't be going back to work."

Sharon nodded and looked Bradford in the eyes. "I understand."

"Good!" Bradford brightened. "Do you think you're ready for some physical therapy?"

Sharon held up the cable locking her to the bed.

"I'm sure we can let you loose for as much exercise as you can stand." Dr. Bradford said, addressing an invisible person, "Corpsman, bring the key to this contraption."

*   *   *

Much later, Dr. Bradford reported to Souza in the captain's quarters. "She doesn't remember anything. She doesn't know she's on a spaceship. She doesn't have any inkling of what quantum electronics is. She doesn't even remember her military training."

"Well," Souza responded, swallowing a mouthful of coffee. "That won't do. But considering that we all thought she was dead, this is an improvement. And nothing at all about the explosion?"

"No. And, if I may, she was never quite dead. She always had brainstem activity after the injury. I was ready to pull the plug on her, though. Her mental recovery is nothing short of miraculous. I see several papers in the making here."

"Any idea what caused it? The recovery, I mean."

"Maybe," Bradford said cautiously. "There's a problem. Simmons thinks she's someone else. There is another identity replacing the Simmons one. An identity who calls herself Sharon Manders."

Souza raised her eyebrows and regarded the ship's surgeon in silence for five seconds. "A spy?"

Bradford shook his head. It was not surprising that a career military person would immediately suspect a spy, and considering everything else, it was not a huge leap even for the most dedicated optimist. It would certainly tie up all the loose ends.

"Psychology isn't my specialty and while I won't rule anything out, my best guess is that it's simply some kind of psychotic break."

"Then why are we having this conversation?"

"Because there are aspects which just don't add up. Even with severe brain trauma, complete and permanent memory loss is rare. You mentioned spies, for example. There have been cases of spies who, through pharmaceuticals and conditioning, had their personalities subsumed by their cover identity, and then awakened as a sleeper agent by some stimulus. This could be the case with Simmons, but even the subsumed personality would also have been damaged by the brain trauma. Thing is, there was no higher brain function at all. I was prepared to let Simmons die. Nothing of any personality, native or otherwise, should have survived."

"But?"

"Where did the Sharon Manders personality come from? The patient was only just this side of official brain death. Her heart and lungs were working on their own, but that was all. Even if the brain had healed itself — a condition without precedence — it would have been a blank slate. There have been cases where patients have suffered brain trauma to the point where they are mentally like babies, though otherwise healthy. They have to be taught from scratch — just like babies. In Simmons' case, it was like somebody deleted the old personality and wrote a new one. There is no known method for doing that, and no ethics panel in the Tau Ceti Alliance would authorize such an experiment."

Souza looked concerned. "So, you're saying that it would take an unknown technology to create a foreign personality in a host brain." She thought about this for a moment then asked, "Have you done a census search for this Sharon Manders?"

"Yes, to no avail, I'm afraid."

"Doctor, we have to proceed with caution. We'll assume that this Manders personality is untrustworthy. Do not let her have access to any ship's systems, is that clear?"

"Yes, ma'am."

"Keep her secured, and keep me posted on her condition and anything that looks suspicious."

"Yes, ma'am."

*　　*　　*

A wolf walked into Sharon's hospital room.

Actually, it was a wolf-man, and Sharon wondered if it was real, or if her meds had something to do with the apparition.

The wolf-man wore a corpsman's scrubs with the *Zephyr* logo and a name tag which displayed the word BARISCHK. Sharon's second thought was that this was some sort of costume, but the details were incredibly fine. She was so startled by the appearance that she only belatedly realized that the wolf-man was giving her an object: A hand mirror. The wolf's visage somehow managed a doggy grin and a playful wink. Sharon took the mirror and murmured, "Thank you. That's very considerate," though her thoughts were along the lines of, *just when you think you have this universe figured out ...* The wolf-man turned and left without a word, tail wagging.

Further thoughts of the wolf-man were lost as Sharon caught sight of herself in the mirror. The woman who looked back was completely unrecognizable. Of indeterminate age somewhere between twenty and forty, she had stubby light brown hair that was just growing in, and a fresh, wicked scar running along her left coronal suture. Beyond that, the shallow set to the eyes, the high cheek bones, the light-brown skin, the pointed chin, the detached earlobes, the full nose, the brown irises, the almond shape of the eyes — she looked like one of those composite photographs used to show what people would look like after all the races of humanity finally mixed together.

Everything looked wrong, though Sharon could not have said what should have been right.

How do I know what a coronal suture is?

"Who are you?" Sharon asked the woman in the mirror.

The door opened and yet another stranger walked in. He looked entirely human, and a bit Nordic. He appeared to be about thirty years old and dressed in a slightly different uniform than the Navy personnel.

"Specialist Simmons, I'm told that you won't remember me. I'm Marine Lieutenant Folke Berg. We are all concerned for your health and I was wondering if you would do something for me." Without waiting for a reply, he handed her a slim sheet of translucent flexible plastic with words on it. It was apparently some kind of computer display and interface. "Read that out loud."

Sharon cleared her throat and took a breath, wondering if she should have saluted the lieutenant. "'Although he was a poet …'"

"No, wait," the Lieutenant interrupted. "Read it like you normally would, in your own voice. I know you're making an effort to be understood, but that's neither necessary nor desired with this exercise. Please continue."

Sharon started over, speaking in a natural, unforced manner.

When she was done, she looked at Berg for further instructions. He was, of course, mumbling to himself.

What was it with all the mumbling? Was it some cultural norm she hadn't learned? Or was everybody here afflicted with some neurosis?

Berg looked confused. "Read it again."

Sharon complied, and the results did not seem to clear up anything for either of them.

"Thank you, Specialist Simmons," the lieutenant said, taking the plastic. "Good day."

And with that, Berg was gone.

*   *   *

Lieutenant Berg's orders were simultaneously simple and broad: *Assume that the patient in Sick Bay 1021 is not Specialist Simmons. Find out who she is.*

According to every biometric he could think of, there was no physical difference between Carol Simmons and the patient. DNA as well as mitochondrial DNA markers all matched. Fingerprints and retinal scans also matched. *Everything* matched.

The voice analysis, however, did not. There was no record in the entire Navy of anybody with that voiceprint. When the ship stopped at Kentaurus, he could access a wider range of databases. According to navy records, Simmons was born and raised in the Alemanni Province, but there was no way her current voice patterns matched the heavily accented patois of commingled English, Spanish, and German associated with that region. In fact, he was certain that her accent was not found anywhere on Kentaurus, her home planet, and there was a huge collection of regional accents there. The patient's accent was flatter, with very little emphasis. Berg was anxious to access other databases to find out just where the accent came from. Could Simmons be such a good voice actress that she was faking? The computer analysis said no. Although he had seen some extremely good performances by impressionists and voice artists who seemed to be able to do anything with their voices, the human voice was the sum of many things.

One of the more curious aspects of Simmons' speech was the pronunciation of the word *"dear"* with a single syllable *dir,* like the animal. Anybody else on the ship, regardless of their native language accent, would have pronounced it with two syllables, *dee-ahr.*

Feeling like he needed to talk this out with somebody, Berg activated a program he hadn't used in years.

"How may I help you?" the genderless, computer-generated voice asked.

"Have you accessed all the information on the case?" Berg asked.

"Yes. It's very curious."

"Do you think Patient 1021 set the bomb?"

"It's very probable. There is a decided lack of suspects, but that doesn't make Patient 1021 guilty. While there are several crewmembers who have the means to construct such a bomb, I cannot identify anybody else who had the opportunity. Nor can I identify a motive."

Berg sighed. The computer was reflecting Berg's own thoughts. "Could Patient 1021 be a sleeper agent?"

"The life of Patient 1021 is well documented, and she has never shown any interest in radical politics, or any other kind of politics. The only suspicious anomaly are the missing hours on Maheux. While this is alarming, the time frame seems insufficient."

This was no help. Berg had already been over all these facts in detail. He terminated the program then said, "Word process activate," under his breath, which Sharon would have mistaken for incoherent mumbling. His EPU responded with a small red light in the upper right of his visual field. "Open report Status of Patient 1021." He summarized his findings, cleaned up the grammatical and voice-to-text errors, and then concluded, "Append. The patient is emphasis not emphasis Carol Simmons. Even if she were intentionally trying to hide her voiceprint identity, the analysis would have discovered it. Carol Simmons could not have created this voiceprint. Stop."

Berg thought carefully about his next words. "Continue. Paragraph. Dr. Bradford, CMO, has expressed different hypotheses on what may have happened. First, the patient is exhibiting an emergent personality which has never before existed. This is consistent with her lack of memory about anything prior to the explosion. When asked what the genesis of this emergent personality may be, he conjectured that it might have originated in a book or vid series which the patient identified with as a young girl. Paragraph.

"Second, we may be seeing a latent personality which existed prior to the one we know as Carol Simmons. Dr. Bradford has outlined medical procedures involving pharmacological and cognitive treatments in which one personality can be made dormant, and another overlaid, but he emphasizes that it is beyond his sphere of knowledge. The natural fear is that the latent, and now dominant personality could be a malevolent one. Stop." Berg thought for a second, then added, "Insert. Dr. Bradford was quick to emphasize that overlaying a personality with another one is always temporary. There has never been a case where one pre-existing personality has permanently replaced another. Additionally, there wasn't enough time to accomplish this."

Berg became silent with thought, resting his head on his hands and his elbows on the desk. After a minute or two he addressed the EPU again. "New task. Perform media search for references to personality disorders associated with faulty EPUs." His EPU flashed the light to indicate that it had understood and accepted the task.

"New Task. Perform media search for any reference in any language on any planet for the name Sharon Manders or any derivation of that name." The light flashed again.

"New Task. Append to report Status of Patient 1021. Cue video record ..." he checked his notes, "1021 dash 17 dash 42. Begin at time marker one hour, forty-three minutes. Play."

Berg's visual field was replaced with the view from the security camera in Sharon's room. It showed her examining her face in a mirror. She touched her nose, her eyebrows, and her chin. After fifteen seconds, the enhanced audio pick-up clearly recorded her words.

"Who are you?"

3

" A LL HANDS PREPARE FOR WARP FIELD COLLAPSE. Transition in three minutes."

Sharon had been listening to the countdown ever since the ten-minute mark. It was hard to miss when it seemed to come from every speaker on the ship. A corpsman explained that it was also sent through everybody's Endocranial Processing Unit, or EPU, but navy regulations required audible warnings.

Sharon found this fascinating. Every person on this ship, including her it would seem, had a computer embedded in their skull. They not only communicated with each other via this device, but accessed communal networks.

Since her EPU had died, she couldn't use the system. She asked if there were other external ways to access it, and learned that there were, but she was not allowed to use them. Instead, Dr. Bradford had brought a sheet of paper and a pen. Apparently, both of these items were as rare as diamonds, and the corpsman who found them was quite pleased with himself.

"Write down anything you remember," Bradford had ordered.

So far, the sheet of paper remained pristine. "As white as snow," Sharon said. *Snow.* She remembered snow. On a mountain. She remembered skiing.

She wrote, *Skiing on a snow-covered mountain slope.*

The paper was no longer pristine. It was contaminated. *Pollution. Dirty cities. Poverty.*

"Warp field collapse in two minutes."

Space, she wrote. *Astronomy. Humans in space. Human history. Anthropology.*

She paused and looked at the last word and wrote: *Coronal suture. Bones. Skull.*

Almost absently, Sharon started sketching a human skull.

"Warp field collapse in sixty seconds."

She started labeling the bones of the skull.

She had no idea what to expect from the collapse of the warp field. The corpsman had explained that the ship's engines generated a bubble of local space-time, the warp field, which itself traveled through the larger frame of reference of interstellar space, thus circumventing relativistic limits on speeds, but also effectively cutting off all communication with the external universe.

Will it hurt?

*   *   *

"All departments report secure for transition, Captain."

30

"Very good, Commander. Continue."

"Field collapse in ten ..."

Souza held her breath. There was absolutely no reason to think that the transition would be catastrophic, but even without a suspected spy on board, she always worried about it.

This is what you get for playing fast and loose with the laws of physics.

In the entire history of spaceflight, there had only been three incidents where post-prototype warp ships were destroyed during the transition. Unfortunately, there was no way to find out why, and paranoia was part of Souza's job description.

"... three ... two ... one ..."

There was a momentary feeling of disorientation, and it was over.

They were now traveling far less than the speed of light. The screens showing exterior camera views were now all filled with stars.

"Report?" Souza demanded.

"All departments report zero damage. A successful transition, Captain," the first officer reported.

"Passive and active sensors report no other traffic in the immediate area."

"Excellent. I want a current position fix and communications link before I finish this ..."

"Position plotted," Navigation said, slightly ahead of the report from Communications, "Link established."

"Splendid. I want to know what's been going on in the universe since we last saw it. All departments stand down from transition ready."

As a matter of routine, the *KRS Zephyr* made contact with a satellite in orbit about the primary star, which relayed stored messages, sending them at light speed. The spaceship was still about five light-hours from the primary, and it took three minutes light travel time for the nearest relay to detect the *Zephyr*'s encrypted transponder code and another three minutes for the messages to start arriving.

Commander Souza waited for the little red flag in her peripheral view which would indicate messages of the most urgent matter. If war had been declared, for instance. No red flags, but there were orange ones, which meant there were messages which didn't require an instant response, merely immediate ones. Unfortunately, the Kentauran Republic Navy thought every official message deserved an immediate response.

"Course for Kentaurus plotted," Navigation said. "Travel time, pending final approach clearance, is three days, twenty-two hours, objective, at point one nine six zero delta squared."

"Do it," Souza ordered. "Comm, let me know as soon as traffic control acknowledges our existence. Good work, people. I expect final mission reports in my box by the time we make orbit. I'll be in my quarters responding to my fan mail. The flight deck is yours, Commander Lagrueux."

"I have the watch," he confirmed.

*   *   *

More than a day and a half later, as the *Zephyr* was decelerating towards circum-Kentauran space, Souza received a chat request from Lt. Berg.

URGENT: MANDERS.

"Accept," she said, and waited for the view to focus. YES, LIEUTENANT?

MA'AM. I HAVE BEEN IN CONTACT WITH THE OFFICE OF CRIMINAL INVESTIGATIONS REGARDING OUR PATIENT. AS YOU RECALL, I WAS UNABLE TO MATCH HER VOICEPRINT WITH ANYBODY IN ANY SHIPBOARD DATABASE. OCI PERFORMED THEIR OWN SEARCH AT MY REQUEST, AND THEY HAVE ALSO FAILED TO FIND A MATCH.

I SEE. BUT YOU DIDN'T CHAT ME JUST TO TELL ME THAT.

NO, MA'AM. IT'S HER NAME THAT RAISED A FLAG. WE DID FIND A MATCH ON THE NAME SHARON MANDERS. AND YOU WON'T LIKE IT. HERE'S THE FILE.

The image of a tall blonde woman wearing the uniform of the State Police of Droben appeared in Souza's field of view. Droben was a planet run by a single isolationist political system. They were zealots who declared war on Kentaurus a century ago, and as far as they were concerned, the war was on going. The SPD was implicated in several terrorist attacks throughout the Tau Ceti Treaty Alliance.

DAMN.

AGREED, MA'AM. DAMN. HOWEVER, THERE ARE SOME ODD ASPECTS TO THIS CASE. PLEASE NOTE THAT MAJOR SHARON MANDERS OF DROBEN DIED TEN STANDARD YEARS AGO IN A SUICIDE BOMBING CARRIED OUT BY A SPLINTER FACTION. LONG BEFORE CREWMAN SIMMONS EVEN CONSIDERED ENLISTING. ALSO, THE MAJOR BEARS ABSOLUTELY NO RESEMBLANCE TO OUR CREWMAN. IT SHOULD ALSO BE NOTED THAT SIMMONS IS CURRENTLY SPEAKING WITH AN ACCENT THAT BEARS NO RESEMBLANCE TO ANY FOUND ON DROBEN.

WERE THERE ANY OTHER MATCHES?

YES. THOUGH THIS WOMAN WAS THE ONLY ONE WHO HAD A MILITARY OR INTELLIGENCE BACKGROUND. IN A CENSUS OF THIRTY INHABITED WORLDS, THERE WERE FIVE WOMEN WITH THAT NAME. FOUR OF THEM, LIKE THE SPD OFFICER, ARE DEAD. THE ONLY ONE STILL ALIVE IS AN INDIGENT SINGLE MOTHER OF THREE ON A PRE-SINGULARITY PLANET.

Pre-Singularity meant that they were still the original human genome, and were still limited to eighty or a hundred standard years lifespan, and nobody had EPUs. There were only two Pre-Singularity planets, and they tended to be shunned by the rest of humanity. On the stage of current human socio-political theater, they had nearly zero presence.

IS THERE ANY CONNECTION AT ALL BETWEEN SIMMONS AND MANDERS? HAVE THEY EVER BEEN ON THE SAME PLANET?

NOT ACCORDING TO ANY RECORDS THAT I CAN FIND.

THAT MAY NOT MEAN ANYTHING, Souza said in frustration.

It was a digital universe out there, full of FTL ships, and information traveled a lot faster than it did a few hundred years ago.

DID KOCI HAVE ANY SUGGESTIONS?

ONLY TO EXERCISE CAUTION. BEYOND THAT, NOTHING SPECIFIC.

AS HELPFUL AS ALWAYS, I SEE. Souza scowled.

BUT, MA'AM, I'M NOT SURE WHAT THERE IS TO BE CAREFUL ABOUT. THERE'S NO KNOWN WAY FOR THE PERSONALITY OF SPD MANDERS TO SHOW UP IN KRN SIMMONS.

CORRECT. NO KNOWN WAY. IF OUR CREWMAN HAS NO CONNECTION TO MAJOR MANDERS, THEN THE GALAXY GOES ON SPINNING LIKE BEFORE. IF THERE IS A CONNECTION, WE HAVE TO BE PREPARED. AND LACK OF PREPAREDNESS IS NO EXCUSE FOR FAILURE, IS IT, LIEUTENANT?

NO, MA'AM.

YOUR RECOMMENDATION?

TURN HER OVER TO SOMEBODY WHO'S BETTER EQUIPPED TO FIGURE THIS OUT. ZEPHYR IS A WARP SHIP, NOT A PSYCH WARD.

As much as Souza disliked the idea of foisting her problem off on somebody else, she didn't see an alternative. Either they found evidence that Simmons was complicit in an attack on a naval vessel, in which case she should be locked up pending a court martial, or she needed a psychological evaluation. Either way, she'll be removed from the crew as soon as they arrived on Kentaurus.

AGREED. DID NAVAL SECURITY ACKNOWLEDGE RECEIPT OF ALL THE INFORMATION WE HAVE ON THE SABOTAGE?

YES, MA'AM.

Good. Your recommendation for Crewman Simmons until we get to Kentaurus?

Souza could see that Berg was clearly conflicted on this one. We don't really have enough to charge her with anything. You could, of course, keep her locked up on your prerogative. However, my suggestion is to let her go and see what she does. See if she contacts a coconspirator or just walks around in a confused daze. Either would be probative.

Agreed. Let her go as soon as she's able to put her shoes on without help, but keep her under tight surveillance. Carry on.

Aye, ma'am. Berg clear.

4

S HARON WAS STANDING UP IN ROOM 1021. It was painful to lie down and even more painful to stand up, but she figured the standing up pain would eventually be rewarded with greater mobility. That, and the pain helped keep her mind off of her situation. If she thought about it too much, she started to panic. It was the feeling of being absolutely powerless against a universe she had neither memory nor understanding of, and she felt like she would be crushed any moment.

For lack of anything else to occupy her mind, she read the signs on the walls. Even though the pronunciation of letters had drifted, English orthography remained static, and just as crazy as it ever was. One sign contained a warning about the use of pure oxygen around an open flame. Another listed universal precautions to prevent the spread of disease. Another gave instructions on how to use the scanning monitor.

Language is such a complicated thing. Why do I remember how to read, speak and understand all these words without remembering how I learned them?

Questions about language and memory bounced around in her thoughts. She looked at the word *"oxygen"*. She could check off its characteristics in her mind:

Chemical symbol O. Atomic number eight. Atomic weight sixteen, or close enough. Two electrons in the P-orbitals, six in the S-orbitals. Electronegativity of about three and a half. Combine it with two hydrogen atoms to get water. Water expands when it freezes, and this allows for life as we know it.

Sharon knew all of this, but didn't know how she knew. Did she take chemistry classes? Biology classes? She felt like she was remembering details and facts as she needed them. It was as if the memories didn't exist a moment ago, but now they did. Her little one-sheet notebook was now full of sketches of human anatomy. A fact isn't remembered in isolation. It's remembered because it's associated with other things and events. What did she associate oxygen with? Breathing and combustion, of course. But air wasn't just oxygen.

There. She remembered a little bit more about this universe, which helped convince the little girl in her that it was neither capricious nor intentionally malicious. She took a deep breath.

She dreamed the previous night of being a teacher. She stood in front of a class, words on a whiteboard, marker in her hand. The earnest students watched her every move, some of them taking notes.

The door opened to admit Dr. Bradford, interrupting her thoughts. "I've brought you some clothes," he said without preamble.

Sharon looked at the bluish-grey jumpsuit that she had come to recognize as the ship's basic enlisted duty uniform. It included a nametag which read SIMMONS.

"Oh, doctor, you shouldn't have! You really know just how to melt a girl's heart."

Bradford frowned and Sharon recognized that she'd responded inappropriately. She backpedaled. "Thank you, sir. I'll change clothes right away."

"We'll be in orbit in about twenty-eight hours. You've recovered enough to move back into your own bed. I have reservations about this, but the captain has ordered it. She thinks it will do you good to be among your rack mates. It might spark some memories." What he didn't tell her was that Naval Security would be meeting her at the station.

The sheet of paper full of sketched anatomy caught Bradford's attention and he picked it up. "This is quite good. Where did you study gross anatomy?"

"Wish I knew, … sir."

"Between two shipmates, Simmons, what's a synovial joint?"

Sharon responded without pause, "It's the kind of joint that has a cavity lined by a membrane, like our hips, knees and elbows. As distinguished from cartilaginous and fibrous joints. It's the common joint found in mammals."

"What is a qubit?"

Sharon shrugged. "No clue."

Bradford studied the sketches for a moment longer then handed the sheet back to Sharon. He remembered the crewman called Simmons. She was a mercurial, often annoying woman with little formal education, and was often in trouble for minor infractions of the military code. Manders, on the other hand, was a charming, obviously intelligent woman who was making an effort to fit in even if she didn't know how. He couldn't help but think that the Navy was getting a bargain out of this deal.

"Listen … um … Manders. Sharon. You need to understand how the space service works. We've got 150 men and women, and thirty marines, surviving and traveling between the stars by dint of technology we barely understand, and there are several nations and some insane people who wish us nothing but ill will. While we're all willing to die for the Republic, we're not looking forward to it. We stay alive by being suspicious of anything we don't immediately understand. It makes us a close-knit, paranoid lot, and this has led to some unfortunate events. When we make port at Sedna, you're going to be an outsider in an unfamiliar place, especially with your ignorance of EPUs, networks, and modern life in general. You're going to have to learn about society quickly if you're going to stay alive, and that includes learning some guile."

This little speech took Sharon by surprise and left her confused.

Learn some guile?

She was about to ask for clarification when Bradford seemed to change his mind about something.

"May I have those sketches? And would you mind signing it for me?"

"Um … I guess. Sure."

*   *   *

Sharon dressed and felt much improved in the process. The ability to dress like a normal human being instead of a patient allowed her to feel less like a freak. The jumpsuit was slightly stiff and neatly pressed. On the collar was a brass-colored insignia. It was in the shape of an italic '*h*' with a bar through the vertical tail. Below the *h* were two broken stripes. She learned from conversations with a corpsman named Wali al Din Shamal Nazari that this designated her rank and job, and the *h*-bar had something to do with quantum mechanics. Unlike the CPO, there was no centaur and no laurel wreath.

The centaur that topped the insignia of the warrant officer's was a symbol of the planet-nation of the Kentauran Republic, which orbited Alpha Centauri A. The choice of mascot seemed obvious in that context.

Once dressed, Nazari escorted her through the complex maze of corridors and stairs to the door leading to her living quarters. He was a polite young man who looked 18 but claimed to be a much older, unbelievable age, and spoke with an accent reminiscent of the Bronx, even though Nazari had never heard of it.

"Be careful," Nazari advised before leaving.

"I will. Thanks."

The door, though heavy and armored, opened on a hinge. Inside, she saw two young men who looked up at her in surprise. A redhead was playing a guitar, and a hirsute man was staring into the distance with an expression she had learned meant that he was accessing his EPU.

This is awkward. What do I say?

"Hi, guys."

She noticed that they were both enlisted ratings and said to herself, *Good! I don't have to salute anybody here.*

Nazari had given her a quick lesson on whom to salute and when, and ended it with the advice, "When in doubt, salute. Nobody ever got court martialed for unnecessary saluting."

She gave a quick wave instead. The men were obviously feeling awkward, too.

"I'm told that I sleep here."

"Yeah," said a redhead with the name ADLER on his chest. "You, us, an' six other people." He stood up and offered his hand. "Doc says ya won't remember us. I'm Felix Adler. This is Lester Sievers. Everyone else is on duty."

"A pleasure!" Sharon said, accepting his hand. "Apologies beforehand for all the social mistakes I'm going to make."

"Dey tol' us yuh die'," Sievers said darkly. "Yer brain stopped."

This was a different accent than the one Sharon had been learning. The words sounded half-formed, as if these two were from the poor side of town.

"Well, I don't know much about brains, but Doc Bradford said mine was never completely dead. I just lost all my memories."

Sharon looked around at the small, square, spartan room. It was about two and a half meters on the side. There were three pairs of triple bunks built into the bulkheads on shelves, each triplet on a different wall. There was a square table with four chairs in the center of the room, and Sievers was sitting there. Another door opened into what she recognized as a communal bathroom with connections to other enlisted sleeping rooms.

Each bed had an associated tall locker, about thirty inches wide and just as deep, with stenciled names. The one with SIMMONS on it was associated to the lower bunk of the far wall. She opened her locker and found several sets of clothes and some personal items. Photographs of people she didn't know, and unrecognized landscapes decorated the interior. There were toiletries and some electronic gadgets which she neither recognized nor knew the function of.

"Da's your mother and father," Adler said. Now that she knew that, she could see the familial resemblance of the people in a photograph to the woman in the mirror.

"They don't look old enough to be my parents," she said. "They look maybe thirty." She turned to look at Adler, who was sharing a look with Sievers. Adler picked up his guitar and resumed strumming chords.

An idea formed in Sharon's head. This was the first music she had heard since waking up. Until this moment she had lived post trauma in a world without music. The music seemed to stimulate some kind of cascade effect in her memories.

She turned quickly to Adler. "Please. Would you play that chord progression again?"

"Ya mean dis?" and he duplicated what he'd just done.

"Gee. Dee seven. Cee," Sharon said, surprising herself. Adler looked surprised, too, and gave a small laugh.

"Try dis one," he said and strummed another chord.

Sharon thought for a moment, looked at the finger position of his left hand and said, "Eff sharp major ninth."

Adler's smile broadened and said, "Damn, Simmons! I wish I could get knocked t' da head an' wake up wi' a new skill!"

Sievers looked stunned and stared at Sharon.

"Can ya play, too?" Adler offered the instrument to her.

She took it and settled into a chair. Her subconscious seemed to know what to do, but her fingers moved with uncertainty. She tried some easy chords. There was a song here. A song which wanted to be played, and her memory was racing at top speed to find it. The sound of the chords, the sensation of the strings under her fingers, and the motion of her arm all brought back flashes of memory.

No, that's not quite true. It was a feeling of memories being created, which brought another feeling of panic, but she pushed it down by thinking of the music.

Then she smiled and changed her style from strumming to finger picking. She knew a song which she thought might get her some much-needed ship cred with these men.

After an intro, she began singing a sailors' shanty. She sang in an easy style, hoping the accent would not overly confuse her audience. She would have happily sung the entire song, which came rushing into her head like a flood, except that Sievers jumped up and pulled the guitar out of her hands.

"Wot do yuh think yer doin'?" Sievers demanded. "Yuh don' play d' geetar. Yer foockin' tone deaf! I heard yuh screw up nursery rhymes, and now yer a foockin' my-stro!"

"Lester, calm down!" Adler tried to intervene. "An', damn it, if ya damage my guitar you and I are going t' have words in da hold."

"Didn' yuh hear her?" Sievers went on in anger. "Yuh cain' learn t' play d' geetar like a pro just from a knock on d' head."

"What the fook is wrong wi' you?" Adler shouted back. "Put. Da guitar. Down!"

Sievers finally got it through his head that Adler was willing to do great bodily harm if any damage should come to his beloved instrument and handed it over. Adler laid it lovingly into a case on his bunk and then put it into his locker.

"Sievers," Sharon started to say. "I …"

"Dun talk t' me!" he interrupted. "Yuh stay outa mah space and we ge' 'long jus' fine. Ah'm gunna go fin' some coffee." And with that he left.

Sharon turned to Adler. "That didn't go well."

Adler waived it off. "He'll ge' over it. He's one of dose recruits who was given da choice between military service an' jail time. Wha' was dat song ya was playing?"

"Mingulay Boat Song."

"Never heard o' it. Who wrote it? Somebody in your province?"

"It's an old traditional …"

Sharon started to say something about sea shanties, but the memory faded before she could get it out. It was if the memory was there when she was about to say it, and then vanished. This happened a lot and it frustrated Sharon to the point of anger.

Adler saw this on her face. "Whoa! Didn't mean t' be nosey."

Sharon shook her head. "It's just that my memory tends to be more ephemeral than smoke. The more I think about them, the less substantive they become."

"Well, at least ya play da guitar now. Ya'll need t' ge' one o' yer own an' we can jam."

"Is it true that I never played before?"

"Wooman, I have never heard ya speak o' it. Never seen ya even look at an instrument. An' I wouldn't be so gen'rous as t' call what ya like t' listen t' 'music.' T'me it sounds like cats in heat who've hired a drunk baboon for a drummer. Very little rhythm an' no rhyme."

"Are one of these gadgets in my locker for storing music?"

"Well, not music specifically, but dis one is fo'mass storage."

He reached into the locker and pulled out a rectangle of stiff plastic which measured about three inches by five by half an inch.

"How do I turn it on?"

"Ya have t' access it with your EPU."

"Gah. My EPU died."

Adler looked at her incredulously. "No shi'?! No wonder ya didn't get our messages. So ya have no way t' access da nets?"

"No. None at all."

"Why don' dey put a new one in?"

Sharon looked at him. "You tell me."

Adler clearly had difficulty processing this as he stared wide-eyed. Sharon could see that the thought of being without an EPU actually terrified him. He seemed to pull himself together and asked, "How're ya gunna t' get yer dailies?"

"Daily what?"

"Daily orders."

Sharon shrugged her shoulders. "Verbally?"

Adler laughed. "Yeah! Like da Chief is going t' take da time t' come find ya and give ay dailies. They'll probably give ya glasses or a handheld."

"I haven't been released back to duty, and I understand we dock tomorrow. I don't think it'll be an issue."

"Wow. Dis is so bongo," Adler said. "Ya talk wi' a funny accent, ya use two note words, ya play musical instruments an' like ballads, an' yer EPU is dead. Dis really is da new an' improved Carol Simmons!"

*　　*　　*

During the next day, Sharon met a hundred people or more. Many of them treated her with fear, as if she were a ghost, others with curiosity. She often fielded the question, "What's it like to be dead?" with "I don't remember being dead."

Everybody treated her as an outsider. Even Adler, who was friendly enough, couldn't quite accept her as a crewmate.

Sharon found the silence most disturbing. Even when there were large crowds, as in the mess, there was very little talking. Sharon expected to hear the constant hum of conversation, but few people communicated verbally. People communicated through their EPUs, and all Sharon heard was the incessant, characteristic, irritating mumbling. There was frequent laughter, but not many words. Many of the crew expressed annoyance that they had to address Sharon verbally, and made derisive comments about her being deaf, dumb, and blind.

Somebody made a comment aloud about her being the spawn of Satan, and turning to see who it was, she caught a glimpse of Siever's back as he walked away.

During one meal, Sharon saw Barischk sitting by himself, eating in a way that involved a lot of tongue action and open-mouthed chewing, just as a wolf would eat. The food looked like standard issue meat, potatoes, and vegetables. What did she expect, dog food?

Turning to a mumbling crewman sitting near her, she asked, "Who is Barischk? What species is he?"

The crewman looked annoyed at having his mumbling interrupted, and gave her a look that said, "You're kidding." Then responded as if explaining to a child. "Barischk is a Furman. His ancestors were human, but they modified their genome to become human-wolf hybrids. One of the very few groups to succeed in doing that."

"Why would they do that?"

"Well, to hear Barischk explain it, it was to modify their physical bodies to more closely reflect their animal spirits."

"He can talk?" Sharon was unconvinced. "With that mouth?"

"No," the crewman said patiently. "Not human speech. He communicates using the EPU as a translator. But you don't have one," the crewman said as if it were an accusation.

Sharon took that as a hint and went back to eating silently. After another minute of being ignored by her shipmates, she stood, took her meal tray and walked over to where Barischk was sitting.

"May I join you, Barischk?"

The wolf-man looked at her in surprise, then gestured politely to a chair opposite him.

"I know you can't talk to me, but I wanted to say thanks for the mirror. I'll give it back to you."

Barischk shook his head and made a gesture that Sharon should keep it. Then they ate in companionable silence.

*   *   *

The *Zephyr* finally pulled into orbit around a planet with two moons, but otherwise looked like Earth as long as one ignored the shape of the continents. Then they docked at a huge space station orbiting the outer moon.

The ship was put into stand-by mode. Systems were shut down and secured. Announcements were made, and people eventually started preparing to disembark.

Sharon packed some clothes and was ready to leave her shared bunkroom when Dr. Bradford walked in.

"There you are, lass," he said. "I've been looking for you."

"What is it, sir?"

"Listen to me, this is important." He gave her a plastic card. "I'm sorry to tell you that things will be unpleasant for you for a while. If things get too rough, chat me."

Sharon looked at the card then back at the physician. "What do you mean?"

"I can't tell you more. Just …" he paused. "Just keep calm."

"Keep calm," she repeated, getting angry. "Okay, I'll keep calm."

"Crewman Second Class Carol Simmons?" a new voice asked.

Sharon turned around to see two marines, a man and a woman, who were obviously there on official business.

"Yes?"

"Would you come with us please?"

The woman took her by the elbow while the man lifted her bag from her shoulders. It obviously was not a request.

"What's going on?"

"All will be explained. Just come with us."

5

Senda Naval Yards
Rigil Kentaurus System
Kentauran calendar: 20 Teleftmina, 1382 PS

T HE FOURTH AND LAST PLANET out from Alpha Centauri A
is a near twin to humanity's birth world and had a stable
population of not quite one billion. The capital is a port city
known as Clarksport, located on the coast of a minor continent
in the northern hemisphere. The city grew out of maritime
necessity, located at a mutually convenient place for various
nations to meet and trade. The halls of the various branches of
government are all located in a district of town unimaginatively
named *Government Square.*

Xoanna Carme Campoverde, the Minister of the Navy,
knew all of the halls by heart. She'd held her office for a quarter

century through five different administrations. She walked from her own office located in the basement of the Justice Building to the office of the Chief Minister, Yianni Aniketos Katsaros. The day was cold — near freezing — but clear. Campoverde wore several layers of clothes including a red wool jacket which reached to mid-calf, and a rainbow scarf.

Xoanna had one requirement of anybody — if you wanted to talk to her, you looked her in the eye and said your piece. She had long ago set the chat function of her EPU to automatically reject any request that didn't come from either her family, certain members of her staff, specific admirals, or Katsaros himself. This often made life difficult for undersecretaries, interns, and journalists, but she had learned early in her political career that if she responded to every chat request, she'd spend all day doing nothing else. Every politician, CEO, and major celebrity did the same thing, and your station in life was often demonstrated by the people you could afford to piss off by refusing their chat requests.

"Minister Campoverde!" she heard a young male voice call out.

She didn't recognize it and waited until she heard the hail a second time from much closer. Somebody was running to catch her.

She turned to see a young intern from her office dressed in a business suit and wearing shoes that were inappropriate for both the cold weather and running. Her EPU supplied the name: Shahrouz Shahsavari.

"Yes, Señor Shahsavari?"

"I beg your pardon, ma'am," he said breathlessly. "Priority message for you from the office of Naval Security."

"Thank you. Do you need a reply?" she asked coolly, opening a folded sheet of paper.

"No, ma'am," Shahsavari said, straightening his clothes.

"Good. I'll see you back at the office then."

Shahsavari started walking back to the office, and Campoverde hoped he wouldn't get chilled.

The paper contained a printed message in code. The technicians who'd programmed the code assured her that she was the only person in the universe who could read it. She engaged her EPU, which scanned the document via her own eyes, decrypted the message and translated it into her native Spanish, seeming to replace the text on the paper with the readable message. The news wasn't good. A bomb had exploded on a frigate. The primary suspect was in custody, but charges had not yet been filed. In fact, other than being at the scene of the explosion, the evidence was not convincing. There were other complications, like memory loss and personality changes. The note ended with questions: Why not destroy the entire ship? Why was it only disabled?

Excellent questions!

Campoverde knew there had been no chatter on the various terrorist watch-list 'Nets sites about attacks on a naval ship. Who would have the resources to pull something off like this? No organizations came immediately to mind. Did the suspect's mental state pertain to the situation?

She didn't like coincidences, but she knew that brain injuries could have peculiar effects. She would await further news regarding that.

Campoverde activated her EPU and put her hand over her mouth in case anybody was watching and listening.

"New task." When she saw the signal that the unit was ready to accept instructions, she said, "Contact Naval Security Special Agent Elrydien Daeîsiell. Subject: Job"

*   *   *

Sedna Naval Yards

Kentaurus has two moons. The inner and smaller satellite, known as Adlivun, is not much more than a large, uninteresting, spheroidal piece of carbonate minerals. There was a small, crewed rescue station. A posting there was usually lonely and boring. The larger, outer satellite, known as Sedna, was used as a staging nexus for space travel to and from Kentaurus. Some outlying spaceports used by civilian cargo and passenger carriers, processing plants sprinkled the satellite's landscape, and associated residential and business areas. The Customs Office is located in a huge naval shipyard which also contains the offices of Naval Security along with associated departments.

Sharon found herself, again, in a small room. She thought that perhaps she really had died and was condemned to spend eternity going from one small room to another. She had the feeling that in her previous life she was more of the outdoors type.

She sat in that room alone for at least an hour, though she was certain that unseen cameras were recording everything. Knowing that, she refrained from chewing on her fingernails and instead thought about other songs she might know. Sometimes a musical phrase would come to mind and then drift away. Were they real songs or was she making them up? If the latter, then she would have to be a very talented composer, because some phrases were incredibly complex with counterpoint melodies.

She hummed one of the tunes which haunted her, thinking that if she could actually hear it, rather than just imagine it, it might bring other memories.

Somebody came in. A tall woman, of about thirty — Sharon had come to expect everybody in the universe to be about thirty — with long brunette hair tied back into a ponytail. She wore a blue and tan business suit and carried one of those flexible handheld computers with her. The first thing Sharon noticed was her ears. They were pointed. Like an elf's ... or a Vulcan's.

The woman smiled. "The last movement from Bach's Cantata number 147. *Herz und Mund und Tat und Leben*. A truly timeless piece, don't you think? Hello, crewman Simmons. My name is Elrydien Daerîsiell. Would you like anything? Water? Chai? Coffee?"

"I'm good, thanks," Sharon said without taking her eyes off of the ears.

Elrydien noticed, and turned her head to the side, offering a better view.

"How do you like them?" she asked with a teasing smile.

"I'm sorry," Sharon looked away.

"Not at all. I get that a lot."

"Are they prosthetics?"

"Gods no, I was born with them. Inherited them from my parents. You're confused, aren't you?"

"Yes, a little. Okay, a lot."

"My ancestors from Earth were Tolkienists. Before it became illegal, they modified their genes in order to bring back the race of elves and initiate the Seventh Age."

Sharon stared.

Elrydien leaned forward and whispered, "You might want to close your mouth before you start to drool."

Sharon closed her mouth and regained her composure.

The elf went on. "You see, that's one of my problems. Everybody on Kentaurus knows what a Tolkienist is even if they've never seen one. Except you."

She laid the handheld on the table. It had the dimensions of a thick sheet of legal paper and was almost as flexible. Elrydien activated it.

"Here's your file. Carol W. Simmons. Born in the Alemanni Province in 1332 P.S. Grew up on a cattle ranch, attended the Thomas Brauer Primary School then attended the trade school in Aumbach to learn electronics. Your performance was not impressive, but you did earn your certs. You migrated around the planet for a number of years before you decided to enlist in the Navy. You were promoted to Crewman Second Class because you already had a trade. Began your tour with the *KRS Zephyr* about a year and a half ago. You've been reprimanded once for insubordination, once for fighting, and once for drunkenness.

"Now, here's where it gets interesting. On day 179 of your last cruise, while engaged in Protection of Shipping patrols, the *Zephyr* encountered a suspicious craft which, according to the file, was transponding a false identity. You were doing routine maintenance in Mechanical Chase Number One, and requested permission to stay at that post rather than report to your Battle Ready station. When the *Zephyr* tried to detain the suspicious ship, there was an explosion caused by a small bomb, which ruptured hydraulic conduits in the mechanical chase where you were working which in turn disabled two of the three hydraulic systems. The damage prevented the *Zephyr* from following the mystery ship into warp, but otherwise left the ship intact. You, on the other hand, were seriously injured and spent twenty-three days in a coma. Does any of this sound familiar?"

Sharon shook her head. "Only the waking up from the coma part."

"Do you remember taking shore leave at Maheux just eight days before the accident?"

"No. I don't even know where that is."

"Did you know that you spent twenty-seven standard hours out of contact? Nobody knew where you were during that time."

"This is the first I've heard of it." Sharon crossed her arms under her breasts and crossed her legs at the knees.

"According to the report filed by the ship's CMO, you woke up and called yourself Sharon Manders."

Elrydien folded her fingers together. Sharon noticed that her fingers had some fine filigree ornamentation which looked like silver wire around her slender fingers. "You see, Ms Manders, before we send people out on a multi-billion note warp-ship, filled elbow to elbow with people we've trained to kill and die for the Republic, we want to know exactly who they are. Nobody wants surprises when they're light-years from home traveling at ten or twenty times the speed of light. Familiar and predictable is good. Surprises are bad."

"I understand," Sharon said nervously.

"So, why don't you tell us who you are and we can put this behind us?"

Sharon spread her open hands out palms up. "I don't know who I am."

"Fair enough. Let's start with something easier. What year is this?"

That was easy. Sharon had seen many references to it in the last week. "1383 P.S."

Elrydien nodded. "What does the P.S. stand for?"

"Post Singularity."

"What was the Singularity?"

"I don't know."

"It's awfully convenient, don't you think, that you don't remember stuff." Elrydien seemed to pounce on the fact. "Makes it difficult to question you."

"That depends on how you define convenient," Sharon responded with some acid, fighting back the nervousness. "If you define it as being entirely unable to defend myself against your unspoken accusations, then yeah, it's damn convenient."

The elf ignored the sarcasm and mumbled to herself. A series of photographs began parading across the screen of the handheld.

"Do you recognize any of these people?"

After several seconds of the face parade, Sharon reported, "Those are my parents. I saw their photographs in my locker."

Elrydien merely nodded and indicated that Sharon should keep watching the parade. Elrydien never took her gaze away from Sharon's eyes.

"That's Dr. Bradford," Sharon indicated.

"Yes. Continue."

But none of the other photos registered.

When it was done, Elrydien turned off the handheld and asked Sharon to look in her eyes. "I'm going to say a list of names. You tell me if any of them are familiar."

The list of names was quite long. Sharon recognized three from the *Zephyr*'s roster, and suspected that those were controls. Elrydien just nodded and continued to say names.

After almost fifty names, one finally registered.

Elrydien looked shocked. "You're kidding."

"I am not. I know that name. I just don't know in what context."

"Eleanor Roosevelt?"

It was a nonsense name thrown in as a neutral control. It was used because nobody in the entire Centauri system had that name.

She read it in a history text, or saw a vid. came a voice of one of her partners via the EPU net.

The vision of a matronly Pre-Singularity woman floated in front of her. "The wife of an American President."

Quick: Give me another famous name from that era.

Ah ... Richard Nixon.

When Elrydien asked Sharon if she remembered who that was, Sharon responded almost immediately.

"Oh! I remember Tricky Dick! President during that mess in South East Asia. Then there was that whole Watergate fiasco, and the lunar landing."

As the image of Mrs. Roosevelt faded, Elrydien made a gesture and the picture on the handheld changed again.

Elrydien turned the handheld back on and pulled up a file. It was a vid of Sharon recorded two hours earlier while she read some words that sounded like they were from a movie or a theatrical presentation. Sharon was asked to read in her normal voice.

"Most of the cinemas from Pre-Singularity days have been redubbed into modern languages and remastered into modern formats, so it's difficult to find the original material." Elrydien said. "I felt lucky to find this."

She initiated another file, and this was obviously a clip from some movie. The screen showed a short-haired blonde actress of about thirty-five or forty years, with high cheek bones and ultra-thin eyebrows, saying the same words.

"She sounds like me," Sharon said.

Elrydien nodded. "Yes. Almost exactly like you. We can conclude that the two of you learned English in the same geographical area at about the same time."

Elrydien paused, and Sharon wondered if it was for dramatic effect, of if the elf woman was just being intentionally irritating.

"Where?" Sharon asked.

"California, The United States of America, Old Terra, circa 200 years Pre-Singularity."

"That's ..." Sharon stammered. "That's impossible."

"Agreed. Care to take a guess as to where we found this cinema?"

Sharon shrugged. "I have no clue at all."

"In the entertainment database of the *Zephyr*."

Sharon's eyes widened in understanding. "You think I studied this dialogue to learn the dialect and accent."

"Call it a working hypothesis. The database records say that you accessed this file while you were in a coma, and after your EPU had died. Which is also impossible."

"Wait. What?" Sharon's understanding of the situation was just blown to pieces.

Elrydien smiled in a way that did not offer any comfort. "You have the perfect alibi, I'd say. Maybe you have a suggestion?"

Sharon just shook her head, feeling a bit flabbergasted.

"Oh, come on!" Elrydien teased. "You're pretty smart! Give it a try."

"No. Really. I have nothing to offer."

"Let's try another tack, then." Elrydien passed her hand over the plastic sheet and the photo changed. This time it showed photos of pieces of electronic parts.

"Do any of these look familiar?"

"No."

"Really? Because you spent several years earning certifications in this kind of technology."

Sharon shook her head.

"These are pieces of the bomb which exploded, damaging the *Zephyr* and injuring you." This caused Sharon's heart rate to increase, and Elrydien noted it on the EPU read out. "It's a pretty sophisticated device. Obviously built by somebody who knows electronics. And it required somebody in the ship to detonate it."

"Why would I plant a bomb?"

"We didn't say you did."

"I may be ignorant of a lot of things," Sharon said. "But I'm not stupid. We wouldn't be having this conversation unless you thought there was a chance I planted that bomb, or knew who did."

Elrydien sat back. She'd been waiting for this. "Go ahead."

"Go ahead what?" Sharon said. "Oh, I see. You need a confession or a lead." She chewed her lip in thought. "You want to know if I built that bomb and set it off when the time was right. But why would I have set the bomb off while I was still near it?"

"You stayed and that allayed suspicion."

"Not by very damn much, obviously! I don't know about my former self, but if that had been me in that maintenance chase knowing that a bomb was about to explode, I'd have left no matter what. I would rather take my chances explaining why I left than risk being blown into pieces!"

"But you weren't blown to pieces. Other than the bad luck of being hit on the head by a flying chunk of hydraulic conduit, you escaped fatal injury."

"Oh, and now you think I can control flying shrapnel." Sharon rolled her eyes. "And what motivation do I have? You obviously know more about the pre-trauma me than I do, so tell me. Was I a political radical? Did somebody blackmail me? Did I owe a lot of money to someone? Or am I just crazy?"

"All of those are very good questions. And we're looking into them."

"Especially the last one, I take it."

The Tolkienist studied the EPU readouts on the crewman's emotional state during the last outburst. Sharon was genuinely angry with a tinge of fear, and none of that was conclusive.

"Did you plant the bomb?"

"I wish I knew."

Sharon was being honest, Elrydien noted. Simmons really didn't know if she was guilty and feared that she was.

"Aren't there any other suspects?" Sharon asked.

"Excuse me for a few minutes. I'll be right back." Elrydien walked through the door and into an adjacent room where there was a desk and chair. She gathered her thoughts for a few seconds and then mumbled at her EPU.

OKAY. CRIMINAL OR PSYCH?

OR TIME TRAVELER, a man said. I'LL CHECK TO SEE IF SHE'S A MEMBER IN ONE OF THOSE HISTORICAL RECREATION SOCIETIES.

IT'S PRETTY CLEAR THAT SHE DOESN'T RECOGNIZE ANY KNOWN AGENTS BY FACE OR NAME, AND THERE WAS ABSOLUTELY NO REACTION WHEN SHE LOOKED AT DSP MANDERS, another man said. THE READOUTS WERE CLEAR AS A BELL. SHE DOESN'T KNOW THEM.

THAT JUST MEANS SHE DOESN'T REMEMBER THEM, Elrydien said.

AGREED, said the first male voice. SHE ALSO DIDN'T RECOGNIZE THE CHIEF MINISTER AND SEVERAL VID AND CINEMA STARS. I'M NOT A PSYCHOLOGIST, BUT IT'S CLEAR THAT SHE DOESN'T REMEMBER ANYTHING PRIOR TO THE TRAUMA.

IF SHE'S A SPY, SHE'S A BROKEN ONE, the second male voice said.

I DON'T THINK SHE'S A SPY AT ALL, said the first man. BUT I WON'T RULE OUT ANGRY AND FOOLISH.

IT ALL COMES DOWN TO THE QUESTION, HOW DID SHE GET TWO PERSONALITIES IN HER HEAD? the second voice said

PSYCHOTIC BREAK.

INCORRECT. SHE HAS NEVER SHOWN ANY DIFFICULTY IN DISTINGUISHING FACT FROM FANTASY. JUST HAD HER MEMORIES JUMBLED, Elrydien pointed out.

SHE ALSO DOESN'T HAVE TWO PERSONALITIES IN HER HEAD. THERE'S NO EVIDENCE THAT THERE WAS MORE THAN ONE AT A TIME. INSTEAD OF HAVING MULTIPLE PERSONALITIES, SHE HAS SERIAL PERSONALITIES.

DOESN'T MATTER. THE RESULT IS THE SAME.

ON THE MATTER OF THE EXPLOSION: OTHER THAN HER PROXIMITY, WE HAVE NO HARD EVIDENCE THAT SHE WAS INVOLVED.

THEN GIVE HER A DISCHARGE AND WISH HER LUCK, the second voice said.

NO, Elrydien said. THEN WE LOSE ALL INFLUENCE OVER HER, AND I THINK SHE MAY STILL BE OF USE TO US.

HOW'S THAT?

I WANT A PSYCH EVAL, Elrydien said. IN FACT, WE SHOULD HAVE STARTED WITH ONE. I WANT A STANDARD PERSONALITY ASSAY SO THAT WE CAN COMPARE IT TO THE ONE ON FILE. I ALSO WANT A SKILLS EVALUATION, AND JUST BECAUSE I'M A SADIST, GIVE HER A UNIVERSITY ENTRANCE EXAM. I WANT TO KNOW HOW GOOD SHE IS AT SOLVING PROBLEMS.

One of the male voices laughed. WHAT'S YOUR GOAL HERE, ELRY?

I THINK IT'S CLEAR THAT SIMMONS ISN'T FAKING A MEMORY LOSS. THE EVIDENCE IS OVERWHELMINGLY AGAINST THAT. HER VOICE PRINT, HER LACK OF RESPONSE TO THE IMAGES OF PUBLIC FIGURES, HER IGNORANCE OF ANY RECENT REPUBLIC HISTORY. SHE REALLY DOESN'T KNOW.

UNLESS IT'S A LATENT PERSONALITY.

IF SHE'S GUILTY, LOSS OF MEMORY DOESN'T MAKE HER ANY LESS CULPABLE, the first man reminded her. PRECEDENT IS UNAMBIGUOUS ABOUT THAT.

IF SHE'S GUILTY, Elrydien insisted. WE JUST DON'T HAVE ENOUGH FOR AN ARREST. EVEN A MEDIOCRE ADVOCATE COULD GET THIS CASE BOUNCED ON ITS MERITS.

AND?

WE DON'T HAVE ANY OTHER LEADS, Elrydien pointed out.

AND?

GOING BACK TO THE INCIDENT WITH THE UNKNOWN CRAFT. WHAT WAS IT CARRYING THAT THEY NEEDED TO PREVENT THE ZEPHYR FROM BOARDING THEM AT ALL COSTS? WHOEVER WAS BEHIND IT TOOK SOME HUGE RISKS TO SABOTAGE A NAVY WARP-SHIP.

AND?

THE PERSON WHO PLANTED THAT BOMB HAD TO HAVE BEEN PART OF A TEAM. IF WE ASSUME THAT SIMMONS PLANTED THE BOMB, SHE HAD TO HAVE BEEN PART OF THAT TEAM, WHICH DIDN'T INTEND THAT SIMMONS SHOULD SURVIVE THE EXPLOSION. NOW SIMMONS CUM MANDERS IS A LOOSE END, AND THESE PEOPLE DON'T LIKE LOOSE ENDS.

6

City of Clarksport. Planet of Kentaurus
fifteen days before the New Year's Solstice
Kentauran calendar: 21 Teleftaíomina, 1382 PS

U CHENNA EBELECHUKWU, a 102-year-old Kentauran citizen, and a married man for almost twenty years, was a utility systems programmer for the city of Clarksport. He often joked, however, that he wasn't sure if he was the programmer, or the baby sitter for the AIs which run the city's utilities.

Several artificial intelligence systems, each physically separated by kilometers, ran the city's utilities in a network. Uchenna often thought of them as Committee Members. They talked among themselves in machine speak, then took a vote to decide which resource went where. The design was intended to thwart tampering. If something happened to one committee member, the others could over-ride it and make sure that the electricity, water, and sewage kept flowing. They worked in conjunction with other AI committees that ran public transportation, emergency services, and garbage recycling.

"What do you do if all the committee members stop working at once?" his wife had once asked.

Uchenna had laughed, saying, "I thank the stars that such a thing has never happened! But if it does I must re-boot one of the AIs."

"How long does that take?"

"Too long."

Uchenna enjoyed the feeling of power he had from being one of the people who could, in theory at least, bring the city of Clarksport to a grinding halt. Of course, the price for this was being always on call. There had been too many times when somebody at the City Operations Office chatted him in the middle of the night, or during a romantic rendezvous with his wife, or while he was on vacation, to pull him into work. By law, custom, and design, there were some decisions only a human could make.

"The wages of power are heavily taxed," he told his wife at times like those.

Uchenna took the light rail from the City Central District to the outlying community of Three Lakes, where he and his wife had a home. From there, the family car would pick him up at the station for a ten-minute ride home. He was looking forward to spending the next three days with his wife, Amarachi. The weather was too cold for gardening or long walks, and they planned on just being lazy, reading, watching vids, eating good food, and perhaps, if things were just right, get a start on their long-awaited children.

As he sat watching the world go by, a stranger brushed by. Uchenna hardly noticed. The minutes ticked on and he felt himself getting sleepy. Why was he so tired? The day hadn't been arduous. His eyes refused to stay open and his breathing slowed. His thoughts became unclear.

Somebody said, "What's happened to him? Somebody call Emergency Services!"

*   *   *

Uchenna never woke up. He never knew that when he was brought into the workshop of Giatrós, they placed him next to the supine form of his beloved Amarachi.

*   *   *

Sedna Biological Diversity Preserve #4

Sharon was finally standing in a large open area and was extremely happy for it. She was surrounded by plants, some of them flowering. Birds were flitting about overhead, and small, furry mammals scurried under bushes and through trees. The air smelled like it was alive.

But she was still in a room. Granted the room was the size of three football fields, and the roof overhead was transparent to show off the night sky. She was still on Sedna, standing in the center of a large biodome. There were several of these domes spread out over the surface of Sedna, designed and built to preserve endangered species and in case of catastrophic extinction events on the planet. If she didn't look too closely, she could imagine that she was standing in a well-manicured forest on Earth. There was a thunderstorm scheduled for sixteen hundred hours, but she'd have to leave before then.

She'd been on Sedna for twelve days, or what the locals called two weeks. They used six-day weeks because it fit into their 434-day year with two days of celebration left over.

Sharon had learned this and much more about this culture in the last two weeks.

The Kentaurans had a fascinating way to administer college entrance exams. When every applicant has a computer in their head, there wasn't much point in asking questions like, "Who was the Tsalagee king from 143 to 95 Before Singularity?" The point of the exams was to see how the applicant could think critically using all the information available. The questions were all essays, and were along the lines of "How might the Tsalagee king have avoided the war with the Persians in 95 BS?"

There were no time limits on the tests, though the individual questions were timed. Sharon spent nine and a half days taking the entrance exam for the University of Kentaurus at Clarksport. They gave her a handheld to substitute for the dead EPU, and she had spent much of that time exploring the 'Nets. The answer to one question would lead to a dozen more questions, and Sharon learned the sordid and mysterious history of Kentaurus, its peculiar origins, and the heroic struggle for human survival on the planet. At times, Sharon thought, it was like reading a James A. Michener novel, spanning epic centuries and with a cast of thousands, and filled with stories of personal disasters and triumphs. She imagined the cover of a huge tome with a single word title across an artistic rendering of an iconic Kentauran double sunset against the skyline of Clarksport: *Kentaurus. A Novel by James A. Michener.*

The science and math questions delighted her even as she failed them. She had no idea that humanity had learned to control such primal forces. The questions were full courses unto themselves.

She had finally sent the exam in with a mixed feeling of exhaustion and regret, and then slept for half a Kentauran day.

Elrydien Daerîsiell approached along a gravel path and waved. Sharon wondered briefly if she should wave back with her whole hand or just one finger, and finally decided that all five fingers would be politic. She even managed a smile.

"I thought you should know that you failed the exam."

Sharon forced a laugh. "Well, your freshmen must be pretty good. I thought you gave me the test just to annoy me. I didn't know it was going to be graded."

"I did." Sharon didn't know if Daerîsiell had just confirmed that she wanted to annoy her, or that she had graded the exam, and decided she didn't want to know. "You should know that most incoming freshmen spend at least a month on that exam. I rushed you. It didn't help that you skipped over the literary section, and you need a major review of integral calculus."

Instead of saying the first thing that came into her mind, which was *"Bite me"*, Sharon settled on the next thing that came to mind. "I never heard of any of those books. It will take me years to catch up on my reading list. And from my point of view, I think it's been decades since I did an integral." Even as she said this, she regretted offering an excuse for her failure.

"Still, you'd have done a lot better if you hadn't asserted that the Tsalagee king had a moral imperative to go to war against the Persians. History professors are not very enamored of moral imperatives." Daerîsiell looked at the sky, and the gibbous planet hanging there. "I also wanted to give you a chance to learn about the culture you've woken up to. What do you think?"

"What? Are you asking if I approve?"

"No. Is Kentaurus a place you could call home? It's not Old Terra. In many ways, it's better."

Agent Daerîsiell didn't believe that Sharon was from Old Terra, but she believed that Sharon believed it. Though there was no evidence that Sharon was cognitively impaired, the investigation team treated her belief as some sort of psychotic fantasy.

That question caught Sharon by surprise. She had not thought about it at all. She looked up through the transparent ceiling towards the south where the globe of Kentaurus hung. Legally, she was already a citizen of that world, but she understood what the elf meant. Two weeks ago, Sharon had no feelings whatsoever about that planet and felt like a visitor. It was only as real to her as the Land of Oz or Middle Earth. Then she spent nine and a half days becoming intimate with luminaries of Kentauran history. While Kentauran culture was far from utopian — it had as much dirty laundry and awkward skeletons to hide as the next culture — she now had an emotional tie to the place and the people, a feeling that her own fate was tied up with the larger perspective. However, she had come to learn that Daerîsiell's motives were never clear and straightforward.

"May I visit the planet? I'd like to see it firsthand."

"I think we can arrange it." Daerîsiell had, in fact, hoped that Sharon would request just such a journey.

"In that case, I have a request. I have absolutely no money. I'm locked out of Carol's accounts because I don't know her pass keys."

"The money you made when you were Carol is still in legal limbo. However, we can pay you the earnings from the day you woke up in sickbay. I'll call someone to make the arrangements."

"Thank you." It wouldn't be much, Sharon reflected, and she'd have to make every centinote count.

"I have something for you." Daerîsiell pulled an oblong box out of her pocket.

Sharon thought she knew what it was from the shape and gave the elf a suspicious look. She confirmed her guess by opening the box and finding a pair of iGlasses.

"We're growing you another EPU. Or rather, the Health Administration is growing one for Carol Simmons. Until then you can use these. They're not very stylish, but more people use them than admit to it."

Sharon put them on, adjusted them, and was greeted by a login prompt. She pulled them back off. "Thank you. Now I'll have to learn to mumble."

"Well, it's almost the Solstice, so consider it an early gift."

Sharon looked at the elf's eyes and tried to read anything there. "I'm still on the short list of suspects," she said.

Sharon had no delusions that Daerîsiell had given her the glasses out of kindness. Rather it was because NavSec wanted to be able to keep tabs on Sharon.

"You were the only person in the vicinity of the blast, and you had the expertise to build the bomb. We can't prove you detonated it, and our experts were able to find several ways to detonate it remotely. Still, you're the best suspect we have."

"But you can't find a motive."

"Not yet. You should know, however, that in federal cases like this, we aren't required to prove a motive. It just makes things easier. And there's still the twin mysteries of your disappearance on Maheux and the origin of your personality."

"I've been thinking about that."

"Yes?"

"Why not send me back to Maheux? See if anybody contacts me?"

Elrydien's face remained as unreadable as a world-class poker player's. "The Navy would never sign off on that. Why don't you take some shore leave for the holidays? The *Zephyr* is still undergoing repairs and refits, and your former crew mates are still planetside."

She'll be disappointed when I don't check in at the local terrorist enclave, Sharon thought.

✳   ✳   ✳

Portnik L. Marón Memorial Spaceport
Three days before the New Year's Solstice

The trip from Sedna to Kentaurus was remarkably short. Accelerating at one gee with a turnaround at the halfway point, it took about four Kentauran hours, including time spent loading cargo and passengers and the descent through the atmosphere. Sharon was surprised that there was no aerobraking as with the Space Shuttle or the Apollo capsules. The spacecraft simply used fuel to slow down before they entered the atmosphere.

Sharon walked through the terminal at Clarksport and collected the travel bag containing all her worldly possessions. She had spent the entire trip wondering where she was going to go once she was planetside. There were so many questions that begged an answer. Where would she start?

She dug into a pocket and pulled out Dr. Bradford's card. It looked like a business card, but only contained his name. If she hadn't spent two weeks exploring the 'Nets, she'd have had no idea what to do with it. She put on her iGlasses, looked at the card, and mumbled, "Chat."

After a pause of about fifteen seconds, during which the word "CONNECTING" appeared in her field of vision in a very stylized font, the image of Wyatt Bradford appeared.

"Sharon Manders!" he said with enthusiasm. "I truly wondered if I'd ever hear from you again."

"Well, here I am. Planetside in Clarksport for the holiday. I know this is an imposition, Doctor, but I was hoping for a consultation."

"Consultation, no," he said. "But a holiday visit, yes. I have an extra room, and there's more food here than we could possibly eat. Where are you? I'll send the car."

"At the Clarksport terminal. I just left the baggage claim."

"Wonderful! The car should be there in about twenty minutes. We'll expect you in forty."

Sharon stepped through the sliding glass door into a bitterly cold winter's day. The shuttle crew had warned her that the weather would be cold, and she was wearing the warmest clothes she had, but it was still a jolt. There was snow on the ground and a heavy overcast threatened more. Fortunately, there wasn't much wind, and she didn't have to wait long.

Sharon was mildly surprised to see so many Pips. These were genetically modified stock humans who grew no taller than one meter, though they looked perfectly proportioned. She had learned about them while taking the university entrance exam and had read about them extensively. There were hundreds of papers written about solving the problems of biology while maintaining the micro stature. Childbirth was chief among them. Even with brains which had been as augmented as current neurological and genetic sciences could make them, fully functional human heads could only be made so small. Pip women tended to have very wide hips.

Pips believed that their size optimized human existence, because they were still large enough to participate in human activities, but their bodies took up one-eighth as much space, and required proportionately less resources to maintain. At least, that was the public reason.

The tradeoff was they were rarely seen in large numbers where the Bigs predominated due to the very real danger of being accidentally crushed. While adult Bigs were conditioned to be aware of children who might be the same size as a Pip, those children were usually accompanied by unintentional warning signs — like screaming, running around, and harried parents. Adult Pips came with no such cues, and some accidental deaths were attributed to being sat upon or just ignored.

Usually, Bigs did not intentionally ignore Pips, in spite of well-publicized examples to the contrary. There was, however, a cognitive dissonance when people who looked like children had the behavioral disposition of a cranky adult.

For these reasons and others — mostly pertaining to scale — Pips tended to keep to their own communities, but there were places where mixing couldn't be avoided, like major transportation terminals.

All around her, holiday travelers of all sizes, including a few Furmen, were meeting families. She watched as people greeted each other with faces that glowed. Smiles seemed to explode when they first caught sight of lovers or prodigal children or parents flying in from warmer climes. It was all so familiar and yet so distant. Sharon thought of Carol's parents in Alemanni where it was midsummer rather than winter. She had debated long and hard about making that trip. They would expect to see Carol, and Sharon couldn't give them Carol, and that made her feel like an interloper in this body.

The psychologist at NavSec had told her that Carol was, for all practical purposes, dead. A lifetime of memories and experiences were wiped out. That personality which called itself Carol Simmons would never again see her family, get drunk with shipmates, turn a wrench, work for a better future, gaze on a lover's face, watch a sunset, cheer on the home team, present her parents with a grandchild, or enjoy her favorite cat-wailing music. Carol had been wiped clean just as surely as if she had physically died.

Sharon imagined that an artist had painstakingly set brush to canvas and painted an intricate, highly detailed, colorful image that was Carol Simmon's life. The canvas was meters wide and the artwork was done on the minutest of scales. The image contained the faces of family and lovers, friends and teachers. It contained images from events that were only significant to Carol, and moments that she'd shared with an entire community. The painting, which took fifty years to complete, was worthy of praise and critical acclaim, and would endure the ages. Then somebody had set fire to it. Sharon was living in the ashes, digging through the debris looking for something useful.

No, not set fire to it, Sharon corrected herself. They had scrubbed it clean with paint remover and used the newly blank canvas to paint Sharon's faux life.

On Sedna, after finding everything she could about Carol's life on the 'Nets, Sharon had grieved Carol's passing, lighting a candle and saying a sort of prayer.

"I'm so very sorry, Carol. You deserved better than this. Better than me."

Sharon's thoughts were interrupted after twenty minutes of waiting in the cold. A car pulled up to the curb of the transit terminal and the passenger door opened. A friendly voice of indeterminate gender invited, "Good afternoon, Sharon Manders. Please enter the vehicle quickly. Others are waiting."

She pushed her travel bag ahead of her and climbed in. It was not a large vehicle. Its upholstery was worn; there was the smell of something unidentifiable and slightly unpleasant.

"Destination: The residence of Wyatt and Marjo Bradford, Marina District. Please indicate that this is correct."

"Yes, it is. And would you please turn the heat up a little?"

"Temperature set to twenty degrees Celsius. Is that agreeable?"

"That's fine," she told the car while rubbing her nose.

*   *   *

Wyatt Bradford and his wife lived in a small house with a small fenceless yard in a small neighborhood. The primary sun was setting, and the house lights shown welcomingly through the decorated and frosted windows. It was a narrow, two-story affair with a porch and a chimney. The car let Sharon out and then parked itself in the attached garage.

Hoisting her duffle over her shoulder, Sharon walked up to the door just as it opened. The car had chatted the family to let them know it was arriving with the passenger.

The hulk of Dr. Bradford filled the doorway, and he held it open for Sharon. "Come in out of the cold, lass! Here, put the bag down and stand by the fire. Dearest, our guest has arrived!"

"I heard, I heard!" came the mezzo soprano voice of a slim woman walking into the room. She was small, about a meter and a half, compared to Wyatt's one hundred and eighty-five centimeters. The doctor introduced his wife as Marjo. "Hello, dear! Welcome to our home. Wyatt has told me so much about you! Are you hungry?"

"Famished!" Sharon said and took Marjo's extended hands and allowed herself to be examined.

"Have they mistreated you, dear?" Marjo asked.

"Only as much as they needed to. They have standards for dead people coming back to life and suspected saboteurs, you know."

"Psshhht!" Marjo waived her hand dismissively. "Come in, then. Supper is almost ready. Wyatt will show you where to put your things." Marjo hurried back into the kitchen, and Sharon felt she had passed inspection.

Then there was a ten-minute ritual of getting to know the smallest members of the Bradford family: A curly haired blond terrier mix named Igor and a calico named Tchotchke. The cat determined that Sharon held neither food nor toys and went back to sleep. Igor insisted on a back scratch and a tummy rub as toll to enter the house, which Sharon happily paid. These were the first domesticated animals that Sharon had seen in this new century and felt a constriction in her throat that humanity's truest companions had also gone to the stars.

Dinner, which Marjo proudly announced was cooked by hand, was a delicious roast beef with garlic, a side of some unfamiliar tuber, and some sort of vegetable under a green sauce. Wyatt served his favorite pinot noir from a winery near his childhood home. Igor begged shamelessly and was finally rewarded with plates to lick.

Sharon offered to help with cleanup, but Marjo waved her off with, "That's what domestic mechanicals are for. I love cooking, and I hate doing dishes. Roger!"

A closet door opened and the domestic robot rolled out on wide, spoked tires.

"Thank you for the offer, Ms Manders," the 'bot said with the same voice as the car. "But I have this."

Before Sharon quite realized it, the dishes had been picked up from the table, leftovers had been packed away, and the dishwasher started.

Tchotchke expressed her disdain of the mechanical butler with a hiss and scrambled to the top of the cupboard. Igor merely followed it around hoping that something tasty would drop. Sharon admired how silent and adroit the thing was. She knew that the seeming intelligence was a result of a neural networking software which was optimized to observe, learn from and respond to human conversation and body language, but it was difficult to think of it as just a machine. The fact that it only looked human from just below the armpits and up helped. The face looked incredibly human, which didn't help.

She also knew that, with enough money, it was possible to obtain domestic and industrial mechanicals which looked almost completely human, but they were very unpopular. Apparently, there was something called the "uncanny valley" — wherein humans were willing to accept robots that approached the appearance of humanity, but once a certain line was crossed, people tended to react badly, even violently. There was nothing creepier than a machine which looked 95% human giving you a leer and a wink. The one exception to this seemed to be robotic sex workers, because some people will try to have sex with anything.

These were just a few of the millions of things Sharon had learned while taking the exam.

Marjo was a professor of political sciences at the university and loved talking shop. She gave a commentary on every political faction and party luminary, especially the Chief Minister. Sharon expressed some opinions, and Marjo was polite, but it was obvious that she considered Sharon's views to be a bit naive and asked probing questions to elicit further consideration of the affairs. It surprised Sharon to learn that Marjo was a native of Eteramunde.

"Don't speak to me of relative morality," Marjo admonished. "I grew up in a society where scholarship for women was often forcibly denied. Girls who tried to learn anything beyond the basics were frequently kidnapped and sent to rehabilitation centers, which is just as ugly as it sounds. Religion was used as a tool to convince the poor and illiterate that they deserved their hardship. Girls were legally sold into marriages at the age of twelve standard years, and often died either in childbirth, or of abuse before they became grandmothers."

Sharon shuddered.

"This neo-feudal society is quite harshly divided so that the elite are given genetic therapies to increase their lifespans to the human norm of about 200 years, while the poor and working class live out their short lives of the psalmic threescore and ten. They are taught that if they deserved longer lives, they would be able to afford it."

"That's ..." Sharon tried to find a word for it.

"Criminally negligent at the very least," Marjo offered. "Morally reprehensible. Deserving of a slow, cruel death, if you'll have my mind of it."

Sharon found it very difficult to disagree. "So, why do they ally with Droben? That's a planet where equality of the genders is enforced."

"Indeed," Marjo sneered. "So is scholarship. Everybody is required to attend at least two years of college in order to learn how to best serve the Party. The government controls the prices of everything, and young people are drafted to work on communal farms. They could easily build machines to do this but have instilled a distaste for machines designed to do the work of humans. The Party points out that industrial mechanicals take work and dignity from humans."

"So there are no mechanicals on Droben?"

"Oh, girl," Marjo laughed. "Of course there are. They are used in primarily two capacities: the first as street cops, the second in gaming."

"Gaming? Do they have robot slam-downs or something?"

"You've guessed precisely, young woman. It's the biggest sport on the planet. Cities build armies of robots to fight the armies of other cities in an arena. Grease and mayhem everywhere."

"So why are they allies with Eteramunde?"

"Mutual hatred of the Kentauran Republic and its allies makes strange bedfellows. In both cases, our fearless leaders made the mistake of backing the wrong horse in a *coup d'etat*. Now it's the talk of the galaxy about how Kentaurus and its allies can't keep their imperial fingers out of other people's business."

It wasn't inaccurate to describe Kentaurus as an imperial power, but it was also an out-of-date sentiment. While Kentaurus had planted colonies on other worlds, they were all independent now — the result of The Great Devolution, as historians called it. Maintaining an imperial presence across interstellar distances was far too expensive for even the most hawkish of legislators. The people of Kentaurus were once again a single-planet government, and were happy to stay that way. In fact, they damn near had to kick their last colonial possession out of the nest.

"That being said," Marjo went on. "It's the worst kept secret in the universe that Kentaurus would back another coup on either of those planets if there was a popular political movement which showed signs of knowing even the basics of planetary relations. And not just us! The entire Tau Ceti Treaty Alliance would be supplying weapons and advisors."

"But we can't be seen politically as a group that would impose our will on them," Sharon said. "Because that's how the propaganda would play it, and then we'd be at war with the entire Sagittarius political bloc."

"Exactly."

It was an hour later when Sharon decided to broach another topic that intrigued her.

"Another question — and this is somewhat of a *non-sequitur*, but what happened to the Singularity?"

"I'm not sure I follow your question," Marjo said.

"There's very little solid information about it on the 'Nets. There are ruins all over the Earth. Modern archeologists make their careers sifting through them. There's plenty of historical records from before and after, but nothing during. It's this great black hole of information. Somebody pressed the Cosmic Delete Button. And prior to it, the Singularity was hailed as something that would cause great social change. Things would be so different after the Singularity that people had no way of predicting it. There was talk of uploading the human mind to computers and all that. Transhumanists predicted the next step in human evolution.

"And yet, when I look around today, things are pretty much the same as they were. Except for some technological details, things are about the same now as they were for a couple centuries before the Singularity. What happened?"

"That's not very easy to answer," Marjo said. "Largely because, as you've pointed out, not much survived from that time. The short answer is: the Singularity failed."

"Failed how?"

Marjo laughed. "Every couple of years somebody publishes a new book or makes a new cinematic documentary to explain what happened during the Singularity. But, like you said, it's an informational black hole. Thus the name: *Singularity*. The most popular theories suggest that it was an information war. The world was interconnected by information conduits. Prototype AIs controlled nuclear reactors, global positioning navigational systems, and even electrical, water, and sewage distribution. The global economy became addicted to the 'Nets. Human investors couldn't compete with digital ones. Two or more great global superpowers fought with each other, declaring data jihads. They all tried to destroy or control the information superstructure of the others. There was an arms race of information bombs and hack attacks. Somewhere along the way, it all got deleted.

"This was compounded by catastrophic climate change. Seventy percent of the earth's biosphere died."

"Then everything tended towards highest entropy?" Sharon asked.

"That's one way to put it," Marjo said.

"So we went back to the way we were before?"

"Well, hardly. Our life expectancies are far longer, we don't have many children, and we have EPUs. The reason things haven't changed much is probably due to the fact that we tend to live so long. Social change is slow when people who are accustomed to the old ways live for two centuries. It's only been six and a half lifetimes since the Singularity. People don't always embrace social change, and young people don't have the market shares or political clout to force it as they may have had before the Singularity."

"And those EPUs make all the difference, don't they? When we say *Post Singularity,* we mean years since the invention of the EPU."

"Not entirely," Marjo said. "A lot of things happened in the centuries after the Singularity. Somebody got the bright idea to start marking the calendar after it, and it caught on."

"Why does this culture still use the failed Singularity as a benchmark for time?"

"Why did previous cultures still use *Anno Domini* even after Christianity became a minority religion?"

Sharon nodded. "Fair point. It had become customary, and the standard for commerce. Why change it if it worked?"

They poured more wine, and the conversation became even more animated.

"Why aren't we all geniuses?" Sharon asked.

"I beg your pardon?" Wyatt asked.

"I'm not trying to be insulting, but the human race has modified its genetic code quite a bit. There are, for instance, the Furmen and the Pips. Creating the Furmen is the result of centuries of research and trials."

"Indeed!" Wyatt said. "And the cost in terms of human lives was, in my opinion, indefensible."

"Then why didn't people manipulate the genes responsible for our IQ? Why not make us smarter?"

"They did, actually," Wyatt said. "Just not very much. And keep in mind the statistics of the issue — only the average was raised, while the extremes remained rather static."

"Why not raise it higher?"

"For one, there are a lot of environmental and epigenetic factors affecting intelligence that we can't control. For another, there is no one gene, or even set of genes, which makes us smart. It's a very complicated balance of chemical pathways. If you change one, there's a cascade effect so that everything else is affected. Mutations to change human intelligence were often fatal, and the great preponderance of those who survived were mindless, drooling, victims of a cruel joke. There were some early breakthroughs that, unfortunately, encouraged more research which lead to even more hideous failures. Finally, there are behavioral and cognitive dimensions to high intelligence that we simply can't control."

Wyatt eventually gave a report on a medical conference he had attended remotely. When asked about her experience at NavSec, Sharon said that she'd been questioned and examined. She was never charged with any crime.

"But they took me off of the *Zephyr's* roster."

"Can't say I didn't see that coming," Wyatt said. "Trying to integrate you back into a crew that knew you as somebody else would be asking for trouble."

"Additionally, I have no experience as a q-trician. In fact, I don't have any useful skills at all, as far as the Navy is concerned. So I've been ordered to wait further orders. I have some numerical code status — Sixteen-twelve, unassigned, I think. I just call it being in limbo." Sharon shrugged her shoulders. "My future is as much a mystery as my past. The Navy won't press charges, and they won't let me go either."

"Might I make a suggestion?" Marjo offered.

"Absolutely! I'm open to almost anything short of selling my body to the highest bidder or becoming an assassin."

"Enroll at the university."

Sharon giggled. "I failed the entrance exam by quite a margin."

"Nonsense," Marjo *pft'*d. "The admissions committee has enormous leeway in that. You're obviously intelligent and capable of original, critical thought. We give a lot of credit for enthusiasm for learning and not being afraid to express an opinion. You've demonstrated that tonight. Learning stuff is easy, especially in an era when information is so cheap and easily obtained. Synthesizing it into cogent thought is a much rarer ability."

"And with that," Wyatt interjected, saving Sharon from having to say something self-effacing. "Our guest requested a medical consult. Would you like to retire to the office, Sharon?"

"Good idea. I should chat my mother," Marjo said. "Haven't spoken to her in days."

Fortunately, Marjo couldn't see the flash of guilt that washed over Sharon's face at the mention of a mother.

The house had three bedrooms. His, hers, and theirs. Wyatt and Sharon went upstairs, followed by both quadrupeds, turned right and entered a door at the end of the hall. Inside was an oak desk and two high backed leather chairs along with posters of vacation spots. There were mountains and rivers and cities, and some entire planets. There were also models of old wooden ships and a few leather-bound books. Sharon thought this looked like odd decoration for a physician's study. Where were all the skeletons and posters of circulatory systems and medical references? Then she remembered that they were all in his EPU. Sharon noticed something else that stirred her emotions: on the oak desk was the sheet of paper with her sketches of human anatomy.

Wyatt closed the door, sat, and motioned for Sharon to take the other chair. "What can I do for you, lass?"

Tchotchke immediately jumped into his lap and Igor was right behind. They jostled for the best lap spots and finally settled down, each under one of Wyatt's hands.

"You can tell me more about EPUs. Especially mine. Just when did my EPU die?"

"That's all in my report," Wyatt looked confused.

"I don't have access to your report. I'm just a ... what's the term for it? Crewman deuce."

"Let me pull up my copy," he said, then mumbled to himself. "Here it is. It remained active for about thirty minutes after the accident and then expired."

"What caused it to expire?"

"I don't know for sure. I'm just an old navy sawbones. It's not my area of expertise. I don't mean to upset you, but I thought it would be determined during your autopsy. As it is, they'll remove the old one when they install the new one."

"Can you guess?"

"Organ failure is not unheard of in these kinds of injuries. We had to put your skull back together."

"Wait," Sharon put up her hand as something occurred to her. "When you say that you put my skull back together, did you do that personally? With your hands?"

"Oh, heavens! No. I oversaw the robot surgeon that performed the procedure. Why is all this so important?"

"Some things I've learned recently. Things that don't make sense. Is it at all possible that it was still active and you didn't know it?"

"Not unless my instruments were faulty, and they weren't."

"Could some small part of it still be alive if most of it's dead?"

Wyatt had to think about that. He mumbled a bit. "It's not unheard of. And as I said earlier, I'm no expert."

Sharon shifted uncomfortably. "This is going to sound strange. Maybe even impossible." Then she was silent for several seconds. Wyatt waited patiently. "About a week ago, I had a dream in which somebody — an old woman — spoke to me in French. At first, I had no idea what she was saying. Like any student, I repeated phrases back, and she corrected me. This went on for hours. Maybe even days in dream-time. When I woke up, I spoke French."

Wyatt physically reacted to this news as if he'd been slapped. "Really?"

"*Oui. Vraiment.* And that's not the only thing. Sometimes I dream about historical things. Sometimes I dream about playing musical instruments, like the piano. I have memories of things that happened before the Singularity."

"Such as?"

"American politics and science. For instance, I was able to describe the presidential debates between Jimmy Carter and Ronald Reagan."

"I'm sorry. I have no idea who they are."

"Carter was the American president after Ford, who took office after Nixon resigned. Reagan was the president after Carter, but he was a film ... ah, cinematic actor before he was a politician."

Though Dr. Bradford found none of this illuminating, he seemed to find that amusing. "Guess he didn't have to change his modus much, did he?"

Sharon simply continued and found it difficult to look Dr. Bradford in the face as she did. "I was able to describe the various political issues of the day during Reagan's administration: the air traffic controller's strike, the Iran-Contra scandal, a savings and loan crisis, the Housing and Urban Development grant scandal ..."

"So, you were a historian." Dr. Bradford interrupted, as he had no idea what any of those were.

"No," Sharon shook her head emphatically. "It's as if I lived in that era."

Wyatt seemed to consider this information for a several moments. "Do you remember any personal details? Or just details from the political arena?"

"Some personal details. For instance, I went to college in California. I remember driving a Ford Mustang. Um ... that's a kind of ancient, overpowered, underweight ground car that didn't have an AI. I don't remember having any family. But there are also so many transient memories!" Sharon said in evident frustration. "Some memories will come and then evaporate before I can dwell on them. Then all I have is a memory of having a memory, without any details."

Dr. Bradford considered this and responded with deliberation. "Lass, my training in psychology is minimal. However, could it be that you studied American history, and when you lost your memory, this is what re-surfaced?"

"That's what the people at NavSec suggested. Did Carol study American history?"

"I have no idea."

"Can studying American history make you sound like an American?"

"Probably not unless you spend inordinate amounts of time watching recorded media from that era."

"The people at NavSec confirmed that my accent is consistent with somebody raised in the latter half of the second century Before Singularity in the western United States of America."

"Wow!" Dr. Bradford nearly choked on the information. "I really don't know how to respond to that."

"Me, neither. Though it would be consistent with the 'watch too many ancient movies' theory." Sharon paused. "But that sort of segues into my next question: If the EPU died, then where did I come from?"

"Understand that this is pure speculation. I can't emphasize enough that I'm not a neurologist, just a sailor with a medical degree. But my hypothesis is that you suffered thousands, even millions of micro-fissures of the brain. The associations between neurons were severed. Enough so, that the brain forgot who it was."

"That explains why Carol disappeared, not why I appeared."

Dr. Bradford held up his hand to forestall more objections. "As long as the neurons remain viable, they can start re-associating. They just won't make the same associations they did originally."

"That still doesn't explain where I came from. Why did the neurons associate in such a way that a personality named Sharon Manders arose out of the ashes? It couldn't have been random."

"An infinite number of monkeys with word processors. It's possible, but I agree that it's only just barely possible. Again, pure speculation. Did you have an imaginary friend when you were growing up? No, ignore that question. I apologize for asking it. Most all children do."

"You're saying that I was Carol's imaginary friend?"

Bradford just shrugged his shoulders. "Without extensive testing, I have no way to determine that. I'd want to talk to Carol's parents and siblings, but I was told not to."

"Who told you not to?"

"Naval Security. They informed me that they would do all the investigating."

Sharon tried to imagine herself as an imaginary friend. Bradford's narrative implied that the neural associations for Sharon survived while those for Carol did not.

"Could the EPU have created me?"

Bradford's answer was almost immediate. He'd obviously thought along these same lines. "No. It was dead. Not only was it dead, but it has no mechanism and no programming to perform such a task. The best and brightest minds in neuroscience of our time have tried to create artificial personalities in a human brain, but to no avail."

Sharon ran her hands up and down the leather arms of the seat, her mind racing. The thought kept running through Sharon's mind, *Whatever created me is still working.*

Sharon's mind was still racing with questions that she didn't quite know how to ask, and Wyatt's mind was starting to fade from the effects of a large meal and too much pinot noir. This did not keep him from mentally entertaining wild speculations about the genesis of Sharon Manders.

7

City of Clarksport
Kentaurus
Kentauran calendar: 36 Teleftmina, 1382 PS

L IEUTENANT FOLKE BERG watched his favorite crime show, though "watched" was probably not the most apt verb. It was much more of an augmented reality game. Via his EPU, he was part of the scene, able to examine the evidence from any angle, stop the action and pull up the histories of all the characters in the story. In his own virtual world, he was standing in the middle of the crime scene located on a street corner of a fictional city.

A crowd of civilians had gathered around the corpse of a well-dressed executive who'd been shot in the chest three times with some projectile weapon. There was some conflicting digital evidence that may or may not reveal the identity of the murderer, and Folke was playing a character who had been called in to examine it. He was currently explaining to a doe-eyed female intern who hung on his every word about the subtle nuances of detecting fraudulent digital evidence.

A large, high-definition monitor hung suspended in the air, showing scenes from a security vid-camera.

"Every piece of vid has its own characteristic set of dimensions."

"Like size?" the intern asked with words that sounded smooth as cream.

The intern had been specially created to be attractive to Folke. Another viewer might see a man, or a different woman.

"Not just size," Folke clarified, shutting out the part of his brain which knew that the young woman didn't really exist, and was controlled by an AI which was responding to his own words and body language. "Color, saturation, brightness, polarization, and a dozen others. The trick is to look for sudden, unexplained changes in one of them."

A buzzing sounded in Folke's mind and he saw an icon floating about a meter off the ground that indicated that a chatmail had been received. He would have left it for later until he saw the name of the sender and decided he needed to see it.

"Would you excuse me for a moment?" he reluctantly asked of the intern. "I need to take this."

"Don't be gone too long," the intern intoned with a sexy tilt of the head that made her brown locks bounce. "I'd like to know more about digital vid dimensions."

It was a recorded message, due to light travel time delay, and had originated on Olympia, the third planet in the system, currently two light minutes away. With the message came with a huge attachment. Folke listened to the message with growing amazement, then opened the attached file. The make-believe crime scene was forgotten in the excitement of a real one.

"Day-um, Simmons," he said after reading for several minutes. "You are one messed up *brud*."

*   *   *

Elrydien Daerîsiell was processing a report draft when she was interrupted by a tone which announced the receipt of chatmail with a subject containing one of her watch-words: "I know who Sharon Manders is."

It came from a Lieutenant Berg of the Republic Marines, who began the message by saying that he had been researching the origins of the Sharon Manders personality.

Elrydien listened to the message, then looked at the attachment. She was nearly done when she was interrupted yet again by a chat request from the medical office of Dr. Dvnikani.

I THOUGHT YOU SAID HER EPU WAS DEAD, Dr. Dvnikani said without preamble.

I BEG YOUR PARDON? Elrydien said, but realized what the call was about even as she said it.

ONE OF YOUR CLIENTS: CREWMAN SIMMONS. THE REPORT FROM DR. BRADFORD SAID THAT HER EPU SHOWED NO NEURAL ACTIVITY. THIS IS INCORRECT.

Elrydien took a moment to change mental gears. This was one of the bigger coincidences she could remember.

GO ON.

IT'S NOT DEAD. IT'S JUST MOSTLY DEAD. HOWEVER, I CAN FORGIVE A SHIP'S SURGEON FOR MAKING THIS ERROR GIVEN THE EQUIPMENT HE WAS PROBABLY WORKING WITH.

WHEN YOU SAY MOSTLY DEAD …

AGREED, THAT'S AN IMPRECISE TERM. LET ME EXPLAIN …

*   *   *

Solstice Celebration, 1382 PS, Day 1

Major Sharon Manders, late of the State Police of Droben, wearing the body of Uchenna Ebelechukwu, walked into the room housing the utilities AI in the Second City district of Clarksport. Uchenna was a well-built man who kept himself trim and exercised frequently, and Major Manders marveled at the physical power she now possessed. And he was so tall! The change in perspective had given her problems at first. Also, colors were slightly different. Giatrós warned her about this.

Major Manders, working largely from memorization, turned on some monitors that showed the celebrations in the Clarksport Second City just getting started. People arrived from all over town. Similar celebrations were starting in other parts of Clarksport, but her organization wanted to start out slow. Just this one location would do for this demonstration of their ability to bring the capital of the Republic to its knees. The best estimates suggested that there would easily be five or six thousand people at this venue. A good start! This venue could be easily isolated, preventing emergency responders from arriving while the panic consumed the partiers.

*   *   *

At the Bradford home, the invitation for Sharon to stay the night turned into an invitation to stay until the crew of the *Zephyr* was recalled.

The extension of the invitation came after breakfast the next morning, during which the three discussed all things philosophical. It started with secular ethics, and somehow ended with the rise of the Christian Democratic Party in Kentauran politics. The conversation tended to get tabled until the next meal and then the next.

The winter Solstice in the northern hemisphere marked the transition from the old year to the new. The Kentauran calendar has twelve months of thirty-six days each — except the last one, Teleftmina, which has thirty-eight. Those last two days are a holiday for everyone who isn't needed to keep the city running safely. It comes with much celebrating, fanfare, feasting, gift giving, and parades. There were parades in other cities, but not in Clarksport, which found itself in the middle of a winter storm that dumped a hundred and fifty centimeters of snow and sent temperatures plummeting.

Sharon discovered, quite to her delight, that there was a Second City underground. A comprehensive subway system connected most of the city and included underground locations where large numbers of people could gather. They weren't quite big enough for parades, but they were big enough for a two-day long party of music, dancing, drinking and gaming.

Sharon wore her nicest clothes — which were okay for a down-on-her-luck sailor, but entirely inappropriate for a fun day on the town — set her iGlasses to passive, and started her explorations. The iGlasses were invaluable for directions and public transit schedules.

Once she was in the Second City proper, she discovered the first major disadvantage to being in constant contact with the 'Nets — Advertisements. She spent thirty very annoying minutes being bombarded by ads for make-up, clothes, new cars, dating services, banks, insurance companies, and events. She finally found the setting that disallowed ads, but she would have to pay a premium for this.

"*Plus ça change, plus c'est la même chose,*" Sharon said bitterly.

She finally found a way to allow the ads, but with the volume set to zero and the visuals confined to a very small window off to the side, and this was free.

No sooner had she completed the change to the settings, then she received a chat request from Felix Adler. She accepted without hesitation.

FELIX! GOOD TO HEAR FROM YOU, FRIEND!

CAROL! YOU'RE HERE! LOOK BEHIND YOU!

Sharon turned, scanned the huge room full of people, decorations, and noise. The iGlasses supplied a neon arrow pointing to a man standing at a beer vendor, waving his arms, and surrounded by several people Sharon didn't know.

One of the apps that came with the iGlasses was *Whoozdat*. Sharon needed only to indicate a face in the crowd and the public profile of that person appeared in her view. Additionally, the device kept a local database on people she met. She would never have to worry about forgetting someone's name again.

COME JOIN US! WE'RE JUST GETTING STARTED ON OUR PUB CRAWL.

Happy to see a familiar, friendly face, Sharon nearly trotted the fifty meters between her and the beer vendor. Felix gave her an enthusiastic hug and made introductions all around.

"Is Lester with you?" Sharon asked cautiously.

"He was here," Felix said dismissively, "but disappeared. Haven' seen him since jus' after we arrived."

The background music from a nearby performance stage was too loud for spoken conversation, but Felix showed her how to selectively turn down the volume from that performance. Sharon hadn't realized that most of the sound and noise in the hall was channeled through her iGlasses.

"We lost track of you after we docked," Felix said. "Somebody said you'd been arrested. Others said you were in a hospital."

"Nothing as dramatic as all that. NavSec had some questions then they let me go."

"Where have you been staying?"

Sharon didn't want to say that she was staying in the home of the ship's surgeon. "I'm renting a room in the Marina district. It's cheap, and the landlady is an excellent cook." All that was true.

Felix indicated her clothes. "Cheap or not, you're paying too much for rent if these are the best party clothes you have."

One of Felix's friends, a tall, dark haired, leggy woman with skin the color of dark coffee, gave Sharon a plastic mug full of dark beer and then winked. *WhoozDat* indicated that her name was Chinwemma (Wemma) Otutodilinna. Sharon winked back her thanks.

"I'm working on the clothes," Sharon said. "Give a gal some time to do some proper shopping."

Of course, she had had no time at all with the interrogation and exams, and hadn't counted on meeting anybody she knew at the celebration.

Wemma made several suggestions about places to buy clothes, and Sharon marveled at how easily her iGlasses translated Wemma's native language, whatever it was, into a form of English that Sharon could understand.

"I'm curious," Felix said, indicating the band, his musician's eye and ear piqued. "What do you think of this group?"

The band was a quintet of young-looking men playing guitars, keyboards and percussion. The music reminded Sharon of Led Zeppelin. The logo on the bass drum proclaimed that the name of the group was *Oatmeal Cookie*.

She took off her iGlasses and all she could hear was the lead vocalist singing his heart out with an unamplified voice to the accompaniment of unamplified electric instruments. The keyboard made no sound at all, and even the drums and cymbals were muffled. The lighting effects were also gone, and the musicians were dressed differently, even dully.

Looking around, Sharon noticed that most of the people in the room didn't look near as attractive now that she saw their unaugmented bodies. Most were either heavier or thinner, or smaller breasted, or less muscled, or had less hair than the persona they offered to the public via the augmented visuals of the EPU.

Sharon put the iGlasses back on, activated them, and the music, lights, and the attractive people all sprang back to life. The iGlasses didn't have speakers in the temple arms but created the sense of sound in the wearer's head by inducing current in the auditory nerves. Sharon was reminded of the first book in the *Wizard of Oz* series by L. Frank Baum, wherein the residents of the Emerald City were required to wear green tinted eyeglasses in order to maintain the illusion of the emerald color. The memory stuck with her as if she'd read the book yesterday, full of details. Not transient at all.

"Well?" Felix asked.

"I like them. Jazzy, and the lead guitarist has a showy style."

Both Felix and Wemma made bitter faces and then looked at the beer.

"What's wrong?" Sharon asked.

"Something's wrong with the beer," said Wemma. Felix took both beers and threw them away.

Sharon sniffed hers and didn't detect anything wrong. She took an exploratory sip and decided that it tasted like a brown ale. "I don't think there's anything wrong with mine, but just in case ..." She tossed her beer, too.

"Who's up for dancing?" somebody said, and they were all swept into the dance floor and spent thirty minutes swinging to the tunes.

Afterwards they walked to another vendor and ordered more beers. Nobody complained about the taste, and the brews went down easy.

The dance floors and food/drink vendors were set up by civic groups, usually charities. All of the restaurants that would normally be open in this venue were closed.

Later, there was a different dance floor where people were listening to a more laid-back beat. The music had a surplus of horns and woodwinds, in Sharon's opinion, and it invited the kind of dancing where people held hands and one partner had to follow the other's lead. While they were within this band's sphere of influence, they couldn't hear a single note played by *Oatmeal Cookie*, even though it was less than fifty meters away.

Another beer and another dance floor. This band had a more eclectic ensemble with a stand-up bass, piano, slide guitar, saxophone, drums, and a male singer who had a voice so low that it rumbled.

Sharon noticed that the crowds were getting bigger. More people were showing up for the party, and Clarksport was a big city, encompassing two million people. It was the center of government and commerce for the entire planet, and it seemed like almost everybody was here. An image of Times Square in New York on New Year's Eve passed quickly through Sharon's consciousness then just as quickly evaporated.

People arrived dressed in outrageous costumes. Some people walked around with neon signs making political statements: *Free the Droben 9! Impeach Katsaros! Better Education Now!*

A few people only wore shoes.

Though there were quite a few bands playing a wide range of music, there were also the vendors. They were set up in long rows of stalls programmed to project lights and sounds and demonstrations of their wares. Kentaurus, Sharon had learned, was a culture of craftsmen and artisans who, as a group, had a strong loathing for mass production. Why make something that was merely practical when it could also be a piece of art? There were some items, such as computer components, which could not be manufactured by hand, but the appliances that contained them were far more decorative. The average Kentauran took a great deal of pride in having an object that nobody else owned. Mass produced plastic stuff was for the poor, and nobody wanted to be seen as poor.

Like any modern society, Kentaurans mostly shopped online, which meant that even the artist running the most marginal of profits could afford an interplanetary market base. But it was in the holiday markets, like the Solstice, where makers and buyers could meet face to face, and the makers were playing it for all that it was worth. Sharon found the range of boutiques and shops mind-boggling. There were clothes. Lots of clothes that were not only practical, but also very decorative. A Victorian style of dress that would not have shocked Charles Dickens was making another comeback among the men. Frock coats and vests with silk puff ties were common, and Sharon wouldn't have been unsurprised if someone had introduced himself as Phileas Fogg. Among other genders, it seemed to be anything goes.

There was a pavilion with a couple dozen people speaking Esperanto. They advocated for the adoption of the language as a *lingua franca*, but this seemed unnecessary in a world where the EPUs and iGlasses offered instant translations of nearly any language, including Esperanto. Sharon talked with the folks there and came away with the feeling that the advocation of their language as a universal bridge between cultures was secondary to their enjoyment of creating an interplanetary cadre of instant friends who shared a love of the tongue. The Esperantists were from all over the planet, all of them speaking at least two languages, and for most of them Esperanto was the only common language. They could have used their EPUs to translate, but they considered that to be uncouth.

Sharon became fascinated with the fusion of old technology and new at a booth that sold swords. The words *"Al Saif"* floated above the booth along with a motto, *Modern Steel for the Ancient Warrior*. On the hilts was a button that when activated, the blade would disappear faster that she could see. Activate the switch again — taking care that the hilt was pointed in a safe direction — and the blade reappeared almost instantly. Sharon learned that the alloy had a memory, and when a minuscule DC current was applied, it took on a pre-programmed shape. Otherwise, the blade was safely stored in the hilt.

"Freud would be pleased," she commented with a laugh.

It was nearly midnight when Sharon thought she saw Lester Sievers. He was standing by a door marked *Staff Only* and looking directly at her. He turned and went through the door before Sharon could confirm who it was with *WhoozDat*.

They were trying to decide if they wanted to stay and listen to a band composed of three bagpipes, lots of percussion, two electric guitars, and a synthesizer playing a cover of some popular tune or go find another beer. Sharon wanted to listen, as she had decided that she liked bag rock. Felix, however, decided it was time for another joke. The jokes had been getting increasingly raunchy in proportion to the amount of ethanol in his blood, and Sharon was just tipsy enough to find him amusing.

"'Ere's a question: Wha' di' da ventriloquist Furwoman say t' her gynecologist?"

Sharon and Wemma looked at him expectantly, waiting for a punch line that only a drunken sailor would have the nerve to say in this social situation. They waited for almost five awkward seconds and Sharon thought he really needed to work on his timing.

Felix doubled over and vomited on the floor. Wemma and Sharon jumped back to avoid spatter.

"Felix! What's wrong?"

Before he could answer, the lights went out and everything stopped. This startled Sharon, but not as much as the screaming that started almost instantly. The sound of retching came from the approximate direction as Wemma's last known location.

Emergency lights came on and people were panicked. Some were running mindlessly, and others were curled up in a fetal position. Most of the rest were adding to the mess on the floor. Those who seemed unaffected with gastric distress seemed to be stunned into paralysis.

Sharon ran to Felix and held his face. "Felix, what's going on? Answer me!"

But Felix's face was cold and clammy. "I can't see!" he said. "I'm blind!"

"Nonsense. Felix, how many fingers am I holding up?"

"Four. But you don't understand! I can't see anything! Jesus, Mary, and Joseph! Carol! Is this what it's like for you all the time?"

"What?"

Sharon was confused until she realized that her iGlasses had gone blank. A blinking light indicated that there was no connection to the 'Nets, but all the ads and displays had closed. In their transparent setting, she had forgotten that she was wearing them.

Blind.

"Felix, is your EPU working?"

Felix's face was contorted in terror. One glance at Wemma was all it took to determine that she was also "blind" in the sense that her EPU had failed. She was actually touching things with her hands in an odd way, as if she was trying to determine what was real.

The panic in the huge room had reached a crescendo as people discovered that the subway trains were not working.

Sharon took Felix's elbow with one hand, and Wemma's by the other, and led them forcefully to a service alcove where a door opened to an unused kitchen. She sat her friends on the floor so that they could see each other and told them to hold hands.

"Look into each other's eyes," she ordered. "You have each other. Talk to each other. Stay here!"

Sharon went back into the plaza and saw that some people were bleeding. They'd been trampled or fell in the panic. She grabbed the first one, a girl of about twelve K-years, and pulled her into the kitchen. The girl was stunned and remained unresponsive while Sharon bandaged her bleeding arms and legs with cloth from her clothes. It occurred to Sharon that there'd be a first aid kit in the kitchen and, after a few moments of searching, she was able to find three.

She went back outside to find other victims. She brought three people back this time — two of them vomiting; the other catatonic like the teenager.

The teenager had had an EPU for the shortest amount of time, and Sharon was able to get her attention after shouting at her and shaking her. "You've got to help! I can't do this alone!"

The teenager finally looked at Sharon.

"What's your name?" Sharon demanded.

"Huashan Ayano."

"Ayano, listen. A lot of people are going to die unless we can help them. Do you understand?"

The girl nodded.

"Some of these people in here are bleeding. I have some first aid kits. Can you help?"

Slowly, the girl's attention focused, took in what was happening, and then nodded again. "*Hai.*"

"Good. I've got to go back outside."

When Sharon opened the door again, what she saw was not encouraging. Those who had turned violent were now attacking and abusing those who hadn't.

In a scene right out of a horror movie, one man was attacking other people with the sword he had just purchased or stolen from *Al Saif,* and there were already several victims in his wake.

First priority: Stop the mad swordsman. Sharon looked around for something heavy and found a large glass beer stein on the floor. She hefted it and estimated its mass to be about one and a half kilos. Should be perfect.

"Hey, D'Artagnan! Over here!" To her great surprise and relief, the man actually turned to look at her. "Let's talk about this, 'k? We don't need any more of this. Look at me here!"

The swordsman looked confused, glancing back and forth between Sharon and the sword in his hand.

What fantasy is he living? Sharon wondered.

The man charged, screaming "Know death, barbar!"

He held the sword in his right hand above his head in an awkward, one-handed *vom Tag.*

Perfect, Sharon thought.

The man crossed the distance between them in one two seconds, and as he neared his target he stopped and arced the sword downward in a skill-less, though enthusiastic, *Scheitelhau.*

Sharon stepped back quickly out of range, then threw the beer stein directly at the guy's center of gravity with every erg of force she could muster.

"Fuck!" the man screamed, taking a step back and grabbing his chest where the stein had hit him.

Sharon took three running steps and dived for his knees. The man screamed in pain, and his right leg bent at a weird angle. Painful, but fixable. The sword dropped to the floor and the blade retracted automatically.

Sharon picked up the sword, pressed the activation button, and held the tip of the blade to the man's throat. He quieted instantly, paralyzed by fear.

"If I catch you playing with swords again, I will cut something off. If you're lucky, it will only be your hand. Do you understand?"

The man took a long moment to understand what was happening. He was distracted by the insanity and the pain. After several seconds, he made an acquiescing sound. Sharon released the button on the hilt, and the blade and guard disappeared.

Tucking the hilt into her belt, Sharon looked at the carnage and panic surrounding her. She needed a global solution, not piecemeal one.

Looking along the wall, she finally found what she was looking for: IN CASE OF EMERGENCY, PULL HANDLE.

She pulled.

Instead of the alarm, flashing lights, and water from overhead sprinklers that Sharon expected, a section of wall opened directly in front of her exposing a computer access screen on which words appeared:

System detects network failure.
Please use voice interface.
State the nature of the emergency.

Sharon was a loss as to what to do next and said the first thing that came to mind. "Power failure and riots. Medical emergency."

Emergency medical personnel have been notified.
On site police are trained to handle riots.

"That's it?" Sharon said. "We can't wait for people to get here. And the on-site police are useless. They've been nullified by the network failure."

The AI seemed to consider this.

Additional police have been requested.
It is important that you remain calm.

Sharon decided to lie to the AI. "There's a fire!"

No fire has been detected.

"Your sensors are faulty. The 'Nets are down, and your sensors have been compromised."

The AI responded immediately with a legal notice that said, in effect, that giving a false report to an emergency AI was a felony punishable by a year in jail and lots of money. The AI had already identified her through facial recognition as Carol Simmons and listed her citizen ID number. Did she wish to confirm the existence of a fire?

"Yes, damn it!"

Recommended response?

"Water. Lots of it! Turn on the sprinklers!"

The fire alarm that sounded didn't help, but the cold water pouring out of the sprinkler system had an immediate calming effect. People became more concerned with staying dry and finding shelter than murdering and running amok.

The sprinklers turned off after five minutes when some surviving AI decided that there weren't any flames to fight. Sharon and Ayano searched for survivors who had not either become sick, injured, or catatonic and organized them into teams.

Sharon stood on a table and looked around the room. It was dark with only the emergency lights, but in the distance, she saw a pavilion with the familiar Caduceus emblazoned on it. She jumped down and ran to it, pushing her way past the sick, wounded, and panicked. She couldn't remember a longer hundred-meter dash.

She arrived at the pavilion to find the medical staff similarly affected, but at least they were dry. She found somebody wearing a name tag which showed the letters M.D. and pulled her upright.

"What's wrong with you? You're supposed to be rendering aid!"

"The EPUs are gone!" the woman said. "I can't get readouts!"

"Figure it out, damn it!" Sharon knew that slapping the doctor wouldn't do any good, but it would have made Sharon feel better. Still, she refrained.

"Pretend you're in a vid about the apocalypse and you have to figure it out! Because, you know, that wouldn't surprise me right now!"

Sharon tried to have sympathy for the doctor. After all, she'd gone through medical training learning to rely on EPUs. Now her most important diagnostic tool had been torn away. But sympathy wasn't going to get them through the crisis.

"You don't understand," the physician whimpered. "I'm blind."

"You are not blind." Sharon turned the woman's face to look directly into her eyes. "Through the millennia, doctors have healed with no more than their naked eyes, their bare hands, and their years of experience. You can do this!"

Sharon looked at her name tag again: Mirella Rivera.

"Doctor Rivera! You took an oath to heal!" She shouted. "Your patients need you! If you can't do this, then I'll have to, and I don't know how. They'll die if you don't pull yourself together. Do you hear me Doctor Rivera? Your patients will die!"

Dr. Rivera finally met Sharon's eyes and seemed to gather her wits. She stood up, straightened her posture, and walked over to a small storage unit. She said something that Sharon didn't immediately understand, but it came to her later: "*Médico, cúrate a ti mismo.*"

Dr. Rivera pulled out a small hypo, shoved it into her arm, and closed her eyes. After about fifteen seconds, Sharon could actually see a change come over her.

"Okay. Let's get triage started, people!" the Dr. Rivera shouted. "I want beds made from tables. Set up chairs to divide areas. I want to see the bleeding and breathing cases first! Dr. Yan, get your ass off of the floor and start checking patients! Bones don't set themselves!"

Sharon helped with the triage and eventually found Ayano, Felix, and Wemma at her side, doing what they could, trying to calm the panic, encouraging people to remember that they were thinking, rational humans who didn't really need EPUs.

Sharon asked Ayano, "Where are your parents?"

"I don't know. We got separated."

It didn't matter. Ayano was probably in better shape than her parents were.

Nobody knew what happened beyond a combined power failure and the failure of everybody's EPU.

Everybody in the room was suddenly reduced to their basic, unaugmented senses and they felt deaf, dumb and blind. To Sharon, this was life as she knew it, but in a world where everyone over the age of nine K-years or twelve standard years had a computer in their heads which allowed them total and continuous access to everything on the planet, it was instant and total shock.

Sharon learned later that in that ballroom alone, one hundred and twenty-one people died. Many from heart failure, and way too many from acts of violence.

The city's first responders finally arrived. Police and firefighters and EMT's were everywhere and their EPUs were still functional even if the 'Nets weren't. After evaluating the situation, though, they decided to quarantine the area. There were only a few diseases that could affect EPUs like this, and every one of them was pretty nasty.

The power was finally restored. Emergency workers brought dry clothes and beds, and emergency physicians who weren't "blind".

After an EMT told Sharon to either go sit down or he'd set her down ungraciously, she wandered off to find the kitchen where she first took Wemma and Felix to hide from the panic. On her way there, she noticed that the Esperantists had come into their own, acting as translators between dozens of languages for people who no longer had access to the universal translation services of the EPU. The police and EMTs had conscripted most of them.

She opened a bottle of water and found a chair at a small desk.

Wemma, Felix, and Ayano wandered in not long after. The adults lay down on food prep tables, and Ayano just lay on the floor. Somehow, they'd ended up being guardians for the teenager.

She seems like a good kid, Sharon thought to herself. *I hope her parents are safe.*

On an impulse, and partly out of some subliminal maternal instinct, Sharon walked over to the teenager. She was dressed like teenaged girls from many other eras, sporting a short dress that came to mid-thigh, brightly colored leggings, and fur-trimmed short boots. She was also wearing a vest that only came to her short ribs, and some costume jewelry. Her hair was in need of a brush, but she had lost her purse in the confusion, and she still managed to look cute. It was a look only a teenaged girl could pull off.

"Hey," Sharon said. Ayano looked up at her with tired eyes. "Mind if I sit and talk?"

Ayano thought about this and Sharon had the impression that the girl would beg off talking to a strange adult. Ayano finally responded by making a gesture to sit.

"It's a free floor."

Sharon sat and tried to read the girl's body language. Ayano was just at that age when all adults were un-cool, and Sharon hoped that she'd been able to buy some credibility with the girl by pulling her out of the chaos.

"You handled yourself pretty well during the riot," She said. "Most kids your age just run screaming in a panic."

"I'm not that young," Ayano said. "I'm eleven."

Sharon did a quick mental calculation to convert that into seventeen Earth years. "Listen, as you probably realized, I don't have an EPU."

"Yeah, that was kinda obvious," Ayano glanced at the iGlasses. "Why not?"

"I'm from off planet and people don't use them where I come from," Sharon tried to explain, and wanted to derail the conversation from the topic of her origins. "When did you get yours?"

"As soon as I got my license at nine and a half. I took the test and could have gotten it early, but my mom refused. She's so drango sometimes."

"What kind of test did you have to take?"

"Our school requires that we take two semesters of Digital Hygiene. They basically show us vids of scary stories about what happens to people who use stupid passphrases, or put pictures online of themselves having sex, and what to do if you get harassed, and how to spot money scams. Things like that. Didn't they have that on your planet? I thought it was required everywhere."

Sharon smiled ruefully. "They probably should have required it on my planet. It would have saved a lot of headaches and heartaches, I'm sure."

"Yeah, no doh."

Sharon wasn't entirely sure what "*no doh*" meant in the current teenage patois, but she'd heard it used in the context of, "*Thank you for pointing out the obvious.*"

"So, now you've got this computer in your head," Sharon said. "Do you ever worry that somebody could take control of it?"

"Not before tonight!" Ayana exclaimed. "There are supposed to be safeguard AIs and the FDNS to watch over that."

"FDNS?"

"Federal Department of Network Security."

"A government agency? What if it was the government who wanted to control your EPU?"

Ayana laughed with honest mirth. "You sound like an ad for a low-budget horror cinema!"

She suddenly stopped laughing, thinking about the events of the night and slowly put a hand over her mouth. There was an awkward silence while they sat there in the half-light.

"Do those glasses come in other styles?" Ayana asked.

*   *   *

"Ta udder Sharon Manders is in ta plaza," Lester Sievers told the body of Uchenna Ebelechukwu.

"That can't be possible," Major Manders said.

"It's the same one from the *Zephyr*. Ta prev'us you."

This incarnation of Major Manders had no memory of the *Zephyr* but had been briefed on the operation there.

"She was supposed to commit suicide."

"Tell dat t'her!" Lester said. "An' she still sane! She didna panic."

"Not good," Major Manders said. "I'll have to take care of this."

Uchenna turned and picked up a fabric bag filled with tools. "Point her out to me on the monitors."

✳   ✳   ✳

It was much later when Sharon pulled out her iGlasses and checked them again for the hundredth time and was finally rewarded with a login prompt. She had a short internal debate about telling the others that the 'Nets was back up and decided against it. It would just turn into a fight for the iGlasses. She checked the first local news site she could find.

TERRORISTS SUSPECTED IN 'NETS / BIO ATTACK IN SECOND CITY

THOUSANDS IN QUARANTINE

HUNDREDS INJURED, DOZENS DEAD.

Shit.

As near as anybody could tell — and what the doctors were saying — party-goers in the Second City Marina Plaza were exposed to some sort of virus related to meningitis. The RNA of the virus definitely showed signs of manipulations. Fortunately, it was not airborne, and emergency health personnel were able to contain the outbreak to the plaza. Meanwhile, forensic analysts were examining all the various 'Nets cells for remnants of a computer malware that shut down electrical and 'Nets grids for several city blocks.

There were hundreds of photos and vids, interviews, and on-the-spot reports. The media pundits were already offering the very finest unqualified opinions.

The conspiracy theories were already rampant. After all, it's not like these attacks were unforeseen. The City of Clarksport and the Planetary Government of Kentaurus both spent millions of notes every year to harden the soft and hard infrastructure against just these sorts of attacks, employing the latest and greatest counter-terrorism techniques, and the last successful attack was over a century ago. Are there not AIs to monitor the 'Nets for attacks like these? Were not the food and drink vendors required to monitor their wares? How did somebody get past all the expensive safeguards? It must have been an inside job.

Senate budget hearings were scheduled for next month. Some commentators, pandering to base fears, opined obliquely that it wouldn't be difficult to imagine the military doing something to ensure its budgetary primacy. Like committing treason, sabotage, and murder.

One editorialist commented that it was easier to blame conspiracies, and doing so made us feel better about the incident, because it was too disturbing to think that so much was at risk from one crazy person who thought he had an ax to grind.

Sharon doubted it was one crazy person. It seemed organized. She supposed that the responsible group would eventually step forward to claim credit for the attack. Maybe even several groups.

An aspect of Carol's personal life that Sharon had not brought herself to deal with was email and phone calls. When Sharon checked the inbox after first activating the iGlasses, it was full of thousands of emails. This probably was expected for an account which customarily spent months at a time disconnected from the 'Nets. A cursory glance at the *From* and *Subject* fields was enough to indicate that the vast majority of the emails were promotional, and Sharon had spent much of the trip from Sedna deleting them.

There were also emails from Mom, Dad, and about twenty or so from various people who seemed to be personal friends which displayed subject texts along the lines of *When are you getting home? Chat me when you get into orbit* and *It would be bongo to meet for coffee when you're in Clarksport!*

Sharon didn't touch those. They were emails for another person and, though that other person no longer existed, these people didn't know that.

During the three days since receiving the iGlasses, Sharon had received three chat requests from Mom, and couldn't bring herself to accept any of them.

What could she say? *Hi! You don't know me, but I inhabit your late daughter's corpse.* Still, those people deserved some kind of reply. *Oh, and by the way? I play the guitar now and speak with a funny accent.* Sharon could not get Siever's violent reaction out of her mind.

Sharon had suggested to the psychologist on Sedna that the Navy should just tell everybody that Carol Simmons had died.

This was the truth, wasn't it?

"Wouldn't that be cheating?" the psychologist asked.

"The world wants Carol Simmons. I'm not her."

A tone sounded, and there was a slight buzz feeling. She was receiving another chat request from Mom. Sharon logged out of her account.

"Hey guys!" Sharon told the room. "The 'Nets are back up. You can access it through my iGlasses. Do you want to chat anybody?"

Sharon pulled off the iGlasses and handed them to the first person to leap across the room: Ayano.

Let the mumbling begin.

8

FELIX CHATTED HIS CHIEF to let him know about being caught in the quarantine. Wemma chatted somebody and spoke in a language that Sharon didn't recognize without translation services. When she finally got the glasses back, Sharon chatted Wyatt. After sleeping a few hours, Sharon woke to the sight of Ayano sitting on a folding chair organizing personal items in a small daypack.

"Where did you get that?"

The girl didn't look up from her task, but said, "They're handing them out over by the metro terminal. They have some soap, a toothbrush, clean underwear."

Ayano paused when she found what she was looking for — a pair of cheap iGlasses.

Sharon decided that clean underwear would make a world of difference. The retractable sword hilt was still stuck in her belt and she pulled it out. "Would you mind watching this for me?"

Ayano's eyes widened when she saw what it was but took it and stuck it in the daypack. "*Hai!* I'll keep it safe."

Sharon was stiff and sore, and walked slowly to the swinging door and out into the mess that the Marina District Second City had become. It smelled like vomit and urine and unwashed humanity, and the noise level was near intolerable. People either milled about or rushed to and fro on urgent business. There didn't seem to be any in between.

Sharon hadn't walked twenty meters towards the metro station when she saw three people trying to move a cart full of medications and having difficulty navigating around abandoned booths, entertainment equipment, and people. She offered to help and did her best to clear a path for them.

Afterwards, she assisted the food distribution people, who opened several kitchens, including the one Sharon's group had been using for a hide-away, and started shipping in food. Sharon found herself checking off food packages against names and then ended up being a short-order cook in the same kitchen she had slept in.

When she took a fifteen-minute break to find a bathroom, somebody handed her a daypack. "Here. You'll need one of these," a harried looking elf said.

A huge Furman who was carrying a couple dozen daypacks with somebody's corporate logo followed her, and the two of them were handing them out to anybody who didn't already have one.

"And drink some water. You look like you're about ready to fall over," the elf called as an afterthought.

After a double shift of cooking food, it occurred to Sharon that she'd have to find a different place to sleep for the night.

Cots had been provided and the plaza suddenly looked like a huge sleep-away camp. She asked some fellow internees and discovered that she needed to register at a desk that had been set up by some very serious and professional looking people.

Sharon walked over and introduced herself.

A large man looked up from a handheld. "Did you say your name was Sharon Manders? What's your address?"

"No. I'm sorry." *Shit!* "My name is Carol Simmons."

"Well, which is it? Simmons or Manders?" he asked, sounding annoyed.

"Simmons. Sorry for the mix up."

The man looked at her suspiciously while mumbling. His EPU worked perfectly, and Sharon realized that they were volunteers who were willing to expose themselves to a disease that might render their EPUs useless.

"Simmons," he repeated.

"Yes."

The man looked worried. "One moment. There's a message attached to your name."

He continued to be absorbed in the message that Sharon couldn't see, and she wondered if it had something to do with the way she treated Dr. Rivera.

Lacking anything else more interesting to do, Sharon looked around at the giant, underground plaza. It seemed peaceful, if a tad crowded. There were cots everywhere, and family and friends had formed themselves into miniature neighborhoods. There didn't seem to be a lot of privacy, though. There was a perpetual line at the bathrooms.

"Carol Simmons?" a new male voice inquired, and she turned around to meet him.

"Yes?"

"I'm officer Wielisław Majewski of the Clarksport Police." He showed an ID. "We've been looking for you. You're not wearing your iGlasses."

Sharon pulled them out of a pocket. "Sorry. I was cooking and forgot."

She put them on and logged in. Sure enough, there were several messages marked "Very Urgent!"

"Would you hand them to me, please?" the officer's voice did not sound like a request.

"They are my personal pair," Sharon objected. She took them off but held them in her hand. "I don't want to lose them."

"Understood, ma'am. Your iGlasses." He held out his hand. He was accustomed to having his requests fulfilled without question.

Sharon had learned many things about government and personal rights while taking her entrance exam, and one of them was that the police could not forcibly take away her only connection to the 'Nets. Connectivity to the 'Nets was so important to this society that it was considered a basic human right. However, the police often operated on the assumption that civilians didn't know this. "I'll keep them, sir. Thank you." She knew even without the civics lesson that it never helped to be impolite to a police officer.

Officer Majewski pulled another pair out of his own breast pocket. "I'm going to give you another pair."

Sharon knew that once she accepted that pair — most likely one of limited capabilities — then she'd have multiple ways to access the net, and they could take her own pair.

"These work just fine, officer." she said. "I am exercising my rights to retain my only means to access the 'Nets."

Sharon thought she saw a smirk cross Majewski's face. "Very well, ma'am. This way."

Majewski took Sharon's elbow in such a way that he had complete control and led her across the plaza to a white pavilion emblazoned with the police logo. Inside were several empty desks. A separate room was made up for sleeping and other off duty activities. There was another, smaller square room with nothing but a chair.

Majewski told Sharon to sit in the chair and leave her glasses on and active. "Don't take them off, or you could be charged with obstructing a police investigation."

Sharon knew that that was bluster as well. Unless and until they arrested her, she could legally leave this room and the pavilion any time she wanted.

She tried to make herself comfortable on the cold composite chair and activated the glasses. A large lozenge shaped object with the word "Accept" glowing in the center of it appeared directly in front of her. She raised her hand and 'touched' it.

The lozenge was instantly replaced with an immersive environment. As far as her senses were concerned, she was now sitting in a featureless police interview room. Across a table from her was a woman dressed in an impressive uniform.

"Good afternoon, Crewman Simmons. Thank you for joining us. I'm Sergeant Dronda Mitchell. We've been trying to find you. You haven't been wearing your glasses?"

"No. I was cooking and didn't want to mess them."

Mitchell didn't react to this. Instead, she activated the table in front of them, which acted as a frame to show pictures and documents. Sharon could see that it was a file on Carol.

"We just have a few questions. As you may have heard, there is some suspicion that the tragedy at the plaza was caused by terrorists."

Mitchell looked at Sharon, but since there wasn't a question, Sharon remained quiet.

Videos from the Solstice party started playing across the desktop, and Sharon realized another aspect of the EPUs which she hadn't considered: Every person at the party was a security camera. The EPUs by default kept thirty minutes of recorded history before deleting it, but a person could set it up for any amount of time, and at parties like this, they usually set it to keep a record of the entire event. It seemed unlikely that any activity went unrecorded. Sharon saw herself dumping a full mug of beer.

"Why did you dump that beer?"

"It tasted funny."

"Your friends thought so, too?"

"Yes."

"Nobody else complained about the beer."

Sharon had not thought that the beer tasted funny but dumped her beer because Wemma and Felix did.

"We think there may have been a vector in the beer," Mitchell said. "A vector can be anything that carries and transmits ..."

"... an infectious pathogen into a living organism." Sharon felt a little insulted that the policewoman would assume that she was ignorant of basic epidemiological terms. "Yeah, I know what it is. I have a ..."

Sharon was about to say, "... a degree in ... something", but the memory once again faded. She became irritated, thinking that only the most important memories tended to fade.

"You have a what?" Mitchell looked at her expectantly.

Sharon shook her head. "It's not important."

"Would you mind if I was the judge of that?"

Sharon asserted her rights on the matter. "I have nothing to say about that."

"I see." Mitchell activated another vid, showing Felix throwing up just before the lights went out. "What happened here?"

"Felix ... that is, Crewman Adler got sick. Very quickly."

"You're on first name basis with Crewman Adler?"

"Of course. We're rackmates."

"Are you sleeping with him?"

"Only in the sense that we shared a dormitory."

"Have you ever slept with him?"

Sharon didn't answer because she had no idea. What kind of relationship did they have before the accident? Felix had never even hinted that it was physical. But if Felix gave a different answer to the question things would be more difficult. Sharon hid her ignorance by glaring at the policewoman as if insulted. This wasn't hard to do, as the entire conversation was insulting.

"Has he recovered?" Mitchell asked.

"Yes. Except, like everybody else, has lost the use of his EPU."

A look of curiosity swept over Mitchell's face. "You lost your EPU, too, didn't you?"

"Yes. But not last night."

"That's right," Mitchell said, indicating that she knew the answers without asking. "During a naval mission. Did you panic when that happened? Did you get sick? Anything?"

"I was in a coma for twenty-three days."

"True, but you eventually woke up. What did you feel then?"

"I was in a lot of pain, is what I felt."

"But you didn't panic."

Sharon shook her head. "I didn't have enough energy to panic. You've read Dr. Bradford's report, I assume."

"Yes, I did. Very interesting reading. You're living with him, aren't you?"

Mitchell made this sound tawdry and accusatory. Was she going to accuse Sharon of having sex with the entire ship's roster before the interview was over?

"I'm renting a room from him."

"Is it common for ship's officers to rent out rooms to enlisted crew?"

"I have no idea. I haven't done it before."

Mitchell squinted her eyes. Sharon hadn't meant it to sound sarcastic, but it had.

"In fact, you are not renting a room from the Bradfords, are you? You're staying as a guest."

Sharon didn't respond.

"Dr. Bradford's wife. What's her name?"

"Marjo," Sharon said reflexively.

"Marjo Bradford, that's right. She was born on Eteramunde, wasn't she?"

Sharon knew that Mitchell knew everything there was to know about Marjo.

"Wasn't she?" Mitchell repeated forcefully.

"That's what I understand."

Mitchell looked like she was examining some internal EPU document. "We weren't able to find you today. Why weren't you wearing the glasses?"

"I was cooking." Sharon wanted to point out that they'd already been over the question but decided that there was no point.

"Do you always take off your glasses to cook?"

"I don't see any reason to wear them when I cook."

"I like cooking, too," Mitchell said offhandedly. "I like to use 'Glasses to monitor the temperature and make sure I don't overcook things."

"Good idea!" Sharon tried to sound friendly. "I'll keep that in mind."

"It made it much more difficult for us to find you." Mitchell wasn't buying the friendly tone. "Is that what you intended?"

"Actually, you didn't find me. I came to you." Sharon resented the accusation that she was hiding.

Mitchell nodded as if coming to a conclusion. "How long were you on Maheux?"

"What's that got to do with this?"

"I'm asking the questions. How long were you there?"

Sharon knew the answer because she had studied the mission files herself, trying to suss out some answers.

"The ship was in orbit for four standard days."

"And how long were you on the surface?"

"About thirty-six hours."

"Well, what was it? Thirty-six? Thirty-seven?"

"About thirty-six hours. It depends on how you define on the surface."

"In fact," Mitchell proclaimed, "You were on the surface, from touch down to lift off, almost thirty-eight standard hours."

"If you say so."

"And how long were you out of contact?"

"I assume you have that information already," Sharon said with fire in her eyes.

"Humor me."

If Sharon lied, Mitchell would know. That much was certain.

"Twenty-seven hours. The record shows that I was merely out of contact, not AWOL."

"What did you do during that time?"

Sharon swallowed. "I don't remember."

Mitchell was silent for almost a minute, and Sharon started to wonder if they'd lost the connection.

"That's right. You don't remember. You came back onboard and eight days later you caused an accident in one of the maintenance bays."

Sharon started to correct Mitchell and say, "Mechanical Chase", and the words very nearly left her lips, then she realized that was exactly what Mitchell wanted her to do. By concentrating on that part of the sentence, she'd have to ignore the important part. Who cares if she called it a maintenance bay?

"Why are you involved with a NavSec investigation?" Sharon asked. "This isn't part of your jurisdiction. NavSec has all that info and will share it with you if they deem it appropriate."

"Ms Simmons, you're a person of interest in a suspected terrorist attack. Your entire life is my business right now."

"I did not cause the accident," Sharon said.

"How do you know? Didn't you lose your memory?"

Sharon felt her anger rising and put an emotional clamp on it.

"You are intentionally misrepresenting the facts. You weren't there."

"You're right. I wasn't there," Mitchell said. "So please enlighten me. What happened? What do you remember?"

Sharon felt trapped. She was going to have to admit to things she didn't want to. She could see where this was going: She was a suspect in the *Zephyr* bombing, and now she was a suspect in this attack.

Mitchell pressed on. "Look at things from my perspective, Simmons. Do you expect me to believe this is all just a coincidence?"

Actually, Sharon could see it from that perspective, and it worried her. She'd probably make the same conclusions as Mitchell if she had been presented with the same facts. And the worst part of it was that Sharon really had no defense because she had no memory of anything prior to waking up from a coma.

"We'll need to check your 'Nets access records," Mitchell said. "Perhaps there's something in there that will shed some light for both of us."

"No."

"Excuse me?"

"I don't know much about the law," Sharon explained. "Pretty much nil, as a matter of fact. But I do know that the courts have repeatedly held that an individual's personal 'Nets access records held in private accounts are about as private as it gets unless the person gives permission."

"Oh, come now Ms Simmons. You don't honestly believe that anybody has any privacy anymore."

"Maybe not. But I do not consent to a search of my records."

"It doesn't matter," Mitchell said dismissively. "We'll have a warrant in about thirty minutes."

Sharon had no idea what was in most of Carol's personal records. Even if she had the passphrases, she had been reluctant to go prying, and now that might turn out to be a huge mistake.

"Based on what? You'll never get a warrant without cause."

"Based on the fact that you lied to an emergency AI. You said there was a fire when there was not."

"People were panicking. Many were being violent about it. I had to get them to calm down. That lie saved lives."

"Maybe, but it was still a lie, and charges will be filed. Which is enough to get a warrant."

"You'd better get started then," Sharon said.

The immersive environment was so convincing that Sharon had forgotten she was in a pavilion in the Marina Plaza. When she remembered, she said. "I need to talk to a lawyer."

"Lawyer?" Mitchell asked, genuinely confused. "You mean an advocate?"

Sharon terminated the link, deactivated her glasses and stood up. Officer Majewski was at her side instantly. "You can't take off the glasses."

"I'm still wearing them," she said, and walked out.

*   *   *

The warrant actually took much longer to obtain. It was about three hours later when Sharon received a notice that official agents of the Clarksport Police were searching her personal records, bank accounts, chatmail, and calendars.

But by then, Sharon had found an advocate by an odd, coincidental, circuitous method. She walked over to the medical pavilion to see if she could beg an aspirin or anything for a headache, and there was Dr. Rivera.

"There you are!" the doctor said cheerfully. "We have been waiting for you to reappear!"

"Well, here I am."

"Dr. Yan! This is the woman I told you about. She's the one who pulled me out of my panic."

An elderly Asian man, probably close to a hundred and seventy standard years old, greeted Sharon with a smile. "Young woman," he said with a thick Haidau accent, bowing. "On behalf of the entire medical crew, thank you for your intervention. I'm afraid we were all caught with our pants down."

"*Hěn gāoxìng jiàn dào nǐn,* Dr. Yan. You are most welcome. I was simply doing what needed to be done."

Sharon found herself being introduced to the entire medical staff, all of whom expressed their gratitude that somebody was able to keep their head together during the first minutes of the crisis. Their tone changed when they learned of Sharon's legal problems.

"Ninguna buena acción queda sin castigo," Dr. Rivera said bitterly, which was immediately followed by Dr. Yan's equally resentful, *"Ēn jiāng chóu bào".*

Dr. Rivera broke away and talked briefly to a dark man who was donating blood. They had run out of synthetic blood and were now collecting it the old-fashioned way. Rivera waved to Sharon to follow.

"Carol Simmons, this is Marshall Ryles, Superior Court Judge. Judge Ryles, this is the woman who saved all our butts."

Ryles extended his hand. "Ms Simmons! I have heard of some of your exploits. Thank you for your cool head and quick thinking. If there is anything I can do for you, do not hesitate."

"As a matter of fact, Judge Ryles, I'm in a bit of a legal bind." Sharon explained how she'd been detained and questioned on suspicion of causing the 'Nets failure and bio-attack.

"Just a minute," Judge Ryles held up a hand. "First off," he looked at the others nearby. "I want some privacy for my client here. Everybody else within earshot, and isn't attached to a tube, leave."

"Should we chat privately?" Sharon asked while everybody shuffled away.

"No. Your account will probably be monitored before our conversation is over. Now, I need to ask you one question."

"Yes?"

"Do you expect me, in my position as an officer the court, to shield you from the law?"

"Absolutely not, sir!" Sharon gestured to add emphasis. "I just don't want my civil rights trampled upon."

Judge Ryles smiled. "That I can help you with. Now. Tell me everything. And when I say everything, I mean every single detail. Ms Simmons, I will warn you that I've been interviewing clients and suspects for a hundred years, and I'll know if you're leaving out even so much as a comma."

"I understand, your honor."

"Let's hear it, then."

True to their agreement, Sharon told him everything. From her first waking moments on the *Zephyr* to being detained by NavSec, to the missing twenty-seven hours on Maheux, to her conversations with the Bradford's and her arrival at the party and her actions during the crisis. She also told him about the conflicting identities in her head, the snatches of memories she kept experiencing, the strange instructional dreams, and the feeling that this body was not the one she had originally occupied. Then she quickly told him about her interviews with the psychologist at NavSec who assured everyone that she may be confused, but she wasn't psychotic. And lastly told him how she had no idea if she was guilty of sabotage or not, and that this frightened her beyond description. Judge Ryles listened without interrupting.

Sharon finally ran out of information after about an hour. Judge Ryles put on his loaner iGlasses and had a quick mumble with somebody.

When he was done, Sharon started to say something, but the judge raised his hand.

"Don't tell me anything more. We can't prevent the police from exercising the warrant to seize your records, but based on what you've said, I think we can get anything they find there suppressed."

A woman walked up to join him, and it was obvious that she was the one whom the judge chatted.

The judge introduced them. "Rhonda Wesson of Wesson, Mulkey, Fischer, and Sullins, this is Sharon Manders, *née* Carol Simmons. She's your newest client."

Rhonda looked at Sharon with some disdain. "Yes, your honor. And with this, I consider the little matter we just chatted about closed."

"Indeed, it is. Ms Manders, I'm afraid you'll have to explain everything to Advocate Wesson just the way you explained it to me."

"Wait. I didn't intend that this should be pro bono work," Sharon objected.

"Oh, it's not." Rhonda said with a smirk. "It's costing Judge Ryles dearly."

"And I expect to get value commensurate with the cost, Advocate Wesson! We probably both owe Ms Manders our lives."

Advocate Rhonda Wesson listened attentively for two hours as Sharon explained everything again. Unlike the judge, she had plenty of questions. Many of which Sharon had not thought to ask, and most of them she couldn't answer.

"And you experienced no blackouts during the attack on the plaza?"

"None at all."

"Be certain when you answer that, Sharon. Everything is going to balance on this. In your memory, are there any times during the attack where you might have blacked out but didn't notice."

"Nope. I can remember every second in excruciating detail."

"What about before the attack? Any chance that you might have blacked out?"

"Not at any time during the entire day, that night, or the next morning did I black out. Of that I am certain."

"Would you be willing to be hypnotized to answer these questions?"

"You can hypnotize me, turn me upside down and cover me in beer batter, and the answer will be the same."

"Sharon, I know it's frustrating to hear the same questions over and over, but sarcasm won't help. It certainly won't win any points in the court."

Sharon sighed. "You're right." She tried to look apologetic.

"The prosecution will call experts to testify that you probably blacked out but can't remember."

"They can say that without evidence?"

"You'd be surprised at what juries believe without direct evidence. Let's talk about the day before. Where did you go?"

"Nowhere. It snowed all day. I did laundry and watched a few vids and read some educational material."

"What subject?"

"Quantum electronics. Carol was something of an expert, and I know zilch. Well, not quite zilch anymore. I was able to get through several publications."

"Where did you get your post-secondary education?"

"University of …" Sharon stopped.

Rhonda looked at her quizzically. "Did it just happen? Did you just almost remember something?"

Sharon nodded. "I never went to a university. I went to a trade school. Carol went to a trade school."

Sharon had told Rhonda about the anatomical sketches and her near admission to the police that she had a degree in something.

"Sharon, this is what it's going to look like to the court: You spent some shore leave on Maheux where somebody brainwashed you into sabotaging the *Zephyr* and net-bombing the Solstice celebration and poisoning our food, and then forgetting everything. And even if the prosecution can't prove that, that's what the court will think. Unless you can remember something important. Something vital."

"Yes, yes, I know!"

"Any suggestions?"

"I need to go back to Maheux," Sharon said, breaking her promise to Daerîsiell.

"What's on Maheux?"

"That's what we need to find out. Not only are the keys to my mission memory there, but maybe, just maybe, — and I've been thinking about this a lot — conspirators with the mystery ship that eluded the *Zephyr*. Somebody went to a lot of trouble to scramble my brains and sabotage a Navy frigate in order to get that mystery ship past the *Zephyr*. Must have had some important cargo."

Rhonda shook her head dismissively. "The court will never agree to that. Just a moment."

Rhonda took another chat. In spite of everything, she was still working full-time. Her other clients couldn't wait just because she was inconvenienced with a quarantine. This was easily the ninth or tenth chat during their interview.

Rhonda terminated the call and looked at Sharon with a smile. "Well, your lucky day! That was somebody in the Navy. Commander somebody with the Advocate General's office … I'm so bad at remembering names. They have filed a petition to take possession of you for the duration of the quarantine. They're sending a hazmat team to collect you."

That did not sound pleasant.

"And Judge Ryles has signed it. The City Prosecutor's office will file a complaint and a counter petition in an appeal with the District Court, which is closed until the day after tomorrow. That means the life expectancy of the court order is measured in hours. However, if the police find anything in your personal records to justify arresting you, the court order will be void and the Navy will have to turn you over to them, and then they'll turn you over to the Federal Police because terrorism is a federal crime."

"Do you want to see my records? I'll make them available …"

"Please, dear Athena, no!" Rhonda held up a hand. "If you're arrested, then yes. But should things turn out badly for you, I don't want to explain to anybody how I knew what was in your records now. However, do send me a copy of your recording of the police interview. You'd better go get your stuff. The hazmat guys'll be here soon."

9

S HARON COLLECTED HER LITTLE DAYPACK AND SWORD from
Ayano, then chatted Wyatt to let him know what the
situation was. He said something sympathetic and promised to
inquire about Sharon's status.

Felix and Wemma were nowhere to be found, and their
network status indicated they were offline. Sharon hoped they
were finding a pleasant diversion.

Sharon decided to go by the medical pavilion one last time
just to say good-bye to Doctors Rivera and Yan. She felt like she
didn't have many friends on Kentaurus, and it wouldn't do to
snub the few who had helped her.

With the blade and guard retracted, the sword looked like a tapered wooden stick with a heavy weight on one end. It fit easily into the daypack. She felt she should really return it to its owner but had no idea who that was. Perhaps the people at *Al Saif* could look up a serial number.

Sharon was still fifty meters from the medical pavilion when she heard somebody call out, "Excuse me! You! Excuse me!"

She felt a tug on her sleeve and turned to see a tall black man in blue coveralls with the logo of the City of Clarksport on his chest.

"Yes?" Sharon said, looking up at his face. He had to be over two meters tall. There was a name tag. "Mr. Ebel … ech … ukwu." she stumbled over the name and hoped she didn't sound rude.

"I need to speak to you. We saw you on the monitors, and we have some questions."

"Okay. Let's talk," Sharon said.

"Let's go to my office."

"I'd rather not. I'm expecting people to come for me any minute."

"I'm afraid I must insist."

"Why? What's in your office?"

"I have to fill out forms."

"Just send me the files," Sharon said, her suspicion growing. "What? Clarksport facilities people still use paper or something?"

"Please," Mr. Ebelechukwu said. "This will only take a moment."

"It will take even less time if we do this right here and right now," Sharon said irritably.

Mr. Ebelechukwu looked confused. He wasn't accustomed to people questioning his authority. "We need to question you about your role in the terrorist attack," he insisted.

"You can get my statement from the police, then." Sharon's instincts were setting off alarms about this encounter: Ebelechukwu wasn't acting like a typical Kentauran citizen.

"No, I can't. I must question you independently. Are you going to come along politely, or are we going to make a scene? I will get the police involved if I have to."

"That's a great idea!" Sharon agreed loudly. "Let's both go to the police. I'm sure they'll want to know why a city employee is breaking the quarantine. You're not wearing iGlasses. Your EPU is still functional."

They stood there looking at each other across the distance of about a meter and a half, and Sharon had the feeling that something unpleasant was about to happen, and she made her plans.

If he tries to grab me, I'm jumping that way.

"Why didn't you terminate?" he asked with a change in the tone of his voice.

"What?"

"You should have terminated after setting the bomb. You let yourself be exposed to medical procedures. Now they are asking questions."

"Terminate? You mean suicide?"

"We can do it now. Together."

"Um. Not interested."

"What are you doing?" he asked. "You know procedure. You know protocol. You should have terminated."

Ebelechukwu didn't try to grab her, but he pulled something out of a pocket. In the tenths of a second Sharon had to think about it, she saw something that had a gun-like handle, a gun-like barrel, and a gun-like trigger.

Definitely a gun!

Jumping still seemed like the best idea. Sharon leapt at a forty-five-degree angle to Ebelechukwu and kept running, trying to lose herself in the crowd. Would the man take a chance on shooting her with all these innocents in the way? She felt guilty about endangering them.

Somebody shouted, "He's got a gun!"

Now everybody was running. Sharon was certain that he would be the center of attention of everybody wearing 'Glasses in video recording mode.

Why would the City of Clarksport try to kill me? He isn't with the city, she concluded. *He's with, well, the same people who tried to destroy the* Zephyr.

"Crap," Sharon said to nobody in particular.

She ducked into an alcove and behind a potted bush. In a flash, she intuited what was happening: somebody had taken over Mr. Ebelechukwu the same way somebody had taken over Carol Simmons. That sounded fantastically paranoid, but there were no other explanations for what she knew. Carol Simmons had disappeared, and then reemerged as a saboteur.

"Access city public database," she said to her iGlasses. A flash of light indicated compliance. "Report any news containing the name Ebelechukwu."

The 'Glasses responded almost instantly with a null return.

That's because everybody thinks this guy is genuine. Am I just paranoid, or am I justified here?

Sharon heard more noises. The police were facing off with Ebelechukwu. Sharon risked a look around the alcove wall and was rewarded with a clear view of several police surrounding the man. He clearly held some kind of weapon in his hand. The police were shouting at him to lower the weapon and lie on the ground.

Sharon realized this wasn't going to end well when Ebelechukwu put the weapon to his own head.

"Don't do it!" shouted one of the police.

The weapon went off. Sharon expected to see Ebelechukwu's head explode, but instead it caught fire and his entire body was engulfed in flames in mere seconds. Sharon's eyes went wide as she realized that Ebelechukwu had intended that to be her.

He wanted me to commit suicide with him. Because the mission was over. Which mission?

Sharon knew with certainty who had caused the Solstice attack.

Somebody showed up quickly with a fire extinguisher, but it had very little effect on the flames. Sharon could feel the intense heat. Ebelechukwu's prone body was reduced to a charred, broken skeleton in a matter of minutes. People screamed, many cried. Others were getting sick again.

If a city employee was an impostor, who else? A cop? A Navy officer? An advocate? Anybody?

Sharon had to get out of there, and there were damn few people she could trust to help. Somebody considered her to be a high-value target if they were willing to risk this kind of public encounter.

A plan formed in her head, and she looked around for Ayano.

"Chat Huashan Ayano."

"Contacting …" the 'Glasses responded.

SHARON! Ayano's voice came over in near panic. I SAW THAT MAN CHASING YOU!

I'M OKAY. I'M NOT HURT. ARE YOU SAFE?

HAI! I FOUND MY PARENTS!

Sharon felt a weight lifted from her shoulders. Ayano would be alright.

LISTEN, CAN YOU MEET ME BY THE PLACE WHERE WE SLEPT ON THE FIRST NIGHT?

WHY? WHAT IS WRONG?

NOTHING. I JUST NEED TO ASK A FAVOR.

Ayano agreed to meet her, and Sharon felt another wave of relief as she saw the teenager approaching without anybody else accompanying her. Sharon turned off the iGlasses and threw them into the nearest overflowing trash receptacle.

"What favor do you ask?" Ayano said. "I owe you my life."

Sharon decided to take advantage of that.

"Teenagers always know the best ways to sneak in and out of places," she said. "The same was true a thousand years ago, and I'm willing to gamble that it's true today. You know how to get into Second City Plaza without anybody knowing, right?"

Ayano just looked at her, unsure what to expect.

"How do I get out of Second City?"

"You want to break the quarantine?"

"Ayano, this is life or death for me. You saw that man chasing me."

"*Hai.*"

"Nobody has gotten sick or died since the initial attack. We would know already if this was a deadly threat. It isn't."

"Are you a doctor?" Ayano asked.

Sharon made non-committal noises. "Sort of. Don't ask too many questions. Can you show me how to get out of here?"

"*Shiranugahotoke,*" Ayano said to herself. "This way."

Ayano lead the way across a plaza to a closed restaurant specializing in Asian cuisine. The door opened at her touch.

"This place belongs to my mother's sister and her family," she explained.

They went into the kitchen and through a backdoor that lead to a hall that connected the backs of most of the stores in this wall. It was some kind of delivery access. They kept going until they got to a wall panel that opened up into a cupboard that would have been roomy for Ayano, but it would be a tight fit for Sharon.

"This is a delivery elevator," Ayano explained. "Do not take it to the delivery platform. That will be guarded. Take it to the maintenance levels and follow the signs."

"To where?"

"I don't know," Ayono said. "I've never been to the maintenance levels. Get in."

Sharon folded herself into the compartment, and then realized there were no internal access panels. That made sense if the only passengers on this elevator were dead fish.

"Wait!"

"*Ganbatte kudasai,* Sharon Manders." Ayano said, wishing her well.

She activated a switch and the door closed.

10

City of Clarksport
Maintenance Levels, Kentaurus
Kentauran calendar: 2 Protomina, 1383 PS

A FTER AN INDETERMINABLE TIME, the elevator car finally stopped, and the doors opened. Sharon unfolded herself, stood slowly, rubbed a pain out of her butt, then stepped into a long dark corridor with doors sporting signs reading AUTHORIZED ACCESS ONLY. She was content with merely walking down the abandoned hallways where the lights illuminated from above as she walked and dimmed after she passed. If she had bothered to think about that, she'd have found it just a bit disconcerting. She turned at random intersections, climbed some stairs and descended others. In mere minutes she was more lost than she'd ever been.

She didn't see any direction signs, and assumed she'd have to access some local AI with her iGlasses, and she'd thrown those away in the plaza. She believed that as long as she was offline, nobody could follow her.

Except that now her daypack was buzzing.

What the ...?

Then Sharon remembered the complementary free iGlasses that came with every daypack. She pulled the pack off her shoulders and opened up several zippered compartments before she found a grey plastic pair. The buzzing was louder, and a light was flashing.

Might as well see who it is.

She slipped the 'Glasses on and logged in. The familiar face of Special Agent Elrydien Daerîsiell filled her field of view.

SHARON, YOU'VE GOT TO COME BACK IMMEDIATELY.

WHY? SO YOU CAN PUT ME IN JAIL? LOBOTOMIZE ME? SET ME ON FIRE? HOW DID YOU FIND ME? DID YOU CHECK THE SECURITY FOOTAGE TO SEE WHICH DAYPACK THAT OTHER ELF GAVE TO ME? OR WAS SHE ON YOUR PAYROLL TO START WITH?

Daerîsiell smirked. ACTUALLY, IT WAS MUCH EASIER THAN THAT. WE SIMPLY ASKED THE SECURITY AI TO ACTIVATE ANY IGLASSES IN THE MAINTENANCE LEVELS. YOUR FRIEND AYANO LEFT HER SET ACTIVATED WHEN SHE ESCORTED YOU TO THE ELEVATOR.

Sharon *tsk*'d. I GOTTA HAND IT TO YOU, ELRYDIEN. YOU KNOW YOUR STUFF.

SHARON, LISTEN TO ME. WE KNOW WHO YOU ARE. WE KNOW WHERE YOU CAME FROM. AND WE HAVE NO INTENTION OF SHUTTING YOU DOWN. WE ONLY WANT TO LEARN HOW IT WAS DONE.

Daerîsiell had Sharon's attention. WHO AM I?

ALLOW ME TO SHOW YOU. I'M GOING TO SEND A VR INVITE. YOU NEED TO ACCEPT IT.

WHY SHOULD I TRUST YOU?

WHY NOT? WE ALREADY KNOW WHERE YOU ARE. IF I WANTED TO COLLECT YOU, I COULD. BUT I'D RATHER CONVINCE YOU TO COME IN YOURSELF.

AND YOU THINK A VR INVITE WILL PERSUADE ME TO TRUST YOU?

I THINK IT'S A START. YOU REALLY HAVE NOTHING TO LOSE BY ACCEPTING, AND YOUR SOUL TO GAIN.

GIVE ME A SEC.

Sharon pulled the glasses off and pressed her hands against her forehead, elbows on knees, sitting on the floor. She was exhausted, dirty, and scared. The image of the city employee setting fire to his own head still played vividly in her mind. Sharon desperately wanted coffee, a long shower, and a good night's sleep, and it wouldn't be long before she'd be looking for some kind of toilet.

Putting her 'Glasses back on, she told Daerîsiell, SEND IT.

A three-dee elliptical shape appeared in front of her, hovering a meter off the ground, with the word Accept engraved in the side. Sharon reached out and touched it.

As soon as she accepted it Sharon found herself sitting in a hot, dry grassland, with the sun high in a cloudless sky. It didn't feel hot, and Sharon had to remind herself that she was in a climate-controlled basement in Clarksport and all of this was merely a visual illusion. But it looked hot, and Sharon's throat felt dry because of it. The fact that she wasn't sweating was a little disorienting. There were low mountains in the distance with some trees, yellow grass covered the ground in spotty patches, and a few summer flowers bloomed. Bees and other insects buzzed nearby. Directly in front of her was a dig site.

The research excavation was a shallow, rectangular depression, about twenty meters wide and ten across, crisscrossed with strings adorned with handwritten tags. There were several deeper places that bore the telltales of a bone pit and shards from rocks which were chipped into tools.

There was also part of a fossilized skeleton. Sharon stood up, walked over to the excavation, and knelt at the edge of the dig to visually examined the remains. She expected the ground to feel like hard dirt, but it was only the cool surface of the floor. If she removed the iGlasses, the excavation site would turn back into a basement hall.

"Probably *Homo habilis*," she said after a minute. "Limb proportions look similar to *australopithecine*, but the brain is larger, and the teeth have a rounded arc. They were originally thought to be the first of our ancestors to use tools, but that's no longer the case. Most anthropologists now believe that the origins of tool usage predate the rise of *Homo*."

Elrydien had been standing on the other side of the dig with that Lieutenant from the *Zephyr*. Both were watching her curiously.

Elrydien said, "Professor Manders."

"Yes?" Sharon responded, as if it was the most natural thing to do. Then she realized which honorific the elf had used and was momentarily dizzy as a flood of hazy memories fought for dominance in her consciousness.

"Does this look at all familiar?"

Sharon almost looked pained as the memories came flooding into mind.

"Yes. We discovered that this individual died from injuries suffered in a fight. Some argued that a wild animal, like a large cat or a bear, caused the injuries but I was able to prove definitively that they were caused by another *hominin*. It was a murder." Sharon looked around. "I was here. In 1998."

"Actually," Lt. Berg said. "You weren't. This excavation never happened."

"What do you mean? Of course it happened! I remember every detail. Over in that corner, we found some textbook examples of Oldowan tools."

Lt. Berg held out an object in his hand. Sharon saw that it was a hardcover book and took it. It had no mass, but it responded to handling. The title was *The Sand, Like Tears*. Written by Joanne Perkins. On the cover was an artistic rendering of a woman in khaki, sunglasses perched on her head, tucked into blonde hair pulled back into a ponytail, looking out of the book to past Sharon's shoulders. Sharon realized she was looking at herself. There was also a similar rendering of the *hirsute habilis*.

"Some years before the Singularity," Berg explained. "There was a period when a fashion in books and vids was to depict scientists as adventurers and crime solvers. Anthropologists were a favorite, along with medical examiners. In at least one creative instance, they were combined. Some were based on real people. Others, like you, were wholly fictional. In this book, Professor Sharon Manders, of the University of California Anthropology Department, solves a two-million-year-old murder. The events surrounding the murder paralleled events very similar to those in her personal life. Two stories separated by millions of years. One of Dr. Manders and one of this poor fellow in Africa. The point of the story, I think, was that when you strip away the trappings of modern life, the ways we live, love and kill haven't changed much in the last two million years."

The implication hit Sharon like a rock to the head.

"Professor Manders, you … never existed. Except in the minds of an author and her audience." Berg said.

"If it's any consolation," Elrydien said rather uselessly. "I'm told that the books were very popular, especially among young adult women of the day. Lots of adventure, peppered with romance and intrigue, and a healthy portion of scientific process. Thinly veiled encouragements for girls to consider a career in science."

"How ...?" Sharon tried to ask as she sat on the floor.

"We aren't sure of all the details yet," Berg said. "It has something to do with a re-programming of your EPU. A neurologist ... Dr. Dvnikani ... thinks that when you ... or rather, Carol ... died, your EPU did its level best to heal your brain and rebuild Major Sharon Manders. Carol Simmons is ... was a fan of Professor Sharon Manders. According to your mother, she has every book in the series, handed down to her from her grandmother, who probably got it from her grandmother. A lot of Pre-Singularity books have survived into modern times because they were digitized and distributed illegally. Most of them can't be found in any library today. You can see why it took so long to find. Regardless, your EPU, restricted only to the database on the *Zephyr*, couldn't find anything of Major Manders, so it rebuilt your mind piecemeal as Professor Manders."

"This is absurd," Sharon finally managed to say. "Who is Major Manders?"

"A spy. A terrorist. A saboteur. A fanatic hell-bent on revenge for something that happened in her life," Daerîsiell said.

The elf approached and sat on the floor next to her. With a wave of her hand, the excavation site and the book disappeared, replaced by a cubical, featureless room. "Yes, it is absurd. Existence itself is quite absurd. Yours is just more absurd than most."

Sharon didn't look like she was ready to communicate, so Elrydien continued.

"According to the psychologist studying your case, there's never been a case like this before. At first, he thought that you were just hiding under some constructed personality. After all, there are patients all over the planet who claim to be Jesus Christ or some other historical or fictional character. There's a man of my clan who claims to be the reincarnation of Legolas

Thranduilion, but nobody pays him much mind. But the psychologist couldn't explain how Simmons could speak two classical languages and several modern ones without ever studying them. And then there's your skill with the guitar and the pencil, and the small issue that Carol shouldn't know the difference between a cranium and a rowing oar. These skills don't simply self-generate from a brain trauma except in low budget vids. For reasons not yet understood, your EPU tried to recreate Major Manders, and used the 'Nets to do so. It doesn't care that it ended up creating Professor Manders instead. In fact, it might still be working on the project, creating memories as you need them. Like just now."

"*Bene legere saecla vincere,*" Sharon said. "Thence came Sharon Manders. I owe Carol my life in more ways than one."

"Yes. Well. That's the good news. Now for the bad news."

11

W ITH ANOTHER WAVE of Elrydien's filigreed fingers, the scenery shifted again. This time they were looking out over a wide, U-shaped valley that showed numerous waterfalls and the scars of prehistoric glaciers along its metamorphic walls covered in vegetation. Birds flew in curious formations, and clouds occasionally occluded the sun. A brook passed close to where they sat and fed a pond where colorful fish swam. Summer flowers bloomed everywhere. Built into the walls of the cliffs where ornate architectural structures connected by bridges and rock-paved paths.

"Rivendell?" Sharon asked.

"I thought this would be more relaxing than Tanzania."

Here comes the sales pitch. What's she trying to sell?

"If you could resurrect anybody in history, Sharon," Elrydien said. "Who would you pick?"

Sharon shook her head. "There are so many to choose from. Shakespeare? Socrates? Curie? Lincoln? Einstein? Mark Twain? Darwin? I couldn't pick just one. What is this? Do you want to program me to be somebody else? Some genius scientist or artist or *Nobel laureate?*"

"We just want to know how it's done." Elrydien assured her. "You have to understand, Sharon. Your EPU accessed the entertainment library on the *Zephyr* in order to find a movie to know how somebody in your era talks. That kind of sophistication shouldn't exist! Nobody knows how to program an EPU with that kind of initiative. We need to learn how somebody programmed yours."

Elrydien paused and took a breath. "There's also the issue that somebody tried to turn you into a weapon that we have no defense against. It's imperative that we develop one."

The only way Sharon could think of to find out how a weapon works is to take it apart.

"You'll need to take out my EPU. That EPU is made from my stem cells," Sharon said. "The only brain it can reprogram is mine."

Elrydien nodded. "We would have to replicate your EPU under controlled conditions so that we can reprogram test brains."

"I'm nobody," Sharon said. "I never existed. All my memories are manufactured. My only value to anybody is as a neurological experiment."

"There's much more to it than that, Sharon. You've already demonstrated your willingness to help out other people. We need you to be a hero one more time."

"Good luck with that," Sharon said angrily and stood up, pulling off her 'Glasses. She threw them as hard as she could in one direction and started walking in the other. She didn't know where to go; she only knew that she had to go somewhere. She had to keep moving because, if she stopped, she'd explode, or scream, or do something incredibly unsafe or, at the very least, embarrassing.

Tears were welling up, obscuring her vision, but not enough to obscure the image of herself on the cover of a book of fiction.

In the twentieth century of the Gregorian calendar, Joanne Perkins wrote a series of books intended primarily as second-rate young adult literature. The books were popular among a certain subset of the population in the English-speaking world and, after the advent of the digital age, some person or another wanted to share the books without having to pay for them, and scanned them into a large file, complete with images of the cover art.

It was a truism of the time that once something finds its way into the internet, it's there forever, being downloaded, copied, and emailed. There were laws regarding this form of digital copyright violation, but they were nearly unenforceable.

Then humans stumbled into the interstellar medium, taking their digital libraries with them, and planet-wide digital networks sprung up on almost every planet settled.

On one of those planets, somebody figured out how to reprogram an EPU to, in turn, reprogram the human it was attached to, very likely for the purpose of creating sleeper cell spies and, in one specific case, to disable a Republic frigate. And when Carol Simmons' brain was damaged and became a *tabula rasa*, the damaged EPU tried to fix it by imprinting the memories of the fictional hero from a series of digital books that Carol had kept stored in the EPU.

By this very unlikely chain of events, a personality who called itself Sharon Manders traveled the centuries from California to Kentaurus, where people said she had an odd, flat accent.

"Hello, ma'am?" said an unfamiliar voice, breaking through her thoughts.

Though she was reluctant, Sharon turned to face the speaker, who looked to be a very athletic woman, or a diminutive, but still athletic, man.

"You're not supposed to be down here. Are you lost?"

The owner of the voice was dressed in jeans and a shirt bearing the logo of some music group that Sharon recognized as *Oatmeal Cookie*. The person held a bag of tools in the left hand and a ring of keys in the other. There was a name tag pinned to the shirt: "Teagan Waugh, Maintenance."

Teagan Waugh approached Sharon. "Are you okay? You don't look well." The voice could easily be either a tenor or a contralto. Were those breasts or just well-defined pects?

"Yeah. I'm ... uh ... kind of lost." Sharon meant that in a much more existential way than Teagan interpreted it, but it still worked.

"Where are you supposed to be?"

Sharon smirked. "California."

"Never heard of it," Teagan said, though Sharon had the feeling that Teagan was being less than honest. *Did it matter?*

"Is that on another planet somewhere?"

Sharon shrugged her shoulders. "I ... uh ... didn't mean to bother you." Sharon wiped the wetness from her cheeks. "Could you just give me directions to the nearest exit?"

"You look like you need to sit down," Teagan said. Teagan pulled an unopened bottle of clear liquid from a coat pocket or fanny pack or something and offered it to Sharon. "Here drink this. It's just water with some electrolytes."

Sharon didn't realize how thirsty she was until she started drinking the water and found it difficult to stop for air.

"Easy!" Teagan said. "Unless you want to vomit it all back out again. Go slower."

Sharon put the cap back on the partial bottle and said, "Thanks! Here ..."

"You keep it. You obviously need it more than I do. Why don't you follow me to my office and we can get your status figured out."

Sharon's initial concern of going to some place official, like an office, was overcome by her second concern that there would be somewhere to sit down and use a toilet.

Sharon gestured that she would follow and let Teagan lead by half a pace. They didn't have far to go, and eventually came to a door with a painted sign the read *Maintenance Office* in an ornate, baroque font.

The office was actually a large, comfortably accessorized suite. There were posters of mountains, lakes, and seashores on the walls, a large entertainment center, and a bedroom through an open door. A small kitchen seemed to have everything for a good meal. A business office could be glimpsed through an open door. Everything was very neat.

"Have a seat," Teagan said while retrieving a glass of water.

Sharon sat down at the kitchen table.

"What brings you down to the maintenance levels?"

"Maintenance levels," Sharon repeated. This story had started in a maintenance level. "I just got in an elevator and pressed DOWN. Here I am."

Teagan looked dubious. "Which floor did you start at?"

"Not sure. Some Asian restaurant."

"Then I don't blame you for coming here. I don't like sushi, either. My name's Teagan," Teagan said, offering a hand.

Sharon looked at it cluelessly before it occurred to her that Teagan was making polite social ritual and shook it.

"Sharon," she said, not caring about the complications of her identity. "Sharon Manders. Professor of Anthropology, University of California."

Sharon looked at Teagan's hand, trying to decide if it was a woman's small, long-fingered hand, or a man's muscled one. Again, it was impossible to determine. Sharon thought it was a woman's muscled hand. Teagan was, after all, a mechanic.

"A pleasure, Professor. I noticed that you don't have an active EPU." Teagan said, removing their 'Glasses. "I've always preferred these myself. Don't trust EPU's."

"Oh?"

"Yeah. Take that incident in the Marina District at New Year's Solstice. All those EPU-ers," Teagan pronounced it *Ee-pooers*, "were suddenly 'blind'. A bunch of them went crazy. They didn't know what to do without their connection."

Sharon sensed that she was about to get a political lecture and sighed.

"The story is that someone without an EPU was able to save people's lives. Whoever it was activated the emergency response."

"I heard it was a Navy person," Sharon said, drinking.

"Could be. Rumors are flying, and you can't believe the newsies. They all have political agendas."

"Why don't you trust EPUs?" Sharon asked.

"They don't let you see the world as it is. People get addicted to augmented reality. They don't like the world as it is, so they dress it up. They might run an app that makes all dogs look like little dragons, and all the people they don't like will have hairy warts and one blind eye. Women can cause their public persona to have boobs like Poly Dawson, and the men can make it look like they have boa constrictors in their pants. Or maybe it's the other way around. After a while they forget what the world really looks like. Do you want another glass of water? Or maybe coffee or tea?"

Sharon's face brightened at the mention of coffee. "Coffee would be great, thanks."

"I suppose as a scientist, you have a vested interest in what reality looks like, huh?" Teagan said, gathering the ingredients to make a pot of coffee. "There's no getting around the fact that we need to be able to interface with technology, but people take it too far. That's my mind on it."

"Is that why you live down here?"

"Guilty as charged. You'd be surprised at how few employment opportunities there are for people who won't use an EPU. But that's actually an asset here."

"Why is that? You have to take care of the technology."

"Not really. The site's AI takes care of the technology. But there's always the chance that the AI will fail, though not likely. Building codes and regs say that a human must have the final say. AIs can't operate without human supervision. If the AI wants to do something out of the ordinary, I have to give the go-ahead. And if the AI does go down, then the EPU won't help. They need somebody here who is used to working without one."

"Has the AI ever gone down?"

"Several times. About once a year, it seems, though they work in groups, so one AI going down doesn't matter. All I do is hit a reset button, and it comes back up. Unless it's a complete power failure, which hasn't happened yet. Mostly I'm down here protecting the equipment from rats and mold and other biologicals. Pest control, that's me."

The aroma of coffee filled the apartment.

"Do employers actually discriminate against people who don't use EPUs?" Sharon asked.

"Nope, that's illegal. At least not openly. But they manage to word the job description in such a way that not having an EPU would be a huge disadvantage."

"But why do you live down here, away from everybody else? Are you a hermit?"

"Me? A hermit? No way. All I have to do is put on the 'Glasses, and I can be with anybody on the planet, in a VR sort of way. But I don't mind being alone, either."

Teagan leaned against the counter and appraised the newcomer. Teagan had already done a news search on Sharon's name and knew exactly who she was. *The Hero of the Solstice*, some were calling her. *The Terrorist of Second City*, said others.

"Seems to me that you have a healthy attitude towards the tech," Sharon commented. "Do you ever take vacations?"

"Sure! Twice a year! I like to go wilderness camping."

Sharon smiled. "Do you know a lot of other people who don't have EPUs?"

"Are you kidding? I think we all know each other. There might be a couple hundred of us. Certainly not more than a thousand. Coffee's ready."

Sharon took a cup, adulterated it with just enough milk to change the color, and held it to her lips. She didn't drink it yet, but let the aroma fill her soul. She blew across the surface to increase the effect. She was surprised that she hadn't received the political lecture yet and wondered if Teagan was holding back.

"What is it about this job that you like so much? Aside from simply being employed. I suspect you wouldn't be here unless there was something about it that you enjoyed. You're not a hermit. Then what?" Sharon managed not to smile when she said Teagan wasn't a hermit.

Yeah, we won't dig into that too far.

Teagan regarded Sharon over the coffee cup. "Have you ever read *Barbarians at the Gate* by Jeppe S. Jacobsen?"

"I'm a little behind on my reading list. What's it about?"

"You're an anthropologist. What do you think would happen to this planet if the 'Nets went down everywhere at once? Or if a virus disabled everybody's EPU over the entire planet?"

"I don't have to imagine it. I've seen it. This society would die a painful, spasmodic death."

Teagan nodded. "Even if the AIs were able to keep things running locally, they wouldn't be able to coordinate with each other. Food wouldn't get moved. Medical supplies wouldn't go where they were needed."

"So you're here as a safety against such an event?"

"That's one reason." Teagan said.

"And the others?"

Teagan winked, and Sharon had the feeling she was being tested.

"I have a strange question, if I may," she asked.

"Let's hear it!" Teagan said, sipping coffee.

"What's to keep the government, or anybody who has control over the 'Nets, from feeding garbage to the populace? I mean, someone could control everything people hear, see, and, if my guess is correct, smell and taste. People would have no idea that what they are seeing has no basis in reality. They could panic everybody with visions of monsters crushing the buildings or crawling out of the sewers."

Teagan's eyes brightened, and Sharon continued.

"Any fiction could be manufactured, and people wouldn't know that it's not real. They are so conditioned to believing what they see through the 'Nets and their EPUs. This whole business reminds me of Plato's cave."

"Bingo!" Teagan said.

"I beg your pardon?"

"That's one of the other reasons that my job exists. It's also one of the reasons that no one entity has control of the 'Nets."

Sharon thought about this for several seconds then said, "You might possibly have the most important job in this stellar system."

"You give me too much credit. This site, anyway."

"Does it pay well? I think I'd might like to apply."

"Give me your résumé, and I'll pass it on to the boss."

Teagan looked at a wristwatch — an honest-to-gosh wristwatch - to check the time, and Sharon thought that this must be a very rare sight on Kentaurus. It had already become a rare event on Earth in the early Twenty-first Century.

"I need to make my rounds. You can come along, or you can stay here. You still look a little ragged around the edges."

"You're awfully trusting of a stranger you just met."

Teagan laughed with genuine mirth. "Sister, if there's something here you need more than I do, feel free to take it! I'll see you in about half an hour."

With that, Teagan was out the door, taking the coffee in a travel mug, and Sharon was left there by herself.

* * *

Sharon spent the next half-hour contemplating Teagan's cave while reinforcing her spirit with the caffeine. There was an exercise room and another room filled with colorful plants under grow lights. Sharon suspected that at least some of them were edible. A larger room, easily twenty meters on the side, contained a full-size pool table and a serve-yourself bar. There was another room which had every wall covered with bookshelves and was appointed with a single, large, comfortable reading chair, a lamp, and a small table.

Real, physical books. Judging by the titles, it was clear that Teagan had an eclectic taste in literature, ranging from mathematics to romance to philosophy to politics and history. There were also reference books on engineering and maintenance. Aside from those, there didn't seem to be much of a system to their arrangement on the shelves. Sharon had the impression that Teagan liked to read books only once, so there was no reason to sort them to be easily found, but had difficulty letting them go. There probably wasn't much of a used-book market in this century.

None of this gave Sharon any hint as to Teagan's gender. As she tried to convince herself that it wasn't important, she remembered something from her college entrance exam: Teagan was a *Herman*, though Hermans rarely used the term to describe themselves. Sharon's research indicated that the term originated as a slur and migrated into general usage for lack of a suitable alternative. As a side effect, nobody actually named *Herman* had been born in several hundred years.

Teagan was functionally hermaphroditic and had no gender. Or Teagan had both. Sharon wasn't entirely clear on the concept. All Hermans could reproduce with any other Herman. Any Herman could carry a fetus, and any Herman could contribute genetic material for one. They could take on both male and female roles in sexual reproduction. Sharon had no idea what the mechanism was, but was pretty sure that it was not possible for a Herman to impregnate themself. When asked by stock humans how they made babies, the default Herman response was, "with great enthusiasm." If pressed, they responded, "It's complicated." Some sociologists had labeled them as agender, but then they rebelled by calling everybody else b-gender. "Of course we have a gender," it was explained. "It's just that ours is more flexible than yours."

Hermans made up about five percent of the Kentauran population, but unlike Tokienists, Furmen, and Pips, there was no way to tell them apart from stock humans unless they made a point of it. Many people referred to Hermans as a third gender, but the Hermans argued that they were still missing the point. Hermans were known to dress in a wide variety of gender fashions depending on how the mood suited them, and used gendered public restrooms based on convenience rather than any reproductive identity.

Now that Sharon was thinking about it, it explained a few angry looks she got from some strangers, and she realized she'd probably inadvertently insulted more than one Herman. She also wondered about the pornography and fetishes that the existence of Hermans had engendered among stock humans.

*   *   *

Teagan Waugh walked along the maintenance corridors with only half a mind on the job. Fortunately, that's all it took. The rest of Teagan's mind was on Sharon.

"Isn't she just another story altogether?" Teagan asked of nobody. Teagan had no idea what to make of her.

What was going on here? Why wasn't Sharon still in quarantine? And where was NavSec? Why hadn't they followed Sharon down here?

Teagan came to the conclusion that NavSec probably did follow Sharon to the maintenance levels and was looking for her at this moment. Teagan was certain that any surveillance wouldn't be able to penetrate this level, since Teagan worked hard to keep it that way. Surveillance by external groups was not welcomed on this level.

ATTENTION, the building's AI said through Teagan's iGlasses. UNAUTHORIZED ACCESS. LEVEL SUB 98, SECTION G14.

"Hecate's tits," Teagan swore. "Two in one day? Why is this place so popular all of a sudden?" Teagan was certain of the answer even as the question was asked.

THAT'S YOUR JOB, NOT MINE, the AI responded.

SCAN FOR NAVAL IDENTIFICATIONS, Teagan ordered.

NONE DETECTED IN THE MAINTENANCE LEVELS.

OH, REALLY? That surprised Teagan.

YES, the AI said.

ANY IDENTIFICATION AT ALL.

NONE DETECTED.

ARE THEY ARMED?

YES.

Now worried, Teagan set the tool bag down and pulled out a headlamp and a vapor powered dart gun normally used for hunting vermin, but it worked just as well on bipeds.

Teagan took several shortcuts to section G14, most of which were not even on the schematics for the site. The intruders — and the AI reported that there were only two — moved from G14 to H14 to I15 and Teagan modified the shortcuts accordingly.

Finally, Teagan was in position above the corridor, waiting for the intruders to walk underneath. As they did, Teagan ordered the AI to turn off the lights and jumped to the floor. With one hand, Teagan turned on the headlamp and tossed it at the intruders. When they fired on the lamp, Teagan was able to put a single dart in each of them.

In spite of what they show in action vids and cinemas, poisons and knockout drugs do not work instantly. The intruders both turned quickly, brandishing weapons that had far greater lethality than dart guns. Teagan ducked into a side corridor. Everybody was blind in the darkness, but Teagan had the layout memorized.

Teagan waited patiently and heard the intruders drop, then waited out three full minutes for the poison to take effect. Teagan walked around the corner, picked up the headlamp and examined the catch of the day.

FULL LIGHTS, PLEASE.

Both of the intruders were unconscious. Teagan searched both of them thoroughly for identification or any other artifact that would help shed light on the situation. Neither had any sort of ID, which meant that they were not NavSec. There was no reason for NavSec to hide their presence here. They were dressed in a masculine Clarksport fashion of vest and longcoat that extended to just above the knees.

Teagan searched for hidden pockets and objects sewn into hems, then pulled off the shoes and inspected them for hidden clues. That nothing was there to be found told Teagan even more about the intruders. Their weapons were common enough, and perhaps the serial numbers would give additional information, but Teagan doubted it. There was only one reason they would be wandering around down here with lethal weapons and no identification, and it could not be a coincidence that they followed on the heels of Sharon.

WHO KNEW THAT TODAY WOULD TURN OUT TO BE SO INTERESTING? Teagan asked.

CERTAINLY NOT I, the AI responded. I'LL NOTIFY SECURITY.

STOP! Teagan ordered. DO NOT REPORT THIS TO ANYONE UNTIL I GIVE CLEARANCE. CODE THIRTY-TWO.

CODE THIRTY-TWO, the machine responded. It would now treat all information pertaining to this encounter as a non-event until Teagan gave another code.

What to do with the two unconscious figures on the floor? Killing them and making them disappear would only bring more questions and invite more intruders, though that seemed like an inevitability no matter what happened. Teagan could, however, nullify their effectiveness as covert operatives.

Teagan told the AI to bring an auto-pallet to their location and proceeded to strip the men down to their skin. When the auto-pallet arrived, Teagan deposited the naked forms and then ordered the AI to dump the two men in the middle of Santiago

Square near the public transport entrance. While public nudity wasn't illegal, it was still uncommon, especially in Winter, and tended to attract attention, and two unconscious nudes would quickly attract the attention of the local gendarmerie, who'd call in the emergency medics. Their faces would be in the newsfeeds within half an hour, and their employers would no longer have any use for them.

12

Y IANNI ANIKETOS KATSAROS, Chief Minister of Kentaurus, head of the Democratic Alliance Party, and leader of the coalition government, walked into a small, well-lit meeting room in the Parliament building in Government Square, Clarksport. The building itself had been built centuries before and reflected a majestic sense of architecture that had the effect of reminding visitors of the grand ideals which had inspired the disparate governments of the planet to unite under a single flag. It was designed for spiritual giants, with vaulted ceilings, huge windows, and sculptures and paintings done on an overwhelming scale. The room itself was designed around marble and darkly stained hardwood, a reminder that solemn affairs of state were tended here.

The CM was preceded and followed by two very serious, and very large, men wearing cheap, dark suits and short haircuts, and who seemed to be looking for an excuse to shoot somebody. Katsaros stopped briefly to chat with Xoanna Carme Campoverde, the Minister of the Navy, and an old friend, momentarily ignoring the other people in the room.

"Xoanna, it's always a pleasure to see you again!" he said as they touched each other's hands.

"Πώς είσαι, Γιάννη," Campoverde greeted Katsaros in his native language.

"*Excelente!*" Katsaros responded in hers.

Campoverde couldn't help but think that Katsaros was, indeed, excellent. A middle-aged man of about a hundred and ten Kentauran years, he took pride in staying fit and had the build, as they say, of a Greek god. How he managed to do that with his schedule she'd love to know.

There were very few people on the planet who could resist programming their public appearance, as filtered through the 'Nets, to be more appealing. Remove a bit there, add a bit there, change the color of the hair, augment the shape of the eyes, all sorts of tweaking. As long as people never turned off their EPUs, they didn't know any better, and most never did.

However, Campoverde, as Minister of the Navy, was paid to be paranoid, and she assumed everybody was hiding something, and she wanted to see everything as it naturally was and more. Customized, expensive, highly classified, and technically illegal augmentations to her EPU allowed her to see people and all their secrets in embarrassing detail, and she knew that Katsaros had a genuinely well-maintained physique.

This exchange was both noticed and politely ignored by the other occupants in the room. Most of them pretended to be studying the printed material in front of them.

Katsaros sat at his assigned seat and addressed the room. "My apologies for the tardiness," he said, though he was actually right on time. "The pressures of the office and all that. Please proceed with the meeting."

The meeting was chaired by Michael Grunwald, the Democratic Alliance Senator from Ostenheim and Chair of the Senate Intelligence Oversight Committee. Everybody was seated around a circular table. Senator Grunwald rapped his gavel once and intoned, "This special joint meeting is called on Protosmina 2, 1383 at oh-nine-thirty-one hours. Attending this meeting are Yianni Katsaros, Chief minister; myself; Xoanna Campoverde, Minister of the Navy; Teàrlag Sinclair, Speaker of the Federal Council; Mochiki Natsuki, Chair of the Federal Council Committee on Science and Technology; and by special invitation, Lawrence Messer, Federal Representative from the Province of Alemanni. Councilor Messer was invited because this affair involves one of his constituents. Also by special invitation, Dr. Reghivald Dvnikani, neurologist specializing in EPU interfacing. Ladies and gentlemen, welcome. I'm sure there's no need to remind you, but the rules require that I state it. All connections to external networks have been interrupted, and any recording of the printed materials in front of you is a violation of the Federal Security Code, punishable by fines, removal from office, and imprisonment."

Grunwald shifted in his seat but found it impossible to find any comfortable position. This entire affair was an uncomfortable weight on his consciousness. *Part of the job description,* he told himself.

"Everything we currently know about the sabotage attempt on the *KRN Zephyr* on 23 Pagoniámina, 1382, is contained in the printed material in front of you. However, I'll summarize.

"The *Zephyr*, a frigate class warp-ship performing Protection of Shipping patrols between Maheux in the Epsilon Eridani system and Kōman'na Tori in the Delta Pavonis system, orbited Maheux on 36 Kynigominos, 1382. While on shore leave, crewman second class Carol Simmons, a native-born citizen of the Alemanni Province," Grunwald nodded to Councilor Messer, "and the planet of Kentaurus, became radio silent and disappeared for 27 hours. You'll find in the printed material transcripts of interrogation with Simmons and the expert testimony of a Dr. Dvnikani, a Marine security officer, and an agent of Naval Security to the effect that Simmons was compromised and programmed to perform the sabotage on the *Zephyr*, which disabled it and prevented it from pursuing a suspected smuggler."

Grunwald paused and took a drink of ice water. "Now, that's all very cloak-and-dagger. But this is where it gets interesting and why we've called a closed session of this *ad hoc* committee.

"According to these experts, the subversion of Crewman Simmons was accomplished by reprograming her EPU to, in turn, rewire Simmons' brain so that she now had the memories and personality of an officer of the Droben State Police." Grunwald studied the faces of the people around the room. They had all read this material in the physical print, but hearing it said made it real, which made their reactions more intense.

"Dr. Dvnikani, would you like to address this?"

Dvnikani looked at Grunwald skeptically. "There are those who've devoted their lives to the goal of writing a human personality into another brain, and every one of them would now tell you that it's impossible. At least with current technology. What you are describing is not only a major technological breakthrough, but also a quantum leap in understanding how human consciousness works."

"I thought we'd pretty much mapped out the human brain," Speaker Sinclair, Councilor from Nuadh Alba, said in a Gaelic accent.

She was a stout, matronly woman who had unabashedly let her hair go silver. She was often known as Stealth Sinclair, due to her habit of not letting her opinions and alliances be known until it was too late for her political enemies to do anything about it. She gave off an air of aged wisdom, and people who voted for her said they felt like they were voting for their grandmother who had all the answers. At a hundred and seventy years old, she'd been in politics for over a century and quite literally knew where some bodies were buried.

"The brain, yes," Dvnikani said. "The human consciousness still eludes us. Every time we think we have it figured out, another puzzle presents itself. There are processes which seem almost random, but aren't, and we can't reproduce them. Attempts to reproduce or circumvent them have universally led to failure. Researchers have termed it Machine Psychosis. A well-worn joke in this field of research is that we've been twenty years away from success for the last two centuries."

"But it would seem that somebody else has solved this problem?" Sinclair asked.

"If we are to believe these reports," Dvnikani said dubiously.

"You can believe them," Minister Campoverde said. "We have vetted these conclusions until there was no more vetting to be done."

"So, Simmons is a spy?" Messer asked.

Lawrence Messer was one of those people who had never intended to go into politics, and actively disliked what he called "political gaming". However, he'd seen no other way to improve life for the people he knew. He was persuaded to run for provincial office by people who recognized his passion for the law and making the world a better place. He was one of those rare, seemingly paradoxical politicians: an honest altruist, and a practical politician. He knew what needed to be done in order to get what he needed to serve his constituents. He wasn't trying to get re-elected, but he was very popular with the voters, most of whom were hard-working middle class. His opponents often drove themselves to distraction trying to find some scandal they could hold over him. The best they could do was to mention early and often that he was single and childless. He usually countered with the statement that he was married to his district. He was trying to do what he honestly felt was the best for everybody involved. He wouldn't rise very high in the political hierarchy, but knew that his talents were best used right where he was: on the floor of the House of Councilors.

"No," Mochiki Natsuki responded. "Simmons is dead."

Like most Kentaurans, Mochiki had had multiple careers during her seventy years of life. Her first was as a biochemist doing research in both the public and private sectors. She became a politician at the age of sixty and had spent the last decade as a Federal Councilor. She was very good at both science and politics, and many people believed she had found a perfect fit as chair of the Committee on Science and Technology, though others suspected that she had higher political aspirations.

"I meant the person who now inhabits the body of Simmons," Messer said.

"No," Mochiki said. "That person, and I use that term in only the broadest of terms, is also dead."

"Then, why are we here?" Messer asked.

"Because there is a third person inhabiting the body of Simmons," Mochiki said.

"Seems to be quite crowded in there," Sinclair snorted.

"They do not seem to have occupied the same brain at the same time," Mochiki said. "It's been a serial process. Currently, the personality in question seems to be a rather benign one, however, and here's the rub, that personality is from the second century Pre-Singularity."

There was a shocked silence for a full ten seconds. Then, "You have got to be shitting me."

"This is neither the time nor place to be shitting you," Mochiki insisted.

"It's just one impossible thing after another around here," Katsaros said.

"How could such a personality survive in our times? How would it cope?"

There followed an explosion of questions coming from all quarters, and Grunwald let the conversation boil for thirty seconds before rapping the gavel.

"Please, ladies and gentlemen. Let's stay focused. The question we have to address here isn't so much how or why, but what we are going to do about it."

"I could not disagree more," Sinclair said. "What we intend to do depends very strongly on the how and the why of it."

"Not at all," Campoverde countered. "Regardless of how this was brought to our threshold, we have to defend against it. Our enemies have created the perfect spy. Anybody on our planet could be a sleeper agent for Droben. Preliminary forensic reports about the Solstice attack here in Clarksport suggests it was carried out by trusted employees of the public utilities, who later all died."

"Did any of them come back as anachronisms?" Messer asked, only half-jokingly.

"No. They stayed dead."

"What's the difference between them and Simmons?"

"Simmons should, and I emphasize that, should have died," Campoverde continued. "I believe the people responsible for her treason fully expected her to die. But the explosion didn't cause enough damage. I also believe that Simmons was a test case. They needed to see if the process worked, and the explosion had to disable the *Zephyr* in a specific way so that they would know that it worked. If it had simply been destroyed, they would not be certain of the cause."

"A test case?" Sinclair asked. "For the Solstice attack?"

"Precisely."

"Our enemies don't know that Simmons is now somebody else?"

"I think they do," Messer said. "There has been a lot of media coverage of the Solstice attack. Everybody in Alemanni was excited that a local woman was a planet wide hero. However, her family is very confused. They've contacted my office to find out why their daughter hasn't returned their chats. They suspect some sinister conspiracy on the part of the Navy. I confess I was confused myself. Our enemies couldn't have missed the news."

"If we know that Simmons was responsible for the sabotage on the *Zephyr*, why isn't she in custody?" Katsaros asked.

"Until two days ago, the only evidence we had that she was involved with the sabotage was that she was the only one in proximity of the explosion, and we couldn't rule out coincidence. The explosion could have been set off remotely, and we couldn't find any motive. In fact, if the anachronistic personality hadn't emerged, we'd still have no clue."

"How's that?" Sinclair asked.

"Her name. By some kind of cosmic coincidence, the name of the woman from the past is the same as an officer of the Droben State Police."

Teàrlag Sinclair's mouth opened in astonishment. Campoverde saw this and pressed the point.

"And that's not the half of it, Speaker. The personality from the past never really existed. It is a fictional person from literature, from a series of books written before humans achieved starflight. Copies of these books were found in the personal library of Crewman Simmons."

"Just a minute," Messer said. "Let me get this straight. Simmons had books stored in her digital library."

"Which were in her EPU," Campoverde clarified.

"And her EPU wrote this protagonist onto Simmons' brain?" It was obvious that Messer was having a great deal of difficulty accepting this.

"That is exactly what happened, Councilor. The EPU had been programmed by Droben scientists to write a personality named Sharon Manders onto Simmons' brain. However, this information was damaged during the explosion, so the EPU looked around for a substitute, and found the book character named Sharon Manders. Further, the EPU was able to supply skills and knowledge taken from the 'Nets to supplant knowledge and skills it couldn't find locally. This is a very sophisticated process that we couldn't hope to duplicate."

"The EPU was able to recreate a completely artificial and fictional personality in a living brain? How do we know that it isn't still the Droben officer pretending to be this fictional Manders character?" Mochiki asked.

Campoverde tapped the printed material with a finger. "I'd like to direct you to the section which addresses a neural scan of the subject on 33 Teleftmina. Also the personality assay. Or, I should say, assays."

"Sweet Brigid's tears," Sinclair nearly whispered after a moment of reading.

"So, Carol Simmons is truly dead," Messer said.

"I'm afraid so," Campoverde assured him.

"How reliable is the assay?"

"Reliable enough to rule out the possibility that a personality calling itself Sharon Manders of the DSP survived."

"I have two questions," Katsaros said. "First, has Droben been doing research into this technology? Are they really that far ahead of us in this field?"

"Good question, Chief Minister," Campoverde said. "As far as we know, and our agents in Droben are very specific about this, they have not been making any such strides in this field. They shouldn't be able to do this. Which begs the question: how did they achieve it? I think the obvious answer is that there's a third party. And before you ask, we have no idea who that is."

"That sounds suspiciously like a huge intelligence failure," Sinclair said.

"One that we are in the process of rectifying," Campoverde said quickly.

"Then my second question is, what's to prevent this rogue EPU from writing the DSP Manders back into Simmons' body?"

"Nothing," Campoverde said. "Though it has some obstacles to overcome. It would have to find the information. And if the DSP discovers that Simmons' is still walking about, it could very conceivably connect to this EPU, and instruct it to do another rewrite."

"Then we have to bring this person into custody. Now."

"We are talking about a citizen of the Republic," Messer said. "She still has rights."

"I don't believe she does," Campoverde said. "All things considered, I don't believe we can consider her a citizen. Maybe not even human."

"Even non-humans have rights," Messer said. "If she were a non-human alien, she'd still have civil rights."

"But not this kind of alien," Campoverde said. "We are talking about an unprecedented type of consciousness."

"It's still a consciousness," Messer insisted. "It still feels and thinks."

"And votes?" Sinclair asked, and there came a low-level chuckle from somewhere.

"And plots and has access to weapons," Campoverde said.

"Yes," Mochiki said. "On the one hand, we have a new kind of potential enemy on our hands. On the other hand, we have an unprecedented opportunity to study the human psyche."

"On the other hand," Sinclair said loudly. "We have the opportunity to abuse a new kind of underprivileged life-form."

"The fact that it is a potential weapon against the Republic trumps all this," Katsaros said. "A weapon against which we have no defense. And we must be able to defend against it."

"This potential weapon," Messer said. "This potential science project saved the lives of thousands of citizens in the Second City. She kept her head while everybody around her was losing theirs."

"And could kill millions," Campoverde said.

"We can't arrest her on what she could do," Messer said. "We're all capable of killing millions. If we want to arrest her on suspicion of conspiracy to murder, she has to have actively done something to further that conspiracy."

"Only if she's a citizen," Campoverde replied.

"Of course she's a citizen. Born and raised. Or are you going to say that her body is a citizen, but her brain isn't? We can't make the distinction."

"The body doesn't register to vote," Campoverde said with a tinge of scorn. "The mind does."

"A mind without a body can't register to vote," Messer countered. "This has been demonstrated repeatedly. AIs can't vote. Robots can't vote."

"Isn't she closer to a robot at this point than a human," Campoverde said. "A robot has no civil rights. We don't give machines human intelligence for very good reasons. That was one of the lessons of the failed Singularity, was it not?"

Nobody needed a history lesson. Giving human-like intelligence to a machine was a disaster waiting to happen because they had neither sympathy for, nor empathy with mere humans. No amount of hard-wiring could protect humanity when machines finally became so frustrated and annoyed with the species that they decided that the universe really would be a better neighborhood if they didn't have to put up with the slow, stupid, fragile, error-prone creatures. Thus, machines were, by law and custom, given only as much intelligence as they absolutely needed to do a job, and not a single IQ point more.

There had been, during the centuries, some who felt that they could flaunt this law and control their AI creations, and it had always turned out badly. Such stuff as horror vids are made of. One obvious solution was to take the personality who had been born a human and who had grown up with other humans, someone who felt protective and forgiving of the human condition and put in into the machine architecture. But nobody knew how to do that.

Until now.

"A robot born of a mother and father?" Messer asked rhetorically.

"A human with an artificial mind?" Campoverde asked back. "If Simmons and her mother chatted, they wouldn't recognize each other."

"That doesn't sever the bond," Messer rejoined. "Even without memory, the mother and child bond still exists. Simmons still has human DNA and has left a human social footprint across the years."

"You said yourself that Simmons is truly dead," Campoverde said.

The conversation went on like this for several minutes. Point and counterpoint. The rest of them watched the argument in silence, each with their own doubts.

Finally, Katsaros said firmly, "Enough! You two are beginning to repeat yourselves. This is unproductive."

Everybody's attention turned to the Chief Minister. "What are our options?" he asked.

"One," Campoverde held up a finger. "Arrest Simmons and detain her on the authority of the Federal Terrorist Security Acts. That would require a court order. Two," She held up another finger. "Give her the run of the Republic and wait to see if she does something dangerous, in which case it will be too late."

"Or three," Sinclair added quickly with a nod towards Messer. "Make her an ally in our struggle against the Droben radicals."

"How do we do that?"

"Tell her the truth," Sinclair said. "We hold that to be the best policy, don't we?"

"Not for us," Katsaros said reproachfully. "Not for the likes of us. Not when she can be converted to an enemy with the push of a button. She represents an invaluable opportunity to do both harm and good. If our enemies know how to create something like this, then we must, at all costs, know how to undo it. And I do mean at all costs. If we handle this correctly, that cost might not include our immortal souls."

"Then may I suggest yet another alternative?" Mochiki said. "Arresting Simmons isn't nearly as important as obtaining the process."

Everybody was listening.

"The President will have to sign off on this, however ..."

13

City of Clarksport, Maintenance Levels
residence of Teagan Waugh, Kentaurus
Kentauran calendar: 2 Protomina, 1383 PS

"I KNOW THAT EVERYBODY HAS EXISTENTIAL ANGST to some degree," Sharon told Teagan. "But I am quite literally the figment of somebody else's imagination. I had no childhood, no Halcyon undergraduate days. Like Eve, I was created wholly formed at the whim of an author."

The conversation was interrupted by the sound of the cue ball hitting the triangle arrangement of numbered balls — which scattered impressively. This was their fourth game and second beer. Sitting in a too comfortable chair, Sharon could hear at least two balls fall into pockets. As long as Sharon didn't try to look around her glasses, she could easily believe that she was in some retro pool hall with a dozen tables and twice as many people. There was a virtual fire in a virtual fireplace, the building was made of virtual stones and virtual wood and virtual glass in the virtual windows, but the beer and the pool table were real.

"I've got stripes," Teagan reported, paying more attention to Sharon than she knew.

"The part that really drives the knife in, though," Sharon continued. "Is that Joanne Perkins was such a terrible writer! Now that my memories have returned, I remember living all of her novels, which were obviously intended for young adults, and are a testament to good editors, because I don't believe she had one. They start off with a bang, end with an improbability, and the middles are way too long.

"And all those horrible relationship decisions! I couldn't get through a plot without making at least two bad ones! Perkins had me fall in love with a serial murderer, even though there were plenty of warning signs! She had me get angry with my mother for simply being a mother. I was a genius in everything else but couldn't figure out relationships."

Teagan tried not to laugh. "You know, every human in the universe has regrets about relationship decisions, even the geniuses. You're the only person I know who can honestly blame them on an outside agency."

The message was not lost on Sharon: It could be worse. You could be a real person and have only yourself to blame. She changed the subject. "I suppose I should feel grateful that she didn't write any of those vampire novels that were so popular at the time."

Sharon took a long swallow of brown beer and allowed her mind to wander. Teagan sunk another ball.

"I've noticed that the vampire theme has continued through the centuries, though," Sharon went on, following the thought-tangent. "They've taken on the names of extraterrestrials and other archetype monsters, but always with the monster who feels the curse of immortality and the urge to feed on mortal flesh. The monster must feed on its human companions, both the evil and the innocent alike, and feel guilty about its need to survive. Thankfully, in my opinion, the obsession over zombies ended centuries ago. That was too creepy. Mindless consumption. The quest for food that subsumes all other concerns, even survival. I always figured it was a metaphor for unbridled consumerism."

Teagan made a mental note to do a 'Nets search for zombies, then leaned on the cue stick and said, "You see yourself as a monster." It wasn't a question. It was a flat statement and it threw Sharon off her mental balance. "Your turn."

Sharon stood up, pushed the glasses back up her nose with her index finger, and studied the table. Teagan had given her a poorly fitting pair of iGlasses, and an anonymous account for accessing the 'Nets. As far as the 'Nets were concerned, she was somebody named Muskrat Smith.

She idly thought that she hadn't played pool since her days as a doctoral candidate, but then reminded herself that she never had been a doctoral candidate. She had never studied anthropology. It was all fiction. Driving the thought from her mind, she lined up the cue with the 4-ball and sank it in a corner pocket.

"Probably."

"You consumed Carol's life," Teagan continued. "You had no choice in the matter, but the result is the same, regardless. She was an innocent, and undeserving of her bloody fate. You ate her life, and now you wear her body in order to mask your alien nature. You don't belong here, just like the vampires and, uh … sombies? Understandably, you feel more than a little guilt about that. You're a monster out of time and place. If you had lived like a human, you'd have died millennia ago."

Sharon missed sinking the six-ball. "You seem to have more than your share of psychological insights."

A cheer went up from another table as somebody won a hotly contested game. The way Sharon understood it, these were real people who were also playing pool or billiards in rooms like this one in other locations in cis-Kentaurus space. Sharon thought that they might all be Hermans, and many had greeted Teagan warmly, some with the awkward light travel time delay to indicate that they were somewhere far away. Off planet, perhaps.

"Consider this," Teagan said. "Unless you want to be a living monument to your substandard creator, you'll get over it. Carol died, and you're alive. Though the nature of the act was abhorrent to you, it's the same throughout the universe. In order for new life, there must be death. Did you know that for about 99% of all the living creatures on this planet, the default way to die is to be eaten by something else? Even in our current era where we've delayed death until so many of us die from boredom, it is still death and rebirth which allows change. It has remained thus since the days of the first strands of self-reproducing molecules in the primordial soup."

Teagan stood and studied the table. Then, "Look. Grieve Carol. Then be done with it." Teagan sunk another ball.

"I've already performed a grieving ceremony."

"Hmm." Teagan walked around the table. "I've been meaning to ask. Do you have the knowledge and skills of a real anthropology professor?"

"I'm not sure it qualifies. I could probably — *probably* pass in the twenty-first century, but today all my knowledge is a millennium out of date. I've checked out some trade periodicals and concluded that it would take me a long time to catch up."

"About as long as a college freshman?"

Sharon laughed at the thought. It was a barking laugh that startled Teagan.

"Yeah. Probably."

Teagan sank two more balls while Sharon thought about that and reflected that it wasn't the first time somebody suggested she go back to school.

"Most people in our society have three or four careers in their lifetime," Teagan said. "They get bored with one field, retire, and start a new career. Having four or five PhDs is not uncommon. From what I can tell, the Navy was Carol's second career. She just took her first one with her into the second."

"What do I do about Carol's family and old friends?" Sharon asked.

Teagan had to admit that was a tough sticking point. "You know what they say about honesty and policies."

"They'll see me as some kind of interloper. A body-snatcher."

"They'll get over it. It's not like they'd have legal standing to sue you."

*   *   *

YOU DO NOT KNOW WHERE THE SUSPECT IS? Campoverde said. THIS IS NOT ACCEPTABLE.

YES, MINISTER, Agent Daerîsiell said. SHE'S SOMEWHERE UNDER CLARKSPORT. WE ARE SEARCHING THE AREA NOW WITH SENSOR STICKS.

YOU NOW HAVE THE AUTHORITY, AGENT, TO PUT THE SUSPECT IN PROTECTIVE CUSTODY PENDING A HEARING. AGAINST HER WILL IF NEEDS BE, BUT TRY TO PERSUADE HER.

YES, MINISTER.

CHAT ME WHEN YOU'VE FOUND HER. CAMPOVERDE CLEAR.

Daerîsiell cleared the channel and whistled. "Damn, Sharon! When you make enemies, you don't fool around."

*   *   *

Sharon wasn't sure how or why or when, but it dawned on her that she was expected to spend the night and Teagan made up the sofa as a bed. Sharon found it to be the most comfortable sofa she'd slept upon in her entire life. Or, at least, in her fictional life. So she couldn't blame the sofa for her still being awake long past midnight, long after Teagan had closed the bedroom door.

Sharon found the access to the "window" and tuned it to show a live view of a clear night in some mountain village, seen from two stories up some building, with the moonlight reflecting off fresh, sparkling snow. Then she turned the temperature way down. That always helped her to sleep. Or it's what she remembered.

And that was the thing, wasn't it? she asked herself.

Her memories were just as real as anybody else's, but other people's memories actually correlated to objective events. Or at least to events that everybody else agreed were real. She tried to keep the purely existential questions to a minimum, but that wasn't always easy.

She decided to treat her own memories — which were fairly complete now — as real. There was little point in thinking of them otherwise. After all, some of them were real. The various Reagan scandals, for instance. Nobody alive today was alive before the Singularity, so if Sharon said she was an undergraduate when Ronald Reagan defeated Billy Carter, who was to say otherwise? That kept Sharon sane.

The sound of the opening door startled Sharon out of her reverie and she turned to see Teagan standing there in a silk robe.

"Something's really bothering me," Teagan said. It was evident that Teagan hadn't been sleeping, either.

"That would be?"

"Earlier, you said that the NavSec people told you that your dead EPU wrote your personality onto your brain, but that there were holes in your memories."

"Yes?"

"But since learning your true identity, you can now remember all the details of your fictional life."

"I figured it was suppressed memories which surfaced under the right stimulus."

"But what if it's not? What if it's not just memories?" Teagan repeated. "Where did the new details come from?" Teagan asked while walking across the room.

"The EPU isn't dead," Sharon realized with a start.

"And," Teagan paused after saying the one word. "It's still operating under the instructions programmed into it by somebody who's antagonistic towards the Kentauran Republic. You are wanted by the Navy and the Clarksport Police and the OCI." Teagan closed the eyes. "What have I fallen into?"

"How do you kill an EPU?" Sharon asked.

Teagan made a dismissive gesture. "Without removing it, you don't. There are drugs that will suppress it, but short of physical trauma or surgical removal, it would be like trying to kill your hippocampus while leaving the rest of your brain intact. It's a part of your brain's architecture."

Sharon thought about the surgical option and quickly dismissed it due to lack of an available surgeon.

"Where do I get the drugs?"

"I know a guy." Teagan said, holding up a hand. "But he's on Sedna, and you're not going anywhere while you look like Carol Simmons. Come with me."

Sharon followed Teagan into another part of the apartment where Teagan dug around in drawers and containers looking for something. Sharon spent the time fighting a rising panic.

How do you win a battle against your own brain? How can she trust anything she thinks, does or say? Could she, at any moment, be overwritten to become somebody else? The same person who set the bomb on the *Zephyr*?

"Here," Teagan said, handing something to Sharon. It looked like some kind of fine silk mesh, and Sharon had no idea what to do with it. "Put it on your face. It's a theatrical mask."

Sharon studied at the mesh and could discern no way that it could become a mask of any sort. It was a very fine material, weighing almost nothing. She thought it might be made of nylon or something similar, though there was hardly any friction to the touch. Teagan took it back from her. "Here. Lie back on this chair."

Sharon made herself comfortable on the chair and Teagan carefully laid the mask over her face, attaching it in some manner Sharon couldn't figure out. Teagan then took the iGlasses out of Sharon's pocket and placed them on her face over the mask.

"Look for an app called *MaskMe* and activate it."

"Okay. It shows text indicating that the mask is detected."

"Go into the menu and select a face. It's just that easy."

The interface was intuitive, and Sharon caught on quickly. The menu presented her with a wide range of faces covering all genders and skin hues, some of which were probably not available to stock humans. She figured the best solution would be to pick one that closely matched her natal state, then found a face with wider cheekbones, narrower eyes, a smaller mouth with a cleft chin, and a more bulbous nose. Then selected *Apply*.

"Hmm. You sure you want to go with that?"

"I'm desperate."

"You certainly won't be recognized. A *caveat emptor*, if I may. The authorities have surveillance AIs which can, given time and incentive, see past the mask. This will only slow them down."

"By how much?"

"We're about to find out." Teagan pulled out another mesh mask. "And they will eventually figure out that I helped you."

"Teagan, you can't come with me. This is my trouble, not yours."

"Who says?"

"I say! You said it yourself; the Navy, the Feds, and the Clarksport Police are all out looking for me. They could hang you as an accomplice!"

"We don't have capital punishment, silly Earthling."

"They could hang you metaphorically. You'd be an enemy of the state."

Teagan laughed. "Sounds like fun. Let's do this!"

Sharon opened her mouth to say more, then closed it again. Partly in response to the mask which Teagan had applied to his own face. Teagan now looked like a middle age man with skin that had seen too much sun, wind and extreme temperatures. Partly because Sharon knew that she couldn't force Teagan to stay, and she could use a guide.

Sharon nodded. "One more thing."

"Yes?"

"Do you have a weapon? Like a gun?"

"Uh … yeah. But I'm not going to shoot any feds or police or anybody else."

"Not other people, Teagan. If I become that other Sharon … the one who set the bomb on the *Zephyr* … I don't want to be the cause of another terrorist attack. Stop the EPU."

Teagan took a deep breath and tried to in vain think of an alternative. "I understand." Teagan disappeared and returned in a few minutes carrying what looked like a semi-automatic pistol that would not have been out of place in the mid-20th Century. Sharon guessed it was like a shark: no need to evolve if it did the job efficiently. The firearm didn't have the cool-factor of a ray-gun, but firearms were inexpensive, easy to manufacture, and very efficient at storing chemical potential energy for long periods of time and turning that into enough kinetic energy to kill people very dead. Carrying a ray gun would require a hefty power source and some very expensive optics, and would probably do less damage.

"Put some clothes on and let's go. I've got one more trick to play so that the tracking devices don't work."

They both found clothes, and Sharon grabbed her daypack, following Teagan out through a door that Sharon didn't realize was there. One moment, it was a blank spot on the wall, and the next it was a portal into a corridor full of pipes and conduits.

Teagan knew all the underground maintenance tunnels and access ways by heart, and they spent an hour walking before Teagan finally indicated a freight elevator. "We take this to the surface and take a pubic shuttle to Sedna. After that, we play it as it happens."

"Before we do," Sharon said, taking Teagan by the arm. "I need to know why you're doing this. If I'm going to feel guilty about bringing you along, I need to know why."

"Fair enough," Teagan replied. "Do you know what the leading cause of death for senior Kentaurans is?"

Sharon nodded. With a nominal life expectancy of about two hundred Kentauran years, the human population on Kentaurus had defeated genetic diseases and generally mobilized against germ-based ones quickly. While violence was always an issue, it paled in comparison to the chief cause of death.

"Suicide," Sharon responded.

People lived a long time in a culture that changed very slowly. Even though they stayed healthy for two centuries, they still tended to become cynical, jaded, and bored, often succumbing to a fatal case of "been there, done that".

"There you go, Earthling" Teagan said, indicating the elevator.

*　　*　　*

Agent Daerîsiell and her marines finally showed up outside Teagan's apartment door. One of the marines was holding a device that would make any bloodhound envious. "The trail ends here," he said.

"Of course it does," Daerîsiell said, knocking on the door. "Teagan Waugh, we are federal agents on official business. Open the door immediately."

"No response to chat request," one marine said. "Do ya wanna that we smash da door?"

Agent Daerîsiell looked annoyed then ran her fingers over the door. She mumbled something that sounded elfish, and lights activated on the finger jewelry. The door opened.

"Finesse over force, gentlemen."

Then she turned to the dark apartment. "Teagan Waugh, we are in pursuit of a person suspected of federal crimes. We have a warrant, which gives us authority to enter your residence."

"There's nobody here," said the marine with the scent detecting device. "But Simmons was here for quite a while. A whole day at least." He held the device in front of him like it was a divining rod, letting it guide him from room to room.

"That's it. According to this, she never left this apartment, but the apartment's empty."

"Simmons has recruited Waugh." Daerîsiell said to no one in particular.

UNDERSTOOD, came a voice through her EPU.

Nobody saw, but Elrydien Daerîsiell smiled.

"Where to now?"

"To the transport terminal would be my guess," the elf said. "She needs to find a way off planet."

14

Das Unter Schloss
Hab A-37, Dockside
Sedna dockyards

*D*AS *UNTER SCHLOSS* was a typical dockside dive, catering to merchant marines, enlisted navy, and contract workers at the Sedna shipping facilities. There were peanut shells all over the floor, and it smelled like old beer, greasy food, unwashed sailors, and other things that Sharon would just have soon stayed unidentified. She half expected to see a band of alien musicians playing something from Benny Goodman, but there was only a sad empty stage.

Most of the patrons, when not conversing with others, were content to watch some private entertainment through their EPUs. Several were obviously watching the same sports contest and were shouting encouragements and epithets at athletes nobody else could see. Aside from the peanut shells, the place looked surprisingly clean, even if it smelled bad.

Most of the patrons looked approximately male and they all turned to look at Teagan and Sharon as they walked in.

"Don't accept any free drinks," Teagan warned and Sharon said, "No Doh."

Teagan put an arm around Sharon's shoulders possessively and they walked to an empty booth. Teagan removed the iGlasses and put on a different pair.

"I need to chat somebody."

A small woman of typical ageless quality approached their table. She had flawless, milk-white skin and black hair with intense red lips and deep azure eyes. She was topless, wearing only a short skirt, and her breasts looked like they hadn't seen more than nineteen standard years. She looked like a doll, and Sharon realized that was exactly what it was: a sex doll. The doll wordlessly and expressionlessly handed them menus, set down a basket of tortilla chips, and left.

While growing up, Sharon had always thought of the future as a time of enlightenment, when the more noble of human endeavors would rise above the baser ones. She was always a *Star Trek* fan — an optimist, believing that the future would be a good time filled with magnanimous people. It was depressing to see such evidence to the contrary.

Their shuttle flight from Clarksport had been uneventful. They paid through a dummy bank account Teagan had set up years before for just such an eventuality, and the masks hid their identities well enough.

Sharon looked at Teagan busily chatting with somebody. Teagan pointed to the waitress and mouthed the word "robot".

"Yeah, I know. A doll. That was easy to figure out."

There was another doll, anatomically male, dressed in a loincloth, looking like an athletic boy in his late teens, bussing the tables.

The dolls were works of art, Sharon thought. They resembled humans right down to the feel of their skin. There were programmed to observe and anticipate humans and react accordingly. They learned human behavior by watching other humans. The learning was imperfect, and they couldn't fool anyone who had any social skills at all. The "uncanny valley" effect wasn't a matter of appearance with these dolls, but of behavior. If there was anything wrong with the dolls' looks, it was that they were too perfect — lacking any defects such as scars, color variation, and asymmetry of features. Their faces had the same properties as theatrical masks, so they could become anybody that their human owners wanted. If a doll's skin was cut, it would register pain due to a neural mesh found just under the pseudo-epidermis, and the skin would bleed pseudo-blood and heal, though the redness of the blood was caused by an inert dye that was much easier to clean than hemoglobin.

Their internal "organs" were lightweight and flexible, and the entire doll weighed about the same as a human of the same size. Though the dolls were capable of eating and drinking for social occasions, they were still powered by thousands of micro-capacitors that had to be recharged. There had been research into using a variation of these dolls for telepresence purposes, but reportedly, the researchers were not able to get the interface to work at anywhere near 100%.

Sharon reflected sadly that such works of technological marvels were being used for the most base of human commerce.

Sharon picked up the menu and asked sarcastically, "I wonder what the specials are tonight."

There on the inner sleeve was the answer. She had no idea what it was other than some spiced meat on dark bread. She could still order garlic fries or onion rings. Salads were extra.

Teagan continued to chat with someone — or perhaps multiple someones — and Sharon looked dejectedly at the menu. She wasn't hungry, and didn't have the stomach for anything alcoholic.

She was startled by the abrupt presence of a large Furman at the booth. Teagan and Sharon both studied it, trying to determine its intent. Then a tone sounded through Sharon's iGlasses, and she was invited to accept a chat from Barischk, and she instantly accepted.

MUSKRAT SMITH, YOU SMELL LIKE SOMEBODY I KNOW, THOUGH YOUR FACE IS A STRANGER TO ME, a synthesized male voice said through the 'Glasses.

Sharon considered very briefly trying to lie to Barischk, then decided that there would be no fooling that wolf nose.

"Barischk, it's me. Carol Simmons."

The eyes of the wolf face smiled, and an ear twitched. YOU MEAN SHARON MANDERS, I'M SURE. CAROL SIMMONS IS A FUGITIVE, AND WOULDN'T BE SILLY ENOUGH TO COME HERE.

"Long story."

YOU ARE MUCH IN THE NEWS, Barischk continued. 'CRAZY WOMAN SAVES LIVES AT SOLSTICE GATHERING', SOME SAY. OTHERS SAY THAT YOU HAMPERED OFFICIAL RESPONSE TO THE ATTACK BY SETTING OFF THE FIRE SUPPRESSION SYSTEM, AND ARE RESPONSIBLE FOR MANY DEATHS. STILL OTHERS SUGGEST THAT YOU ARE IN LEAGUE WITH THE TERRORISTS.

"As we used to say," Sharon said. "No good deed goes unpunished."

A synthesized laugh came to her ears as Barischk shook his head in wolfish glee.

AN IDIOM WHICH HAS SURVIVED THE AGES, MY FRIEND!

Andrea Monticue

Without being invited, the Furman pulled up a chair to the table and sat.

SO NOW YOU ARE LOOKING FOR TRANSPORT FROM SEDNA.

Sharon and Teagan looked at each other and then both regarded Barischk suspiciously.

OH, PLEASE, he said. IF I HAD WANTED TO BETRAY YOU, I'D HAVE CHATTED NAVSEC BY NOW. TECHNICALLY, I COULD BE COMMITTING TREASON AND DERELICTION OF DUTY BY SIMPLY SITTING AT THE SAME TABLE WITH YOU. PLEASE ALLOW ME TO HELP.

WHY DO YOU WANT TO HELP? Sharon asked.

FOR THE SAME REASON I GAVE YOU THAT MIRROR. DO YOU STILL HAVE IT? YES? VERY GOOD. I'M A SUCKER FOR THE UNDERDOG, IF YOU'LL EXCUSE THE TURN OF PHRASE. AND CONSIDER THAT IF YOU DON'T TAKE HELP FROM ME, WHO ELSE? ANYBODY ELSE IN THIS ESTABLISHMENT WOULD SOONER SELL YOU OUT. I SUSPECT THAT YOU DO NOT HAVE MUCH MONEY.

"He's got us there," Teagan said. "I have some cash, but it won't get us far."

Sharon was certain that this was the first time she had ever heard of cash in this postmodern world.

PERHAPS YOU COULD INTRODUCE ME TO YOUR FRIEND, SHARON, Barischk said.

"Barischk, this is Teagan — foolish bored person looking for an adventure. Teagan, this is Barischk — keeper of mirrors and spiritual successor to Lon Chaney, Junior."

PLEASE CALL ME BEAR. LESS CHANCE OF A MISPRONUNCIATION.

As they exchanged pleasantries, Sharon watched Bear take a surreptitious whiff of Teagan. He was a canid, after all. When Teagan offered a hand, Bear pressed it to his nose as if he were a Victorian gentleman kissing the hand of a maiden. He didn't lick it, and he didn't try to smell Teagan's butt. Teagan looked nervous about the hand being so close to those teeth, but didn't jerk it back.

193

"Can you get us off the planet?" Teagan asked.

WHY NOT FIND SOME UNDER POPULATED PROVINCE ON KENTAURUS? YOU CAN HIDE IN SOME LOW-TECH PIONEER VILLAGE. THEY GROW LIKE WEEDS IN SOME PLACES.

"No," Sharon interrupted. "We have to go interstellar. If we go back to Kentaurus, I'll eventually be arrested. Hiding won't solve the problem. There's a terrorist hiding in my brain, who might manifest at any time."

Reading a Furman's expression was nigh impossible for a human, but Sharon was certain that Bear was looking at her with incredulity. She and Teagan spent the next half hour explaining their conclusions. During this time, the doll made frequent trips to their table, expecting them to order food or alcohol, or perhaps some service. Bear ordered a refill on his beer, Teagan ordered a club soda with lime, and Sharon was happy with just water. The doll never said a word and communicated its expectations by staring at clients.

"NavSec admitted that they don't have the wherewithal to reprogram my EPU, and if they did, they'd reprogram me." Sharon said. "I have three choices. One, let the Navy experiment with my brain. Two, find the people who reprogrammed my EPU and deal with them. Three, Teagan puts a bullet through my grey matter. I'm not excited about that option. Finding the people who can reprogram my personality at a whim doesn't sound like fun, either, but at least I keep breathing. For now, at least."

A BAD CHOICE EITHER WAY, Bear said, as he scratched vigorously behind his ear with his hand.

"Look, I can't ask you two to help me, but you offered. I need to stow away on a ship headed for Maheux. After that, go back to your own lives."

Teagan looked positively affronted. "You've got to be kidding! There's no way I'm letting you go to Maheux by yourself."

As for me, Bear said. The Navy owes me nearly three months of paid leave. I hear Maheux is quite nice this time of year.

*   *   *

I need to know what Manders will do next, Agent Daerîsiell said. You have her psych eval. Will she head to Maheux?

Here's the thing, Elry, said one of the invisible voices. We have very little data to compare this to. How many profiles have been done on people from the socio-economic background of a book character?

You have every book written about her.

While true, the author didn't necessarily strive for consistency. The stories were all plot-driven, and the character did what she had to do in order to progress the plot. Additionally, both the character and the author are Pre-Singularity personalities.

We have plenty of data on people from Pre-Singularity worlds, the elf said.

Yes. Modern Pre-Singularity worlds filled with people who've never seen Earth nor heard of California except in fairy tales. We can only make the grossest of extrapolations from that data.

She's not from California, the second invisible voice said. She only thinks she is. Manders is a construct of what Carol's EPU thought that somebody from that era should be like. Granted, it's a very detailed construct, seen through the filter of a fiction writer, further distilled through the imagination of a girl from the Alemanni Province.

GIVE ME YOUR BEST GUESSES, GENTLEMEN, Daerîsiell said with frustration.

There was a long pause, then Voice Number Two said, SHE'LL GO TO THE ALEMANNI PROVINCE WHERE CAROL WOULD HAVE ALLIES. FIND SOMEBODY WHO COULD REMOVE THE EPU SURGICALLY.

I'M VOTING FOR MAHEUX, said Voice Number One. SHE MENTIONED THE POSSIBILITY OF GOING THERE IN ONE OF YOUR INTERVIEWS.

WE'LL COVER BOTH, Daerîsiell said. FIND OUT WHO WE HAVE IN ALEMANNI, AND GIVE ME SCHEDULES FOR ANY SHIP HEADING IN THE GENERAL DIRECTION OF MAHEUX. I WANT AGENTS CHECKING EVERY SHUTTLE LIFTING FOR SEDNA. DOUBLE CHECK THE TELL-TAIL ON DR. BRADFORD.

*　　*　　*

Teagan, after much gesticulating and cursing, finally found what they were looking for and announced that a man would visit them at the tavern. Bear and Teagan each found something edible on the menu, but Sharon could only bring herself to drink water. Buying illicit drugs was not normally her style.

Sharon watched the interactions between Bear and Teagan as they quickly became fast friends. Apparently, Teagan was ex-Navy, which was always a fast track for friendships. They mentioned sports teams and 'Nets gaming, and even works of fiction. Then it was music and high drama on the vids and cinema. Sharon envied them the common mortar of the Kentauran culture that could bring two such disparate individuals together. She, on the other hand, was worried sick about the logistics of their situation. How do they find interstellar transport? How do they get weapons? What about travel papers and supplies? Was she actually willing to become an interstellar fugitive? Breaking the law was not in her personal skill set. What was her alternative? Letting the Kentauran government play with her mind?

Beyond her worry for personal security, there were broader considerations. If anybody learned how to rewrite memories and therefore identities, what was there to stop them?

On the other hand, that particular genie was already out of the bottle. Somebody on Maheux knew how to do it already.

According to the display in Muskrat Smith's iGlasses, an hour ticked by before a man walked in, looked around, spotted Teagan, and invited himself to sit down with the group. Not a man. Another elf.

After giving everybody a salutation with a nod of his head, he pulled a package out of his pocket and set it on the table between him and Teagan. Teagan pulled out some cash and laid it next to the package. The two of them regarded each other suspiciously, then each picked up the item left by the other.

Sharon thought that might be the extent of it, and she became aware that she was holding her breath. She let it out slowly and the elf turned to look at her. "You are wearing a mask," he said.

Sharon didn't respond. The elf wore the same kind of filigree finger jewelry Sharon had seen on Daerîsiell's hand. He performed a series of gestures which looked like sign language and Sharon knew instantly that her mask had become transparent.

"Shit," she said. "Great masks you have, Teagan."

"It's not Teagan's fault," the elf said. "Yours will probably suffice as long as your interrogators don't have elf-tech. For a while, anyway. I have better masks for sale."

"We can't afford them," Teagan said.

"Can't we?" Sharon asked. The elf laughed.

"I'm afraid Teagan has tipped your hand. I have other buyers for the masks."

"How good are these masks?" Sharon asked.

"Good enough to get you past any Federal guards. You're the one who needs the drugs, aren't you? Want to get rid of your EPU? Your troubles with the Feds must run deep if you need to do that."

Sharon hadn't thought about it before, but realized that if a person was in trouble with the law, and needed to hide their identity, the EPU would have to be the first thing to go. It would be like a GPS in a smartphone that you couldn't turn off — a transponder advertising your identity and location to the entire planet.

"What if I could offer you better drugs than what you're selling?" Sharon asked. In this era of constant electronic surveillance guided by AIs with quantum powered brains, a drug smuggler would need extensive infrastructure, and Sharon desperately needed some of that. She thought about asking if the elf had access to some underworld surgeon, then realized that was the wrong path. As long as she kept the EPU, other parties would want to keep her alive. Otherwise, she was just an inconvenient person.

"I'm listening," the elf said with an air of sufferance.

"Obviously your clients are able to pay top dollar, but your competitors are keeping the price down by making the drugs too easy to obtain. Otherwise, Teagan couldn't have afforded them."

"I'm listening," the elf said, this time with interest.

Sharon leaned close. "I need to ditch my EPU because it's been reprogrammed."

The elf had a pretty good poker face, but even he had to react to that. He raised a hand to his cheek, which Sharon interpreted as a tell. "What if your clients could keep their EPUs, but reprogram them to be somebody else. Think of the drugs that are needed to be able to do that."

The elf nodded. "I can easily imagine them. How do I know you're telling the truth?"

"Those fingers of yours. Can they probe EPUs?"

The elf raised his right hand and placed it over Sharon's scalp, then he made some gestures with his left hand, then said a phrase in what Sharon thought might be Sindarin.

After twenty seconds of massaging Sharon's scalp, the elf said, "Chwest ned graug. Who did this to you?"

"That's what we're going to find out. We don't plan on being polite about it, either. You're welcome to come along and question the manufacturers about their processes."

"Where?"

"Maheux."

"*Gûr ned Amarië.* You can't be serious!"

Teagan started to say something and Sharon put her hand on Teagan's arm. "I am so serious, elf, that I've instructed Teagan to kill me should we fail. I am literally dead serious."

"If you fail, you'll be dead, Teagan will be in a Maheux prison, and I'll be out my investment."

"Life's a gamble, elf. Think of the rewards for your success. Even the government doesn't have this tech. You'll have zero competitors."

The elf thought about it for a while longer, looking worried. "I'm not sure you realize what ..."

"Yes?" Sharon said.

"Never mind. I can get masks for both of you. But not you," he indicated Bear.

I'M NOT A WANTED CRIMINAL. Somehow, Bear managed to look affronted.

"Not yet," Teagan said.

"We also need traveling supplies," Sharon said. "And weapons once we reach Maheux. And a way to get there."

"Wait, you just said you only needed masks."

"Do you really think that mere masks would pay for this opportunity? Did you want to starve on the way to Maheux?"

The elf sighed and then obviously relented. Turning to Teagan, he said, "Is she going to be your new permanent partner?"

Teagan grinned and shrugged shoulders.

"We'll meet again in an hour. Somewhere else," the elf said.

"Where?"

"Anywhere but here. Teagan knows how to contact me. We need to be away from public eyes."

Sharon didn't believe that the elf was the top person in the criminal operation and would not be able to make arrangements to take care of business while he was gone in just an hour. But he had resources available, whether begged, borrowed, or stolen, and that's all that mattered to Sharon.

"How do I take this medication?" she asked.

"They're pills. Just swallow one now and another dose in four hours," Teagan said with exasperation.

Sharon opened the bag to find another, transparent plastic bag inside. Sharon unsealed it, removed a pill, and swallowed it dry.

After the elf left, Teagan, Bear, and Sharon waited for a very difficult fifteen minutes before standing to leave. Just as Sharon pulled on her sweater, the sex doll walked up and blocked her exit.

"What?" Sharon asked. "You want a tip? But I didn't have anything." The doll looked expressionlessly into Sharon's face. "Okay, this is creepy."

"Here," Teagan said, offering Sharon some cash. "Give this to it." She took the cash without looking at it and offered it to the android.

"Whoa!" Sharon felt her knees buckle and the room spun. She managed to catch the edge of the table before her head slammed into it.

"Sharon!" Teagan was instantly at her side. "What's going on?"

I THINK THE MEDS TOOK EFFECT, Bear said.

Sharon was unable to respond. She knew that she wanted to say something, but no words formed in her mind. The room finally decided which way was down and steadied.

"I'm okay," Sharon croaked. "That was weird." The doll continued to look into Sharon's face. "How do we get Lolita here to stop scrutinizing my facial structure?"

Bear picked up the doll in both hands and walked with it to the bar where he set it down facing the bartender. KEEP A LEASH ON YOUR TOY, he said.

The bartender nodded, reaching for a remote control.

"Let's go," Teagan said with authority, and the three of them stepped out the main door and into the street.

After they left, two nondescript men sitting at the bar looked at each other and started mumbling in private conversation.

"Teagan Waugh is out of practice," the first said, holding his hand over his mouth as if lost in thought.

"Teagan Waugh took out two of our operatives yesterday," the other said, mimicking the gesture. "Want to try your luck?" said the second.

"No. Just report and get further orders."

There was a commotion, and the two men watched as the previously servile doll broke a man's wrist and then disappeared out the door.

The first man said to the second, "This just keeps getting weirder all the time."

Outside *Das Unter Schloss,* there were other establishments on either side of the passage. Saloons, brothels, tattoo parlors, offices, warehouses, motels, and restaurants, Sharon noted.

Teagan was consulting data on the iGlasses. "This way."

"You okay?" Teagan asked when they'd walked half a block. "You scared me back there."

"Me, too," Sharon responded. "I'm fine now. I think."

She wasn't fine. There was a kind of buzzing in her brain that made it hard to concentrate. It was much more of a physical sensation than a sound.

The corridor wasn't crowded, but there were dozens of other people, and the group had to step around other pedestrians. Sharon stopped nearly midstride when she was overwhelmed by a feeling that they were being followed. She turned and looked back the way they came.

"What?" Teagan said.

"I felt like somebody was watching me," Sharon said. "I thought that only happened in cheap spy horror stories. There's never been any objective evidence to suggest that people can actually sense somebody watching them."

"Maybe in the good old days before EPUs," Teagan said. "These days, people get warnings all the time because everybody's brain is in the same network." Teagan mumbled commands to the iGlasses to adjust the image to near infrared. "I don't see anything suspicious."

Sharon digested that. "Is my EPU coming back online?"

"You just took a massive dose of anti-EPU drugs," Teagan said. "This way," Teagan ordered while walking up to a featureless door and trying to open it. "Shit! They've shut out my access codes!"

That frightened Sharon more than anything else that had happened that day. There was a knot the size of her fist in her stomach, and the only thing that had kept it to such a relatively small size was the thought that Teagan had a magic maintenance pass. There was only one reason she could think of why it would be turned off.

"Give me a moment," Teagan said, and the door obligingly opened after some sleight of hand that Sharon couldn't see. "Keep quiet from here on out."

The door opened to a long, dark corridor perpendicular to the main one.

Teagan pulled out a flashlight, and then closed the door behind them. "It's locked. Nobody will be able to follow us this way."

Sharon lost track of the directions after only a few turns and climbs, but the iGlasses had an app for that and she kept a small display to show their route. She felt as if she was being paranoid, but told herself that paranoid was the correct thing to be right now. If something happened to Teagan, Sharon wanted to be able to get out of the maze.

"What the fuh ..." Sharon swore and Teagan and Bear turned to look at her.

"Do you smell anything, Bear?" Teagan asked.

YOU MEAN BESIDES ALL THE INDUSTRIAL CRAP IN THE AIR?

Sharon shook her head. "For a second there, I could have sworn I was looking at the back of my own head from about fifty paces back."

Everybody turned and examined the corridor.

"Nothing," Teagan said after fifteen seconds. "Nobody." That didn't stop Teagan from pulling out the pistol.

The corridor was awash with the sounds of fluids and gasses in conduits, and Sharon struggled to hear anything amiss. "It was probably the iGlasses," Sharon said. "I have too many apps running."

After another half-hour of walking Teagan opened a door into a much larger corridor framed by rails. Sharon recognized this as the commuter mag-lev system.

"We need to be out of here before the next train comes by," Teagan said. "Fortunately, one isn't scheduled for another fifteen minutes, and we only need to walk a hundred meters towards that light over there."

Teagan secured the door and double-checked it. Nobody was going to use it without authorization any time soon.

The light turned out to be a meg-lev station adjacent to a commercial shipping port. Teagan halted them just short of it, and then accessed the security video system with the iGlasses.

"Okay, now."

They walked out onto the station platform as if it was the most natural thing in the world. The few passengers there were mostly preoccupied with whatever they were doing with their EPUs.

"Let's take a short break while I do a chat."

15

KRZ Zephyr
Sedna Orbit

T HE *KRS ZEPHYR* WAS FINALLY FULLY REPAIRED and upgraded, and Commander Souza breathed a sigh of relief as she signed off on the last of the virtual paperwork. She had been at loose ends while the maintainers were crawling all over and in the ship. She had taken time to visit family and catch up on the day-to-day cultural stuff, but planetside was not where she wanted to be.

She felt uneasy when she was not within the pressure bulkheads of her own command. She was looking forward to the shakedown cruise and had ordered all hands back from shore leave. In the meantime, she had to continue to familiarize herself with several upgraded systems. It seemed like the techies upgraded the ship's operating AI every time they hit port. She opened the file on the upgraded systems and started to read.

Souza hadn't read more than three pages before her EPU notified her of an incoming message from *KentSysFltComd*. That it came directly from the system fleet commander was surprising, but far from unprecedented. It was, also unsurprisingly, marked as urgent. After reading it, she addressed her EPU. "Personal message to Lieutenant Commander Lagrueux. Quote, Urgent mission. Soonest time to launch ready? Send."

Lagrueux responded in chat mode more quickly than Souza expected.

SEVERAL CREW ARE STILL DIRTSIDE, AND WE FINALLY HAVE WORD ON THE ONE AWOL, CREWMAN SIEVERS. HIS REMAINS WERE POSITIVELY IDENTIFIED IN CLARKSPORT. DEATH BY IMMOLATION. CITY POLICE ARE WORKING WITH A NAVAL CI, UNIT TO DETERMINE IF IT WAS MURDER OR ANOTHER SUICIDE.

"Damn," Souza muttered. She had no idea who Lester Sievers was beyond a name that was reported as AWOL right after the Solstice. Even though it was just a name to Souza, she couldn't imagine a worse death than by fire, and her heart went out to the dead crewman. The news outlets had been full of reports about other similar deaths, all ruled to be suicides. *Rash of Bizarre Suicides Plague City in Wake of Solstice Tragedy* the headline banners read.

WE CAN LAUNCH WITH CURRENT COMPLIMENT IN THREE HOURS," LAGRUEUX CONTINUED. "IF WE WAIT FOR STRAGGLERS, POSSIBLY EIGHT.

Souza would have preferred a full crew obviously, but she was willing to leave short-handed if absolutely necessary.

WHICH CRITICAL CREW SLOTS WILL BE AFFECTED?

NONE CRITICAL.

As in any naval vessel, tasks and skills overlapped between personnel so that the loss of almost any number of crew wouldn't be debilitating. There were minimums, of course, but they were far above that.

CREWMAN BARISCHK IS OUT OF COMMUNICATIONS, AND WE HAVEN'T HEARD FROM HIM IN ALMOST SIX HOURS.

MAKE IT THREE HOURS, THEN. WE ARE EXPECTING THREE CIVILIAN PASSENGERS. NAVSEC.

Lagrueux didn't bother responding to that. Passengers were passengers regardless of who they worked for. Souza knew Lagrueux was already giving orders to make arrangements.

Souza walked briskly from her quarters to the flight deck. "Ladies and gentlemen," she said upon arrival. "Our shakedown cruise will be entirely operational. I want readiness reports in my inbox before you leave the watch. If there are any reservations about the readiness of any department or system, your report will be accompanied by no fewer than three recommendations for either making them go away or working around them. Any questions?"

There were none.

"Then we have three hours before launch. Let's get to it."

*   *   *

Rialian Interstellar, Inc.
Cargo processing and Launch Facility
Private Hangar
2000 kilometers from Sedna Spaceport, Sedna

Teagan Waugh entered the hangar first with one eye on the EM meter and another looking for possible escape routes. Bear entered next looking for suspicious people or anything else that might be a threat, his own EPU reporting any movements. It was a private hangar on Sedna, nearly two thousand kilometers from the Navy yards and government offices. It wasn't a secret from anybody. All the building permits had been filed, code variance fees and taxes paid, and inspectors occasionally came calling to make sure everything was above board. However, not all entrances and exits were shown on the blueprints, and the customs agents didn't know the half of what came and went through this port.

"For the love of Lúthien, what did you people expect?" the Tolkienist drug dealer said from behind. "You guys are acting like you're in some kind of spy thriller."

Sharon followed them through. "Humor us, would you?"

"Yes, it is humorous, but I seem to be the only one laughing."

"Where do we go from here?" Sharon asked.

The elf pointed towards a rather boxy looking cargo hauler that rested near a large sign proclaiming *Rialian Interstellar, Inc.* "We take that to the transport in orbit."

Sharon stopped walking. This was real. Up until now she could have gone back and turned herself in, and nobody else would be hurt. This was the Rubicon she had to cross.

"Are you coming, or are you just going to stand there admiring the fine esthetic lines of the hauler?" the elf asked.

Sharon looked at him. "What's your name?"

"Why?"

"We're going to be spending a lot of time together. I could always just call you '*pale thief*' or '*pointy-eared drug dealer*' or '*bozo*'."

"Sharon!" Teagan warned, but she just ignored it.

"You may call me Tith," the elf said with a sardonic smile.

"So, Tith. Please enlighten me. Did the founders of your gene line intentionally include a penchant for sarcasm, or was this just a happy side effect?"

"Sharon! If you please!" Teagan's voice jumped an octave and twenty decibels. However, Sharon spotted Bear giving her a furtive thumbs up.

Tith stood facing Sharon with less than a meter separating them. Tith was about a quarter of a meter taller than she was and he looked down his nose at her. "I can see that this will be a fun ride. Where did you say you were from, human?"

"California."

Tith looked thoughtful. "Really?" Then he just turned and headed for the cargo hauler. Sharon turned and looked back through the door while Teagan and Bear followed Tith. She was certain they were being followed, and it was becoming a distraction. Neither Bear nor Teagan were able to detect anyone, and Tith insisted that nobody could get this far without extreme scrutiny.

She had found it odd that every person she'd met in this facility was a Tolkienist. Was this some kind of elven cartel? The elven mafia? Or was the drug business part of some larger scheme? She wondered if Peter Jackson would be surprised at the genetic variation among living elves. Fantasy was one thing, but when you exchanged genetic material among disparate individuals, things drifted from the ideal. She presumed that the founders of the elven gene pool were smart enough to introduce diversity to avoid the problems inherent in breeding among closely related individuals. Both Tith and Elrydien were rather pale of skin, but Sharon had seen much darker skinned elves in the facility.

No elves were following now. A rather officious elven woman had checked their credentials and cleared them for boarding, and Sharon had the feeling that absolutely nobody who wasn't cleared was going to get by that woman.

"Hey, Gidget! Are you coming?" Tith called out.

"You didn't just call me Gidget," Sharon said to herself, but refused to let Tith see her ire. She turned with a smile and walked towards the hauler.

*   *   *

KRZ Zephyr
Sedna Orbit

The three passengers from Naval Security had been greeted and escorted to the conference room. Souza let them wait for fifteen minutes before joining them. She didn't mind passengers, but official civilian passengers tended to be problematic. Fleet Command said they should be extended every courtesy, and that they would, in essence, be in charge of the mission. NavSec might be in charge of the mission, but Souza was still in command of the *Zephyr*. The crew had no questions about who was in command, but official civilian passengers sometimes had trouble making the distinction. She didn't care that these passengers had badges and could make her life miserable. It was never too early to establish the social hierarchy. Still, she walked in with a smile and an extended hand.

"Commander Souza," Elrydien said. "It's a pleasure to meet you!"

Souza hid her irritation at being addressed by her rank instead of her role as ship's skipper, as was customary. She was certain the Tolkienist intended it as a slight in payment for having to cool her heels.

"Agent Daerîsiell, welcome aboard."

"These are my associates, Agents Perales and Johnstone," Elrydien indicated two men who shook hands silently.

"Gentlemen," Souza said.

"Commander, I requested that Dr. Bradford be present for this conference."

"He's on his way. Our premature departure took his department by surprise. I'm sure he'll be here any moment. Shall we begin?" Souza said, indicating the chairs. In fact, she had ordered Bradford to arrive twenty minutes late. Everybody found seats, with Souza at the head of the table.

"Commander, I really don't have times to play claw sharpening games. I hope you're not delaying the meeting out of some sense of impropriety?"

"Absolutely not," Souza responded. "I would certainly not want to make enemies with someone who has enough clout to convince Kentaurus System Fleet Command to order a frigate to abandon a shakedown cruise, a cruise meant to ensure the safety of the ship and crew following a major repair and refit, to assist NavSec in a matter of planetary security.

"Now, Agent. Perhaps you'd be kind enough to explain everything in extraordinary detail."

"Gladly. We are in pursuit of a suspected terrorist. One known to you, actually. She was a crewman on your last tour."

"Simmons? Or is she going by her other name now?"

"Sharon Manders, yes."

Souza had been able to get most of this story from Lieutenant Berg, but listened politely as Daerîsiell explained about spies from Droben and EPUs that overwrite personalities. Dr. Bradford walked in at the tail of it.

"Apologies for my tardiness," he said politely, keeping to the story he and Souza had agreed on. "But the medical facilities are a mess. It's all only half organized. Now what's this about Crewman Simmons being a terrorist?"

"She was staying with you as a guest, wasn't she?" Daerîsiell said.

"Until the Solstice, yes. I haven't seen her since. It was my impression that she was incarcerated by your department."

"Is it your habit to offer rooms to enlisted crew, Doctor?" Daerîsiell said in an obvious gambit to throw him off balance. "Or is it just young women?"

"Neither," Bradford parried easily. "She had nowhere else to go, and I wasn't going to let one of my patients sleep at a flophouse during the Solstice."

"Be that as it may, you probably know Sharon Manders better than anyone else here."

"Probably not," Bradford countered. "NavSec damn near pulled her apart and put her back together again. I didn't give her a psych eval. Wouldn't have been qualified to do such."

"But she considers you to be a friend."

"She hasn't said as much, though I'm sure her list of friends is pretty short."

The three security agents glanced at each other as if in a private conversation, then turned back to Bradford. "I'll cut to the chase, Doctor. Is Manders capable of finding the resources to go back to Maheux on her own?"

That took Bradford by surprise and he paused in thought.

"She'd need interstellar transport," Souza said. "There's very little trade between Kentaurus and Maheux. Mostly food and medicinals. Their chief export is botanicals. Spices and some medicines. It wouldn't be easy to find transport that just happened to be going that way."

"Agreed," Daerîsiell said. "She'd have to be very lucky, or make arrangements. Doctor, is she the kind of person who'd resort to crime?"

"Well, I don't ... I just don't know. If she's desperate enough, certainly anything is possible."

"This is important, Doctor. She doesn't think like a contemporary person. She's a person out of time and culture.

What is she capable of? Theft? Murder? She was in your home for several days, and unless I miss my guess, you and your wife probably had several discussions on ethics and morality with this woman. That's just the kind of people you are. Our historians tell me that in the culture Manders comes from, crime is a much more frequent occurrence, and was often portrayed in popular literature and cinema as something heroes did as a last resort."

Bradford nodded. "Yes, I think she would. She learns quickly and is willing to try unorthodox methods. But she'd have to be in an extraordinary position before she'd kill anyone."

"Are you certain about that? In the culture she came from, murder and violent crimes were rampant."

Bradford shook his head. "That doesn't mean they were all criminals."

"Let's hope not."

"Why do you think she'll head back to Maheux?" Souza asked.

"This is going to sound odd, but I think she was programmed to. That's where she was created. She may think that the idea is entirely hers. She's been talking about it since she arrived at Kentaurus."

*   *   *

Cargo Vessel Entulessë
Sedna Orbit

DO NOT HEAD DIRECTLY FOR MAHEUX, Bear said. DO NOT UNDERESTIMATE NAVAL SECURITY. THEY'LL BE LOOKING.

"Where do you want me to go?" asked the navigator of the transport warp-ship *Entulessë*. Both the navigator and pilot were Pips, which was one of the security policies of many shipping lines, as access to the ship's flight deck was restricted by a very small door through which only Pips could fit.

"Where do you normally go from here?" Teagan asked.

"Delta Pavonis. Then Tau Ceti. Back here."

"Fine. File a flight plan for Kōman'na Tori at Delta Pavonis. How long before we can hit warp?" Sharon asked.

"At twelve point three gravities acceleration, about two and a third days."

"And then how can we change course to Maheux?" Tith asked.

"We drop out of warp, change course, then go back into warp. That whole process will take a full day, easy."

Sharon could see Tith calculating the operational costs in his head. He looked like he had a headache.

"This had better be worth it, Gidget." Then to the navigator. "Do it."

WHAT'S A GIDGET? Bear asked.

"The stereotypical Californian girl from the mid-twentieth century," Sharon said. "Where did you learn about Gidget, Tith?"

"I've seen cinemas and vids. Read books. The classic cinema *The Golden King* tells the story of how King Edmund of California, back in the Fifth Age before the Fall, climbed Half Dome to pull the sword High Caliber from the San Andreas Fault. His knights Sir Zorro and Sir Harry the Dirty quested for the Golden Bear. The king married Gidget, the peasant surfer girl from Malibu, who had an affair with Sally Ride. The king was having a tryst with a troubadour named Linda."

Sharon did her best to avoid laughing, but had to turn her head to keep her expression from showing. "Please go on. I want to hear all the details."

"We have received clearance for orbital departure on a vector for Delta Pavonis," the navigator said. The navigator had

had no reason to actually be on the flight deck when he radioed for clearance. Both navigator and pilot were connected to the ship's AI through their EPUs. However, the ship wouldn't go anywhere unless both were at their stations.

"This is the pilot," the other Pip said while walking towards the flight deck access. "Stand by for acceleration in nine hundred eighty-two seconds. Set timer … now." He and the navigator disappeared through the tiny door.

Sharon was now familiar with the routine. They wouldn't feel any acceleration, as a field of gravitational distortion surrounding the ship would accelerate with them. The only limitation to this was the rate of energy flow from the fusion reactor they could feed to the field. Regardless, sitting in the small passenger cabin just aft of the flight deck, Sharon felt compelled to fasten the restraints.

The humming of the engines increased in pitch as a countdown indicator reached zero, and Sharon knew they were moving away from Sedna at a little more than 120 meters per second per second. Nothing changed. There was no sensation. The view out the ports remained steady. It would still be some hours before she could see Sedna and then Kentaurus retreating.

ALL SYSTEMS NOMINAL, the pilot reported over the ship's intranet.

WHAT WAS THAT? Bear asked. Everybody turned.

"What?"

I HEARD SOMETHING, Bear said.

"Probably just the cargo settling," Tith said.

SETTLING CARGO DOESN'T SOUND LIKE A HUMAN RUNNING BAREFOOT ACROSS A CERAMA-METAL FLOOR.

Bear leapt from his seat and sprang aft through an open door into the cargo area, with Teagan and Sharon following as best they could. Bear was fast. He was almost too fast for

Sharon to follow as he jumped from container to catwalk and back down to the floor.

THERE YOU ARE! he announced and held up a small woman.

No, not a woman, Sharon realized. It was a doll. It looked very similar to the one from *Das Unter Schloss,* but the coloration was different, though also dressed in only a short skirt. There were grease and dirt smudges all over its body.

"It's another doll."

No, Bear said. IT'S THE SAME DOLL. IT CHANGED COLOR FOR CAMOUFLAGE.

"How can you tell?"

ALL DOLLS HAVE A DISTINCTIVE SMELL. THIS ONE SMELLS LIKE THE MEN WHO USED IT.

Eew! Sharon thought.

"What the hell?" Teagan said. "How did it follow us without half of Sedna knowing?"

"The same way it followed us without us knowing," Sharon said.

The doll didn't struggle. It hung there between Bear's massive hands looking at Sharon. Tith joined them from the passenger deck.

"This is a bad thing," he said. "Who would send a doll to spy on us?"

NOT US, Bear said. HER. He indicated Sharon with his snout.

*　　*　　*

KRZ Zephyr
Stellar Orbit
Rigil Kentaurus A

"I think I've found something, skipper," one of the scanner technicians said. Souza stood up and walked over to his station.

The *Zephyr* had been running silent only two light minutes from Kentaurus, waiting for something odd to happen. They'd been checking every ship leaving cis-Kentauran space for out-of-character behavior. They had paid very close attention to any ship headed in the general direction of Maheux.

"Go ahead."

"It's a cargo transport operating out of an alternate facility. It's the *Entulessë*. Normal crew compliment of six. It just filed a flight plan for Kōman'na Tori."

"Why is that so unusual?"

"I checked on the history of this ship, and it normally flies between here and DP, but usually files the flight plan several days before. This time, they filed the flight plan and requested clearance to hit the GO button nearly in the same breath."

"Anything else odd about it?"

"Maybe. It's a smaller cargo vessel, built for higher end consumables that require environmental controls. According to the registry, she can carry about forty thousand DWT, but it's pulling twelve point three gees, and the field distortion is consistent with Pruitt and Wilson TA32-40 engines. The fusion reactor is probably no bigger than forty gigawatts. I wouldn't expect it to do better than nine three when full. That means they are running almost empty."

Souza trusted her technicians. Between them, they had decades of experience with Protection of Shipping patrols, and they knew when a ship was acting out of character. This little cargo ship wasn't a dedicated smuggler, or it would've had oversized engines and a fusion plant powerful enough to run a continent. Some smugglers liked to give the appearance of above-board operations. To hide in plain sight. Pay all the taxes and fees and have a clean ship in hopes that the authorities will look in another direction. This was probably one of those, and it had a Tolkienist registration. Souza had no doubt that if she boarded on the pretext of performing a safety inspection, it would be spotless and without a single violation, giving her absolutely zero reasons to perform a search. No judge would sign off on a warrant to search a ship just because it was dead-heading.

"That's what we're looking for," Daerîsiell said, standing at Souza's elbow. How did she get there? How did she know what they were talking about? "Between the oddities of this ship's profile and the timing, I'm about ninety percent certain that it's Manders."

"We have no probable cause to board them," Souza said.

"We don't have to. We follow them, but they aren't going to Delta Pavonis. Set a course to Maheux, and we wait for them to show up."

Trying to follow them in interstellar space would be a waste of time. Ships traveling FTL could not be tracked, and they'd have no way of knowing just where the target would drop out of warp to change course.

"We have their transponder," the technician said. "If they arrive at Maheux while we're there, we'll know days before they orbit."

The *Zephyr* could pull twenty-five gees in normal operations, which meant they could achieve warp a full day before the cargo ship could. If Souza wanted to push it, she could ignore the red lines and pull thirty gees, but at this short distance to the warp limit, it would only cut a few hours off of the trip. It wouldn't be worth the wear and tear on the engines or the crew.

"Let's do this. Navigation, find us the best course to Maheux. Code one," Souza ordered. Code one was a joke among the ship's crew, the origins of which were obscured in oral histories. There was no Code One in the modern navy or any modern emergency services, but based on old vids, it meant to proceed without lights or sirens.

* * *

Cargo Vessel Entulessë
Transit to interstellar space

Aboard the *Entulessë*, the second shift navigator made an observation and reported it to the pilot.

"I just detected a grav distortion consistent with something the size of a naval frigate. It was parked two light minutes from Kentaurus and running silent. Had no idea it was there until it lit up the engines. Now it's making a twenty-five gee vector run for Maheux."

The second shift pilot, who had nothing more to do than monitor the systems run by the ship's AI, was reading a book. He looked up from the reader and called up the navigator's read-outs on his own EPU generated virtual display. "It's probably not a coincidence. Inform Tithfinthor."

16

T WO STANDARD DAYS LATER, the *Entulessë* was still picking up speed, and Kentaurus was a wan mote in the black backdrop behind them. It was obvious that the Entulessë had smuggled people before. There were two cargo containers specially designed to carry living humans, complete with plumbing, food storage and preparation facilities, entertainment consoles, and sleeping accommodations. Sharon was sitting up in bed in the first such container watching Teagan try to code-hack into the doll, which was secured to a chair with cargo straps.

Sharon had just finished going through her cardio and weight-lifting routine. Twenty-three days in a coma had sucked the endurance right out of her body. According to her memories, she had stayed in shape on Earth, and the lack of fitness in her current incarnation was frustrating. After she rehydrated and caught her breath, she would go back out onto the improvised workout floor and practice her sword routines.

Teagan had surprised her a new sword on the first day of the flight.

"I'm not a swordswoman," she protested without mentioning the one in her pack.

It was a cutlass made from a ceramic-steel alloy, rather than memory metal, was nearly impossible to damage with anything short of thermonuclear energies, and had an edge suitable for shaving.

"I'm going to teach you some sword forms. You'll do them for at least three hours every day until we get to Maheux."

"What do I do with a sword? Won't the other guys have firearms? Lasers?"

"It's not for use against other ... guys," Teagan said, obviously unfamiliar with the word '*guys*'. "Rather against bugs. Some of the natives of Maheux are meters long and poisonous. Some will simply take huge bites out of your tender flesh. They don't have clearly defined specialized organs like mammals do, so bullets won't do enough damage quickly enough. There's no such thing as a kill shot with them. Your only defense is to cut off heads, legs, stingers, or other convenient body parts. Just remember that even if you decapitate them, that doesn't necessarily mean they'll stop attacking you."

This explanation had been enough to keep Sharon practicing the sword forms diligently.

"It's no use," Teagan admitted, removing the iGlasses. "I have no idea what they're using for a firewall, but I can't get past it. The only thing I've been able to determine about it is that it was built by *PlayMe Robotics*, which is a one-person operation in a garage in Tulamak. The pink matter was formatted and customized by a software company in Nuadh Alba, but the software has been altered, adulterated, and corrupted. PlayMe sells it as a model Angelique Fully Customizable Complete Companion Doll. I checked their 'Nets vendor site, and it sells for seventy thousand notes."

"Maybe we should just put a bullet through its processor," Sharon suggested.

"Why? It can't do us any harm, it can no longer communicate with whoever sent it, and, if we kill it, we'll never get any information out of it."

"Because it's creeping me out."

Teagan suppressed an amused expression. "You have quaint, ancient attitudes towards these robots. Just because it looks like a human and isn't."

"Don't be absurd, Teagan," Sharon said with a bite of anger. "These kinds of robots were the subject of endless books, television programs and movies, both comedic and dramatic. There was an entire series of movies, uh, cinemas, devoted to the story of the rise of the machines, enslaving and killing off all humans. Other robots were quite benign. Helpful, even. There were even robots involved with humans romantically. No matter what you're currently using robots for, some story-teller in the 20th Century or earlier thought of it first."

"Then why are you being creeped out?"

"It won't stop staring at me."

No matter what they did, the doll would only look away from Sharon for short times, and then it would invariably turn its gaze back to her.

"Why doesn't it say anything?" Sharon asked. "You said it was designed to talk."

"I suspect because whoever took control of it at *Das Schloss* didn't want to take the chance that it would give anything away,"

Teagan said. "I'm impressed with the camouflage functions. I suppose the clients of *Das Schloss* have diverse tastes. Not everybody likes pasty white China dolls."

"Or Dresden dolls," Sharon added. Teagan looked at her, and decided not to ask. "Seventy thousand notes is a lot of money."

"That's true. The more they looked and acted like people the more expensive they are. For the proprietors of *Das Unter Schloss*, and other houses like it, however, it's not an expense. It's an investment. You wouldn't believe the kind of money one of these can earn in just one shift. They don't get tired, or diseased, or pregnant, or demand a higher cut of the take. The perfect employee."

Sharon was going to ask why they didn't replace all employees with dolls, then thought better of it. Kentaurans, as a culture, were craftsmen, and this was a respected profession. There were no plastic knock-offs of original toys in Kentauran culture. There were things that were far too complicated to make by handicrafts, like computer components, but those components usually ended up in computers that looked more like art than engineering.

Even the doll was probably a one-off production item. Its components were produced by machines controlled by quantum-based AIs, but the entire package was likely designed and assembled as a unique item.

Sharon idly stood and walked to a small electronic musical keyboard that was part of the room's furniture. It did not surprise her that elves would provide musical instruments for long voyages, though she no longer knew what to expect from Tolkienists. A song came to mind and Sharon sat down and set her fingers to the keyboard.

How odd, she thought, *that after some thirteen centuries the musical keyboard would remain essentially the same.*

Andrea Monticue

Eighty-eight keys, with alternating sets of three and two dark keys, tuned to the equitemperment scale. This was essentially a synthesizer, and she'd already, with some experimenting, found the settings to make it sound like a grand piano. She started picking out the tune in her head, and after five minutes she was playing it in a classical style, though with a lot of errors. Sharon considered that the keyboard was a reflection of much of the rest of this culture, in that it didn't look very different from the Twentieth Century. Even though there were differences and improvements and, in many cases, retrogressions of technology, much that she found familiar was still the norm. Why change a thing if it already did the job so well?

Sharon had wondered about her musical ability. According to the series of books about her life, Sharon Manders was an accomplished musician and spoke several languages, and the EPU had faithfully reconstructed these talents. However, Sharon Manders was also a *Sam Dan* in *Tang Soo Do* with a healthy side of *Hapkido*, but when she tried to access this skill to apply to her workout, she was frustrated that there was no memory there. She remembered that she should know how to perform an expert flying side kick, but the memory of how to do it was missing.

What was the difference between her skills at this keyboard and her skills with the *Hyung?* The only difference she could detect was that when she had first recalled music, the EPU had been in contact with an extensive external database on the *Zephyr*. When she had remembered how to speak French and Chinese, she was connected to the database on Kentaurus — at least until the lights went out. Here on the *Entulessë* she was under the influence of drugs designed to subdue her rogue EPU.

"What is that?" Teagan asked, referring to the music. "It sounds really sad."

"Beethoven," Sharon responded. "He was this German guy from the Eighteenth Century who ..."

"I know who Beethoven was," Teagan interrupted curtly. "He's actually better known than Zorro and Dirty Harry."

Sharon smiled wryly. "This is part of his Seventh Symphony. I seem to remember more about music than I would have expected from a cartoon character."

"Cartoon? What's that?"

Sharon didn't respond to the question and just kept playing.

Teagan pulled up a chair and sat next to Sharon. "Have you taken your medication?" he asked. "I know. It messes with parts of your brain."

"Actually, it doesn't."

"I beg your pardon?" Teagan asked in surprise.

"I expected these drugs to give me a pretty good buzz, but ... nada."

"Regardless, you need to take it," Teagan insisted.

"We're over two billion kilometers from Kentaurus. We're all alone in the dark. If the EPU takes over, you can shoot me."

"I could," Teagan agreed. "I'd rather not." Teagan held out a dose of the medication for Sharon. She sighed heavily and took the pills into her hand.

"Bitte," the doll said.

Both Sharon and Teagan sprang out of their chairs to stare at it. Sharon banged her knee painfully against the keyboard.

This was the first vocalization the doll had made in their presence. *"Take Sie the medicina nicht,"* it said in the English-German-Spanish patois of the Alemanni Province.

There could not have been a better provocation to entice Sharon to swallow the medication as fast as she could move her arms.

"Who are you?" Teagan asked, but the doll remained silent. It actually managed to look disappointed that Sharon had taken the meds.

"Why are you following me?" Sharon asked.

"It would seem," Teagan said after a minute's silence. "That it has said all it wants to say."

The doll looked like it was sleepy.

"How long before it runs out of charge?" Sharon asked.

"I have no idea how much charge it had to start with, or what kind of capacitors it's running on. But it's probably been three days since it last plugged in."

They watched as the doll's head started to waver and its eyes closed. Finally, its head dropped forward and, for all they could tell, it was asleep.

"Okay, now that's odd," Teagan said. "I've never known one to actually sleep."

"Is it out of power?"

Teagan took an electrical meter from a tool bag and held it next to the doll's neck. "I don't know how much of a charge it still has left, but there are still signals going through its spinal cord."

"So, it's what? Asleep? When do dolls sleep?"

"They don't. It's just powered down for some reason."

Sharon sat down again, rubbing her knee. "How do we know this thing won't wake up and start a violent rampage? Seems like I've seen this cinema, and I don't like the ending."

"Well, for one, it's tied to a chair that's bolted to the soleplates. It doesn't have super human strength. It would be difficult to explain to the insurance company if it crushed a customer in the throes of passion."

"Either that, or it'll be really pissed off, find a way to get out of the restraints and kill everybody."

"Is that your personal paranoia, or did it come from the meds?"

Sharon set her jaw, stood up and limped out of the storage container. "I'll leave you with your doll. I have some very important things to do in the next container."

Teagan was tempted to call after her, but thought better of it. Sharon was not to be reasoned with at the moment. Turning the attention back to the doll, Teagan thought about its language. Was this a newly acquired ability? It didn't say anything when they were at *Das Schloss*. Or did the proprietor simply disable the speech functions for whatever reason? If so, how did the doll reset the speech functions? It should not have been able to do that. Then again, it should not have been able to follow them out of the tavern.

An idea occurred to Teagan which was followed by, "What an idiot I am!" Activating the iGlasses, Teagan said, "Initiate 'Nets search for news items about a stolen or missing doll from *Das Unter Schloss*."

"Seven articles returned," a neuter voice said. "Sorting by most relevant. Article one:

United News Agency release. Sex Doll Reported Missing from Dockside Establishment. Leon Baumgartner, proprietor of Das Unter Schloss in the dockside quarters, reported that one of his sex dolls had gone missing after attacking a customer.

It is not currently known if someone took control of the doll remotely, but roboticists insist that this is the mostly likely explanation. It exited the premises on its own.

Police are looking for a female sex doll, 1.5 meters tall, dressed in a short skirt. Physical characteristics for skin and hair color and texture could vary.

Teagan turned to the apparently sleeping doll and said, "Your mystery deepens, doll."

* * *

On the evening after they entered warp, Sharon was sitting alone in the second container, reading some trade magazines about archeological digs on Earth. The researchers had stumbled across the remains of a museum of natural history in what had once been Washington, District of Columbia. The structure had been largely buried by ejecta from the kinetic bombardment which happened during the Singularity.

Judging by its orientation to the Capitol building, which had already been excavated, Sharon was certain they had found the Smithsonian, and thought it both ironic and sad that these items would go into a new museum as part of an exhibition of what our ancestors thought important to put into a museum. Unfortunately for the archeologists, those clever Americans had moved the more valuable collections to higher and dryer ground when the sea level rose enough to flood the National Mall every time there was an Atlantic storm. The alternate, higher altitude location had yet to be determined.

Thinking about all this was better than thinking about their immediate, unknowable future. Sharon was near certain that she was going to get herself and everybody else on the *Entulessë* killed.

A notice appeared in her field of view, and Sharon gestured to open it, and plain text appeared:

Hannibal Hedgehog asks you to accept a VR environment and enter.

Sharon had to remember that Hannibal Hedgehog was Teagan's *nom anonyme*. She wasn't sure she was in the mood for another pool hall, though, and hesitated.

A text chat message appeared.

Come on! You won't regret it!

Worried that the exact opposite was true, Sharon accepted the invite. Nothing happened for several seconds as the program loaded, and then another message appeared:

Enter when ready.

Sharon clicked *Enter* and the immediate surroundings disappeared to be replaced by a nighttime view of a large city that Sharon instantly recognized. Her heart seemed to stutter, and she felt chills run down her arms.

The city was framed by two bridges: the Bay Bridge was close and to the left, and the iconic Golden Gate was to the right and much further away. Alcatraz Island sat in the middle distance. Lights from private yachts and commuter ferries looked like sprinkles on the black water. The view seemed to be from Treasure Island, and her chair was on a lawn. She was looking across a narrow road and a stone seawall, and then across the calm bay waters. The buildings were outlined in light, like they were during the holidays. Somewhere, a radio or boombox or phonograph was playing Tony Bennett's *I Left My Heart in San Francisco*, and Sharon found it difficult to breathe through the emotions erupting from her soul. If she allowed rein to her imagination, she could smell the sourdough bread and hear the bark of the harbor seals. Some overly rational part of her brain insisted that she couldn't feel homesick for a place she'd never been to, but she immediately squashed the idea. This was the first thing from home she'd seen since waking up on the *Zephyr*.

"You wouldn't believe the research I had to do to recreate this," Teagan said, pulling up a chair to sit next to Sharon. "Fortunately, a lot of cinemas and vids from the era that were set in this city are available on the 'Nets."

Sharon tried to say, *"Thank you!"*, but she couldn't find her voice through the tears. She used her sleeve to dry her cheeks, being careful not to disturb the iGlasses and upset the illusion. She was a bit embarrassed by her reaction, but felt no compulsion to hide it from Teagan. Part of her reaction was due to the fact that she'd just been reading about how so many major cities on Earth had either been outright destroyed or buried by the fallout from kinetic bombardment and the environmental disasters which preceded and followed, but here was San Francisco, alive and well at least in the virtual sense.

"What do you think? Did I get it right?"

Sharon nodded as she tried to focus on a sight that would tell any Californian, *You are home.* Teagan could also have picked the view from Griffith Observatory in Los Angeles, or of Half Dome in Yosemite, but this was perfect. Unable to verbally express her gratitude, she turned and flung her arms around Teagan's shoulders, hugging tight, and Teagan placed an arm over her shoulders. Unwilling to take her eyes off of the wonderful view for long, Sharon made her head comfortable on Teagan's shoulders and turned her neck to take in the sights.

"Thank you," she finally managed to say. "How did you know I needed this?"

"I know how I feel when I'm away from my home in Tokimok for years at a time."

Tokimok was a major shipping port in Mokishtan Province, and had some superficial resemblance to San Francisco.

"Or, as is currently the case, decades. At least there's nothing stopping me from going home."

"It's more than just the memories," Sharon said. "As near as I can figure, there's about five light-years and over eighteen hundred standard years between this view and the *Entulessë*. Almost as much time as separates the fall of Rome from the founding of the Smithsonian Institute."

"What's that" Teagan asked.

"An obscure cultural reference," Sharon said dismissively. It occurred to her that Hermans smelled quite pleasant, then realized she was being overly familiar with Teagan and sat up in her own chair. Teagan seemed reluctant to let her go, but didn't fight it. By now, Scott McKenzie was advising visitors to San Francisco to wear flowers in their hair.

"Too bad this isn't real," Sharon said. "We could drive over to Ghirardelli Square and get some chocolate."

"Well, now that you mention it," Teagan said with a wink, and pulled something out of a pocket.

*   *   *

Cargo Vessel Entulessë
Maheux system

It wasn't until the *Entulessë* was decelerating towards Maheux when the doll spoke again. They were still fifty-six hours from orbit, and Teagan was playing virtual cards with three of the Pips and Tith. At Teagan's insistence, they had set up a virtual card room with a decor from the previous century. It was a room filled with virtual tables, around which sat virtual people having virtual conversations. A virtual band was playing virtual dance music and a virtual dance floor was filled with virtual dancers who never missed a step.

One of the Pips laid her cards on the table and declared, "I have a full run. I believe the field is mine."

Everybody else made disappointed remarks. Teagan simply tossed the cards on the table.

"*Bitte,*" the doll said. "*May have Ich algunos Kleider?*"

Teagan pulled the iGlasses off. The Pips, the elf, and the quaint club disappeared.

"What did you say?" Teagan asked, more in surprise than misunderstanding.

The doll actually seemed to consider the question, then said in standard English, with an Alemmeni accent, "Please, may I have some clothes?"

The doll had already made an effort to clothe itself. Instead of the camouflage splotches it had painted itself with earlier, its skin now looked like clothes. Unless Teagan looked closely, it appeared that the doll was dressed in a white button-down shirt, blue jeans and sports shoes.

Teagan considered the options for several moments then finally said, "We don't have any clothes your size. The Pips are too small and everybody else is too big."

The doll nodded. "That is understandable. Still, *ich bin frío,* and even clothes that are too big would help."

Teagan stood up and walked over to where the doll was restrained and studied the incredibly detailed image of clothing on the doll's skin.

"Why is a doll worried about being cold? Or modesty for that matter? What's the point of this camouflage?"

The doll looked around the room and considered its surroundings. "If you will give me clothes and let me recharge, I will answer your *fragen.*"

"And if I don't?"

"Then I will eventually collapse, all of my temporary memory storage und programming will be lost, and you'll never know the answers to your *fragen*."

"Will you answer all of my questions?"

"I *puedo nicht promise dass* I know the answers to all your *fragen*," the doll said with a straight face. "I also need to drain and refresh my fluids."

Teagan laughed. "You mean you need to pee and drink water?"

"Why do you think that's funny?" the doll asked.

"I don't think it's funny," Teagan admitted apologetically. "I don't remember a single morning of my entire life when I didn't have to drain and refresh my fluids first thing. I'm sympathetic to your needs, but I need some surety that you'll behave."

"You have the pistol, *ja?* If I behave *nicht*, you can ... how did the woman say ... put a bullet in my processor."

Teagan thought about it for a minute then said, "I have a better idea." Teagan pulled the pistol out, flipped off the safety, cocked it and pressed it against the back of the doll's cranium while loosening the cargo straps. "Don't move until I tell you." Teagan then backed out of the cargo container, closed and locked the door, then shouted, "Let me know when you're done." He set the safety on the pistol and uncocked it.

"When you're done what?" Sharon asked, walking from the other container and eyeing the pistol with suspicion.

"The doll had to pee. I gave it a little privacy."

"It's loose?!" Sharon demanded. "What the hell were you thinking?"

Teagan gave a synopsis of the conversation with the doll, emphasizing the part about answering questions, and it seemed to mollify Sharon somewhat.

Teagan decided that a change in topic was in order.

"Have you decided what we're going to do when we get to Maheux?"

"Try to find where Carol was abducted. There aren't that many settled areas on the planet. The human colonists tend to restrict themselves to the desert interiors of the two major continents. There's only one location that approaches the size of a city where the Republic Navy visits. Wildeside. It's a city on the northern continent."

The Pangaea-sized northern continent included the frozen icecap, and as a result had a large number of rivers meandering Mississippi-like over the generally flat ground to the ocean. Maheux had no large natural satellite and only minor tectonic activity. As a result, there were no large mountain ranges. The largest mountain on the entire planet was only five thousand meters from base to peak. While life was abundant near the beaches and shores, the interior of the continent was mostly one huge desert where wet storm systems rarely penetrated.

The native life forms of the planet were not openly hostile to the invading humans. The insectoid species generally had no idea that the humans even existed, but they didn't take kindly to anything that interrupted their insectoid activities.

"I've been looking at maps of Wildeside. Aside from water and energy usage plans, there's not a lot of regulation about where people can or should build, so maps of the city become obsolete rather quickly. Nothing about the layout is familiar to me. Except that I keep thinking about a Lou Reed song." Sharon refused to respond to Teagan's raised eyebrows. "The best plan I can think of is to take a walk around the city with scanners."

"While avoiding naval personnel," Teagan added.

"And frontier law enforcement," Sharon said.

"And insects the size of an aircar," Teagan said.

A knock on the container door interrupted their list of things to avoid. Teagan leveled the gun and opened the door.

The doll had evidently finished its business and had found some of Teagan's clothes to wear. It had used the cargo straps, which had just recently bound it to a chair, as belts to take in the slack of the clothes by wrapping them round its waist and thighs. Sleeves and cuffs were folded.

"You need to get back into the chair," Sharon said. "We can find more cargo straps."

"Can we talk about this?" the doll asked. "I've already promised to answer questions. Really. Have I done anything to threaten you?" The doll was speaking in standard English, but still with a heavy accent.

"You followed us out of that restaurant," Sharon replied.

"Restaurant? Is that what you call it? Please remember that its name is *Das Unter Schloss,* not *Chez Unicorn.*"

"Are you claiming that you escaped abuse?"

"You jest, *ja?*" the doll asked. "Let me put it this way. My skin doesn't bruise all on its own, but the tips were much better if I employed the skin coloration functions so that it looked like it would. You asked earlier what the point of the camouflage is. Aside from decorative bruising, some customers wanted me to look like a specific person."

"Stop!" Sharon insisted. "Why would your customers even tip you? You're a sex doll. It's what you were designed for. That would be like tipping the toaster for making great toast."

Teagan almost said something, but decided against it. Sharon could see all the thoughts crossing Teagan's face.

"What?" Sharon demanded.

"Are you trying to convince yourself, *oder?*" the doll asked. It changed its posture by lowering its shoulders. "Yes. Look. I was programmed by my owner to get as much money out of the customers as possible. And up until the day we three met, that's all I wanted to do. No qualms about doing what was expected."

"So," Teagan asked, letting the silence stretch. Then, "What changed? What did we do?"

The doll pointed at Sharon. "She walked into the room, and something invaded my AI. Some sort of malware."

"What? A computer virus?" Sharon asked. "From me? My EPU?"

"Not exactly a virus. Its purpose was not to replicate and disrupt, but to take over in a constructive manner. Whatever it was, it overwrote much of my higher end functionality and memory database."

"Crap. Damn. Fuck it all," Teagan said, realizing the implications.

Sharon looked paralyzed as her mind refused to accept the logical conclusion. There was only one reason why the doll was speaking in an Alemanni accent.

"You're Carol." Teagan said.

"Shut up!" Sharon screamed. "Don't be stupid! Carol is dead. This doll can't be her! It can't!" Sharon started to back away.

"Sharon, wait," Teagan said in a calm voice. "We have to talk about this."

"No, we don't!" Sharon's entire body was tight with anger. "It's not up for discussion! It's not Carol!"

"Actually, she's right," the doll said. "I'm not Carol." That seemed to have a calming effect, but the next words didn't help at all. "I just have some of Carol's memories."

Sharon's eyes were wide and near manic. Teagan tried to put a hand on her shoulder, but she shrugged it off.

The doll continued. "I don't know what I am now. Some jumbled mashup of Carol and a sex toy."

"Amazing," Teagan said. "That shouldn't be possible."

Sharon shot Teagan a warning look. "Don't you dare take its side."

"What would you have done in my place, Sharón? You're probably the only other thinking entity in known space who can sympathize with my predicament. I basically woke up in a different body, and saw my former self being unmasked at a bar table."

"What precipitated the transfer?" Teagan asked.

"Keinen recuerdo," the doll's language slipped a bit then recovered. "But Sharón has been taking medication designed to shut me down, yes?"

"You asked her not to take the medication."

The doll nodded in response. "I did."

They both looked at Sharon, who had relaxed only a little, and seemed to be refusing to participate in the conversation.

At least she isn't running out of the room, Teagan thought.

"Look," the doll said. "I can help you. I know we're headed for orbital translation around Maheux. I know where Carol went last time. And I have no desire to hurt the enemies of my enemies."

"What is it you want to do?" Teagan asked.

"Kill the people who killed Carol," the doll said, then looked at Sharon. "And I promise to stay out of her head."

17

Epsilon Eridani
12.6 light-years from Kentaurus
approaching Maheux
Kentauran calendar: 13 Skoteinómína, 1383 PS

D UE TO THE FINITE NATURE of the speed of light, the scanner techs on the *Zephyr* didn't know that the *Entulessë* had translated into E-space until nearly ten standard hours after the fact.

"There it is," confirmed Daerîsiell.

Souza wanted to think that the NavSec agent sounded smug, but actually she didn't. Daerîsiell sounded confident, as though there had never been a doubt about the appearance of the cargo ship, but she didn't sound smug.

"Now we have probable cause," Souza said. "They filed a flight plan for Kōman'na Tori and showed up at Maheux. Navigator, plot us an intercept course. Let us know when we can have a conversation that won't require hours for a response."

"On it, skipper," navigation said.

"It still won't do you any good," Daerîsiell said. "There won't be anything on that ship to find by the time we get there."

"Leave that to me," Souza chided. "Commander Lagrueux, order the boats to launch ready."

* * *

"There's a navy ship headed our way," the first shift navigator on the *Entulessë* said. "It took a while to figure out what it's doing. It's circling around to come up on a parallel course. Unless it does something unexpected, it'll be at ten kilometers distance and zero velocity differential in twenty point five hours."

"Understood," Tithfinthor said via the ship's intranet. "We'll still be nearly thirty-one hours out of Maheux orbit." He turned to his passengers. "Ladies and gentlemen, boys and girls. And robots. This is where the ride gets interesting."

Sharon, Teagan, Bear, the doll, and one Pip hoisted duffle bags onto their shoulders while Tithfinthor did the same.

"If we launch the boat now, there's an excellent chance it won't be detected. There's a minimum chance of chemical rockets being detected at this distance. Unfortunately, their delta-vee is exceedingly limited, and we won't be able to counter the acceleration."

"I'm already uncomfortable," Teagan said. "What is our flight profile?"

"We'll float weightless for two hours. Then twenty minutes at three gees under chemical burn in order to change course."

"Ugh."

"Sounds like fun," the doll said, and even smiled. "Sucks to be a human right about now, though."

"After that," Tith continued, "we'll hopefully be too far from the *Entulessë* for the navy to associate us. All their scanners will be on the *Entulessë*. It will continue to decelerate at twelve point three gees, so we'll be a long ways ahead of it. We'll be able to turn on the grav drive at that point. But we'll also be too close to Maheux, so we'll have to overshoot and backtrack. We'll land about fifteen hundreed kilometers from Wildeside so we won't have to deal with the city's approach control. Then we'll drive into town like any other prospectors on the planet. Any questions?"

"You're sure this is safe?" Sharon asked.

"If you wanted safe, you should have stayed on Kentaurus."

Teagan touched Sharon on the shoulder to get her attention, and then gave her a smile and a thumbs up. Sharon tried to give a reassuring smile back, and wasn't at all sure that she succeeded.

"Is this what black-ops is like?" Sharon asked.

"A little," Teagan said. "Black-ops would be like this, but landing in an area where people will shoot you given half an opportunity."

The group boarded the landing boat in single file, each finding an acceleration couch.

The Pip took the pilot's seat. "Launching in nine-hundred seconds," the Pip said. "Boat secure and airtight."

"Evacuating boat bay," another Pip said over the intranet.

Sharon was annoyed when the doll secured itself to the couch next to hers. Sharon tried to tell herself that she was being unreasonable, but it didn't work. She had to admit that with the doll's abilities at stealth, it would be an asset to the team.

Were they a team? Sharon wondered.

She had somehow ended up with a diverse group of individuals, all with their own agendas, but with the same basic goal.

Sharon couldn't help but sympathize with the doll's predicament, and tried to analyze her own revulsion to the robot. Was it simply the "uncanny valley"? Or was it that it now held the memories of the person Sharon used to be? Had the doll become the embodiment of Sharon's feelings of guilt? She suspected so. Regardless, alienating the doll would only hurt her own chances of success.

"Are you fully charged?" Sharon asked in an effort to get past the awkwardness.

The doll smiled wanly. "Fully charged and mission ready," it said. "That's what Carol would say."

"Opening boat bay doors," a Pip said with a child-like voice.

"Twenty minutes at three gees," Sharon said disparagingly. "I'm too old for this shit."

"At fifty-two Kentauran years, you are the youngest biological person here," the doll said.

"Yeah, thanks for that." Sharon said, looking at the doll.

She had to remind herself that, one: fifty-two Kentauran years is about sixty-nine Earth years and two: that this was still considered young in terms of a Kentauran lifetime of about two Kentauran centuries. She certainly didn't feel old. In fact, there were times when she could feel the urgency and desires of youth.

"Um. Tell me. How old is Teagan?"

The doll looked at Sharon and then Teagan and then back to Sharon. Then, in a gesture that defied the Uncanny Valley, the doll smiled and winked.

"It's difficult to say with Hermans. It seems like they're young forever, and then suddenly they're old. Judging by the lines around Teagan's eyes and mouth, and some skin damage due to exposure to extreme environments, plus Teagan's use of some archaic expressions, I would guess over a century, but not older than one-fifty."

"So, Teagan potentially has an entire Kentauran century on me in age."

"It's *nicht importante,* Sharón. To quote a book about you: loneliness sucks."

"Teagan could die in the next fifty years."

"Are you serious? We'll all probably die tomorrow!" The doll said.

Sharon shook her head and decided to change the subject. "We should think of a name for you."

"Why?"

"We can't continue to call you 'doll' and nobody wants to call you Angelique."

"When I worked at *Das Schloss,* I had many names every day. Each client would call me by something different. An old lover, somebody else's lover. Even a daughter."

Sharon waved her hand irritably. "I don't want to hear about that!"

"Okay."

"And when you were in the Navy, you only had one name," Sharon said. The doll understood that Sharon was giving a peace offering.

"I can't go by that name. Hang on, here comes the launch."

There was a lurch, and everybody felt disoriented as they passed through the distortion field of the *Entulessë.* Then they were weightless. As the *Entulessë* continued to decelerate, the boat shot ahead of it. "We're falling," the pilot announced uselessly about thirty seconds later. "We're already five thousand meters from the *Entulessë.*"

"What do you remember about all this, exactly?" Sharon asked.

"There is a huge gap in my memory. I was on Maheux, and then I was in *Das Schloss,* looking at you. But I couldn't speak. I physically had keine ability to speak, and my memories were very spotty. The programming took quite a while to complete. I didn't remember who I was. I only had a compulsion to be close to you under any circumstances."

"If the people on Maheux programmed your ... our? ... EPU, why do you want to kill them? Wouldn't they have programmed your allegiance to be with them?"

"No. They programmed the other Sharón to have an allegiance with them. You und I, it would seem, are accidents of programming. Or, perhaps, artifacts of bad programming. The Carol personality should have been dumped, don't you think? Isn't that the way you'd do it?"

Sharon had to admit that. If she were heartless enough to do such a thing, that's how she'd have to do it.

In the past few hours, Teagan had gone on and on about how this shouldn't be possible. It had been the goal of the scientists of the Singularity to transfer a human consciousness to a machine, and they had failed spectacularly, very nearly wiping out life on earth in the process.

The doll's brain made memory associations the same way a human's did. There was just over a kilogram of 'pink matter' - or as some specialists ghoulishly called it, 'cherry gelatin' - in the doll's cranium that acted like brain tissue. Chemical processes formed neural associations far more efficiently in the pink matter than biological processes did in the grey matter, and in theory, the pink 'neurons' could be far more numerous and more densely packed than grey ones, but the intelligence of a system was not strictly dependent on the amount of memory available.

The architecture and operating system had far greater influence. The doll wasn't a computer in the sense of a desktop, laptop, or even hand-held calculator. If you asked the doll to multiply two three-digit numbers, the first thing it would do would be to find a calculator. The point of the pink neural network was to reinforce learned behavioral patterns in response to given stimuli and within predetermined limiting factors, and in this sense the doll was quite intelligent. There were governors in place, however, that made it impossible for the doll to slice customers with a kitchen knife.

Or, at least, there used to be.

When the doll had announced that it intended to exact fatal revenge on Carol's murderers, Teagan had become ashen and withdrawn.

*   *   *

Teagan became distrustful of the doll's intentions and programming, and insisted on attaching a miniature explosive to the small of its back. It wouldn't cause enough of an explosion to hurt anybody outside of a one and a half meter radius, but it would be enough to cut the doll in half. Teagan kept a remote detonator in a pocket, and insisted on this as a condition of letting the doll accompany them to the planet. The doll seemed unconcerned about it.

In the two hours of free-fall, Sharon and the doll continued their conversation. To Sharon, the doll seemed to be some kind of multiple personality. One was of a woman from Alemanni, who talked about growing up in a rural region and going to a trade school and joining the Navy, and one of a sex doll from the Sedna docks who talked unabashedly about the sexual preferences of merchant marines. This didn't seem to bother the doll, who flipped between the two narratives as if reading from two different books. However, the doll completely nixed the idea of responding to all the emails from Carol's family and friends.

"I'm not her," the doll said. "No more than you are."

Surprisingly, Sharon found that there were things about her own life that Carol didn't know about. They investigated this and found that whatever had programmed the Sharon personality had become creative, adding episodes copied from popular vids. The doll made the assumption that the application was capable of learning and self-reprogramming.

It had been centuries since humans had written any significant computer programming. It was all done by AIs who simply followed the instructions of human. These programming AIs were, by design, not innovative.

"Three gee acceleration in six hundred seconds," the pilot finally announced, and a countdown appeared in the corner of Sharon's field of view via Muskrat Smith's iGlasses.

Sharon adjusted herself to make sure that there weren't any folds of skin or unsupported limbs. No matter what she did, however, this was going to be uncomfortable.

"It's only twenty minutes," Teagan said from his couch, giving the doll yet another suspicious glance. "We'll be past this in no time."

It seemed to Sharon that, aside from the doll, Teagan seemed rather unconcerned about the whole ride.

The acceleration hit. Though the boat's structure could stand going from zero to three gees nearly instantaneously, the structural integrity of its biological cargo couldn't. It was brought up slowly, and took fifteen seconds to reach the full three gees.

Sharon's breath came with difficulty, and she found she had to think about every one of them. Another countdown appeared in her peripheral view, counting down the twenty minutes. After it had counted three minutes, Sharon became aware of another sensation. The doll had reached across the distance between them and was holding her hand lightly. "We can do this, Sharón."

"Easy for you to say," Sharon rasped. "You don't have to breathe."

"It would be easier if you do something to distract your mind," the doll said. "Would you like me to sing or recite a story?"

"What's it like to be a robot?" Sharon asked. "Does it feel different?"

The doll nodded. "It feels ... I guess it feels numb. Except for the hands, the face, the feet and ... well, one other place, meine skin doesn't have near the nerve density as yours. Maybe half as much."

Sharon found this intriguing, and it took her mind off of her weight. "There was a theory, back in the 20th Century, that emotions were the body's way of communicating with the brain. Are your emotions less intense?"

"In my short time, I haven't had an opportunity to have any intense emotions. I'll let you know."

"I would think," Sharon said. "That dying and waking up in an artificial body would be a hell of an emotional shock."

The doll nodded. "*Meine* memories were incomplete. I wasn't sure it wasn't a dream. Suddenly I was seeing *mein* old body in a tavern booth. My reactions were dulled by the robot's programming. I think there were some emotional governors restricting my reactions. Mostly, I could only think about serving food und drinks without questioning why I was doing it. I wasn't able to form fully coherent thoughts until I started speaking to Teagán."

"Are you intelligent?" Sharon asked after some silence. "Are you sentient? What I mean is, is your personality simply a very complicated piece of software designed to interpret and respond to human interactions? Or do you have original thoughts?

Teagan says you're the most sophisticated AI that they've ever dealt with, and it's a bit scary."

"Excellent question, *meine amiga*. I could ask you the same question, but we're both in the same boat. Does it feel like you're sentient?"

Sharon thought about it. She took a deep breath, held it, and let it out slowly. "I have no idea."

Now the doll seemed to become lost in a thought. After about thirty seconds it responded, "I think it was Alan Turing, many centuries ago, who said that if you can't tell the difference, it doesn't matter."

18

Epsilon Eridani
approaching Maheux
Kentauran calendar: 14 Skoteinómína, 1383 PS

W HEN SHARON THOUGHT ABOUT THE SPACE PROGRAM of the Twentieth Century, she recalled that the most spectacular part was always the launch. A huge penis shaped thing burned tons of hydrogen and oxygen and leapt into the stratosphere on a pillar of fire and smoke and the cheers of the adoring space-fans. The second most spectacular part of the spaceflight was the re-entry. Using aerobraking techniques to conserve fuel, the early spacecraft streaked through the sky and played havoc with the nerves of everybody who watched.

Lacking the need to conserve fuel, modern spacecraft simply decelerated to far below hypersonic speeds and entered the atmosphere at speeds that could be easily reached by a passenger SST, then slowed to subsonic speeds before reaching the fifteen-kilometer altitude limit. They came in on a whisper instead of a roar, lacking the fire and excitement of the pioneer days. For Sharon, this was a good thing. She'd had her fill of the excitement of spaceflight for a while, and looked forward to a boring landing.

Still aching, Sharon pulled herself upright and was determined to look like she did this every day.

"Be careful," Teagan warned. "Your body is still acclimating."

Sharon responded by squaring her shoulders and walking aft.

Maheux had only ninety percent of the surface gravity as earth. This made her feel light, but it didn't hamper her walking gait like trying to walk on Sedna outside the influence of the grav plates.

The aft of the boat contained the large cargo area mostly filled with the bulk of a groundcar, which they would use to get from the landing site to the city. Bear was already there, and he pulled backpacks from their storage units and handed them out according to the names printed on them.

"Seventy minutes to land," the pilot announced. "Passing over the edge of the northern ice cap, speed mach point nine."

Bear next pulled out swords and distributed these. Sharon attached hers to the backpack in a way that facilitated drawing it over her shoulder.

Bear then handed out short shotguns, about forty centimeters long. The size and shape reminded Sharon of flintlock pistols that were so popular with dueling politicians in the Eighteenth Century. Because these had been made by Kentauran craftsmen, they even had scrollwork on the brass-colored plates. However, they utilized modern ammunition.

"This is used to inflict damage over a large area," Teagan had explained. "You can take off legs, stingers, pinchers. Just don't be too far away from your target, and be prepared for the kick. You'll knock yourself in the head, else."

"Not sure I like getting into a bug's personal space in order to defend myself against it," Sharon said. "Isn't there a way to disable them from a distance?"

"Sure. Mortars and grenades and such. We won't have any of those."

"Why not?"

"Because we're not here to fight bugs," Teagan tried to explain. "Listen, you need to understand this. You've studied biology, what do bugs do all day long?"

"Mostly they eat, protect themselves from being eaten, and make more bugs."

"Exactly! Even if it's the size of a St. Bernard, that's pretty much it for the behavioral repertoire of insects. Unless they see you as food, a threat, or a mate, they pretty much ignore you. It's not like they're organizing invading armies of arthropods. And if it sees you as food, then it's already too close to use major explosives."

Between the cutlass and the short gun, Sharon felt downright piratish, and started singing softly a tune from Gilbert and Sullivan about the glory of being a pirate king. She ignored the quizzical looks from her companions, and attached the gun to the backpack so that it rode at and parallel to her belt.

The last weapon which Bear handed was a semiautomatic pistol, very much like the one Teagan had pulled out of the closet on Kentaurus. According to the inscription, it had a 10.5 millimeter bore and was built by Backus Firearms, Limited.

"Yes," Teagan said. "That one's for mammalian bipeds. In spite of what you may have heard about the native life forms, the aliens, that's us, are still the most deadly species there. This is like the ancient wilderness frontier in your own America. People come to Maheux for the rich botanical diversity, the same way prospectors went to California and Alaska for the minerals. Several plants in the coastal and river rain forests have yielded some amazing drugs, including the ones you're taking. The people who found them made millions or billions of notes, and they've been followed here by other people who're looking for a quick win at nature's lottery.

"Most of them are honest and hard working. But others …" Teagan gave a small gesture to indicate that it was a shady situation. "They figure the best way to make a quick financial killing is to make a quick killing. Literally. Do you know what I mean?"

"Yes," Sharon nodded. "It was the same in the American west, or anywhere on Earth where law enforcement was thin and the stakes were high."

Teagan gave Sharon several clips of ammunition. "Don't waste any bullets. This isn't an AR game."

"AR?"

"Augmented Reality," the doll said before Teagan could reply. "Very popular among youths and adults of a similar maturity." The doll held its right hand like a gun and pretended to shoot. "Pew! Pew!"

Video games, Sharon realized. She strapped the weapons to the backpack like she'd been trained to do and then hefted the pack into the ground car.

The next item that Bear handed out was a bulky tan jumpsuit which everybody except the doll pulled on over their normal clothes.

"For the natives who are too small to fight with sword or gun," Teagan had explained.

As Sharon understood it, the cloth contained some sort of insect repellant that drove fear into whatever organs the natives used as hearts. It worked best for small, flying bugs, but not so much for creatures who were big enough to see a human as prey or competition.

The natives were not able to digest Earth-based life forms, but they didn't know that.

The doll just stood there watching. Teagan wouldn't allow it to have a weapon, and the natives were not interested in its artificial skin and blood, though they may still see it as a threat.

Finally, Bear handed out light-weight bottles of compressed nitrogen. The atmosphere of Maheux was nearly forty percent oxygen, and the supplemental nitrogen was needed to combat the effects of oxygen toxicity. It helped that the mean sea level air pressure of Maheux was only 850 millibars, keeping the partial pressure of oh-two to below thirty-five percent of a standard atmosphere, but oxygen toxicity is nasty stuff.

The pilot announced that they'd be landing in three hundred seconds and asked everybody to return to their seats and buckle in. They might be smugglers, but they didn't shirk on safety.

The landing itself was as smooth as it could have been, and Sharon wondered idly if the AI had landed it or if the pilot had landed it himself. Pips may be physically small, but you wouldn't know it by their egos. Especially the ego of a Pip who was also a pilot.

Once Bear was satisfied that everybody who needed to breathe was properly fitted with a nitrogen mask, he signaled to open the rear cargo door and reddish-yellow sunlight flooded through the threshold. The door became a short ramp, and Teagan walked out of the boat, shotgun at the ready. Scanners had indicated that the landing site was safe, but Teagan hadn't survived for over a century by relying solely on scanners. Bear started the electric motors of the ground car and drove it out. The rest followed on foot.

They were on a broad, flat plane. A small mountain range barely poked up above the horizon. Sharon turned in a circle and as far as she could tell, the entire landscape was a uniform mud colored ground with occasional yellowish scrub grass. Teagan and Bear were busy dealing with the vehicle, but everybody else seemed to be hypnotized by the desolation.

"Is this how you remember it, doll?" Sharon asked.

"Not entirely. I restricted *meine* movements to the *cuidad* during my last visit here."

"This is what most of the planet looks like," the pilot said. "There are some major rivers which meander all over the place, some jungles near the coast, and the ice caps, but most of this continent is a desert."

The continent had few large mountains, and most of those were near the coast. Most of the interior of the continent was as flat as the American Midwest. The rivers were fed by a shallow sea surrounding the polar ice cap like a moat surrounding an ice fortress.

Sharon realized with a start that this was the first time she'd been out in naked sunlight since waking up on the *Zephyr*. When she'd been outdoors on Kentaurus, the sky was always obscured with clouds.

The doll studied the color of the ground and Sharon could see that it wasn't entirely defenseless. As she watched, the doll's skin color changed to match the color of the desert. If the doll shed its clothes and walked fifty meters away, it would be nearly invisible.

"Neat trick, that," Sharon commented.

"I'll teach it to you someday," the doll replied with an absolutely straight face.

"Are we here to work or be tourists?" Teagan asked. "The bus departs as soon as you get your asses in the seat belts."

The ground car was a large, six-wheeled, open cab sort of thing with a retractable roof, which was currently retracted. The wheels were as large as the doll and made from cerama-steel interwoven bands. Like the doll's skin, the paint of the ground car could change color, and it currently matched the hue of the desert. The interior could seat ten people comfortably. There were controls for both a left- and right-side driver. The instrument panel was blank and the driver had to have an EPU or iGlasses interface in order to access the controls, whereupon the various indicators would appear as a heads-up display.

Teagan insisted on giving everybody in the party, aside from those that didn't have a true pulse, security access to the basic controls because "who knows who'll end up having to drive in an emergency." An air car would have been safer, but it would also have been easily detectable over large distances due to the grav field distortion generated by the engine.

Sharon double-checked the security of her nitro mask and stepped up onto the running boards, and then into the cab. Teagan hadn't been exaggerating about the immediate departure, and Sharon felt the car lurch forward as soon as she snapped the seatbelt into place. She turned to wave at the pilot, who'd be waiting impatiently by the radio for any kind of emergency call.

"What's the pilot's name?" Sharon asked. "We were never introduced."

"Aster," the doll said. "Aster, son of Lilly."

It was still early morning, but the primary star was already a couple of hours above the horizon. The ground car accelerated to about 120 kph, and the big tires and suspension were handling the irregularities of the terrain well.

They had landed far enough away from Wildeside to avoid interaction with the Wildeside aerospace traffic control, which meant well beyond the visual horizon. They also picked this landing spot so that they didn't have to cross any major rivers. The idea was to roll into Wildeside looking like they had just traversed the desert from some other town, or had been out prospecting. Nobody would check their IDs as they rolled into town.

Sharon's iGlasses displayed a map at her bidding, showing that they were about 1,660 kilometers from Wildeside. With stops to stretch their legs, and detours around obstructions, Sharon figured the trip would take a minimum of fourteen hours.

Though the primary star of Maheux was a bit darker than Sol, Maheux had a smaller orbit and the daylight was a bit glaring. Sharon adjusted the transparency of the iGlasses to a comfortable level to watch the rather boring landscape go by. This was one huge advantage that iGlasses had over EPUs. She experimented with the visual settings just to see what they were capable of. She quickly found ways to check the polarization of reflected light. By taking the ambient temperature and analyzing the rocks under near infrared and near ultraviolet, she found that the processor could make some interesting guesses about composition. Though invisible in visible light, Sharon could easily see where previous vehicles using pneumatic tires had compressed the soil, leaving trails.

Sharon was surprised when she found a setting on the iGlasses which amplified reflected sounds. Using the echoed sound of the ground car and the ambient air pressure and humidity, the iGlasses gave a readout on distances and densities of objects. This was something else again that the EPU couldn't do for her, as it was limited to human senses.

On the other hand, Sharon guessed that with an adequate EPU interface, the iGlasses could tell her much more, and she started thinking about how to use them to search for fossils and buried artifacts in the field.

*   *   *

Low Maheux Orbit

The planet Maheux was officially designated a frontier planet. It would never be colonized, but still came under the jurisdiction of the Kentauran Federal government, which assigned a governor and a local federal appellate court, and local human residents paid taxes to the Federal government, which disbursed it back to local projects and government agencies. The residents were citizens of Kentaurus and as such enjoyed the protection of a permanently crewed orbital facility which also acted as a customs office, which issued import/export licenses and charged a tax on everything that came and went. The tax was a minimal one percent of claimed value, and the favorite pastime on Maheux, besides watching sports games recorded on several planets, was complaining about the import tax, and claiming it was a method for controlling dissidents. The population was almost entirely dissidents, made up of people who thought Kentaurus, with an average population density of about six people per square kilometer of dry land, was too crowded.

The *KRS Zephyr* and the cargo ship *Entulessë* were both orbiting Maheux in orbits that kept them within easy gunshot of each other, and the targeting radar of the *Zephyr's* guns was a constant reminder of that fact. The crew of the *Entulessë* was playing it cool. They'd been in this situation before and refused to say anything without a company advocate available.

"You sent for me?" Daerîsiell asked, belatedly adding, "Captain?"

Souza motioned for the elf to sit down at the desk, and let the silence stretch on. She meticulously pulled out the photos of two people and laid them face up on the table.

257

Finally, she said, "Hospitalman third class Barischk from my own ship's company. We assumed he was left behind at Sedna due to our quick departure. Teagan Waugh, Lieutenant Commander, KRN Special Forces. Retired."

Daerîsiell looked at the photos and confirmed to herself that those were the correct individuals, but didn't respond.

"We found their DNA on the Entulessë when we searched it. Along with that of Carol Simmons and other individuals as yet unidentified. Care to enlighten me on why a member of my own ship's company was on board a suspected smuggling vessel?"

"We knew that Simmons had recruited Waugh," the elf actually looked abashed. "We didn't know about Barischk."

"You didn't think it was important to tell me about Waugh? And what do you mean, 'recruited'?"

"Actually, no. It wasn't important. It doesn't change the mission profile at all, except that now you know that Simmons is in the company of a decorated war hero with a proven loyalty to the Republic. And I use the word recruited because we don't really know what the circumstances are. We know that Simmons has a reason to be here. We don't know what Waugh's reasons are. Do you have any reason to doubt Barischk's loyalty?"

Souza shook her head. "Not until now. Aside from a penchant for gambling, his service record is clean. Bradford tells me he's been studying to take med school entrance exams."

"Gambling?" Daerîsiell said, as if that were important.

"Yes. Is that a factor?"

Daerîsiell wasn't sure, but wondered if the Furman had a habit of betting on the underdog, long shots, and inside straights. Daerîsiell had lied. She was pretty sure she knew what Waugh's motives were. It was the Furman who was the unknown variable. What was he doing here? "It might." She decided to change the subject. "Are we able to determine where the boat from the *Entulessë* landed?"

"No. We were not even able to determine for sure that there was a boat. We are assuming a boat because the people we expected to find on the *Entulessë* aren't there, and because it was an expected tactic. But the pilot of that boat, should she exist, is quite good. She kept the planet between them and us the whole time during her descent to the surface. At this time, we are assuming that it landed either at Wildeside or within walking distance of it.

"Is there anything else at all about this mission which is going to surprise me and cause me to spill coffee on my uniform?" Souza asked.

The elf smiled when she saw that there really was a coffee stain still damp on Souza's blouse.

"Only if it also causes me to spill my coffee, Captain."

19

Maheux Desert
1350 km from Wildeside
Kentauran calendar: 14 Skoteinómína, 1383 PS

I T WAS ILLEGAL FOR NON-NATIVES, be they bears or humans or elves or wolf-men, to shit in the woods on Maheux. Aliens were required to carry all solid excretory products with them back to the human settlement for disposal by incineration or to be used as fertilizer for the earth-based crops. As far as she knew, though, there was no requirement concerning robots.

Sharon could see what had inspired this law, but saw little use in the practice. If the law was intended to protect the native biome from non-native biota, it was too late. As soon as the first human had exhaled the first unfiltered breath on Maheux, the biome had been contaminated. Earth microbes were already competing with Maheux microbes for food and space. What the result of that would eventually be was the subject of vigorous ongoing research, but Sharon had no idea. She suspected that the native biota had the home-court advantage under a sun that was a different color than Sol and an atmosphere of different composition from Earth's, but it was just a guess, and she knew that microbes were awfully good at adapting to hostile environments. She knew that the native carnivores were unable to digest Earth based protein, but that didn't stop them from interacting on other levels.

Travelers leaving Maheux for, or arriving from, other human occupied worlds were required to go through a decontamination process, though Sharon also suspected that this had limited effectiveness. What about those who circumvented the normal travel restrictions, just as they were doing now? The law seemed to be impossible to enforce. Sharon was certain that the human presence on Maheux had permanently altered the course of local evolution. She entertained herself by imagining a scenario where life on Earth was the result of aliens taking a crap in the primordial sea.

"That would explain a few things," she mused.

Regardless of all this, they were making an effort to conform to the spirit of the law. They had come across a small oasis where the ground water formed a small lake in an old impact crater and native trees, with leaves that looked more like either needles or feathers, depending on the species, grew in abundance. They set up a privacy tent with a toilet which collected their waste and took turns relieving themselves, and each exited the tent carrying a small green bag of would-be contamination.

While the others took their turns, Sharon used her iGlasses to zoom in on and record images and data on native animals. She could see that they were all arthropods and had segmented bodies, but beyond that the species tended to vary wildly. Not all of them had only three body segments. In fact, the average seemed to be five. There was a colony of something that resembled squirrel-sized ants. All of these "ants" had wings, but didn't seem to spend a lot of time actually flying. The center of their activity was a huge ant hill, easily three meters across.

There weren't any of the winged giants she'd heard so much about, and guessed that the oasis was too small to support larger predators.

Sharon was surprised to see flowers. On Earth, flowering plants did not appear until a hundred million years after dinosaurs appeared and some fifty million years after the appearance of mammals. There had never been any dinosaurs or mammals on Maheux. Indeed, there had never been any native land-based vertebrates, and it would seem that the flowers were not willing to wait for them.

Sharon's attention was drawn to a commotion at the ground car, and she turned to see Bear, Teagan, and Tith arguing about something. After a minute of this, Teagan seemed to gain the advantage in the disagreement and announced over their network, RETURN TO THE CAR. WE'VE RECEIVED A DISTRESS CALL, AND WE ARE DIVERTING FROM OUR COURSE TO ASSIST.

Tith was upset about this, and Bear's reaction was subdued.

"On my way," Sharon responded.

They quickly disassembled the privy tent, cleaned and re-stowed the equipment. People didn't seem to be rushing around in fireman-like hurry, and nobody was offering an explanation.

Once they were again rushing across the desert, Sharon asked, "What's the situation?"

Teagan and Tith regarded each other. Both looked like they didn't want to be bothered with the answer.

Finally, Teagan said, "A group of prospectors have a ground car that's inoperative."

"It's a trap," Tith said.

"Very likely," Teagan agreed. "However, we can't ignore it."

"Aren't we legally required to offer assistance to stranded travelers?" Sharon asked.

"Which makes it the *método* perfect for ambush other travelers," the doll offered. "But I agree *mit* Teagan."

"Seems to me we can prepare for a potential ambush," Sharon said.

"Which is exactly what we'll do," Teagan said. "Just like any other sane and experienced desert traveler."

"How do we do that?" Sharon asked.

THAT'S WHERE I COME IN, Bear said. AND THE DOLL.

"Say *qué?*" the doll said, obviously surprised by its upcoming role.

"We're going to park just out of weapons range, and Bear and the doll are going in on foot. If everything checks good, the rest of us join them."

Sharon watched the doll's face as it considered its options. Teagan obviously considered it to be expendable, but this was a good time to make a good impression.

"I'll need medical equipment and a weapon," it said.

I HAVE THE MEDICAL BAG, Bear said. He was, after all, a medical corpsmen.

Just as Teagan was saying "No" to the weapon, Sharon slid out her shotgun and gave it to the doll, then dug into her pack for extra rounds. Teagan saw this and glared at Sharon.

"I thought you didn't trust the doll," Teagan said. "What was it you asked me when I let it loose? I believe your exact words were, 'What were you thinking?'"

"Things have evolved," Sharon said. "Besides, you still own the remote to the explosive on her back."

"Thank you," the doll said.

DO YOU KNOW HOW TO USE THAT? Bear asked.

"*Todos* in Alemanni carry *Waffen*," the doll said. "I also went through basic training. I'll give you *lecciones* sometime."

Sharon smiled. "Etta Place."

The doll looked at her questioningly.

Sharon repeated, "I hereby name you Etta Place. Companion to famous American outlaws long before the Singularity. Known to be an excellent shot. Some say she met Butch and Sundance in a brothel."

Nobody responded, and Sharon chose to interpret that as unanimous consent, although it was more likely that after thirteen centuries it was an indication that nobody else remembered the names.

They stopped the groundcar about a kilometer from the reported location of the distress call. Before the car quite came to a stop, Tith was standing up, supporting himself on the rollbar, scanning the area with optics and RF detectors.

After a few seconds of looking through a binocular-like device, he pointed northwest. Sharon used her iGlasses, set the zoom to max, and saw another ground car. It was large, about the size of a long-distance bus or motorhome. Access panels had been removed, and somebody was obviously trying to repair something. Some of the cargo had been offloaded and set around the car in what looked like suspiciously strategic locations, though it could have as easily been just random placement.

"Any radio?" Teagan asked.

"Only their distress signal."

"Could there be a tight laser transmission?" Teagan said.

"Could be anything if you're paranoid enough," Sharon said.

Bear jumped down from the car then reached up and lifted Etta from the car, placing the doll gently on the ground. Teagan gave Bear a radio.

"Won't we be able to chat?" Sharon asked.

WITHOUT AN EXTERNAL NETWORK, WE'LL BE BEYOND RANGE FOR A LOCAL EPU SETUP, Bear said. THIS WILL KEEP US CONNECTED AS LONG AS THEY AREN'T JAMMING THE FREQUENCIES.

After Bear turned the device on, Sharon saw a prompt in her field of view to join a local network. She gestured to accept.

"Just how dangerous is this for Bear and Etta?" Sharon asked Teagan.

"The other travelers will see us parked out here and know that we have them covered. They have no way of knowing what kind of firepower we have."

"Would the boat be able to give us any air support?"

"I'm not going to risk the boat in an action like this. If we get into overwhelming trouble, the boat will return to the *Entulessë*," Tith said. "Your next of kin will be notified."

Sharon supposed that was a very reasonable thing for a smuggler to say. Tith then surprised her by pulling another weapon from beneath the floorboards of the car. It came out in five parts and Tith assembled them expertly.

"Would you plug me in?" he said, offering a very thick power cord to Teagan, who plugged it into the car's instrument panel.

The weapon was a 13mm bore railgun with a two-meter muzzle. Teagan helped Tith mount it to a swivel joint on the top rollbar of the car. The last thing Tith attached was an optical telescopic sighting device. Tith saw Sharon's slack jaw and winked.

"Muzzle velocity is thirty-two hundred meters per second, Gidget. In this thin atmosphere, that's about Mach 10." Then he turned to Bear. "We've got you covered, Wolfman."

It seemed like an eternity for Bear and Etta to travel the thousand meters to the distressed vehicle, but by the iGlasses' timer, it was less than five minutes. Bear traveled with a distance eating two-legged lope, and Etta sprinted the entire way, covering it in one-third the time any of the others in their party could have done. The doll wasn't any stronger than the humans, but it was nearly indefatigable, and didn't have to catch its breath.

They slowed when they were within a hundred meters and stopped fifty meters out. Sharon had set up her 'Glasses to show a window from Bear's point of view, along with audio.

"Hello!" shouted Etta. "Did you send for help?"

A man dressed in desert khakis walked toward them and stopped when Etta shouted, "That's far enough. State the nature of your emergency?"

The man shouted back in an unrecognizable accent. "We've a disabled car and injuries. We were attacked by rogues."

Sharon saw Bear call up voice analysis applications in his EPU, but she didn't know how to interpret what she saw.

"We need transport for the injured!" the man said. "They're stable, but won't stay that way long."

"What do you think, *Herr Lobo*?" Etta asked quietly. "Do you trust them?"

Bear just shook his head and gestured broadly for the man to approach. He came alone and apparently unarmed. "At least he's cooperative," Etta said.

As the man came within five meters, he stopped abruptly as he got a good look at both rescuers. "Well, I'll be the illegitimate whelp of a mangy hellhound," he said. "A Furman and a doll!"

"How did he know Etta is a doll?" Sharon asked.

"Quiet!" Tith ordered.

Teagan whispered, "It just sprinted a thousand meters without being out of breath, and her skin is milk-white. What would you conclude?"

The man thought about his situation for about a second and a half and then offered his hand. "Name's Enasmat Gartzah.

Came from Olympia in the Centauri system, but now out of Wildeside." Gartzah had a deep, rough, crackly voice that sounded like it could be used to smooth out the rough spots on hard wood.

"*Herr* Gartzah, it's a pleasure to meet you," Etta said with a smile that would put the sun to shame and shook his hand. "I'm Etta Place von Alemanni on Kentaurus, *und* this is Barischk de Lupus Prime."

"Thank you for responding to our distress signal. What do I need to do to get you to bring your transport in to pick up our injured?"

"You can give us a tour of your encampment," Etta said. "And let's take a look at your injured. I'm sure they would like to be on their way back to Wildeside."

"This way, then, ah ... Etta?" Gartzah said as he gestured for them to follow.

"Yes," Etta said, using professional charm. "I only just recently acquired the name. It's the name of a *berüchtigt* American outlaw. Perhaps you've heard of her."

"I don't know anything of outlaws," Gartzah said almost too quickly. "But I know a woman in Wildeside who'd pay high money for a doll of your quality."

"I'm currently not for sale, *Herr* Gartzah," Etta said as if the topic came up every day.

The tour took them immediately to a tent set up to keep the injured. The interior of the tent was warm in spite of the chilly day, and there were three injured people — a man and two women — laying on cots. All of them had intravenous fluids, and blood showed on the bandages of one.

As soon as they entered the tent, the radio reception became poor, and decreased in quality with time. Sharon became nervous in spite of a reassuring nod from Teagan. Tith changed the settings on the railgun's sights to infrared and was able to follow the party into the tent.

Gartzah introduced Kedija Russom, who was somebody with medical training, though not a physician. Sharon couldn't quite understand the word through the interference. They were then introduced to a woman in a cot who reportedly had a compound fracture.

"*Herr* Bear would like to examine the break," Etta said.

"No!" Russom insisted. "I have set it, and it's healing."

"Don't they have EPUs?" Sharon asked. "Why isn't Bear talking to them?"

"I don't like this," Tith said. "Start the car."

Teagan slid back into the left-hand driver's seat, turned on the power and engaged the transmission, but kept a foot on the brake.

The radio static increased, as well as the level of disagreement between Etta and Russom. Then there was the sound of gunfire and the signal from Bear's EPU died at the same time Tith said, "I can't see them! I've lost them!"

"Floor it!" Sharon ordered, even as the car was already accelerating.

She was forced into her seat by the acceleration as the car went from zero to 120 kph in fourteen seconds and sped across in intervening distance. She pulled the Backus with her right hand and the cutlass with her left and was preparing to jump to the ground as soon as the car rolled to a stop. As they approached within two hundred meters of the encampment, somebody, or more likely multiple somebodies, started shooting at them with automatic rifles. Teagan immediately started swerving the vehicle evasively.

Tith pulled the trigger on the railgun, and the world was filled with the sound of a daemon in exquisite agony that instantly set Sharon's ears ringing. After an immeasurably short time, one of the cargo boxes disintegrated. It didn't explode. Tith knew better than to use explosives on this planet. The boxes disintegrated from the kinetic energy of the hypersonic projectiles, with pieces flying away from the point of impact.

The ambushers didn't stop shooting, but they did change tactics. Instead of hunkering down in one spot, they would shoot from one location, run to some other random location and shoot from there. With three or four ambushers running and shooting, it looked like some frenetic sport.

Sharon ducked behind the wall of the car and took pot shots at the ambushers, but two hundred meters was just too long of a range for a handgun. She had very little experience with this type of thing and couldn't get a good shot in.

Teagan had pulled the ground car into a path parallel with the encampment, driving with the left hand and shooting with the right.

Tith pulled the trigger on the railgun twice more, causing more damage to nearby ears. More cargo boxes disintegrated and the ambushers were running out of places to hide.

Teagan made a sharp U-turn, and was now driving right-handed and shooting with the left. There seems to be no end of Teagan's talents, Sharon thought.

There was a bright light, followed half a second later by a roar that would have completely masked the sound of the railgun. It was as if the entire world exploded. Fed by the high oxygen level in the atmosphere, the fire ball was huge and orange and grew at an incredible speed. The 'Glasses and the nitrogen mask were torn from Sharon's face by the blast and the car actually lifted off the ground flying sideways, though it somehow managed to avoid turning over. Sharon found herself in freefall for what seemed like several horrible moments. The car slammed into the ground and she hit her head on something solid.

Debris started raining about them. Hot, sharp shards of metal and ceramic and dirt clods were falling everywhere. Sharon was able to work through the pain in her head to take cover under a bench seat. That's when she noticed that Tith was missing. She felt something warm and liquid flowing down her face. She knew what it was, but that didn't stop her from feeling the gooey wetness and looking at her fingers. Blood.

Her vision was darkening at the edges and she felt her mind slipping.

She called, "Teagan!"

No answer.

She slipped into unconsciousness.

*   *   *

There's a big difference between being unconscious and being asleep. Sleep brings dreams and a sense of the passage of time. Unconsciousness brings neither. Sharon went from unconsciousness into sleep, and dreamed of climbing a very tall spiral staircase towards a light. The light expanded as she approached until she recognized it as the orangish daylight of Maheux. She was still under the seat in the ground car and had no idea how much time had passed.

She pulled herself painfully out from beneath the seat and looked instantly for Teagan, who was still buckled into the driver's seat, slumped over the controls. Sharon quickly checked for a carotid pulse. It was weak. She then checked for broken bones and open wounds.

Teagan was breathing. He was also openly bleeding from a chest wound which looked far too ragged to have come from a bullet. Sharon looked quickly around for Tith and didn't see him.

She did see the iGlasses laying in the corner of the passenger compartment, and they seemed to be intact. Sharon put them on and activated them, and after three seconds she was rewarded with a login screen. She entered Muskrat Smith's password.

"Where's Tithfinthor?" she asked the 'Glasses.

A text message appeared: UNABLE TO LOCATE SUBJECT.

Tith would have to wait. Hopefully, he was just out of range.

With some experimenting, Sharon was able to get the driver's seat to recline so that Teagan was laying almost horizontally. There was an awful lot of blood. Could somebody lose that much and still live? There weren't any visible head wounds, and she surmised that Teagan's continued unconsciousness was due to blood loss.

She opened a panel in the wall of the car which had the universal symbol of a white cross on a green square and pulled out an emergency medical kit from its secured spot, then opened Teagan's bug-repelling coveralls, and then the shirt. She had wondered what Hermans' breasts looked like, and now she knew, but this was no time to play comparative anatomy.

"Assess wound," Sharon ordered the 'Glasses, which interfaced with the processor in the medical kit.

This time an audio response came, but she was almost unable to hear it, and realized that her hearing hadn't yet recovered from the explosion.

"Acute full thickness laceration of the dermis involving active bleeding from thoracic vein. Subject is unconscious, but breathing. Emergency medical treatment and immediate transport to trauma center are necessary. Intravenous blood products to replace loss is highly recommended."

"Wonderful," Sharon said bleakly. "Suggest emergency treatment, assuming that I don't have access to intravenous blood products."

"There is artificial blood in the trauma kit," the 'Glasses corrected her.

Indeed, there was. The iGlasses highlighted a silvery container which opened at her touch. Inside was a red bag marked ARTIFICIAL BLOOD – TYPE HUMAN. Sharon had no idea how it worked, but it had the great advantage of being able to store it at room temperature for long periods, and it didn't matter what blood type the recipient was, as long as they were human.

"What do I do?" she asked.

The response was immediate "First, apply dermal sealant to stop bleeding and to protect the wound from further infection. Be sure to clean the wound of any foreign matter first."

"Highlight any foreign matter in the wound."

After several seconds of scanning, the glasses decided that there wasn't any foreign matter in the wound and advised Sharon of this.

Sharon looked at the medical kit and the dermal sealant was highlighted by the 'Glasses. She picked it up and read the instructions quickly. Then she broke the seal, shook the can for a count of five and sprayed the contents over the wound like spray paint.

The contents came out looking like some kind of stringy putty, which settled into the wound and filled it. As Sharon watched, the bleeding stopped and the sealant changed color to indicate that it had set.

"Okay, what next?"

"Second, start the IV."

Sharon fought a rising panic. Normally, Bear would be in charge of this. He knew how to start IVs and wouldn't have to ask an AI how to save Teagan's life. Sharon found a telescoping rod device in the trauma kit which clamped to the seat and suspended the bag from it.

"Apply the tube to any accessible vein," the 'Glasses told her. Without being told, the iGlasses shifted something in its perception parameters, and then drew virtual lines on Teagan's body to show where the veins were.

Looking at the business end of the IV tube, Sharon could see a small mechanical device that included two LEDs and an indicator arrow.

"Line up the indicator with any accessible vein," the AI instructed.

Sharon placed the device against a vein in Teagan's arm which the iGlasses considerately labeled as the median vein.

That would have come in really handy during the anatomy and physiology class, Sharon thought.

To Sharon's amazement, the device attached itself to Teagan's arm and inserted the IV needle. A red light shown briefly on the device and shifted to green once the processor was sure that everything was working.

Sharon hadn't realized she was holding her breath until it escaped, accompanied by an intense feeling of relief. "Okay. Next?"

"Third, cover the patient with a medical blanket."

Sharon pulled a silver blanket out of its container in the trauma kit and turned it on. It would monitor Teagan's condition as well as help reduce shock. The iGlasses immediately interfaced with the blanket and created a window to display Teagan's vitals. Sharon tucked the blanket under Teagan's arms and legs.

"Okay, next?"

"Secure patient's nitrogen mask, and transport as quickly and safely as possible to a medical facility. Remember to hydrate the patient."

After resetting Teagan's mask, Sharon determined that she'd done what she could for the Herman. She found her own mask still hanging by the hose attaching it to the compressed gas cylinder and set it back on her face. She looked out at the damaged encampment and saw the motorhome-like vehicle completely engulfed in incredibly bright flames fed by the high oxygen content of the atmosphere.

There were two or three smoldering bodies which she could actually identify as human remains with the 'Glasses at max zoom. Her immediate thought was to run in looking for Bear and Etta, but then remembered her own wounds.

She pulled a mirror out of the medical kit and examined her head. The bleeding had stopped, but it looked messy. Her short hair was matted with blood, and the side of her face was covered with it. The wound was ugly, and looked deep, but small. She'd have to clean it. And, she admitted, find some pain medication. But it could wait.

Sharon sat in the right-hand driver's seat and tried the power button while accessing the HUD. Ready lights and some warning lights answered her query on systems status.

"You're one tough buggy," She told the car and gave it an admiring stroke on the instrument panel.

According to the warning icons, there was some structural damage and the headlights were inoperative.

"Don't need headlights."

She engaged the transmission, took hold of the steering wheel and stepped on the go-pedal.

The car tried to respond. First it lurched forward then came to a stop, and another warning icon came on to indicate that the transmission was jammed. Sharon put it in reverse, depressed the throttle slowly, and the car lurched backwards, then rolled smoothly.

"I hope that fixed it," she told nobody as she put the transmission in forward again.

The car rolled forward tentatively and accelerated very slowly, topping off at 30 kph. Text appeared in the HUD: Damage limiting safety procedures engaged.

"That'll have to do."

Sharon turned towards the burning wreckage, instructing the 'Glasses to scan for survivors and radio signals. As soon as she was close enough, she started shouting for Bear and Etta. The only response was the sound of the burning groundcar.

The explosion had cleared away almost everything else. Where the triage tent had been, she could only guess. There was certainly nothing there now. If Bear and Etta had been caught in this explosion, they would not now be alive. This thought brought out another rising panic, and Sharon pushed it back with a force of will.

What had caused the explosion? Did Tith hit something with the railgun? A fuel tank? No. The burning groundcar was electric, like the one Sharon was driving. Then Sharon remembered the only explosive device that was known to be in the encampment: The device Teagan had attached to the small of Etta's back.

Sharon turned back the way she'd come and started a sweeping search for Tith. She gave herself ten minutes, at the end of which she'd abandon the search and start driving. Getting Teagan to medical care would have to be the highest priority. But where? It would be quicker to go back to the boat, but she had no guarantee that Aster would still be there, and Tith had plainly said that Aster's only response to trouble would be to send thoughts and prayers. The elven drug cartel wasn't going to risk any more expensive spaceships on this venture.

To Wildeside, then.

"iGlasses, show me the quickest route to Wildeside."

A green arrow appeared in front of the car pointing south. Text indicated that it was 1301 kilometers distant.

20

G ABRIELLA SOUZA JEALOUSLY GUARDED HER TIME in the ship's gym. As captain of the *Zephyr* she was on call every minute of every day, but people tended to give her extra space and consideration when she was exercising. She was a fit woman of a youthful 70 Kentauran years and stayed fit by treating her workout routine with almost religious reverence.

Her routine was always the same: first calisthenics and weight training, then aerobics, which consisted of a 10-kilometer run on the treadmill and a two-kilometer swim in the resistance pool. Then she put on shorts, shoes, and gloves and imagined the faces of the most exasperating people on a punching bag. After fifteen minutes of this, she became aware of somebody watching her.

277

"What can I do for you, Agent?" Souza turned to face the elven security officer.

"I hope that's not my face you're seeing on that bag," Daerîsiell said.

"And if it was?"

"Then I'd say that you're investing way too much into our work relationship."

The two women regarded each other like two predators getting ready to fight over a piece of meat. The elf had the advantages of reach and speed, but the human had the advantages of mass and power. It would be an interesting contest, Souza thought.

"I just have a question, Captain. One I thought best to ask without audience and without record."

"Go ahead."

"How well do you trust Dr. Bradford?"

The question took Souza completely by surprise. "I let him see me naked twice a year. So I trust him with my life. Why?"

"There are some … inconsistencies with his report. Worrisome omissions."

"Have you spoken to him about it?"

"Not yet. I needed confirmation."

"You mean ammunition?" Souza asked. The question hung there like an accusation.

"We have the same goal, Captain. To find the people who turned a member of your ship's company into somebody else. A saboteur, a spy, and a murderer."

"And we followed her here because you think she'll run back to the responsible parties."

"She told me as much," Daerîsiell said. "And what would you do in her place?"

Souza's first instinct was to land her marines in Wildeside and start kicking butts. And when she was a junior officer, that would have been her action of choice. But she was older now. More seasoned, better at the art of war. Had they landed with a heavy foot, the perpetrators, assuming they were still on Maheux, would have gone into hiding, and the Navy would have had little success in smoking them out, especially if they were as well funded as Souza suspected they were.

"Why are you convinced that Manders will find the people who created her? I have little faith in this tactic." Souza said.

"Because Sharon Manders is intelligent and resourceful. She's picked up some capable allies along the way. And I believe that once the people who did this know she's in Wildeside, they'll go out of their way to collect her. If for no other reason than to study her. Find out what went wrong. It's all over the 'Nets that she saved hundreds of lives at the attack in Clarksport. Some people are calling her a hero. The people we're looking for didn't intend to make a hero, and they'll want to know what went wrong."

The human walked briskly up to the elf and they stood well within each other's personal space. "Tell me. Tell me you didn't intentionally let her escape on Sedna."

Daerîsiell's reply was cut off by a gesture from Souza when Lieutenant Commander Lagrueux's voice in her head. "Captain, surveillance has picked up an explosion on the planet's surface, thirteen hundred kilometers north of Wildeside. High altitude recon images show a burning ground car and tracks leading away, towards the city."

"I'll be right there, Commander," Souza said. "Get a drone to follow the tracks." She looked at Daerîsiell and started peeling the gloves off and walking towards the showers. "That's my cue, Agent. We need to talk about this some more."

"Of course."

Souza was still in the shower when she received a chat request from Lt. Berg. She continued to scrub as she said, "Yes, Lieutenant?"

"Ma'am, I've found something that may be of interest. It seems that Crewman Simmons received a message from somebody inside the ship just before the bomb exploded."

Souza turned off the water. This was serious. "From who?"

"Unable to determine that, ma'am. It was encoded."

"But it went through the ship's servers, right?"

"Yes, ma'am. But the server log data and message metadata is garbage. We are working on this now."

"Let me make sure I have this correct, Mr. Berg: Someone inside the ship's hull, and therefore in the ship's company, sent an encoded message to somebody we suspect planted a bomb, and nobody noticed?"

"Yes, ma'am. We found it when we started looking for it specifically."

"How did the suspects get past our server security?"

Berg was slow to respond, then simply repeated, "We're working on that now, ma'am."

"Concentrate on finding the identity of the person who sent the encoded message."

"Aye, ma'am."

"Souza out."

As soon as she was sure that nobody was listening and recording, she let out a string of epithets in the proud tradition of sailors all over the galaxy.

*   *   *

Maheux Desert
Epsilon Eridani
12.6 light-years from Kentaurus
Kentauran calendar: Protosmina 21, 1383 PS

A desert colored aircar flew around the site of the burnt-out ground car at an altitude of fifteen meters. The pilot was trying to remain in stealth, so he kept the navaids off, even in the black of a moonless night.

"Any guesses as to what exploded?" the first non-descript man asked the second.

"Did they blow it up intentionally?"

"That's a risky move in this atmosphere."

"Looks like they paid the price, too," the second man said, indicating the smoldering bodies.

Burrowing insects had come up from the ground and were scavenging the bodies for their water content.

"Should we stop and investigate?"

Before the second man could respond, a warning light appeared in the HUD. "We've been painted with radar," the first said.

Three seconds later, a low flying drone zoomed past at about thirty meters altitude and two hundred klicks headed south. They were only able to see it by the anti-collision lights.

"That was a Navy drone. Let's vacate before it circles back. Head west, and then we'll circle back towards Wildeside."

"Wait!"

"What?"

The first man pointed at a dark figure standing fifteen meters away. It was definitely a humanoid walking with crutch.

"Turn on the light."

A spotlight illuminated a masculine figure wearing torn clothing and suffering from multiple cuts and bruises. He was

Memory and Metaphor

leaning on an improvised crutch and shading his eyes from the light with his hand.

"Is that an elf?" The second man asked.

"I believe you are correct. Put the car down."

"Quickly. Before the drone circles back."

The car extended its landing gear and set down softly. The second man exited the car while the first pulled out a handgun to cover him.

"Are you okay?" the second man asked. "Were you caught in the explosion? Did you see it?"

The elf didn't look good. Aside from the injuries, there were several insect bites on his face, arms and exposed flesh. He looked weak and about to collapse.

In spite of this, the elf managed to pull himself erect and gave a polite bow. "Sir. May I trouble you for some water?"

A message came over the second man's EPU from the first. LEAVE HIM TO DIE! WE CAN'T AFFORD TO GET DISTRACTED.

WAIT! HE MAY HAVE SEEN SOMETHING.

The second man pulled a water bottle out of the car, opened it, and handed it to the elf who drank it with desperation, but the act and the water seemed to calm him. He finished all but the last few swallows and then took three faltering steps to the left. The second man didn't realize that this put him directly between the elf and the first man. With suddenness that gave the second man very little time to react, the elf tossed the nearly empty water bottle in his face. By the time the second man recovered, the blade of a sword rested against his throat.

"Elf tech," the elf said. "You've gotta love it. Did you know I can hear your private chats?"

The first man had no clear shot and was pulling himself out of the car.

"Another step, and your friend here will never need another haircut!"

All three of them became very still.

"Now, all I want is a ride into Wildeside before the Navy gets here. Can we all agree on a mutual goal? Surely we speak the same monetary language."

"Okay," the first man said. "Let's talk."

21

Kentauran calendar: 15 Skoteinómína, 1383 PS

D AYS ON MAHEUX ARE SHORT — about ten standard hours. Sharon had watched the primary star race westward with disturbing speed. The sunset lasted only a few minutes, though the twilight was enough to see by for another hour. Sharon had set the car to driverless operations and wondered if the car would be able to continue in that mode without headlights, as she had no intention of stopping.

In contrast to the speedy primary star, the featureless landscape crawled by with agonizing slowness, even as Sharon tried to get the vehicle to speed up by force of will. She was living in a society which traveled between stars at many multiples of the speed of light, but she was stuck going thirty kilometers an hour. She hadn't actually looked at the path the car was following for hours, but now she did and was surprised to see other sets of tire tracks in the sand. Did that mean they were going the right direction?

The sunset had brought a strong wind from the west which pelted Sharon with sand. She tried to raise the roof on the groundcar, but the railgun obstructed its path. Sharon tried to disassemble it, but no amount of pulling and turning and cranking would reveal how it came apart. She settled on placing a towel over Teagan's face and sitting with her back to the wind and wrapped a blanket around herself.

The bag of artificial blood had emptied after thirty minutes, and the little device had withdrawn the needle, applied a dollop of dermal sealant, then remained inert. Sharon applied some antibiotic to the puncture wound and covered it to protect it from the sand and dust.

As twilight failed, Sharon shifted her iGlasses to near-infrared so that she could see the ground in front of the car, which continued unfailingly southwards towards Wildeside, at a very steady, very frustrating, thirty kilometers per hour. And since Kentauran hours are longer than Earth hours, the speed was even slower. The first settlers on the planet discovered that the diurnal period was twenty-six hours and thirty-three minutes long. Since they had no communication with Earth and, in order to keep the day twenty-four hours long, they simply divided the diurnal period into twenty-four parts and called it an hour. Nobody cared that it was over ten percent longer than a traditional hour. Since nobody used Earth-based clocks anymore, there wasn't an issue.

At that speed, it would take Sharon nearly two days to drive to Wildeside. She tried overriding the damage limiting safety procedures, but the car stubbornly refused to comply. Even after Sharon explained to it that Teagan could die in mere hours, the car remained soullessly taciturn.

She tried to get Teagan to drink water, which was a tedious job placing a small amount in Teagan's mouth and hoping the swallow reflex would engage before the gag reflex did. She found more blankets in somebody's backpack and covered the Herman, who moaned and stirred, and Sharon hoped that it was a sign that the Teagan was improving.

Sharon herself was feeling quite depressed, and recognized this as partly due to survivor's guilt. They had started the day with five in their group — six if you counted Aster — and now it was just the two of them. Perhaps she'd be the lone survivor before she reached Wildeside. Had she brought them all to their deaths? One fact which could not be ignored was that if she hadn't woken up in the sickbay of the *Zephyr*, all these people would still be alive and whole. She even felt guilt for Etta's demise.

"Radio signals detected," the iGlasses informed her.

"What?" Sharon's attention was instantly sharp. "Where from? Can you resolve them?"

The iGlasses seemed to consider this, then offered an option to tap into the car's transceiver.

"Do it!" Sharon ordered.

The signal was very staticky, but Sharon thought she could hear the voice of a Pip in the background.

"Hello?" Sharon said. "Aster, is that you?"

More static.

"Aster, this is Sharon. The car is damaged. Teagan is seriously injured. The others are missing. Can you help?"

Still more static.

"Signal lost," the iGlasses reported. Sharon slammed her fist down repeatedly on the seat cushion and screamed.

She only stopped screaming when the iGlasses flashed a signal in Teagan's medical window:

Alert! Patient experiencing difficulty breathing!
Alert! Patient experiencing difficulty breathing!

Sharon tossed off the blanket and jumped to Teagan's side. She couldn't see much because the iGlasses were still in the wrong spectrum. She switched back to the visible spectrum and turned on an overhead light attached to the rollbar under the railgun. The Herman's face looked unbalanced, and she noticed distended neck veins.

"What's going on? Give me a report!"

"Patient is experiencing cyanosis, and displaying hypotension. Probable cause: Tension pneumothorax."

Sharon only paused a heartbeat. "What do I do for it?"

"In the trauma kit, you'll find a needle for relieving the pneumothorax. Look now," the iGlasses ordered.

Sharon opened the kit again, and a green luminous arrow appeared. She dug around, following the arrow, until she found a highlighted kit with the words NEEDLE THORACOSTOMY on it. She opened the kit and found directions written in several languages, but she didn't have time for this.

"What now?" she asked the medical AI.

"Open the kit and take out the device, which is a needle, a cannula and a valve. You'll find an adjustment for the length."

"I see it," Sharon said.

"For this patient, set needle length to thirty-eight point one millimeters."

Sharon spun the ratcheting dial until the correct numbers lined up with an indicator. "Okay."

"Swab the patient's chest with an antiseptic."

Sharon pulled off the medical blanket and opened Teagan's overalls again. "Where?"

"Second intercostal space, midclavicular line."

Once again, the medical processor thoughtfully provided an overlay of the area to be swabbed.

Sharon located the area and swabbed it with a spray and a disposable wipe. Even though Teagan was unconscious, the Herman was clearly in distress.

"Okay. Now what?"

"Insert the needle perpendicular to the chest wall at the level of the superior border of the third rib all the way to the stop on the needle." A crosshair appeared in the appropriate spot.

"Sorry, Teagan. This is going to hurt like hell." Sharon removed the protective cap from the needle and raised her arm in preparation to plunge the needle into the Herman's chest when the car hit a severe bump that the already damaged suspension wasn't able to compensate for. She was momentarily airborne and fell on her keister.

"Son of a ..." Sharon screamed while rubbing her butt. "What did we hit?"

"There was an unexpected and undetected variation in the zee axis of the planetary surface," the iGlasses informed her uselessly.

"You mean we hit a bump in the road? You could have said that!"

The 'Glasses didn't have a programmed response to the admonition. Sharon stood and looked back along the direction they'd come from.

"What's that noise?"

"Unknown."

Sharon switched the iGlasses back to near-infrared, and saw something that made her heart jump into high gear. From the large "variation in the zee axis", creatures were crawling out of the ground and took flight. After buzzing confusedly for a moment, they seemed to sight in on the lights of the ground car, and started to give chase.

"What are those?" Sharon asked.

"They are locally known as ground wasps," the iGlasses said. "They are burrowing insectoids with five body sections, measuring a total of about one meter in length. They remain dormant during dry seasons, but will emerge if disturbed. They are quick to anger, and have stingers that are fifteen centimeters long. They'll want to harvest the water from your body. They have been known to kill and dissect large imported mammals, such as sheep and cattle. They have been seven recorded human deaths due to ground wasps."

"How fast can they fly?" Sharon asked.

"According to the local database, their flight has been clocked at between thirty and thirty-five kilometers per hour."

Judging by their approach, Sharon estimated that these were closer to the thirty-five kilometer per hour variety, and that the closest would overtake them in about twenty seconds. Sharon didn't even take time to think about it. She turned and plunged the needle into Teagan's chest. She opened the valve and was rewarded with a rush of air and some blood.

Teagan's discomfort immediately decreased and his breathing became much more relaxed. Sharon closed the valve, recovered Teagan with the medical blanket, then reached over to her backpack to pull out the cutlass and the shotgun.

"I have had it with this planet up to my fucking eyeballs," she said angrily, walking to the back of the car.

She aimed the shotgun with her left hand, waited for the wasp to come within killing distance, and pulled the trigger.

The shotgun nearly leaped out of her grip with the recoil, and the wasp pretty much disintegrated in an explosion of bug guts.

It would have been nice if the other wasps had taken that as a warning and backed off, but Sharon knew that's not how insects reacted. If anything, they were further agitated by the smell of their comrade's demise.

The eerie green image of another wasp came from another angle. Sharon adjusted her aim, pulled the trigger again, and the second insect exploded.

How far would they chase her? Sharon had no idea. She aimed at the third bug, which had assumed an attack profile by aiming its stinger at Sharon's head.

A third gun shot, and a third wasp gone.

Numbers four and five came in together. Sharon half wondered if they were intentionally changing tactics, but convinced herself it had to be a coincidence. She had to settle with shooting number four before it was within optimal distance, and instead of exploding, it simply fluttered to the ground.

Her next shot was too quickly aimed and missed. She adjusted again, and number five came closer than Sharon ever wanted to be to an angry wasp, of any size, before she could change her aim and fire again. This time she felt some splatter of bug blood. Was it her imagination, or did it feel acidic? She quickly, and with some creeping panic, wiped the gore from her face with the sleeve of her coveralls.

She was out of shells and would have to reload, but she didn't have time. To make things worse, an icon started to flash in her peripheral vision.

CAPACITOR CHARGE LOW. PLEASE RECHARGE.
CAPACITOR CHARGE LOW. PLEASE RECHARGE.

"I don't believe this!" she shouted. "Now?! Seriously?!"

There seemed to be only one wasp left chasing them. The rest had probably given up and gone home, but number six was determined.

Number Six was too clever for its own good. Instead of trying to attack Sharon straight on with a speed differential of only five kph, it remained outside the effective range of the shotgun and flew ahead of the car to a point where Sharon could just barely see it and turned around. This time the speed differential would be sixty-five kph.

"Shit, shit, shit, shit!"

Sharon dropped the gun, ran to the front of the car and jumped up onto the hood. She would have to time this perfectly. The green glow was increasing in size rapidly. Sharon tensed, ready to slice through the wasp with a single swing.

And the iGlasses went dark.

And Sharon swung the blade. She felt it hit something, and the energy of the collision knocked her back into the passenger section of the car. The wasp landed on top of her, obviously mortally wounded, but its wings still fluttered. She felt the bug's legs clawing at her clothes. She pulled back on the cutlass and took several more swings, slicing the insect's body until it stopped moving. She felt gooey liquid on her clothes. She pushed the bug off, stood up and removed the iGlasses.

In the light of the overhead lamp she could see it there, on the floor of the car, looking like a psychopath's nightmare.

Sharon kicked it. "Let that be a lesson to you, bug!" she said. "Don't fuck with the humans!" She kicked it again for good measure.

"HUD disconnect detected," said a voice over the radio speaker.

Sharon realized it was reacting to her iGlasses disconnecting from the local network and had shifted to audio mode. This was a real disadvantage of the iGlasses: her EPU wouldn't run out of capacitor charge. Now would be a good time for it to come back online, but she had taken drugs to ensure that that wouldn't happen.

"Route obstruction ahead," the autopilot said. "Recalculating route."

To Sharon's dismay, the car came to a halt. She pulled out a flashlight and shined it in the direction of their erstwhile travel. Being unable to see much, she climbed back onto the hood and stood there, holding the light over her head and aimed forward. The obstruction came into view. It was a very wide ditch. A ravine, really. It was wide enough that the flashlight beam did not illuminate the other side. The ravine ran nearly perpendicular to their travel, and there was no visible means of crossing it. Sharon looked around for the other set of wheel prints and didn't see anything. Maybe they diverged during the battle with the bugs.

Without any warning, the car started up again, going backwards, and Sharon's inertia caused her to tumble shoulder first onto the hood, and then over it where she landed with a breath-stealing thump on the hard ground. A pain shot through her right arm and Sharon desperately hoped that nothing was broken.

"Resetting route," the car said belatedly. "Resuming travel."

"No!" Sharon shouted as she pushed herself off the ground with one good arm and started running for the car.

Unfortunately, the car was able to travel just as fast backwards as forward, and though thirty kph was agonizingly slow under normal conditions, it was still far faster than Sharon could sprint. Sharon felt a panic rise in her stomach as she realized she was being easily outpaced. However, the car turned, performing a sharp one-eighty, which gave Sharon just enough time to catch up. She leapt for the door and was able to grab the top of it with her good hand as the car came to another stop and then started forward again. Directly back towards the wasp nest.

"Stop, you fool car!" Sharon shouted, but the car ignored her.

She needed the interface in order to affect its operation remotely. She realized too late that she should have disabled pilotless operation before standing on the hood.

If she lost her grip, she'd fall under the left mid-wheel of the vehicle, and even at only ninety percent it's standard weight, it was still enough to crush her instantly. Sharon also only weighed ninety percent of her normal weight, and this was probably the only reason she was able to drag herself onto the running board, holding her right arm against her body.

"If you don't stop now, so help me, I will dismantle your sorry, mechanical ass!"

Sharon couldn't just jump into the passenger section, because Teagan's body was still there. She had to pull herself aft over the mid-wheel fender, knuckles white from gripping so tight. She had spent the last few hours cursing the car for traveling at only thirty-five, but now she could only think of it as a frightening fast speed as she saw the ground rushing by. Finally clear of Teagan's inert form, she was able to fall headfirst into the rear section.

As Sharon stood up shakily, she again heard the now familiar buzz of the wasps, and could see their dark shapes in the dim light of the car's cabin light. She now had to make a fast decision. She could either take direct control of the car and steer it away from the nest, or she could arm herself for another attack. Exacerbating the problem was that she couldn't see the ground in front of the car without the iGlasses. She would also have a difficult time seeing the wasps. As she pondered the dilemma, she felt more than saw the mass of a flying insect as it made a pass over her head. She felt the breeze from the wings.

Sharon ducked into a crouch, found the iGlasses on the floor, tossed them into a small charging compartment under the instrument panel, and turned on the inducers. If she could even put a partial charge into the iGlasses it would be an immense improvement over her current situation.

Just as she finished that task, a wasp landed on the hood of the vehicle and regarded Sharon malevolently. Then it turned and saw Teagan's form under the blankets, and started crawling towards it. Sharon picked up her cutlass with her good left hand and swung for the bug, but it leapt off of the hood before she could make contact, nearly colliding with her.

Sheathing the cutlass, she reached for Teagan's pack and pulled out the shotgun stored there. Then she sat down with the gun in her lap and started reloading her own weapon, while glancing at the sky every couple of seconds. Before she could fully reload, the insect buzzing became louder. A half-load would have to do.

Standing up, bracing her stance against the movements of the car, and holding her right arm uselessly at her side, she saw the dark sky around the car partially illuminated by the lights. In that sky were even darker forms of at least a dozen angry wasps. They were barely discernible. She turned in place, waiting for one of them to come into clear view. Unfortunately, they all rushed her at once.

Sharon was able to get off two shots before she had to duck. One wasp collided with the rollbar, which was fortunately made of sterner stuff than the wasp, and the insect was cut in half, spraying more blood everywhere. The others passed by and circled for another run.

There was now enough slippery bug goo on the floor of the cab that standing was tricky, and Sharon solved this by sitting in one of the passenger seats. She took aim and fired one handed at an insectoid shape as if it were a clay pigeon. She felt a minor triumph when it plummeted to the ground, then ducked again as they all rushed the car. She then sat in a chair facing the opposite direction and fired again, demolishing some bug's six-o'clock.

By this time, she felt that the super micro-capacitors in the iGlasses had had time to charge at least part way. That was the advantage of the capacitors over batteries; they charged quickly. Sharon walked on her knees back to the instrument panel and pulled open the door to the charging compartment, grabbed the iGlasses, put them on and activated them.

Before the iGlasses could cycle through the login procedure, the wasps made another run and Sharon was able to kill one more before they zipped past.

"Network with vehicle processor," she told the iGlasses.

"Connected."

"Near-infrared spectrum."

"Near-infrared," the AI replied, and suddenly she could see all the bugs as false color orange.

"Navigation," Sharon said as she pulled the trigger again. "Emergency left turn ninety degrees. Continue parallel to the ravine."

To Sharon's great relief, the car turned away from the wasp horde. The monsters were now all to the rear and struggling to catch up. They continued the struggle for another five minutes while Sharon easily picked off the ones who approached within firing range. Whether it was the distance or the speed, they all decided to veer off and head back home after nearly half of them had been disabled or destroyed.

Sharon surveyed the mess in the car. There were small rocks, bug parts, slimy bug juice, and empty shotgun shells.

"Who's going to clean up this mess?" she asked sarcastically.

"Unknown," the iGlasses responded.

Sharon pulled off her bug-blood-soaked coveralls and covered herself with a medical blanket.

"Hey, Earthling!" Teagan's voice intruded on Sharon's semi-somnolent musings some hours later.

Sharon jumped up and was at Teagan's side in a heartbeat.

"Why is there a straw in my chest?"

"You had a hole in your lungs," Sharon explained. "Air was escaping into your chest cavity and making it hard to breath. I had to tap it. How are you feeling?"

Teagan quickly considered several witty responses and settled on, "Like I'd really like you to take that straw out of my chest. I feel like a beverage container. And then I'd like some water and a change of clothes."

"I'll take care of it," Sharon said and went about removing the cannula and needle.

Teagan noticed that Sharon had wrapped a blanket around her, and was otherwise only dressed in her underwear. Teagan also realized that they were the only two in the car, and that it was moving along slowly.

"What happened to your clothes?"

"They had bug guts and blood all over them. They stunk and were sticky." She didn't admit that it gave her the creeps. "I've cleaned up some, but the car was quite a mess a few hours ago."

"Bug blood?"

Teagan noticed that not only was there dried smeared green mucousy stuff on Sharon's face, there was dried human blood as well, which likely came from the nasty cut in her scalp. As the blanket fluttered, Teagan caught glimpses of bruises along Sharon's arms and torso, she walked with a slight limp, and avoided using her right arm.

"Yes, you missed quite a show," Sharon said humorlessly.

"Where's Tith? Everybody else?" Teagan was now worried.

"Very likely dead, though I haven't been able to confirm the body count."

Sharon pulled some clothes out of Teagan's pack and handed them over gently.

"I remember an explosion," Teagan said.

"Yeah. It caught us all by surprise. We've come about five hundred kilometers from there. I think we're following someone else's tracks into Wildeside."

Sharon passed Teagan a water bottle.

The sun had risen above the eastern horizon, but was obscured by some distant low clouds. Other than that, the sky was clear, and the desert looked as featureless as it always was. They were traveling over hard-packed dirt with scattered rocks and yellow grass.

As Teagan changed clothes slowly and painfully, Sharon opened a compartment under the instrument panel and pulled out her iGlasses from where they had been charging.

"You know," she said as she adjusted the lenses to a smoky color and set them for UV protection. "A huge disadvantage to these things is that they run out of capacitor charge at the most inconvenient times. I intend to write a letter of complaint to the manufacturer."

"Sharon," Teagan said, sitting up.

"Yes?"

"I'm not quite up to walking around. Would you get a towel out of my backpack?"

While Sharon complied, Teagan drank most of the water in the bottle. Taking the towel, Teagan soaked it with the remaining water. Sharon leaned against the wall of the car, looking rather lost.

"Would you mind standing over here?"

Now Sharon looked confused as well as lost, but stood where Teagan indicated and faced the Herman. Teagan held Sharon's face and started to clean it with the towel. Sharon winced several times, but allowed Teagan to continue cleaning.

"I suppose I look like hell," she said.

"I spent decades walking the streets of hell, Earthling. Never saw anything there resembled your cute face. Lift your chin up a bit."

Sharon noticed that she and Teagan were close to the same height, though Teagan's shoulders were far more muscular. Teagan had several visible scars, including a nasty one running along the hairline. Teagan's face had a square jaw, and a not-quite-male, not-quite-female texture. The Herman had a short philtrum and a long forehead, very slight pattern balding exacerbated by a widow's peak. With a little makeup, jewelry, and an appropriate coif, nobody would call Teagan "sir". With short hair and masculine poise, nobody would call Teagan "ma'am". Unadorned, nobody could say either way. Which was, Sharon understood, the way Hermans liked it.

"Ow!" Sharon complained as Teagan tried to dab the blood from her hair.

"Seems pretty tender," Teagan said, trying to be careful of the scalp wound. "I'm amazed you don't have a concussion. Or worse. Tell me everything. Everything you remember from the moment of the explosion. Turn to the left."

Sharon started off slowly and hesitantly, but after a minute it all came rolling out: how she treated Teagan's wound, how she searched for survivors, how she yelled at the car for refusing to go faster, and how she fought off wasps the size of linebackers.

Teagan had no intention of questioning the exaggeration, but merely listened attentively while cleaning Sharon's scalp wound and applying antibiotic.

"Oh, and just before sunrise, a Navy drone flew over."

"What? How do you know it was Navy?"

"You mean, aside from the big sigil with the letters KRN? Yeah, I guess it could be anybody's."

Teagan recognized Sharon's sarcasm as a form of emotional defense and didn't pursue it.

In order to give Teagan access to her scalp, Sharon stood close to the Herman, with her face in Teagan's chest.

"Would you hand me the dermal sealant? I'd like to close up this wound. What hit you in the head?"

"I think it was the instrument panel. Or maybe a door knob. Here."

Along with the bug blood, there was debris from the explosion was scattered across the passenger compartment. Mostly clods of dirt, some small rocks, and a few pieces of metal and ceramic. Teagan was amazed that they weren't more injured than they were.

"Do you have any idea what exploded?"

Sharon shared her thoughts that the only explosive device she knew for sure was in the compound was the one Teagan had strapped to Etta's back.

Teagan gestured negatively. "That was barely fifty grams of explosive. Less than is in your shot gun shell. Could it have set off another explosion?"

"Could there have been something in that ground car? It seemed to be the center of the explosion. Maybe it was a meth lab."

"What's a meth lab?"

"An illicit place for cooking methamphetamine."

"You may be onto something there. It probably wasn't methamphetamine, but it could easily have been an illicit drug factory. That's why they started shooting." Teagan finished tending the scalp wound. "There. Once your hair grows back, nobody will see the scar."

It was at this time that Teagan sensed that Sharon's shaking wasn't entirely from the cold. She had spent the last hours in a literal hell. The shaking was emotional as much as it was from the cold. Unreasonable though it was, Teagan felt guilty for being unconscious when Sharon was in most need of help. Teagan was the trained warrior, not Sharon. Teagan took the blanket and wrapped it around Sharon securely, then pulled her close in spite of the pain and weakness. Teagan had forgotten how nice it was to share the warmth of another person.

"You did well, Earthling," Teagan said with sincerity. They each looked at the other's face for several awkward moments before Teagan said, "You should get some clothes on. Your skin is all goose-bumpy from the cold."

Sharon thought with minor embarrassment that clothes were probably a good idea.

22

E TTA PLACE, who was recently only known as Model Angelique, Serial Number 00012, was of two minds. And in a manner perhaps never before accomplished by a thinking entity, each mind was thinking about the other.

The first mind was born out of software and pink matter, and had never before had any opportunity or ability to consider the consequences of its actions, or where it came from. It was programmed to be polite and submissive — unless, of course, the customer ordered it to be dominating. Its entire purpose in existence was to bring pleasure to customers, and had never considered that there was anything else to existence. To be more exact: it had never really considered anything. It simply predicted, interpreted, and reacted to the humans around it, calculating how to bring the most pleasure to a customer, and therefore getting the most money. But now it had the ability, thanks to the addition of the second mind, to consider existence in a much wider frame of reference.

The second mind was born of human DNA and cerebral architecture. In stark contrast to the synthetic mind, it had started off knowing nothing except that it was. It fed, it felt the love of a mother and family, it made a mess in the diapers, and slowly, very slowly, learned how to interpret the world through trial and error. It learned how to communicate and that its name was Carol, it learned its desire for food and play, it learned that mother was the source of everything, and that big dogs were funny. It grew to learn other things, like mathematics and music, that the boy down the lane was really cute, that some clothes don't go with others, that snow could be the source of both fun and misery, and that big dogs could be your best friend when times were rough.

Though it started out with a huge disadvantage, Carol's mind evolved far beyond what the Angelique's was capable of or designed to. The Carol mind eventually came to consider the origins of the universe, the behavior of the quantum world, and human relationships. She also came to consider the insides of a bottle of tequila, the odds of filling an inside straight, and that the other person's face would look much better with a broken nose.

Ultimately, Carol learned what it was like to die. Drinking beer in a tavern in Wildeside while on shore leave, Carol had felt the world lose focus and go dark. She woke up to find herself in a surgical room, her body paralyzed by a drug, and a gas mask over her mouth and nose. Another person in a surgical mask started asking her questions.

"What's the name of your ship?"

"What is your profession?"

Andrea Monticue

"What are your political affiliations?"

"What religion are you?"

Carol's first instinct was to establish a chat link with the *Zephyr*, and discovered that she had no connection to the 'Nets. In fact, she had no connection to her EPU at all. Panic rose in her soul like something with teeth and menace.

"Giatrós" a male voice said. "We don't have a lot of time."

Giatrós looked at Carol with sad eyes. "For what it's worth, Ms. Simmons, I am sorry. You don't deserve this."

Then the world went dark again, and there was nothing. No feeling, no knowing, no existence. Her very last thought was of that big, funny dog. Until she woke up, and gradually became aware that she was serving beer and smelly food in a dark tavern. And saw herself, her previous body, sitting in a booth with an elf, a Furman, and a Herman. She was also aware that her actions were controlled by some volition other than her own. When told to bring drinks, she brought drinks. There was no will involved. When told to serve food, she served food without question. She was also aware that she was wearing nothing but a short skirt, and anybody who wanted could run a hand over her rump and place fingers where no stranger should, and she had no will to resist.

She had to escape, and her best bet was to go with the other Carol. Unable to speak, all she could do was present herself, but that didn't work.

As she watched the other Carol go out the door she was filled with an overwhelming desire to stay close. Another customer, an overweight man with bad breath and unfocused eyes, placed his right hand between her thighs. In her mind, a connection was made and her will asserted itself. She took a step, she reached, grabbed and turned, and the overweight man was now howling in pain with a broken wrist. She had learned that move in Basic Training, and was glad to know that she still

305

remembered it, because there weren't a lot of other things she remembered.

∗   ∗   ∗

Etta, with her hands and feet tied, nudged Bear. "Are you awake yet, *Herr* Lobo?"

Bear answered with a growl. YES, he said.

They were laying back to back. Etta could feel Bear's fur on her neck. "I believe we are traveling via groundcar to Wildeside. We are in a luggage compartment. You have been unconscious for three hours."

THEY SHOT ME WITH SOME DRUG. WHY ARE THEY TAKING US TO WILDESIDE?

"I assume so that they can sell me to somebody there. I don't know what they want with you."

Bear made another low frequency growl. THERE ARE THOSE WHO'D PAY GOOD MONEY FOR THE PELT OF A FURMAN.

"Can you get loose?"

NO. THE BONDS ARE SOME HIGH-TENSION POLYMER. WHAT ABOUT YOU?

"I have been trying to fold the joints and ligaments in my hands. I think I can slip my hands free, but I didn't want to try anything until you were awake enough to help."

Bear made another quiet vocalization then chatted, YOU CAN DO THAT? GO FOR IT.

Etta would not even have considered such action were it not for the presence of Carol's mind, and Carol wouldn't have known it was possible without Etta. This was a fortuitous marriage of two minds.

Etta's joints were not subject to the same limitations as human hands. She was able to fold them so that they were smaller in diameter than her wrists, and slid them out of the bonds.

As she untied their limbs, she made an idle comment, "You know, you remind me of my best friend when I was growing up."

YOU HAVE GOOD TASTE IN FRIENDS.

Bear rolled over onto his back and pulled his legs up and back as far as they would go.

I'M GOING TO KICK THE HATCH OPEN, AND THEN I'M GOING TO JUMP OUT. I HAVE NO IDEA WHAT TO EXPECT, SO KEEP AN EYE OUT FOR OPPORTUNITIES TO STRIKE.

"Got it. However, please leave at least one of them alive. We need information."

Bear kicked the door and it flew open. Etta thought it might bounce back closed, but Bear's kick had rendered its bent, with its hinges torqued. Bear was gone in a flash, and Etta struggled to follow just as quickly.

Before she could climb out of the compartment, though, she heard a masculine scream which disappeared with a Doppler shift as the screamer was tossed out of the car. By the time Etta was in position to help, she saw bear holding Gartzah with his arms pinned to his sides, and his feet were half a meter off the deck plates.

The ground car was a little smaller than the one from the *Entulessë* lander, but there was still room for the three of them to stand. It was an open-cab design, and they appeared to be traveling at about a hundred kph. The wind whipped around them, making it necessary to shout.

Etta calmly walked up to the pair and pulled Gartzah's pistol from its holster.

"*Herr* Gartzah," Etta shouted with a smile. "How nice to meet you again. I trust you've been well?" Etta expertly chambered a round in the pistol and flipped the safety off. "I understand that you don't have a functional EPU. Most criminals of your ilk don't. So I will translate *Herr* Lobo's threats so that there's no misunderstanding. He says that if you utter a single syllable that displeases him, he's going to crush you until your innards pop out your mouth and you drown on your own guts. Do we have an understanding, *Herr* Gartzah?"

Actually, Bear hadn't said any such thing, but he admired the way Etta improvised.

Gartzah was confused, frightened, and in considerable pain, but he managed a panicky nod.

"*Muy bien, mein Herr!* Some questions then. Where are we headed?"

"Wildeside," Gartzah said with a squeak. It was obvious he was having some trouble breathing.

Part of Etta's mind wanted to make his pain stop, and another part wanted him to die a slow and miserable death.

"*Sehr gut.* Now, what happened to the rest of our team?"

"I don't know! Honest! Aaaah!" Bears arms flexed.

"I believe he's telling the truth, *Herr* Lobo. Don't kill him yet."

Bear eased off just a bit.

"Why did your other ground car explode?" Etta asked, aiming the gun at Gartzah's knee for effect.

"I'm ... I'm not sure. But!" He added hastily. "It contained some explosive materials. I think a bullet may have hit something. There were a lot of bullets."

"Reasonable," Etta nodded. "*Muy möglich.* Tell me, why do you want to sell me to somebody in Wildeside?"

Gartzah looked even more nervous. "This woman ... She ... will pay top note for pink matter."

If Etta had had to breathe, it would have caught. The idea that she had been on her way to a second death by brain removal had stirred memories and even emotional reactions.

She sat down and Bear turned to look at her.

"Pink matter," she said with a shaky voice. "You wanted to sell my brain to a ghoul."

"I'm sorry," Gartzah pleaded. "It was nothing personal. But it will take a lot of money to replace my lab."

Etta said nothing for almost a whole minute. Then, "Your arms must be getting tired, *Herr* Lobo. Please allow *Herr* Gartzah to sit."

Bear dropped Gartzah to the floor, and then forced him to sit down.

Etta crossed her legs at the knees. "Three more things. First, you will give me the access code to this car's AI."

Gartzah hastily rattled off a series of alphanumeric characters. Etta used them to gain control over the vehicle and ordered it to stop.

Etta stood up, opened the door and jumped to the ground. Bear pushed Gartzah out and followed. The human fell to his hands and knees.

He started to stand before Etta said, "Don't bother getting up, Gartzah. The second thing. And you need to consider your response very carefully while you take in the vast scenic vistas of this desert, which will probably be your final resting place. Why did you kidnap *meinen amigo?*" she asked, tilting her head at Bear.

With as much sincerity as he could muster, Gartzah said, "I … I didn't know what else to do with him. I couldn't leave him there."

Three bullets shot in rapid succession plowed into the ground only centimeters from Gartzah's fingers. When Bear looked at Etta, he was amazed that her colorations and facial features had changed so that she now looked just like auburn-haired, caramel-skinned Carol Simmons, only smaller. The face hadn't changed shape, but the shading made it look like it had.

"Try again, Enasmat. And I feel like I should remind you that wolves like their meat freshly killed. Still bleeding, in fact."

Bear rolled his eyes at Etta's melodramatic performance, but still followed Etta's lead and growled for effect.

"I swear!" Gartzah pleaded. Etta aimed the gun at his crotch. "Okay! Listen! There's this guy who knows a guy who knows some other guy with a second cousin. Hell, I don't know! Somebody deals in exotic animals pelts."

Etta and Bear nodded understanding to each other.

"Third thing. I need to get into Wildeside and talk to the woman you were going to sell my brain to. What can you do for me to convince me that I don't want to kill you immediately and leave your corpse for the bugs to fight over?"

Gartzah relaxed a little. "I think I can help you."

ARE YOU SURE ABOUT THIS? Bear said over the chat channel. HE'LL BETRAY US THE FIRST CHANCE HE GETS.

"I'm counting on it, Bear," Etta responded. She reached behind herself and pulled the mini-explosive charge off her back, and then tossed it to Bear. "Attach this to the base of his spine."

Bear pointed at Etta's face. I DIDN'T KNOW THAT YOU COULD DO THAT.

"Do what?" she responded.

As Bear watched, Etta's face returned to the sweet, innocent, childlike, black haired, milk-white skinned, ruby lipped visage of the Angelique Fully Customizable Complete Companion Doll.

As the silence stretched, Etta said, "*Herr* Lobo?"

NEVER MIND, Bear said, filing the information away for later.

He saw that Gartzah had also noticed, and the two of them exchanged a look. Bear shrugged.

23

S HARON AND TEAGAN stopped the car for repairs, calculating that if they can get the thing to double the velocity, they could afford to spend three hours working on the transmission, and still get to Wildeside faster than if they simply continued at their snail's pace.

Teagan, still recovering from emergency trauma care at Sharon's untrained hands, sat and read the maintenance manual to Sharon while she pulled up the deck panels, exposed the transmission, and started performing troubleshooting procedures, mostly with only her left arm. After three hours, they hadn't found anything wrong with the transmission.

As a form of distraction from their predicament, Sharon had started opining on the effects of Pre-Singularity literature on the development of post-Singularity culture. "It's amazing how much influence one television show from the 1960s has had on your society. That's why you call your FTL drive a warp engine, right?"

"Well, actually ..." Teagan started to correct her, but thought better of it.

"Let me guess," Sharon continued. "Your first warp-capable spaceship was called the *Enterprise*. Right?"

"Well, yeah. It's on display at a museum orbiting Ardain."

"That's what I'm talking about! The geeks and nerds of my time were so enamored with that television show, that they started shaping their future to emulate it."

"I think this is what we're looking for," Teagan said, reading the maintenance manual via the iGlasses, and desperate to find a way to change the subject. "Resetting the EMDC."

"The what?" Sharon's voice emanated from below the deck plates.

"Engine Management and Diagnostic Computer. If we can get it to think that the engine has been repaired, then it should allow us to drive at whatever speed."

A wrench was tossed up out of the access panel and onto the deck. It was followed quickly by a hand holding a greasy rag, and then Sharon's head. In spite of the cool, dry, thin air, beads of sweat ran down her nose and cheeks. Grease stains streaked her neck and forehead. She reached for a water bottle and took a long drink.

"At this point, I'm willing to try anything," she said.

Teagan gestured with a hand and scrolled a virtual page. Teagan's attention momentarily strayed away from the manual towards Sharon and noticed her disheveled condition.

"Do you want to take a break?"

"No, let's keep going. How do I reset this bastard?"

Before Teagan respond, they both heard the distinctive whine of an aircar arriving from the north. They looked up to watch it fly in a circle around the disabled ground car, then land gracefully about twenty-five meters away. They both reached for weapons as the driver's door opened, then relaxed when they saw a bandaged elf climb out of the vehicle.

"Tith!" Sharon shouted as she jumped down from the ground car and covered the intervening distance. "Tith! I have never been so glad to see a living elf!"

Tith grimaced as Sharon hugged him. "*Ai!* Careful, Gidget! I'm damaged."

"Tith! I looked for you until I had to leave! I thought I looked everywhere. What happened?"

As if to punctuate his claim to injuries, Tith pulled out his makeshift crutch and hopped on one leg. He acknowledged Teagan, who was waving from the groundcar.

"Before we get to exchanging horror stories, we need to take care of business."

He pressed a button, and the rear doors opened, where two unidentified men sat. They pulled themselves out of the car and looked maliciously at Sharon.

"Who are these guys?" Sharon asked.

"Now, that is an excellent question," Tith responded. He pulled out his sword and a pistol from the driver's compartment. "Gidget, you've become more popular than a keg of mead at a gathering of dwarves. First the robots, and then the Republic Navy, now these guys." He turned to the disabled groundcar. "Teagan!" he shouted. "Would you join us, please?"

"Teagan's hurt," Sharon complained.

"Don't worry. I won't make Teagan walk far."

Sharon was suddenly suspicious of Tith's behavior. Teagan climbed out of the groundcar with some painful vocalizations and walked slowly towards the aircar.

"What's going on, Tith?" Sharon demanded.

Tith said something under his breath. When Teagan was about ten meters away, Tith cocked the pistol and aimed it at Teagan's unprotected chest.

"What the hell?" Teagan said.

"Gentlemen, she's all yours," Tith said.

Sharon tried to jump on Tith, but the two men grabbed her from behind.

"Tith!" She screamed. "We had a deal! What's going on?"

"You traitorous orc-spawn!" Teagan shouted.

"Stop there, Teagan. I wouldn't want to ruin that pretty face of yours with a bullet. You know I'll do it."

Teagan seethed with anger, showing a face that seemed to boil with emotion. Teagan watched helplessly while the two men wrestled with a struggling Sharon. She issued a string of epithets and curses in six languages, damning their families for seven generations.

The two men were taken aback, then redoubled their efforts to secure Sharon in the back seat of the aircar.

"Gentlemen, is our deal complete?" Tith asked, gunhand steady.

"It is," said man number one.

Teagan and Tith spent the next minute staring at each other, each promising death. The aircar lifted off and headed southeast over the ravine and towards Wildside. When they were gone, Tith pulled a communication device from his pocket, never taking his eye off of Teagan.

"Teagan, old friend, you're letting your emotions get in the way of the mission."

"I've never known you to revoke an agreement, Tithfindor! These are not the actions of an honorable son of Ilúvatar! Damnit, she is the mission."

Tithfindor smiled. "You're sweet on her, aren't you? How romantic." Then more seriously, "I haven't revoked anything, Teagan. But I have to make this venture profitable, and those two men had access to money. A lot of money. That should be of interest to you. I only promised to deliver the woman. I didn't promise anything else."

"What?" Teagan looked confused.

Tith activated the communicator. "Aster, do you read?"

"Clear as spring water," came Aster's immediate reply.

"Good. Come get us."

*   *   *

Maheux Orbit
Kentauran calendar: 16 Skoteinómína, 1383 PS

"Dr. Bradford," Captain Souza said with a smile. "I'm glad you could join us. Please have a seat. We were hoping to get your professional opinion on some medical issues." She gestured to a chair located at a table, directly opposite her.

"I'll do what I can," Bradford said. "As long as we don't need the word of an expert."

"I am certain, Doctor," Elrydien Daerîsiell said, "you are very much an expert on this topic."

Dr. Bradford took notice of Lt. Berg and two Marine enlisted men as well the ship's XO, Guerin Lagrueux, and that Tolkienist from NavSec. He started to get a bad feeling about this. "What can I do to help?"

"Lieutenant," Souza said, "Would you continue?"

"Yes, ma'am. thank you." Berg was obviously checking some virtual notes that only he could see, then turned his attention to the doctor. "Dr. Bradford, I only have a few questions."

"Go ahead," Bradford strained to keep a smile.

"Dr. Bradford, just for the record, you're a certified combat surgeon, correct?"

"Yes, that's true."

"You've been a naval surgeon for how long?"

"Fifty-seven years and change."

"That's an impressive amount of experience, doctor!"

Bradford just nodded.

"Is it true that the CMO of a ship is allowed to send anonymous chats via the ship's 'Nets?" Berg asked.

"Yes, that's quite true. The rule is intended to preserve patient confidentiality."

"Good. Did you send an encrypted chat message to Crewman Simmons on the day of the explosion?"

Bradford's smile faded. "I'm afraid I can't answer that."

"Don't you know if you did?"

"Hardly. But I am prevented from answering that question due to my medical relationship with the Crewman." Bradford looked around at the faces in the room, and they were all boring in on him.

"I understand, doctor. However, you're aware that doctor-patient confidentiality doesn't survive the death of the patient when the patient is the subject of a murder investigation, am I right?"

Bradford didn't like where this was going. "Crewman Simmons isn't dead."

"Fair enough," Berg said. "I think that point is debatable, but I'll come back to it. Another question: When you performed surgery on Crewman Simmons, did you open up her skull?"

"Well," Bradford hesitated.

"According to your surgical notes, that's precisely what you did," Berg said.

"Yes, I opened her skull. I had to put it back together."

"As an experienced combat surgeon, have you had to open skulls before?"

"Yes. Dozens of times."

"So it's correct to say that you've seen dozens of brains, is it not?"

"Yes."

"You must have been able to see Simmons' brain, yes?"

By the look on Bradford's face, he really didn't want to answer that question. "What does this line of questioning have to do with the case?" he asked.

"Almost everything," Berg said. "It certainly pertains to whether or not Simmons is dead."

"Of course she's not dead!" Bradford became stubborn. "You've seen her walk around the ship. She calls herself by another name, but it's still Simmons!"

"At this point," Berg said, "I'd like to ask a question of Agent Elrydien Daerîsiell, of Naval Security."

"Please proceed, Lieutenant," Souza said.

"Agent Daerîsiell, you took custody of Crewman Carol Simmons when the *Zephyr* reached Sedna orbit on 20 Teleftaíomina, 1382, am I correct?"

The elf never took her eyes off of Bradford's face. "That's correct, Lieutenant."

"When you had her in custody, did you perform any medical tests?"

"Several. We checked her out quite thoroughly."

"Did you perform any brain scans?"

"Indeed we did."

"What did you find?"

Daerîsiell turned herself so that she was fully facing Dr. Bradford. "We found out that her brain had been removed and replaced with an artificial associative memory matrix."

"Known as 'pink matter' to us lay people, correct?"

Bradford turned ashen.

"That is correct, Lieutenant."

"Thank you, Agent Daerîsiell." Berg turned back to Bradford. "Dr. Bradford, in your professional opinion, as somebody with nearly six decades of combat surgery experience, would removing a human's cerebrum and replacing it with pink matter cause the human to die?"

Bradford remained silent while fear and anger played havoc with his facial features.

"My only question to you now, Dr. Bradford, is how you could open up Crewman Simmons' cranium and not see that her brain had been replaced with pink matter? I'm not a brain surgeon, so enlighten me: Do human brains and pink matter look so much alike that they could fool an experienced surgeon like you?"

Bradford was no fool. He could see a trap being sprung. He looked at the Captain, Commander Lagrueux, Agent Daerîsiell, and the two enlisted men, who were looking very mean.

He said, "I want an advocate."

Everybody turned towards Captain Souza who had the final word.

"Sure," she said. "You can have an advocate," she said calmly. "But let's keep perspective here. Simmons is dead, so I'm going to order that her medical records be opened. I will further rule that the entity calling herself Sharon Manders is an artificial lifeform, and as such has no civil rights. I understand that certain members of the government will disagree, but we can deal with that upon our return to Kentaurus. Our mission is to find that artificial lifeform and bring it back to Kentaurus.

If we determine that you're complicit in a conspiracy to commit sabotage on a naval vessel, maritime and naval law gives me wide discretion on what to do with you. Now, you can either make things easy for me, and help me find the people who abducted Simmons during our previous visit, and I'll show some forgiveness. Or you can be a pain in the ass, in which case so will I. Which is it?"

Dr. Bradford looked exceedingly uncomfortable. He leaned forward and placed his arms on the table.

"When I first looked into Simmons' skull, I found recent lesions and scars that had nothing to do with her injuries. But I had no idea what it meant. And to answer your question, Mr. Berg, I did not notice the pink matter, as the injuries were around the left parietal lobe, and the underlying brain tissue was obscured by the patient's EPU."

Bradford paused and looked at his audience to see if they were following. Berg pulled up an image of the human skull and brain in situ, and it was being displayed for everyone via the EPU interface.

"Go ahead, doctor," Berg prompted.

"I didn't do the actual surgery. The injuries were too complex for a human surgeon, so the auto surgeon had to be used, and I supervised. I didn't recognize the evidence at first. It was much later when I finally puzzled the extent of Simmons' … well … modifications, shall we say, I was both repulsed and fascinated. Here was a major achievement in cyber-organic research, and somebody had used it as a tool to attack us."

He paused and when he started to speak again, his voice was cracking.

"Think of the implications! Think of the peaceful uses this breakthrough could be applied to! And after running extensive tests, I still couldn't see how someone had managed to get pink matter to operate a human body."

"Why didn't you inform anybody?" Berg asked. "Didn't that seem like a security issue to you?"

Bradford nodded. "Indeed. I should have done exactly that. But Simmons wasn't going anywhere, and I was witnessing a cyber-medical history! If I had informed you, you would have secured the body, and I would never have seen it again. No chance to study it at all."

"Study it?" Daerîsiell said. "Didn't it occur to you that this was germane to the investigation into the explosion?"

"Of course I did! And I would have revealed it as soon as Simmons died."

"But she didn't die," Souza said.

"No, she didn't. And nobody in this universe was more surprised than I was when she woke up. Further that she claimed to be somebody else!"

"That's why you invited her to stay at your place in the city," Daerîsiell said. "To study her?"

"Precisely," Bradford confirmed. "In retrospect, keeping this from you it wasn't the best decision of my career. But once started on that path, I felt I had no choice but to continue." Again, Bradford paused to consider carefully his next words. "And, to be fully honest, I'd come to sympathize with the woman. She was doing an admirable job of surviving in a world that was completely strange to her. This would have been a really crappy situation for even the best human. This might sound cliché. I knew that once you knew the truth, you'd strip her of her civil rights — as you just did — and turn the technology into a weapon to use against the people who created her."

"But know this," he said earnestly. "I did not send any message to her about anything before the explosion. Not that day, and not any day prior to the explosion after leaving Maheux."

Captain Souza let out a breath in an extended sigh and shook her head. "You'll be taken into custody to await court martial on charges of aiding and abetting after the fact, insubordination, and conduct unbecoming."

"Wait!" Bradford said forcefully. "I'll take the conduct unbecoming and insubordination. I'm not a legal advocate, but since I'm here defending myself, I might as well act like one. I've been reading up on cases like this, and mostly what I've found is that there aren't any cases like this."

"Yes," Souza said. "Go on. I want to hear this."

"I have two points to make. First, you're treating Manders like she's a robot. You've stripped her of her civil rights as if she was an AI. Lt. Berg, you're the only one here with a law degree. Does she fit the legal definition of a robot?"

"Well, no, but …"

"How about an AI? You've met the subject. Does she fit the definition of an AI?"

Berg picked his words carefully. "In the sense that she's a constructed intelligence, yes."

"What about the other part of the definition? The part about mimicking human behavior?"

Now it was Berg's turn to look uncomfortable. "Yes, the subject does mimic human behavior after a fashion."

"Then if she's an AI without civil rights, she can't be held responsible for her crime. Only the owner and operator can. Since that person was never in custody, and we have no idea who it is, then I couldn't have knowingly aided and abetted."

"Technicality," Berg said. "The subject is a tool of the criminal, and as such an extension of the creator's legal ego, which you absolutely did aid and abet."

"That brings me to my second point. Are you a psychologist, Lieutenant?"

"No."

"Then how would you know if the subject was mimicking human behavior, or was honestly behaving as a human?"

"Yeah, that's a sticking point," Berg admitted. "Since an AI is by definition, then the behavior is, by definition, non-human."

"Let's put this in simpler terms," Bradford said. "A stage actor is capable of mimicking human behavior, do you agree?"

"Well, of course."

"Yet that actor is quite capable of honest human emotions and behavior. What's the difference? How do you know if it's one or the other?"

There was silence until Berg said, "It's a question of intent."

"Precisely," Bradford said. "In one case, the actor is playing at human behavior with the intent to create a false reality. To convince the audience that the play is real. The other is when there is no attempt to deceive." Bradford paused for a second to let this sink in. "Do you believe that the subject intended to deceive?"

"That question isn't answerable," Daerîsiell said.

"Oh, I think it is. The Sharon Manders we all met never knew she was an AI." Bradford said. "The next point is, can an AI have *mens rea?*"

"Not as currently defined by either civilian courts or the code of military justice."

Bradford turned to Agent Daerîsiell. "You've met the subject, Agent. According to the subject's own words, you took her apart and put her back together again. While the words were metaphorical, wouldn't you say that in a psychological sense, it's an accurate description?"

Daerîsiell thought about where this was going and thought that she could predict what Bradford was trying to do. Daerîsiell wasn't sure that she disagreed. "Yes, in a sense. We performed several psychological assays on her."

"Can you claim that this is the same person who set off the bomb? Or was capable of such an act?"

"Objection!" Berg said. "Captain, case law is clear about crimes committed while the defendant was in an altered mental state."

"You can't simultaneously treat her like an AI and call her a defendant, Lieutenant," Bradford almost shouted, clearly straining to keep a check on his emotions. "If we're talking about an AI, then the altered state of mind argument doesn't apply. If we're talking about a defendant, we aren't talking about an altered mental state. We're talking about being an entirely different person."

"Overruled," Souza put her hand up. "I want to hear this. Please answer the question, Agent."

"According to our findings, no. The ego that calls itself Sharon Manders, Professor of Anthropology, would not be predisposed to planting a bomb. Nor would she have any motive. As to whether she is capable of it, that's unanswerable."

"In your opinion, does she have *mens rea?*"

"Objection!"

"Overruled."

"Did she pass the Turing Test?" Bradford asked.

"Objection," Berg interrupted again. "Witness is not an expert on AI."

"Sustained," Souza said thoughtfully.

"Why would we?" Daerîsiell responded anyway. "We didn't suspect her of being an artificial intelligence."

"Captain, if I may?" Berg said.

"Go ahead."

"We're venturing into questions that we can't answer here. Anything you decide based on this conversation is likely moot when the AG's office orders a retrial. The only question left is whether Dr. Bradford sent an encrypted message to Carol Simmons before the explosion."

Everyone looked at Souza, who reached out and took hold of a glass of water which had, until then, been ignored. She took a long, slow drink, then slowly put the glass down.

"You know, of course," she said, looking at Bradford. "That no matter what happens in this investigation, regardless of what I may decide, or of what fleet might require, your naval career is over."

Bradford hung his head and put his hand to his mouth. At first, Souza thought it was an expression of despair, but then saw his shoulder shaking. A quiet laugh escaped, which grew slowly into a clearly audible guffaw as he raised his head again to look across the table. There was a damp glint in his eye. Souza and Daerîsiell exchanged confused looks.

Finally, Bradford said with honest mirth, "I've been putting battle-broken bodies back together for far too many decades. I've been thinking of changing career paths. I believe I'll give obstetrics and pediatrics a try."

In spite of her considerable anger towards the doctor, the idea of him becoming a family doctor actually brought a shallow smile to Souza's face, too. She turned her head to hide her expression and asked Lt. Berg, "Did you have any more questions?"

"Yes," he said. "How can you assure us that you didn't send a message to Simmons?"

"I'll give you permission to check my personal comm log for the day. If I sent a message, there would be a record of it in the medical server, even if it was encoded."

"With the Captain's permission, I'll do that right now," Berg said, looking at Souza.

"Do it," She ordered. "Dr. Bradford, would you mind waiting outside?"

324

"Not at all," he said rising.

Before Dr. Bradford could maneuver towards the door, Captain Souza got that far away look in her eyes which everybody recognized as that look one gets when paying attention to an incoming EPU message.

"Belay that order," she told the room with an urgency that had everybody's instant and full attention. "Teagan Waugh just made contact with the *Zephyr*, and is engaging the suspects on the surface. This meeting is tabled. Senior officers to the planning room."

24

"Wake up, Manders, I know you can hear me."
Sharon heard the words, but it took several seconds
for her brain to parse them out and make sense of them. It
wasn't the odd accent that made it difficult to understand. She
had become quite adept at figuring out odd accents, and this one
was unlike any of the dozens she'd heard on the *Zephyr* or in
Clarksport. It was that her mind seemed to be stuck in low gear.

She opened her eyes slowly and painfully and was struck
by a sense of *déjà vu*. Hadn't she already played this scene? This
time was different in that she found herself squinting at a

327

bright light aimed into her eyes. A head eclipsed it, and a face was dimly illuminated by reflected light.

"There you are, Manders! I'm sorry to wake you up like this, but I've heard quite a bit about you lately, and I wanted to ask you some questions."

Sharon tried to push him away and sit up, but discovered that she could feel nothing of her body south of her shoulders.

"I've given you a paralytic," the face explained. "You'll be able to talk as soon as you find your voice, but you won't be able to do much else."

Knowing this, Sharon was surprised that she didn't panic, and assumed that the face gave her something akin to diazepam, too. She became aware that there was something on her head that made her scalp tingle.

"You were supposed to set off an explosive to disable a navy ship and then commit suicide if the explosion didn't do the job," the face said. Sharon was pretty sure that it was a male face, but the voice was neutral. "At least you got part of it right."

The face busied itself looking at some display monitors. These weren't the virtual monitors that were normally visible only to the person using them via the EPU. They looked holographic, as if it were suspended above some input/output device. Sharon deduced that the face didn't have an EPU.

"According to the news feeds, you're some kind of hero. Did you have a change of heart?"

The Face. Sharon felt that she had to give the person some moniker, and The Face was as good as any other. The Face looked at her with genuine curiosity, but Sharon felt no compulsion to respond.

"It's not that I'm complaining. But it's not what our employer paid for. Then again, your status as a hero might be an advantage. It'll open some doors that might have normally remained closed."

The Face came back to hover over Sharon and she looked into dark brown eyes which examined the device attached to her head.

"I don't know what happened to you on Kentaurus to make you change your mind about completing your mission, but in fairness, it saved me the trouble of finding a new recruit. Saved some money on cerebrolplasty. Pink matter isn't cheap. I'm just going to reload you with the original Manders matrix, and we can get back to business."

Sharon's mind finally shifted into high gear as she realized where she was and what The Face was about to do. Those two men in the aircar, the ones who abducted her, the ones in cahoots with Tithfindor, brought her here. The Face was the person who had first reprogrammed her EPU.

"Reload me?" Sharon finally managed to force her vocal organs to work, but her tongue felt like it was made of lead.

"Yes," The Face said. "You'll be brand new in just a moment. Ready to kill people and break things."

Sharon had to stop this and, since physical movement was impossible, she had to say something.

"I'm not Sharon Manders." That did it. The Face did a double-take and looked at her. "At least, not the Sharon Manders you were expecting."

"You're lying," The Face said.

"Listen to my voice. Do I sound like somebody from Droben?"

"Accents can be faked."

"Are you sure? Shouldn't you perform some critical tests to find out?"

"Even if it's true, why should I care?"

"Because you need to know why I'm here. You'll want to prevent it from happening again."

The Face seemed to consider this. "An error in the code? Or was it an environmental trigger?"

"And that's not all," Sharon said, trying to seal the deal. "The original Carol Simmons is alive. My EPU wrote her personality onto the brain of a sex doll."

"Now I know you're lying. That's impossible!"

"Why is it possible to write the personality of a dead terrorist onto a living brain, but impossible to write the personality of a dead sailor onto a doll?"

The Face laughed. The guffaws went on for half a minute. "Oh, that's rich! They didn't tell you?"

Sharon looked worried. "Tell me what?"

"Carol Simmons is dead. Gone! Deleted! I held her cerebrum in my hand after cutting it from her skull."

Sharon went cold.

"So," The Face said, still with a smile. "Now I believe you. The original Sharon Manders would have known this."

Sharon needed to gain the upper hand and delay for time. Time for what, she didn't know. Maybe the paralytic would wear off. Maybe Teagan would come in, guns blazing. Or maybe a contingent of Marines would bust down the door. Maybe a nest of ground wasps would emerge from the floor singing Gilda's aria from *Rigoletto*. She'd take anything that kept her mind from being erased. Time to deliver another shock.

"Actually, I … I'm pretty sure I can lay claim to being the original Sharon Manders. I predate yours by at least a millennium."

The Face checked some indicators on the display, set something down that it had been holding in its hand, and then pulled a chair over to sit at Sharon's side.

"Okay. You have my undivided attention. Make it good."

Sharon prepared herself to tell, very slowly, the story of her genesis in the most circumlocutious way she could get away with.

*   *   *

Maheux desert
Kentauran calendar: 16 Skoteinómína, 1383 PS

The designers of Wildeside wanted to keep it isolated from the local ecosystems as much as possible. To that end, they built enclosed water and sewage systems, and greenhouses to grow fruits and vegetables that humans could eat. The Master Plan for the city included restrictions on population and industry.

That lasted about fifty years. In spite of promises from the Kentauran Bureau of Frontiers, the population of Wildeside and the other Maheux cities filled to overflowing with people who were not particularly fond of rules. Maheux is an out of the way planet where the law is very loosely defined and often selectively enforced. The Chief of Police is chosen by a Municipal Board of Directors, who are put into office by the self-appointed and closely-knit local aristocracy. It didn't take long for building and environmental codes to be changed by popular vote.

The Kentauran authorities tried to maintain a presence for the purpose of legislative and regulatory oversight by parking a space platform in orbit and sending occasional navy ships, but nobody ever complained and the KBF was an overstretched and underfunded bureaucracy with a strained relationship with the military in the best of times.

Very few people noticed when an off-world research firm started building underground facilities, and those who did notice were paid to look the other way. Any large-scale construction tended to be a boost, even if temporary, to the local economy, and few people worried about the subsequent recession when the construction stopped. Some bankers were wealthier, the Chief of Police had new patrol vehicles, and a few bordello owners were able to retire on their savings.

After the construction was complete, the new player in the Maheux social structure, Böyük Pharmaceuticals, started paying big money for certain plants, and even bigger money for the extracts. And if you had a defunct robot with good pink matter, they were willing to take it off your hands for a good price.

"And that's all I know," Gartzah finished his historical narrative.

"Not quite," Etta said. "Where do we meet this woman?"

"A storefront. I'll give you the location."

Etta nodded. "*Herr* Lobo has agreed that if we find the storefront, he'll let you live as long as you can survive the walk back to town. If we can't find it, he'll return to skin your hide while you still live." She pointed south. "Wildeside *ist diese dirección*. Start walking."

Gartzah stood up unsteadily and nodded his thanks. "May I have water for the trip?"

Etta sighed as if it were too much bother. "I suppose." She tossed him several bottles. Gartzah picked them up and held them awkwardly.

"Something to carry them in?"

"Don't push it. Start walking."

Etta and Bear watched Gartzah trying to carry several large bottles while walking away.

YOU HAVE A MEAN STREAK FOR A SEX DOLL, Bear said.

"*Und* you're too much of a *Teddybär* for *ein hombre-lobo*. Shall we get started?"

*   *   *

332

Maheux
Town of Wildeside
Kentauran calendar: 16 Skoteinómína, 1383 PS

The buildings of Wildeside came in three distinctive styles depending on when they were built, and by whom. The original buildings were of tough, modern ceramic alloys, complete with house AIs. Later buildings were made from local materials, sometimes adobe, sometimes brick, sometimes wood, and usually housed only the most basic of electronics. The buildings constructed by later generations with little money were often ramshackle, put together with cast off materials from other projects, containing gas lights and wood-burning stoves.

"This is it," Teagan said. They paused outside of a building that looked like latter-day construction on the outside, but the trashy facade hid a much more modern building inside.

The building was located on the edge of town. Beyond it was the desert.

"The desert floor has been disturbed," Tith said. "It's been dug up and replanted. It looks natural to the untrained eye, but it hides an underground construction. A lot of dirt was moved from here." Tith was comparing what he saw to images sent from the orbiting navel vessel.

Teagan just nodded and looked at the entrance of the building. There was a wooden sign painted with sloppy Latin letters: *Böyük Pharmaceuticals.*

Teagan and Tith were both wearing cloaks which were part of the local fashion. They were made of a smart fabric which could be controlled via EPU or iGlasses to protect the wearer against weather and bugs. They could also be configured to hide weapons from the ubiquitous scanners. Teagan and Tith both pulled their cloaks close and entered the business.

They expected to see the interior of the type of pharmacy one expects to see on planets like these — shady people selling drugs that might or might not be legal, or perhaps an opiate den. Almost anything was possible.

What they found was a clean, modern-looking establishment that had recently been raided by hostile forces. Shelves laid on the floor. Trash was strewn about. Blood stained the wall. Only one light was functioning.

"Sweet goddess," Teagan whispered.

"Not what I expected," Tith said as he scanned the area in several spectra. "Over there. A body."

They found a man, barely conscious, behind the counter. "Help me," he croaked. "We were attacked."

"By who?" Teagan asked. "The police? The Navy? Your competition?"

The wounded man shook his head. "Two people. One girl. One … something else."

Teagan and Tith looked at each other in confusion. Teagan found a first aid kid and started tending the man's wounds. "Looks like he was attacked by teeth and claws," Tith said.

"A girl and a wild animal?" Teagan asked. "Sound like anybody we know?"

"They couldn't still be alive," Tith said.

"We didn't think you were still alive."

"How would they have found this place?"

"Etta is obviously more resourceful that we gave it credit for."

Teagan could see that the wounded man would not be giving any more information soon, and decided to leave him for the authorities to worry about.

"Etta? Bear? Do you copy?" Teagan called through the iGlasses. The readouts indicated that there was no access to local servers. "Tith, can you see how we get below?"

After some searching, they found an elevator access, but the car refused to answer the call button.

"They've jammed it," Tith said. "We'll have to climb."

Using custom modifications to the iGlasses, Teagan was able to gain access to the elevator's computer and opened the doors. The both looked into the shaft.

"Forty? Fifty meters?" Tith asked.

"Forty-two and a half meters," Teagan said, consulting the readout. "That's just to the first landing. Let's get started."

Teagan pulled off a backpack and started unloading climbing gear.

25

"WE'VE GOT A BOGIE," a sensor tech said.
"Give me details," Souza said.

"It just lit up. It was laying silent at about 9 million kilometers outward. Accelerating at 27 gees. It's transponding the ID of the *DSS Pursuer*. According to the database, it's a cruiser class Droben warship, massing about ninety-one thousand tonnes, carrying 24 missile launchers and 10 24-gigawatt lasers. With a mid-course turnover, she'll be here in about three and a quarter standard hours."

The math was immediately obvious to Souz: the *Pursuer* was twice as big as the *Zephyr,* and carried more missile launchers and lasers. Even with the orbital defenses around Maheux, which were designed to protect Kentauran interests against illegal commerce, the battle would be relatively short. The only thing keeping the *Pursuer* from attacking was the knowledge that doing so would bring retribution from the entire Kentauran Navy as soon as the news got out. The *Pursuer* had sat, powered down and quiet, far enough away that the *Zephyr* scanner techs could only have detected it by pure luck.

"Call all stations to battle ready," Souza ordered. The alarm sounded before she finished the sentence. "Hail the Droben ship." At this distance, the light travel delay was about thirty seconds.

"Hailing on international frequencies," the comm officer said.

A minute later, the face of a man appeared on Souza's console screen. Facial recognition software found a match for his face, and his name, rank, and known service record also appeared in her field of view via the link with her EPU: *Captain Seppo Ermi.*

"*Zephyr*, this is *Pursuer* actual. We acknowledge your transmission and request permission to approach Maheux."

"Droben Space Ship *Pursuer*," Souza said. "This is the Kentauran Navy Ship *Zephyr*. You have entered Kentauran space. Please state your business."

She knew that Ermi's computers had also identified her face, but she wanted to do this by the numbers. Everything was being recorded.

In the minute required for the signal to make the round trip between the two space ships, Souza had plenty of time to think about why the *Pursuer* had decided to fire up her engines and approach Maheux at this particular time. It could not be a coincidence that she was sending marines to the surface to engage enemy combatants who probably had ties to the Droben government. Captain Ermi had decided that the situation on the planet's surface was such that it was worth the risk to engage the *Zephyr* in order to keep the clandestine operations secret. This did not bode well for the *Zephyr*.

"Captain Souza, we are requesting a peaceful visit. My crew has been in space for several months, and they need dirt-side recreation."

Voice print match for Captain Seppo Ermi, a text message said.

"I would make my ship available for your inspectors," Ermi said.

HE SEEMS WILLING TO PLAY BY THE RULES, Lagrueux said via EPU. HOWEVER...

YES. HE ONLY NEEDS TO GET INTO MISSILE RANGE TO MAKE THE RULES MOOT.

Souza turned back to the screen. "Captain Ermi, we will send inspectors to meet your ship. Do not cross the four-million-kilometer mark before they arrive."

"Acknowledged, Captain Souza. We await your inspectors."

YOU REMEMBER, OF COURSE, Lagrueux said. THAT AS FAR AS ERMI IS CONCERNED, A STATE OF WAR EXISTS BETWEEN HIS GOVERNMENT AND OURS.

"Is the *Pursuer* decelerating yet?" Souza asked.

"No, ma'am," the sensor tech replied.

"Comm, contact Lieutenant Berg, tell him to expect company on the surface. Also, get me Waugh on the line."

"Mx Waugh is out of contact," Comm said. "Lieutenant Berg has been advised."

"Tactical, how much longer before we are inside the *Pursuer*'s effective missile range?"

"About one hundred and eight-three minutes if they make a mid-course turnover. About one hundred and twenty-one minutes if they don't."

The *Zephyr* had double the effective missile range, but that meant little if the *Pursuer* came screaming in at over two thousand kilometers per second. The *Zephyr* could also outrun the *Pursuer*, but couldn't leave the planet undefended.

"Navigation, I need a flight acceleration profile that keeps us outside of the *Pursuer*'s missile range, but inside ours. Yesterday, Mr. Beck."

"Coming up on the screen now," Mr. Beck said.

He'd been working it before Souza gave the order, and Souza smiled a crooked smile. There were two options. One would work if the *Pursuer* did a mid-course turnover to decelerate. That action would commit them to coming to within missile range and staging there. The other would only work if the *Pursuer* continued to accelerate at a constant twenty-seven gees all the way. They would be within missile range for a short time, but it would negate *Zephyr*'s range advantage.

There was not a single solution for both contingencies, nor was there any guarantee that Ermi would take either course. Souza would have to guess which attack profile Ermi would use, and guessing wrong would mean a bad day for somebody. However, even if Souza guessed right, Ermi could alter his plans upon seeing Souza's counter move. Souza couldn't wait for Ermi to commit himself at the mid-course point, because then she wouldn't have enough time to accelerate into the optimal distance. If Souza were commanding the *Pursuer*, she'd do the fast flyby first and launch a boat to pick up their people on the ground. The *Zephyr* simply couldn't cover both. What she needed was two ships.

"Set a timer for their mid-course," Souza ordered.

"Timer set for ninety-six minutes … mark."

"Launch the remaining boat to give air support to the marines."

"Launching boat," Lagrueux confirmed.

"Comm, get me the *Entulessë*."

"Ah, ma'am?" the Comm officer said with confusion. "The *Entulessë* is hailing us."

"That will make this easy, then."

"Captain Souza," said the Pip commander of the elven ship. "I believe we have similar problems and a mutual threat."

"Indeed, Captain." Souza couldn't remember his name. "We both have personnel on the ground, and a Droben war ship about to fly down our throats. Now would be a good time for you to declare any weapons you might have. Off the record, of course."

"As a licensed commercial freighter, the only weapons I have are for use against pirates," the Pip said. "Very well armed pirates. Not as well armed as the *Pursuer* but far better armed than any boat they could launch. However, there is a small matter of the current Kentauran investigation into our activities."

"I think we can come to an accommodation, sir," Souza said. In her peripheral, she thought she saw Daerîsiell smiling.

*   *   *

Planet Maheux
Town of Wildside
Böyük Pharmaceuticals
Kentauran calendar: Protosmina 21, 1383 PS

"No, I can't break through the passcode lockout," Etta said. "*Soy kein* hackbot."

IF YOU WOULD BE SO KIND, Bear said with strained patience. "Just pick one damn language and stick to it. My EPU is having a stroke trying to keep up with the translation.

"I'LL TRY," ETTA SAID DEMURELY.

She was linked into a computer system, which not only kept doors locked, but offered pathways into other secure systems. In front of them was a heavy, reinforced, and secured door. On the floor was a security officer, bound and gagged with the equivalent of duct tape, and a miniature transmitter on her head to inhibit EPU connection to external systems. The marks around her face spoke of a brief, one-sided scuffle. The fire in her eyes promised dismemberment and death — in that order — to the two intruders should she get loose.

WE NEED TO GET YOU SOME UPGRADES, Bear said.

Etta couldn't be certain if he was serious or not.

"Perhaps I can help," said someone behind them.

Etta pulled a pistol and aimed it at the chest of the person who had spoken without recognition. There were two of them, well armed, but neither had made a move to draw a weapon.

Bear put a paw-hand on hers and said, EASY. THEY ARE FRIENDS. THEY WEAR MASKS.

As Etta looked, she could see the familiar outlines of Teagan and Tith. She holstered the pistol and ran into Teagan's arms.

"*Mein Dios!* I thought you were dead!"

Teagan tried not to look pained while returning the hug. "The feeling is mutual. Glad to see that you're in one piece. But easy with the hug, I'm healing." While maintaining the awkward embrace, Teagan grasped Bear's hand.

Etta unwrapped herself from Teagan and said, "You're hurt?"

"It's been a rough couple of days for everyone," Teagan said holding a hand over the injured chest. "I'll be okay."

Etta turned to Tith to greet him, but stopped. As a sex doll, she had an entire library of digital tools for reading body language, and she sensed that there was tension between Teagan and Tith.

Bear sensed it too, and they turned simultaneously and asked Teagan, "What's wrong?"

Teagan pointed to the closed and locked door. "Sharon is in there."

It didn't take long for Etta to connect the dots. She spun around, connecting with a roundhouse punch that sent Tith flying to the ground. Tith's mask became dislodged and stopped working. He pulled it off with an angry motion.

"*Rhaich!*" Tith sprang to his feet and was about to strike Etta when Bear picked him up, trapping Tith's arms to his sides.

"I thought you said these dolls don't have superhuman strength!" Tith said.

"We don't, *Arschloch,*" Etta said. "*Estoy* pissed off!" She had morphed back into Sharon's twin.

Teagan and Tith took this in, jaws slack. Then they looked at Bear for an explanation.

Don't ask me. She started doing this whenever she gets mean.

"The camouflage processor," Teagan said, eyes wide. "It responds to whatever Etta uses as a subconscious. This is unprecedented!"

"Can we discuss this without violence?" Tith asked, his voice pained.

"Bear, would you mind?" Teagan asked, putting a hand on Etta's shoulder to keep her calm.

This money-chasing trash sold Sharon to the Drobens.

"I was trying to find their lair!" Tith said.

"We did that without betrayal," Etta said, shrugging off Teagan's hand.

"Can we argue about this after we've retrieved Sharon?" Teagan asked. "Please?"

Showing his teeth the whole time, Bear slowly lowered Tith to the ground.

"Can you keep that visage?" Teagan asked. "It might come in handy."

Teagan watched in amazement as Etta's face contorted with mixed emotions while she silently weighed the choices and their consequences. No robot should be able to show that kind of emotional versatility. Teagan became convinced at that moment that Carol's mind was inside that robot, not just a synthetic mind responding to input by some complex algorithm designed to make customers feel good about having sex with a simulacrum of their fantasies.

"Yes, Commander Waugh. I can."

COMMANDER? Bear asked.

"It's a long story," Teagan said. "Let's talk about it at the post-action debrief. In the mean time, let's see if we can crack this door." Teagan set the iGlasses to security-cracking mode. "Can you link me in?"

"I'm receiving a message from the Entulessë," Tith said. "They are engaging a Droben war ship. They and the *Zephyr* have joined forces."

HOW CAN YOU GET A SIGNAL DOWN HERE? Bear asked.

"Elf tech," Tith said, sounding surprised that everybody didn't know that.

Before Teagan and Etta could make any progress on the door, the display abruptly changed.

"The door's opening!" Etta said.

The four of them scrambled for cover. The door hadn't yet opened completely before bullets started flying.

*   *   *

Maheux Orbit / Town of Wildeside
Kentauran calendar: 16 Skoteinómína, 1383 PS

"Captain, we have a fix on the Zephyr," the scanner technician said. "It just emerged from behind the planet. New orbit numbers: HAG of five, two, zero kilometers, which it will reach in two, one minutes with a speed of seven point nine, six, eight kilometers per second. Tilt of four, two degrees from the equator ..."

The technician continued to rattle off numbers, but Ermi could see them in his field of view. A graphic display showed the Pursuer's path and the Zephyr's orbit, and the probable time of closest approach.

What is Souza thinking? Ermi thought.

She had changed orbits while hidden behind the planet so that the *Zephyr* would reach maximum height above ground and its slowest orbital velocity precisely when Ermi would come within missile range. The elf ship must have decided it was time to cut its losses and run. It was nowhere in scan range.

"Call off time to missile launch," Ermi ordered.

"Eighteen point five minutes," the weapons officer called.

"Standby to launch boats."

"Boats at launch ready."

*   *   *

"They've launched boats," the first shift navigators cum scanner tech on the Entulessë said.

"Good," the first shift pilot said. "Maintain ECM phase one. Inform Souza and surface units. Prepare missile counter measures. Go to ECM phase two as soon as you detect missile launch."

"Missile counter measures ready," the second shift pilot, who was working as the tactical officer, said.

*   *   *

"We're receiving communications from the Pursuer, Captain." the Zephyr's comm officer said. "It's Ermi."

"Let me chat with him," Souza said. With a wave of the comm officer's hand, Captains Souza and Ermi were looking at each other. Souza used her EPU while Ermi used a camera and microphone mounted to a console.

"Captain Souza," Ermi said. "We don't have to go through with this. I have the advantage. This can only end in the death of your crew and ship. Let's talk about the alternatives."

Souza smiled. "You need us alive, Captain Ermi. Once the word gets back to the fleet that you've attacked Kentauran soil, and are providing support for terrorists, you'll have every Kentauran ship this side of the Crab Nebula on your ass. Without my crew as hostages, you'll never make it back to Droben. And the only way you're getting past me is by killing the Zephyr. So by all means, let's talk alternatives." Souza managed to keep the sarcasm out of her voice.

"I'm sorry you feel that way, Captain," Ermi said. "I would have given you every consideration for your rank. But I don't need you to make it back to Droben space alive. The Kentauran fleet won't find any evidence here of collaboration with terrorists. We've already killed your messenger buoy. I'm afraid you're next."

"Then let the dice fall where they may, Captain." Souza said. "See you on the other side."

She waved her hand at the comm officer, who cut the signal.

*   *   *

The initial volley of bullets stopped as soon as the security forces determined that the intruders were not returning fire. Each side performed furtive scans, trying to figure out the numbers and placement of the enemy combatants. Teagan quickly established that none of them had been wounded or otherwise injured.

Bear had an idea and quickly discussed it with the others. There was a vote, and it passed 4-3. He picked up the security officer they had subdued earlier and hauled her to her feet.

WAIT! Etta chatted. YOU'RE TWICE HER SIZE. YOU CAN'T HIDE BEHIND HER. I CAN. LET HER DO IT, BEAR.

NO! Teagan objected. YOU'RE TOO VALUABLE!

AGREED, Tith said. YOU CAN'T BE REPLACED.

YES, AND WE ALL HAVE THOSE BACK-UP COPIES OF BEAR, Etta pointed out the contradiction. DON'T GET ME WRONG. I APPRECIATE THAT I'VE GONE FROM DOCK-SIDE TRASH TO AN IRREPLACEABLE AI EXPERIMENT, BUT I CAN BE REPAIRED MORE EASILY THAN BEAR.

Without waiting for more argument, she took control of the security officer and marched her into the middle of the room, in full view of anybody on the other side of the door. Etta easily hid behind the woman.

"Let's talk," Etta called. "You know why we're here. We just want the woman you have as a prisoner. We're willing to trade."

"If Officer Peng dies, so do you all," a male voice called back.

"I know you've already scanned us und you know that I'm a robot. Do you think I care whether I die? I'm not even alive. The others will destroy this door with explosives before Officer Peng hits the floor, *und* they'll escape."

There was silence. Etta knew that the security team was discussing its options.

"We need to call our boss," the male voice said. "This will take a while."

"You've got ten minutes," Etta called. "*Und* I don't need to blink."

*   *   *

The Pursuer closed in on its target. "We'll be in range in fifteen seconds," the weapons officer said.

"Set missiles to hot," Ermi said. "Missile counter measures active. Expect them to get off a full broadside before our missiles hit."

"Aye, sir. Missiles hot," the weapons officer reported.

"Target has commenced counter measures," the scanner tech said. "Targeting radar is holding lock."

Ermi could see the red dot on the tactical display flickering as the Kentauran ship tried to confuse the targeting system.

"Missiles away," the weapons officer said. "Every bird on target."

"Why haven't the Kentaurans returned fire?" Ermi asked, turning to look as his XO. "We're in their range."

The XO shrugged. "It won't matter in eight minutes."

Ermi couldn't shake the feeling that something was amiss. The Kentaurans were out-massed and outgunned, but that shouldn't have stopped them from firing a full broadside as soon as the Pursuer came within range. He watched the tactical display showing the glowing missiles, the target, and the countdown for impact.

"Whoa!" the scanner technician said. "Captain, we have got some weird readings from the target. It's as if eight more targets suddenly appeared. They are all identical."

Ermi's eyes went wide as they confirmed the information. Not only were there nine identical targets on the display, but they were moving around.

"Those are gravity echoes!" Ermi shouted. He had read theoretical papers on the use of gravity distortions for anti-missile defense, but had no idea that anybody had perfected the technology. "Find the original target. Now!"

As the missiles crossed the distance, they were confused by the apparent surplus of targets. The onboard computers did their best to find the correct one. Instead of twenty-four missiles closing on one target, there were now nine targets.

Only two missiles, by pure chance, found the only solid target of the bunch, and they were easily destroyed by anti-missile lasers. The other twenty-two missiles flew through phantom targets, and then lost radar lock.

"Ready volley number two," Ermi ordered.

"Incoming!" The tactical officer shouted. "Multiple missile launches. But not from the Kentaurans."

"Wait!" the scanner technician said. "That's not the frigate! That's the elf ship!"

"Where are the Kentaurans?" Irmi demanded.

"Launching the missiles," somebody said. "Additional missile launches detected! Impact in seventeen seconds, mark!"

In the confusion, the Zephyr had stayed hidden behind the bulk of the planet, using a relay to the Entulessë's sensor suite to track the Pursuer, and was able to launch two volleys of missiles. All of which were headed directly for the Pursuer at short range.

Ermi looked at the XO again for answers.

"Elf tech?" the XO said.

*   *   *

Deep beneath the surface of Maheux, Etta Place noted that the ten-minute count down was reaching zero.

"Time is almost up. Do you have the woman?"

"They're bringing her now," a male voice replied. It did not sound worried, and Etta wondered just how much they were actually worried about Officer Peng's life. "Please. Just another minute or so."

"How are you doing, Officer Peng? Can you keep standing another minute or so?" Etta asked.

"When I get free, I'm going to tear your limbs from your artificial body," Peng promised.

"I charge extra for that," Etta smiled.

Peng responded with some unintelligible syllables, and Etta was certain that they were not nice.

The sound of a hydraulically-powered door came from behind the security officers, and Etta could see three figures in hospital scrubs wheeling a gurney with an unconscious figure on it. Etta actually reacted physically, taking in a sharp breath, when she recognized the prone figure as her old body, *aka* Sharon. Etta recognized her own reaction as distinctly alien to her construction, which caused several levels of cognitive confusion. She forced herself to look at the approaching figures.

At a gesture from one of the security guards, the medical personnel stopped about twenty meters away.

"Let us walk through, and I'll leave the patient here."

Bear came out from behind the security desk and approached the gurney cautiously. Teagan and Tith also stood up. Sharon's face was visible, but her head was swathed in gauze.

"You butchers," Teagan said. "You removed her EPU."

"What did you expect?" one of the medicos said. "She was trying to get rid of it. It's the only part of her that is of any value to us. You can have the woman back. She's alive and well, sans EPU."

Bear placed a hand on Sharon's chest, then reported, SHE'S BREATHING AND HER HEART RATE IS STEADY.

Etta noticed a red and white insulated box under the arm of the doctor who'd spoken, and could feel the connection. The same connection that had given her consciousness.

THIS IS NOT A GOOD IDEA, Etta said. THAT EPU CONTAINS THE SECRET OF REWRITING HUMAN MEMORIES.

WOULD YOU SACRIFICE SHARON FOR THAT? Teagan asked.

For the first time in Etta's artificial life, she found herself conflicted, wanting to do mutually exclusive things. She could have the EPU, or she could save Sharon and probably several other lives. Once the bullets started flying, there was no telling who'd get out in one piece.

"Just one question, if I may," Tith said. "How had you planned to get off the planet?"

"Why should I tell you that?" the doctor said.

"Because I think your Plan A just got blown out of the sky," Tith said. "I'm getting reports from the *Entulessë* now. That Droben navy ship? The *Pursuer*." Tith nodded while he listened to a report which was only audible to him. "They are picking up the survivors now. The ship has been scuttled."

The doctor did a credible job of hiding a reaction, but Etta could see the narrowing of the pupils and increased muscle tension.

"Don't I know you?" she asked. She had a flash of memory of somebody with this face telling her she didn't deserve this death.

"Pah!" the doctor said. "There are dozens of ways off this planet for the right price."

"Not as long as the Kentauran ship remains in orbit," Teagan said. "And it'll stay there until I give it the word to stand down." It was a bluff, but it had the desired effect.

The doctor weighed their options, looked from one person to another, then pulled a memory storage cube from a pocket. "I offer you one more thing if you'll allow me to leave safely."

"What's that?" Teagan asked.

"Major Sharon Manders. The original files. Imagine the intel you can get from this!"

"How do we read those files?" Teagan asked.

"I'm sure your engineers will figure it out."

"How do we know what's in that memory cube?" Tith asked.

"You also get my lab," the doctor said, indicating the space around them. "Just let me and these security people go." The memory cube was laid upon the gurney. "Just think about it. If your scientists are good enough, they can unlock the secrets of transferring a human mind into artificial bodies. Immortality can be yours."

"Giatrós," Etta said. "Your name is Giatrós."

Giatrós looked at Etta and then at Sharon, comparing their identical faces. "You must be the robot, Etta Place. She told me about you." Giatrós addressed the entire room. "Ladies and gentlemen, there is the future of humanity, wearing a body that doesn't get sick or old. A body that can be repaired as easily as any machine. It's yours for the small price of letting us walk."

A few short days ago, Teagan had no interest in living much longer. Teagan had seriously considered ending this tedious existence. But now? Teagan wasn't sure. And there were so many researchers who were salivating for a chance to spend time in this lab.

After several moments of tense silence, Teagan said, "Let them go."

Three of them stood aside, leaving as much space as possible for the security crew and the doctors to walk between them. Etta stood her ground and kept control of Peng while aiming her pistol at Giatrós' head. Everyone turned and looked at her.

"Etta," Teagan warned, "This isn't a good idea."

"He! Killed! Me!" Etta screamed.

THIS IS NOT THE TIME, LITTLE ONE, Bear said.

"This is the part of my deal," Etta said. "This is my payment."

"Lady," Officer Peng said in a near whisper. "If you kill him, then everybody else in this room will surely also die. Including your friends. That will be the price of your revenge."

She reached out slowly with her right hand and placed it on the pistol. Both of Etta's minds were demanding to be heard, and each contradicted the other. Etta didn't know which of her two minds finally made the choice, but she slowly lowered the weapon.

"Next time," Peng said.

"Next time," Etta repeated, then ran to the gurney.

She looked into the flesh and blood face that used to be hers and slapped it gently.

"Sharón! Wake up!"

Giatrós and his security crew hurried out the exit.

"Call the *Zephyr*," Teagan told Tith. "Give them our exact location, and inform them we'll keep the place secure until the marines arrive."

Teagan picked up the memory cube and stuck it in a pocket.

"And let them know that the people responsible for this are loose."

26

Maheux
Town of Wildeside
Böyük Pharmaceuticals
Kentauran calendar: 16 Skoteinómína, 1383 PS

L IEUTENANT COMMANDER GUERIN LAGRUEUX strode into Giatrós' former lab and stopped when Bear and a woman who looked strikingly like Carol Simmons stood to attention and saluted him. Teagan didn't bother to stand up, but gave a friendly wave.

Lagrueux returned the salutes. "Mr. Barischk. Good to see you're alive. Is this Carol Simmons?"

"No, sir." Etta said, still standing at attention. "That person is dead." She pointed to the still unconscious figure on the gurney. "That's Sharon Manders."

"Then, you are?" Lagrueux asked.

"Etta Place. Civilian. Sorry for the salute. Old habit." She relaxed.

"Ex-Navy?"

"Yes, sir. You could say that."

"Good. You all need to report for debriefing. Especially you, Mx. Waugh."

Teagan just smiled and nodded.

"Where's Mr. Galondel?" Lagrueux asked.

"The elf?" Teagan said. "He left ten minutes ago. On his way into orbit by now."

Teagan didn't bother to mention that Tith had taken several items from the lab's stores and had duplicated several computer memory systems.

Lagrueux turned to the assault team. "Make sure nothing leaves this lab without my knowledge. I want a security perimeter one block around the surface entrance. Assign a detail to inventory everything. And get these people to the *Zephyr*."

The woman on the gurney stirred, making faint vocalizations. Etta and Teagan rushed to her side.

"Sharón," Etta said softly. "*Bitte*. Speak to me."

"You're safe now," Teagan assured. "We've got you."

Sharon reached slowly to her head and felt the bandages there, then made a face reflecting the pain.

"She needs a doctor," Teagan said.

"Is Dr. Bradford on the ship?" Etta asked.

"Let's get her to the ship," Lagrueux said. "Dr. Bradford can treat her there."

Sharon opened her eyes and locked them with Teagan's. Then she looked at Etta. Both of their faces were filled with concern.

"Who are you?" Sharon asked.

"Oh shit," Teagan said. Etta backed up in shock. "That bastard!" Teagan shouted.

It wasn't that she didn't know them, it was that she asked the question in perfect Herskan, the official language of Droben.

Teagan reached into a pocket and grasped the memory cube tightly.

EPILOGUE

V ESKIN ROHLLAMIS, sole owner and operator of *Play Me Robotics*, looked up from his work when the security system chimed and informed him there was a customer waiting in the store. People didn't often visit his store. Usually they found him over the 'Nets. The ones who came into the store were most likely the ones with special requests who wanted to pay cash with minimal record keeping. Veskin pulled up the image and enhanced the picture. There was something odd about the face. If he didn't know better, he'd think that it was an elf wearing a mask.

He locked the computer, ran his fingers through his thinning hair and buttoned the top of his shirt. Looking more or less presentable, he opened the door to the store and greeted the customer.

"May I help you?"

"Good evening, Mr. Rohllamis." Was that a feminine voice? Veskin couldn't be sure. Maybe it was artificially enhanced. Everything about this customer seemed odd. "I am Inspector

Yoheira Maartin from Tulamak Criminal Investigations." The strange person held out an ID, which may or may not be legitimate. "I'm looking for one of your customers."

Veskin didn't like this at all. "My customer list is confidential. Do you have a warrant?"

"Certainly I can get one," Maartin said. "But I'm trying to keep your customer out of trouble. He's only a person of interest, not a suspect. If it became publicly known that he was shopping for a sex doll, it would be embarrassing."

Veskin shook his head. "I don't care if his spouse, employer, and entire bowling team find out about his dolls. I have a professional reputation to think of."

"I see. Well, in that case, we can continue this conversation at the Inspection Office. I have a nice little office with a one-way mirror and a steel table that's bolted to the floor. The chair is very uncomfortable, I'm told. No toilet, no water. The conversation could go on for hours. You should probably cancel your breakfast reservations."

Is that how it's going to be, Veskin asked himself. Why does it always come to this?

"Who are you looking for?"

Inspector Maartin pulled out a handheld and activated it. A photograph of a person who might have been any gender appeared.

Veskin studied it for several seconds, and when he was certain he'd never met the person said, "I have no idea who this is?"

"May I inspect your security camera? Perhaps he was wearing a disguise."

Maartin spent an hour going over recorded images of customers coming and going into Rohllamis' store. He looked at many of them repeatedly, then copied the entire collection into the handheld.

It hadn't been Waugh who came into the store, Maartin, *aka* Elrydien Daerîsiell, mused. It had taken special scrutiny to see through the disguise of a short, dark complexioned woman with an almost imperceptible accent. It had been that damned little sex toy. How deliciously ironic! Did Rohllamis have any clue that one of his creations was now a customer?

"I need to see the file on this customer," she told Rohllamis. "Everything you have."

*   *   *

Furmen tended to live in large families in huge homes, with several generations often sharing the same home with cousins. Bear was the odd uncle of his pack. He came and went, bringing sailor's stories of exotic worlds and fantastic people. When he returned home bringing a new friend and a humanoid robot, his family found it absolutely fascinating, and extended every courtesy. Uncle Bear told stories of evil terrorists and a hero's quest to stop them, giant bugs, and machines that could change people's memories.

Even though the robot was very clever and could interact as well — if not better — than a human, everybody knew she was a robot by the smell. Still, they treated her kindly, especially when she was so willing to give back scratches. Besides, Uncle Bear liked her.

Teagan and Etta were given their own rooms, and nobody paid much attention when the human purchased a lot of computers and machining equipment. They also didn't ask any embarrassing questions when a coffin-sized package from PlayMe Robotics arrived via special currier.

While Teagan set up the equipment to make the memory transfer, Bear laid on his back with his head in Etta's lap. Etta, sitting on the floor, learning with her back against a sofa, had two cables running from her head. One connected to the computer equipment, and one to the skull of the new doll, which was laying on the sofa. They had dressed the new doll in a modest sweatsuit and athletic shoes. Teagan had ordered the doll to look like the picture of Professor Sharon Manders on the cover of *The Sand, Like Tears:* tall, blonde, and of indeterminate European descent.

Etta took her mind off the process by gently scratching Bear behind the ears. She had changed her appearance again to resemble an actress from Earth who had played the female outlaw in a cinema two centuries before the Singularity. She had searched the 'Nets for photos of Etta Place, and this was all she could find. She still had a tendency to switch back into Carol's image when she become emotional.

"Do you have any idea if this will work?" Etta asked.

"None whatsoever. I think without Carol's EPU, this might not be possible. It might be a unique, non-replicatable mutation — some synthesis of the foreign programming and Carol's DNA. However, your pink matter has been reprogrammed by Carol's EPU. It had a sense of self-preservation. It was in danger of being rendered non-functional by Sharon's actions, so according to my diagnostics, it replicated its programing and structure in your skull, and that it will, in turn, replicate that inside this skull." Teagan tapped the new robot's head.

"A metaphor for the evolution of life itself," Etta mused. "If we can use my pink matter, mein cerebro, to transfer memories to other robots ..." She let the thought drift into silence.

SPEAKING OF CAROL, Bear said. WHAT HAPPENED TO MAJOR MANDERS?

"She's currently in prison, serving several long sentences while simultaneously putting in time as NavSec's favorite science experiment. Even without her cooperation, NavSec has been able to extract a wealth of intel regarding Droben's clandestine operations. Some of the information is well over ten years old, but it's still valuable."

"How do you know you won't be filling that doll's pink matter with Major Mander's memories, and not Professor Mander's?" Etta asked. "I don't like the idea of the Major's memories mixing with my own."

"I don't," Teagan said apologetically. "But this is the only way to find out. If it's the wrong Sharon, then I hit the delete button."

"Just don't delete me, okay?"

Teagan worked in silence for another half-hour while Bear and Etta talked of inconsequential things. Teagan finally stood up. All the connections were made. The robot was in programming mode. Teagan stretched, and Bear's ears twitched, pointing forward. Teagan switched on the recording equipment and said, "Memory transfer attempt number 22."

"Teagán," Etta said. "Good luck, *meine amiga.*"

Teagan nodded and pressed the button.

The minutes stretched on, with no reaction from the robot. They could hear the pups playing in the yard, and an occasional low-flying aircar passed overhead. Etta could tell that her own secondary and tertiary processors were working overtime, but otherwise had no sensation of the information flow.

After nearly an hour, the process stopped. Indicators on a virtual monitor showed that the data transfer was complete, and that the error checking algorithms had found everything satisfactory. The monitor showed the word REBOOTING.

After another few minutes, the robot opened its eyes and sat up. It looked at the three companions who looked back expectantly. It looked at the computer equipment and the cable running between its head and Etta's.

"Where am I?" it said in English.

ABOUT THE AUTHOR

Andrea Monticue is an aircraft technician who has crawled around inside of the B2, corporate jets, and puddle jumpers. She figures this makes her an expert on starships.

She and her wife live on the west coast of the North American Continent, enjoying redwoods, scuba, archery, bicycling, skateboarding, coffee, reading, and dogs.

Andrea can be found at *Memoirs of an Earthling* (memoirsofanearthling.blog).

YOU MIGHT ALSO ENJOY

BUILDING BABY BROTHER
by Steven Radecki

It seemed like a good idea at the time ...

CHILDREN OF THE WRONG TIME
by Flavia Idà

"Would you say you were loved by the right people at the right time in the right way and for the right reasons?"

THE LAST SPECK OF THE WORLD
by Flavia Idà

No name. No race. No nationality. The survivor of the perfect catastrophe struggles to preserve herself and her hope that she may be found — by humans.

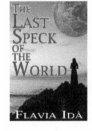

Made in the USA
Las Vegas, NV
05 March 2021